I0732927

Proud Mary

LUCINDA BRANT BOOKS

—The Roxton Family Saga —
NOBLE SATYR
MIDNIGHT MARRIAGE
AUTUMN DUCHESS
DAIR DEVIL
PROUD MARY
SATYR'S SON
ETERNALLY YOURS
FOREVER REMAIN

— Alec Halsey Mysteries —
DEADLY ENGAGEMENT
DEADLY AFFAIR
DEADLY PERIL
DEADLY KIN
DEADLY DESIRE

— Salt Hendon Books —
SALT BRIDE
SALT REDUX

'Quizzing glass and quill, into my sedan chair and away —— the 1700s rock!'

Lucinda Brant is a *New York Times*, *USA Today*, and *Audible* bestselling author of award-winning Georgian historical romances and mysteries. Her books are renowned for wit, drama and a happily ever-after. She has a degree in history and political science from the Australian National University and a post-graduate degree in education from Bond University, where she was awarded the Frank Surman Medal.

Noble Satyr, Lucinda's first novel, was awarded the $10,000 Random House/Woman's Day Romantic Fiction Prize, and she has twice been a finalist for the Romance Writers' of Australia Romantic Book of the Year. All her novels have garnered multiple awards and become worldwide bestsellers.

Lucinda lives in the middle of a koala reserve, in a writing cave that is wall-to-wall books on all aspects of the Eighteenth Century, collected over 40 years—Heaven. She loves to hear from her readers (and she'll write back!).

lucindabrant@gmail.com	lucindabrant.com
pinterest.com/lucindabrant	twitter.com/lucindabrant
facebook.com/lucindabrantbooks	youtube.com/lucindabrantauthor

Proud Mary

A GEORGIAN HISTORICAL ROMANCE

Roxton Family Saga Book Four

Lucinda Brant

A Sprigleaf Book
Published by Sprigleaf Pty. Ltd.

This is a work of fiction; names, characters, places, and incidents
are the product of the author's imagination or are used fictitiously.
Resemblance to persons, businesses, companies, events,
or locales, past or present, is entirely coincidental.

Proud Mary: A Georgian Historical Romance.
Copyright © 2017, 2020 Lucinda Brant, all rights reserved.
Editing: Martha Stites, Cathie Maud Cabot & Rob Van De Laak.
Photography, art & design: Sprigleaf & GM Studio.
Cover models: Megan Channell and Paul Marron.
Custom jewelry: Kimberly Walters, Sign of the Gray Horse
Reproduction and historically inspired jewelry.
Cotswold Harebell fleuron design by Sprigleaf.

Back cover images: Stanway Manor House Image ©Laura Facchini, used under licence,
"Child hoop rolling at Colonial Williamsburg" ©Emanuel Tanjala, used under licence.

Georgian couple silhouette is a trademark belonging to Lucinda Brant.
Sprigleaf triple-leaf design is a trademark belonging to Sprigleaf Pty. Ltd.

Except for brief quotations embodied in articles and reviews,
no part of this book may be reproduced in any printed or
electronic form without prior permission from the publisher.

Typeset in Adobe Garamond Pro.

Also in ebook, audiobook, and other languages.

ISBN 978-1-925614-82-4

10 9 8 7 6 5 4 3 2 Studio Art Perfect Bound Paperback Edition (s.iii) I

for

Marguerite
&
Wendy

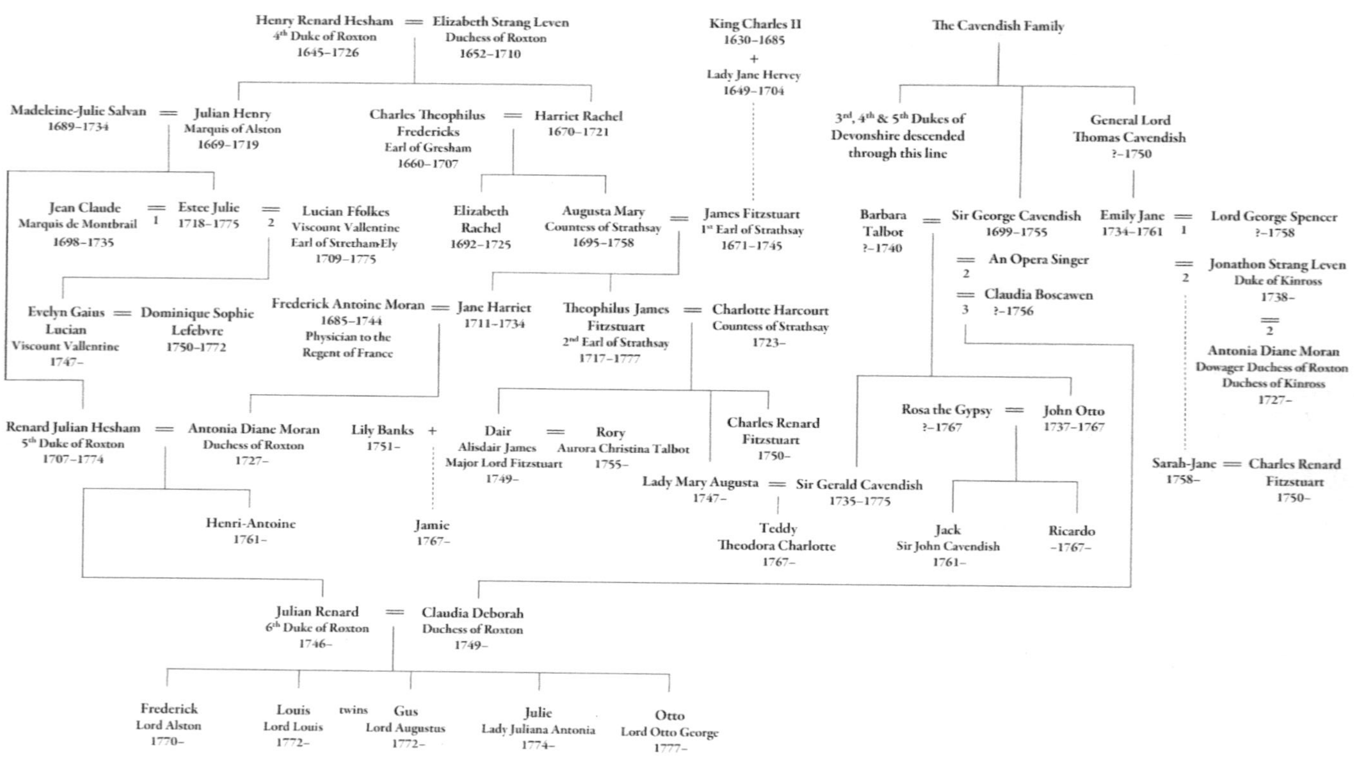

The Cavendish Family

Henry Renard Hesham
4th Duke of Roxton
1645–1726
= Elizabeth Strang Leven
Duchess of Roxton
1652–1710

King Charles II
1630–1685
+
Lady Jane Hervey
1649–1704

3rd, 4th & 5th Dukes of Devonshire descended through this line

General Lord Thomas Cavendish
?–1750

Madeleine-Julie Salvan
1689–1734
= Julian Henry
Marquis of Alston
1669–1719

Charles Theophilus Fredericks
Earl of Gresham
1660–1707
= Harriet Rachel
1670–1721

Jean Claude
Marquis de Montbrail
1698–1735
= Estee Julie
1718–1775
1   2
= Lucian Ffolkes
Viscount Vallentine
Earl of Stretham-Ely
1709–1775

Elizabeth Rachel
1692–1725

Augusta Mary
Countess of Strathsay
1695–1758
= James Fitzstuart
1st Earl of Strathsay
1671–1745

Barbara Talbot
?–1740
= Sir George Cavendish
1699–1755
= An Opera Singer
2
= Claudia Boscawen
3   ?–1756

Emily Jane
1734–1761
= Lord George Spencer
?–1758
1
= Jonathon Strang Leven
Duke of Kinross
1738–
2
=
2
Antonia Diane Moran
Dowager Duchess of Roxton
Duchess of Kinross
1727–

Evelyn Gaius Lucian
Viscount Vallentine
1747–
= Dominique Sophie Lefebvre
1750–1772

Frederick Antoine Moran
1685–1744
Physician to the Regent of France
= Jane Harriet
1711–1734

Theophilus James Fitzstuart
2nd Earl of Strathsay
1717–1777
= Charlotte Harcourt
Countess of Strathsay
1723–

Rosa the Gypsy
?–1767
= John Otto
1737–1767

Renard Julian Hesham
5th Duke of Roxton
1707–1774
= Antonia Diane Moran
Duchess of Roxton
1727–

Lily Banks
1751–
+

Dair
Alisdair James
Major Lord Fitzstuart
1749–
= Rory
Aurora Christina Talbot
1755–

Charles Renard Fitzstuart
1750–

Sarah-Jane
1758–
= Charles Renard Fitzstuart
1750–

Henri-Antoine
1761–

Jamie
1767–

Lady Mary Augusta
1747–
= Sir Gerald Cavendish
1735–1775

Teddy
Theodora Charlotte
1767–

Jack
Sir John Cavendish
1761–

Ricardo
–1767–

Julian Renard
6th Duke of Roxton
1746–
= Claudia Deborah
Duchess of Roxton
1749–

Frederick
Lord Alston
1770–

Louis
Lord Louis
1772–
twins
Gus
Lord Augustus
1772–

Julie
Lady Juliana Antonia
1774–

Otto
Lord Otto George
1777–

PART I

THE GHOST

ONE

GLOUCESTERSHIRE, AUTUMN, 1777

Mr. Christopher Bryce sat at his desk in the steward's office reading a letter. As was his practice after riding across to Abbeywood Farm from his estate in the next vale, he had removed his frock coat and hung it on a peg behind the door. His assistant always kept the room too warm. Sitting in his shirtsleeves was preferable to watching the thin little man huddled at the end of the desk shivering with cold.

Unconsciously, he raked long fingers through his untidy curls and felt the hair ribbon come loose between his fingers. Without taking his gaze from the letter, he pulled his shoulder-length hair back to his nape and retied the crumpled piece of black silk. His stock, like the hair ribbon, was also crumpled, the folds of linen wrapped loosely about his strong neck. And while he had scraped the soles of his jockey boots clean to enter the house via the servant's entrance, the leather was splashed with the mud and filth of having led his mount through to the stables. The mare had thrown a shoe.

But it was not this misadventure which could be blamed for his want of dress. Squire Bryce always appeared to have dressed in haste, grabbing whatever garments were to hand, and never to have glanced in a looking glass before greeting the world. *Disheveled* was a word that often tripped off the tongues of the local gentry matriarchs. Had he been any other farmer in the district, he would not have come under such scrutiny. But he was not like any other squire—far from it. He was master of a Jacobean manor house—a local landmark in fact— Brycecomb Hall, and owned several prosperous cloth mills. Also, he had recently—eight years was considered yesterday to the inhabitants of this sleepy pocket of the Cotswolds—returned from more than a decade of living abroad. Most vital of all, he was unmarried.

It was of little concern to the parents of unmarried daughters that Mr. Bryce was approaching forty, or that upon first acquaintance he proved a disappointment. It was not that he lacked a profile worthy of immortalization in oils, because he was exceedingly handsome. He had a fine nose, a determined chin, and a pair of damp brown eyes that had something of the lost-puppy look about them. And his auburn curls were so thick they were the envy of many a female. Maidens had upon occasion gone weak at the knees at the sight of him. This was particularly so when he was astride his horse, hair wind-tousled, long muscular legs shown to advantage in soft leather riding breeches that looked to have been applied by a painter rather than his tailor. Mamas reprimanded daughters for their unladylike gawking, yet secretly sighed at what might have been, had they been their daughter's age.

It was not Christopher Bryce's looks, but his lack of engagement with his neighbors, most particularly their eligible females, that was cause for disappointment. That he was handsome and unmarried only made his detachment that much more palpable. He was impervious to the attentions of even the most charming of hostesses, who did their best but failed to ignite the Squire's interest in their unmarried female relatives. He was not disagreeable, but he was not agreeable, either. He might smile and politely reply to any enquiry put to him, but he made no attempt to further the conversation, which was concluded before it began. It was not what the local gentry was used to in a squire of Brycecomb Hall.

Henry Bryce, the present squire's father, had been the most congenial of fellows, and when his wife was alive, many routs, shoots, and social gatherings were held at the Jacobean manor. Those old enough to have been acquainted with the Bryces and to have attended such events, also knew that their only child had been, in his youth, just as sociable as his elderly parents. But all those years living on the other side of the Channel amongst foreign types had changed the son.

Christopher Bryce had spent so many years in foreign climes his neighbors had expected him to return to the vale with a wealth of stories about the people he had encountered, and the places he had visited. But Mr. Bryce neither offered, nor provided when prompted, any anecdotes about his travels. It was as if he had never been anywhere beyond Stroud, and even then he only ventured to town on market days. His topics of conversation remained decidedly provincial. This satisfied his fellow farmers, but dissatisfied their wives, their sons, and most certainly their daughters who craved a little excitement in their daily routines. It was left to fertile imaginations to wonder at what sort of life Squire Bryce had led far from the vale that he had no wish to discuss any part of it.

And imagine they did, in whispered conversation when he happened to pass them in the village street astride his mount, acknowledging them with a nod but never stopping. Or when he quietly slid onto the family pew for Sunday service, neither looking left nor right, the vicar pausing mid-sentence at the collective sly glance of the congregation in Squire Bryce's direction. Even the vicar's wife was heard to remark to a clutch of female parishioners, as Mr. Bryce strode away setting his tricorne in place, that the squire was an enigma. His sartorial efforts left much to be desired, but watching him in motion was something to behold. He was the arresting sum of his extraordinary parts. Every female eagerly nodded in agreement, pulse racing.

For it was when he was animate that Christopher Bryce's true masculine beauty became apparent. The village's female inhabitants confidently put their finger on precisely what it was about the squire's movements that set him apart from his fellows—it had everything to do with the way in which he carried himself. He did not amble or lope like a youth, and he certainly did not trudge or plod. Nor did he slouch or shove his hands in the pockets of his frock coat. He moved with an elegance and ease which was unhurried, upright, and unself-conscious. It underscored the years spent among foreigners; as did the fact he no longer spoke in the Cotswold vernacular of his youth.

Christopher Bryce might pretend to remain insensible to the effect his clothes, his person, his time abroad, and his deportment had on his neighbors, particularly the females, but he was acutely aware of the consequences his decisions and actions had on others. Thus he may have had the appearance of being wholly absorbed in the letter in front of him, but he had heard the raised voices on the other side of the office door, had a fair idea what the commotion was about, and knew his assistant was sufficiently distracted by it to have left off his arithmetical reckonings.

The little man's quill remained poised over the inkwell.

"You had best invite her in, Mr. Deed," Christopher said without looking up.

"Who, sir?"

"Lady Mary."

Mr. Timothy Deed was skeptical. Not only because he had not discerned Lady Mary's voice amongst the din, but because in his two years employed in this household, the mistress had never visited the steward's office. If her imperious little ladyship wished to speak to Mr. Bryce, she summoned him to her drawing room, which was right and proper. She certainly did not trespass into the servants' domain, nor raise her voice in ill-lit corridors. Thus Mr. Deed hesitated to do as he was told and voiced his surprise.

"Lady Mary, sir? Here? Why?"

"We will find that out when you open the door and let her in." When there was silence after this flat reply, the Squire lifted his gaze to his assistant's quizzical look. He offered an explanation. "Perhaps you forget that John Twisell, Jethro Tanner, and the Blandfords had until today to accept their altered circumstances?"

At the mention of four servants who had been at Abbeywood since before the death of its owner, Sir Gerald Cavendish, Mr. Deed's eyebrows shot up in understanding.

"None have accepted?"

"There are still a few hours left in the day. But given the hubbub, that would seem to be so."

Mr. Deed's eyebrows came down and he ground his teeth. "Then they are not only lazy but fools!"

"But given false hope perhaps…?"

Mr. Deed's gaze darted to the door. Though there seemed to be an angry mob gathered outside, he still could not hear the voice of the mistress of the house.

"By her ladyship…?"

Christopher Bryce did not answer the question, but his silence said everything. He set aside the letter, and took from the small pile beside the standish one with its seal intact. It was from His Grace the most noble Duke of Roxton, the same correspondent who had written to him and whose letter he had been reading. This letter was addressed to Lady Mary Cavendish. He was very sure no two letters could be so different in tone and content, and he itched to toss this unopened correspondence to the flames in the grate. He did not. Instead he tucked it out of sight under his letter from the Duke, shook his thoughts free of that nobleman and looked at his assistant to find him staring at him. He hoped his features did not give away his thoughts, when he said evenly,

"The door, Mr. Deed."

Timothy Deed nodded, quickly set his quill in the ink pot, and scraped back his chair. Pulling on the points of his plain knitted waist-coat as he crossed the room, he squared his shoulders at the door, as if steeling himself for what and whom lay beyond, then wrenched it open.

A blast of cold air made him take a step back, so did the clamor of a cluster of squabbling servants. The noise ceased almost immediately, replaced by the silence of fearful expectation as to what would happen now that Squire Bryce had been roused, and without one of them with the good manners and courage to scratch at his door to seek an audience. It said as much about the Squire as it did about them when everyone in the room, bar one, took a step back when Mr. Bryce's smooth baritone was heard from deep within the room.

"Mr. Deed! Do not keep her ladyship waiting."

It was then that the assistant noticed the Lady Mary, the only one in the room to stand her ground. She was regarding him in silent expectation that he would instantly shift out of her way without the need to speak, which he did, and with a bow. And after she had passed into the room, neither looking right nor left, Mr. Deed regained enough of his composure to order the clutch of silent downcast servants not to linger, and to get about their business. And he did this with an imperious wave of a thin hand before shutting the door in their faces.

Christopher was on his feet before the Lady Mary swept across to his desk with a firm tread, hands clasped in front of her gauze apron, chin level with the floor. He wondered how many hours she had spent arguing with herself as to whether she should summon him to her, or she go to him. And by her mulish look, taking the monumental step of coming to him had been an internal struggle of epic proportions.

After all—and he knew she believed this implicitly—it was not the right and proper action for the mistress of the house, the daughter of an earl no less, to cross the household divide that separated master from servant. There was a correct order to life. Everything and everyone had a proper place. And Lady Mary's proper place was at its apex amongst the nobility—those who governed and gave orders. Everyone else—Mr. Christopher Bryce of Brycecomb Hall included—belonged to the periphery of this elegant and dazzling world, out of sight and out of mind until wanted and called.

And because Christopher Bryce did not doubt Lady Mary's expectation that those who lived on the periphery would come when called was as natural to her as breathing, he was prepared to give her ignorance of a more enlightened worldview some latitude. After all, he did not think her inherently intolerant or unkind. It was just the way she had been raised by her noble parents, a rigid upbringing reinforced as wife of a pompous self-important bigot. But that did not mean he would conform to type or allow her to interfere in his decisions. Far from it. What her ladyship needed, and he was only too willing to provide, was to have her outlook given a shake now and again.

But he was wise to the fact it was not one of his little shakes that had brought her to his door on this day, but something that must have greatly upset her. And so he had Mr. Deed fetch her a chair and waited for her to sit upon it. But she ignored his offer and the chair and came right up to the front of his desk, saying without preamble,

"Is it true you have dismissed four more of the household servants?"

"No, my lady. I did not dismiss them."

"Oh?! I thought…" Her shoulders relaxed and she let out a sigh of relief without realizing it. "Then there has been a misunderstanding. The Blandfords say they were given notice and so too, old Jack Twisell, and the Tanner boy."

"They should not have bothered you. Won't you sit, my lady?"

Again she ignored his offer, and so he and his assistant remained on their feet.

"They did not, Mr. Bryce. They rightly spoke to Mrs. Keble, and when she was unable to find a suitable resolution, she brought the matter to me, which was the right thing for her to do."

Christopher's eyebrows rose slightly at mention of the house-keeper. He suspected Susanna Keble of inciting the servants against him whenever an opportunity presented itself. The woman had a misplaced confidence in her authority. Mrs. Keble was under the delusion that her illicit affair with Sir Gerald—of which he was well aware, but was certain Lady Mary was not—and the fact Lady Mary would not hear a word against her, gave her special status and privileges at Abbeywood. He had quickly disabused her of this notion. She had even tried to seduce him, but he was deliberately blind to her tawdry attempts. He would not have been male had he not noticed she was pretty, but it was a brittle prettiness that hid a cold heart and a calcu-lating disposition. She was cunning enough to hide her below-stairs machinations to undermine his authority, and in his presence was always biddable. Mrs. Keble's days were also numbered in this household.

"Mrs. Keble had no right to bother you, my lady," he replied evenly. "I am sorry, but in this matter there are no alternatives to discuss. I cannot be persuaded to change my mind."

Lady Mary blinked at him in surprise, and then she surprised him.

"Why would you think I came here to persuade you otherwise, Mr. Bryce? I never expect to be consulted on matters that are considered *important.* I never have in the past. My opinions have rarely been sought, and I don't single you out in this."

Though I had hoped—indeed when I first met you I had thought—you were different… said the voice in her head. She quickly shook herself free of wishful thinking and continued.

"So when you say you will not change your mind, I accept that as a given. Sir Gerald never consulted me—he *told* me. As you are telling me now. But that does not mean, just because I cannot do anything about it, I do not have an opinion, or feelings, or wish for a different outcome."

This speech was met with silence from both men, who were unable or unwilling to add to her observations because there was nothing to add to the truth. Yet, her final comment did elicit a response from Christopher, who said quietly,

"If it will ease your mind, my lady, I have not turned them out, friendless and penniless. They have employment and shelter elsewhere."

"Employment and shelter—*elsewhere*?" she repeated. "But… The Blandfords have been at Abbeywood since before I came here as a bride. Does not loyalty count for something?"

"Need you ask me such a question? It is just as important to be gainfully employed. Which the Blandfords, young Tanner, and Old Jack were not. And now they will be, and housed. Please sit, my lady."

Lady Mary remained standing.

"And the eight servants you dismissed while I was away at my brother's wedding? Are they gainfully employed and housed elsewhere, too?"

"Yes. They—"

"Mrs. Keble told me you put them to work in your mills. Is that so?"

"I offered them employment at my cloth mills, which they accepted. And you will excuse me for correcting you. Those men were not your servants. Sir Gerald hired them. The positions they had within this household were unnecessary and wasteful. In fact they were leading meaningless lives and their minds had become stagnant. Inanimate companions had more life and occupation than those men. And as you are well aware, Abbeywood's finances, such as they are, can ill-afford to pay for the board and paint from which such figures are formed."

Again he glanced at his assistant. The elderly man now had hold of a corner of the desk to keep himself upright, so he said more curtly than he intended, "Sit, my lady!"

"I do not wish to sit, Mr. Bryce. And I do not understand why you insist I do." She suddenly felt uncomfortably warm under the Squire's steady gaze, looked about her, saw the well-lit fire in the grate, and frowned. "Nor do I understand why this room is permitted to be kept as warm as a kitchen on baking day when, as you say, this household cannot afford to be wasteful. And do not tell me it is not overly warm in here because you, Mr. Bryce, have stripped to your—to your—*shirt-sleeves*, which is a most impolite way to receive visitors—"

"I was not in expectation of a visit from you, my lady," Christopher cut in blandly, though he was quick to stifle a smirk at her expression of affront at his social solecism. "Perhaps if you'd sent word of your coming I'd have roused myself to the trouble of throwing on my frock coat to sit sweltering, waiting your arrival?"

"How droll you are today, to be sure, Mr. Bryce."

He inclined his head. "A rare occasion indeed, my lady. Not as rare as seeing me upon a dance floor, but today is not a day for dancing either."

Or witnessing me swim naked in a mill pond. Though I suspect such a prim little thing as you, my dear Lady Mary, would faint at the sight of provincial masculinity gloriously on show.

Christopher was not a betting man—he was too cautious with his money, and even more so with what belonged to others—but he would've laid good odds that her late husband Sir Gerald would never have had the bad manners, or the bravado, to remove his nightshirt in his wife's presence, even in the most intimate of situations, and stand naked before her. After all, carrying out his marital duty was just one of the chores Sir Gerald, as baronet, was obliged to perform. So he had confided in Christopher after a long night of heavy drinking.

For Christopher there had been many such long evenings in his neighbor's book room, listening to Sir Gerald drone on about his self-consequence, his place in the "grand scheme of things", and how he intended to make his mark on the world that would surprise his wife's relatives, and leave them—the Duke of Roxton in particular—speechless.

Christopher had been tasked to discover precisely how Sir Gerald intended to leave his mark, knowing it had to do with the war in the American Colonies. The Spymaster General Lord Shrewsbury suspected Sir Gerald of high treason for passing state secrets to the French to help their new-found friends, the American patriots, win the war against their English masters. Christopher was to get the proof of this treason, spending more hours than he cared to remember keeping company with his drunkard neighbor.

Information gleaned from these conversations was written up in reports to the Spymaster. But there were some details Christopher kept to himself. Details he would rather not know, intimate details about his neighbor's marriage, and the Lady Mary. And it confirmed Christopher's private opinion: Such a pretty little redhead as the Lady Mary was wasted on the likes of the boorish Sir Gerald. What was the point of making love if all the senses were not engaged? Bedding her should have been an honor and a delight…

To gaze upon her stripped out of corset and chemise, feminine curves bathed in the soft yellow glow of candlelight, glorious red hair tumbled to the small of her back… To have her hips moving with desire as he—

"Mr. Bryce—Mr. Bryce, are you attending me?" Lady Mary demanded, taking a step closer to the desk when he did not blink or answer immediately. "I knew my coming here would cause considerable curiosity, but I could think of no other way of speaking with you in private because I—Mr. Bryce?" She peered at him, frowning, realizing his thoughts were anywhere but in his office. "Are you certain it is not too warm in here because your face is flushed and you are looking—"

"No. It is not too warm!" he blurted out rudely, lust and the guilt which came with illicit longing making his tone harsher than he intended. "I may, may I not, keep my office as warm as I please *and* work in my shirtsleeves—or-or *nightshirt*—if I so wish it!?"

"Yes. Yes, of course you may," she stammered, shocked by his unexpected and uncharacteristic incivility.

Yet when she continued to stare at him, his guilt increased, wondering if indeed his expression had in some bizarre way reflected his deepest unattainable desire. So ludicrous it was laughable, and pathetic, because it would never occur to her, not in a thousand full moons, that a Cotswold squire's daydreams were filled with wanton thoughts of her.

But because Mr. Deed was also staring at him as if he had had a momentary mental lapse, he offered up a convoluted explanation, one designed not only to allow him to regain his equilibrium in mind and body, but which would also reinstate—even if it was only his thoughts which had wandered across the social divide—the societal distance required of him as steward and a nobleman's daughter; their disparate births, her rank, and his position demanded it. So he stated the obvious, which she already knew, and which would surely reconstruct that metaphorical stone wall of icy cordiality and formality that must exist between them.

"I should not need to remind you that this estate is in dire financial circumstances—"

"I am well aware of its-its—*circumstances*, Mr. Bryce. You remind me at every opportunity—"

"—because Sir Gerald lived well beyond his means," Christopher continued tonelessly. "Your husband's wants far exceeded his needs and his income. He spent excessively on all manner of impractical objects —snuff-boxes, Sevres porcelain, and expensive carriage clocks—items of no use to the effective management of this estate. He also kept a vast number of servants, employed to perform the most menial of tasks— an unnecessary conceit, and one he could ill-afford. No doubt the government's new tax on male servants to pay for the war in the colonies will have little effect on the size of His Grace of Roxton's household retinue. The burden of such taxation, as always, falls on those least likely to be able to carry it. I know you do not wish your nephew to be presented with an encumbered estate when he comes of age."

"Mr. Bryce, you are correct. I do not want Jack to inherit an economic ruin. Nor do I require another lecture on Sir Gerald's excesses. But perhaps you require reminding that acting as steward, it is your business to balance the books, not to pass judgment on my husband's character. Nor do I understand why you have singled out His Grace of Roxton for particular censure. The Duke has graciously permitted you to do as you please where this estate is concerned, even though he could, if he so wished it, remove you from your post and put another in your place."

Christopher opened his mouth to comment when the thud of a chair hitting up against the wall turned his attention to his assistant. Mr. Deed stumbled backwards but in two strides Christopher had him by his bony elbow and pulled him to his feet. He quickly set the chair to rights and eased the elderly man onto it, telling him in an under-voice to remain seated. He then returned to stand behind his desk and pointed to the chair set out for Lady Mary.

"Sit. I am not asking you. I insist. In doing so, I may sit. And Mr. Deed may remain seated and ease the pain in his arthritic knees. I know you do not wish to be *impolite*. Nor would you deny him the warmth of a good fire so that he may do his work on behalf of this estate without pain."

Instantly, Lady Mary was contrite and sat as requested. She spread her quilted petticoats and perched on the very edge of the chair, back straight and hands in her lap. Her glance and small nod of acknowl-edgment at Mr. Deed softened Christopher's mouth, and he leaned forward in his chair, clasped hands on his desk, and addressed her as if she were the only person in the room.

"I don't wish to argue with you, my lady," he said quietly. "But you have been misinformed if you believe the Duke of Roxton has any power over me. I have taken on the role of steward because Sir Gerald, in his last will and testament, charged me with this duty and I accepted it. If you wish me to go over that document with you—"

"No. No. I could not bear it. Not again. It is enough of a humiliation my husband saw fit to draw up such a despicable will. That my daughter and I are left to the mercy of a stranger—"

Christopher's eyes went dull and he sat back.

"A stranger? Not quite. Surely, as your neighbor, I have not been a stranger to you these past eight years? But, please," he purred, the metaphorical societal wall between them well and truly back in place, "tell me in what way you are at my mercy?"

"You know perfectly well what you have done!" Lady Mary retorted, and immediately had to rack her brain to come up with at least one plausible example of the Squire's interference in her day-to-day life that would not make her sound petty and ungrateful.

After all, she and Teddy remained at Abbeywood under his good graces, and if she were truthful, their lives had changed minimally since Sir Gerald's death. Except perhaps where their freedom of movement—her daughter's in particular—was concerned. So she latched on to this tangible example, one that continued to frustrate and confound her.

"It is a mystery to me—indeed to my family—why Sir Gerald appointed *you* as Teddy's guardian, and not a member of her family. My brother—*her uncle*—would have been a more suitable choice. Teddy loves her Uncle Dair, and they have similar temperaments, both preferring to be out-of-doors and physically active. I grant Dair was unmarried at the time of Sir Gerald's death, but you, too, are a bachelor, Mr. Bryce. And of longer standing than my brother, who is newly married. And his wife, the Lady Fitzstuart, is the sweetest creature imaginable. Regardless of his unmarried or married state, he would have welcomed the opportunity to be T—"

"At this moment Lord Fitzstuart is on his way to Barbados. So he is not only an absent husband, but you would have him an absent guardian, also."

"He did not leave his bride to sail off to the Barbados by choice! As I told you in my letter from Treat: He's gone in search of our father. The Earl has been missing since a hurricane devastated the island. Many thousands are said to have perished, and every structure and

living thing flattened to dust! That is the worst of possible circumstances, and in all probability our father is—our father is—*dead*, and
he—Dair—he will have the gruesome task of identifying a rotting
corpse! And you have the-the *impertinence* to suggest because he is
doing his duty he would not be a fit guardian for my daughter?"

"Yes. And I am sorry for it," Christopher replied, leaning across his
desk and offering her his plain linen handkerchief.

While she had been talking, Lady Mary had grown increasingly
agitated, shoving her hands under her apron and into the slits in her
petticoats, searching the two pockets for, he presumed, her handkerchief. So he was pleased when she took his and dabbed at her eyes. He
hated seeing her in tears, and loathed himself for causing her distress.

"It was not my wish to upset you, only to make the point that had
Major Lord Fitzstuart been Teddy's guardian—and he now absent
from England—you would be without his guidance should you require
it. And he does not need the added burden while carrying out his duty
to his father, of worrying over his niece. He can at least breathe easy,
knowing her interests are being taken care of, and concentrate on the
distressing task before him. That he has had to leave his young bride a
month after their honeymoon is surely more than one man should
have to bear."

Lady Mary nodded, a good deal calmer, the folded linen handkerchief now in her lap.

"That is true, Mr. Bryce," she conceded. "But if not Dair, then Sir
Gerald did not have to look further afield than my cousin Roxton. The
Duke is head of my family. Indeed he is head of a great many families
connected by birth or marriage to the dukedom. He has been guardian
to Sir Gerald's nephew and heir Jack for almost ten years. And he is a
most excellent and loving papa to his own children. Surely you must
see that Roxton was the right and proper person to be named Teddy's
guardian."

"I do not see it, my lady."

Christopher had never met the Duke and hoped he would never
have cause to do so. Amongst Sir Gerald's alcohol-fueled confidences
had been many an anecdote about Lady Mary's cousin, and none of
them complimentary. He had learned that Roxton was the reason Sir
Gerald had withdrawn from Polite Society. While he had little respect
for the man—and he was certain Polite Society did not miss Sir
Gerald's self-important pontifications—he did have some sympathy for
the Baronet's shabby treatment at the hands of his wife's relative. Sir
Gerald's confidences about the lascivious behavior of Roxton and his
ilk came as no surprise, but Christopher did not believe for one

moment the more salacious rumor that the Duke, and not Sir Gerald, was Teddy's true parent. If for no other reason than he did not believe the Lady Mary capable of deceit, carnal or otherwise. Her conceit would never allow her to stoop to being a man's mistress, not even if that man was a duke. That was Sir Gerald's drunkenness talking. Though he was very sure Sir Gerald had been utterly sober when he stipulated in his will that his only child, Theodora Charlotte Cavendish, must spend the years until her twenty-first birthday, or her marriage, whichever was the sooner, at Abbeywood, under the guardianship of his neighbor, Mr. Christopher Bryce, or forfeit a dowry of four thousand pounds held in trust.

"If you were to accept the Duke's invitation and visit Treat," Lady Mary argued, "and if you were to allow Teddy and me to accompany you, I am convinced you would agree that the estate is the most suitable place for her—for us—to live."

"You are free to live where you please, my lady. But Teddy will remain here, as was Sir Gerald's wish."

"If you were a parent you would understand that I am *not* free. Nor do I wish to be free if it means being parted from my daughter. I am her mother, and even you are aware that I love her very much, and so I must live where she lives."

"Then we are in accord, my lady. You both will remain here at Abbeywood. And if ever you desire to visit your cousins, you are free to do so. Now, if that was why you came here, to try and persuade me, yet again, to allow Teddy to go live amongst her Roxton cousins, then, yet again, I must disappoint you."

He extracted the Duke of Roxton's sealed letter out from under the one he had been reading before Lady Mary had interrupted his morning's schedule, and held it out to her. He hoped it would banish her mulish expression and any ill-will she was feeling at what she no doubt considered his high-handedness. He then made motions to stand.

"This came today, and it is from your illustrious relative. No doubt it contains the news you've been waiting to hear. Now please excuse me; there are quite a few persons waiting to see me."

It said a good deal about her preoccupation with her thoughts when she exchanged his handkerchief for the letter with a perfunctory "thank-you", then slipped it into a pocket. So he patiently waited for her to speak, surprised at her unresponsiveness. Usually when he handed over correspondence from her relatives she was all smiles, and so breathless with anticipation to read their news that she could hardly wait for him to quit her company so she could read in private.

Not today. And so he silently waited for her to tell him why she had made the journey to his office at the back of the manor house.

"Mr. Bryce, I had hoped to speak to you entirely alone, but I also do not want to inconvenience Mr. Deed by having him leave the warmth of this room, so if he can assure me what I have to say will go no further, then I will confide in you. I have no wish to upset the servants—"

"My lady, you have my complete confidence!"

"Thank-you, Mr. Deed," Christopher stated at his assistant's outburst, and nodded to Lady Mary. "How may I—how may *we*—be of assistance?"

Lady Mary sat up very straight before leaning forward, as if not wishing to be overheard. Her violet eyes widened and her mouth trembled. Christopher could not help but lean forward, too, his gaze not on her lovely eyes but on her plump lower lip and that tremble. Her voice was a whisper, and he strained to hear her every word.

"Mr. Bryce, there is—that is—I am very certain—Sir Gerald's bedchamber is-is *haunted*. There is a-a ghost!"

TWO

"A-A—*GHOST*? YOU SAW A GHOST?"

Christopher resisted the urge to roll his eyes and huff his disbelief. A ghost!? God grant him patience. He had interrupted his busy morning schedule for this. Correction. He had interrupted it for *her*. But she was talking fanciful nonsense.

Yet, in the years he had known her, *fanciful* was not a word he associated with the daughter of the Earl of Strathsay. Prim, and practical, yes. And proud—oh yes, the Lady Mary was *very* proud. But fanciful? Never. So there had to be some basis in fact for her belief in a ghost, the fear in her eyes told him so. She truly believed it. And he believed her. It was just that he did not believe the house was haunted.

So he took a moment to compose himself, lest he appear supercilious, and awaited further explanation.

Lady Mary took his silence for condescending disbelief.

"I did not *see* it, Mr. Bryce. I *heard* it."

MARY KNEW THE MOMENT SHE UTTERED THE WORD *GHOST* THAT Mr. Bryce did not believe her.

It was not so much his tone as the way in which his square jaw clamped shut, and his nostrils flared as he pressed his lips together, as if forcing himself not to smile. She was surprised he hadn't punctuated his incredulity with a roll of his fine eyes. It must have taken all his self-control not to laugh out loud, too.

But she was not deterred by his skepticism. She had expected it; would have been surprised had he reacted in any other way. She had been incredulous herself. But it was the only explanation that made sense. After all, no one had used Sir Gerald's rooms since his death two years ago. And if anyone did enter them, it was the servants during the autumn cleaning in preparation for winter, to dust what was not under holland covers, and to check that the fireplaces, one in the bedchamber and one in the dressing room, were not inhabited by rodents or birds. And then the servant door by which they had entered was locked again, and the key given to the housekeeper. The main door to the bedchamber, which led onto the corridor, had been locked and this key given to Lady Mary on the day of her husband's funeral. She had not unlocked it since.

The autumn clean had been over a month ago now. And there was no reason for any of the servants to enter those rooms again, nor had they. She had checked with the housekeeper. And certainly no one would enter them at night, which was when she had heard the noises. And so she told Mr. Bryce, doing her best to appear as if she were discussing the everyday, and not something incorporeal. And because she was delaying for as long as possible confiding in him what she feared most.

"And where did you *hear* this specter, my lady?"

"I was in my bedchamber. The noises came from Sir Gerald's dressing room."

"Thank-you for the clarification. What time was this?"

"At night. It was late."

"You were not—*dreaming*—perhaps?"

"No. I thought so at first. I thought I was having a nightmare. But when I was fully awake I knew I was not dreaming, which was far more disturbing than any nightmare."

"Did you hear these—*noises*—just the once?"

"No. I was woken again later that night by similar noises. Which is why I-I decided to come to you."

"Do you think that perhaps what you heard was a cat on the roof, or a bird nesting in the tree outside your window? Or indeed, it may have been a branch of that tree scraping against the window pane?"

Mary considered this for a moment, then shook her head.

"No, Mr. Bryce. The noises could not have been made by those things. The sounds were different entirely. And it was a still night—has been still all this week. So there was no wind to stir the branches, or whistle through the sills."

"What precisely did you hear, my lady?"

"My first thought, when I was still half-asleep, was that it was Sir Gerald come through from his bedchamber to visit me. To do so he must walk through his dressing room, which is the room that divides his bedchamber from mine…"

"And so you heard footfall?" Christopher gently prompted when Mary's voice trailed off and she looked down at her hands.

Mary shook her head again, then slowly lifted her gaze to his brown eyes.

"No. Not footfall. It was the banging of a door that woke me. Thinking back on it, it must have been the door from one of the clothes presses. And the second sound was a thud, like a chair being knocked over and hitting the floor. That's what woke me the first time. The second time was when someone or something was moving about the dressing room. Only this time drawers were pulled open and then slid shut, many times over, as if it was searching for something. In my half-waking state I presumed it was Sir Gerald—how I always knew when he was coming—I would be awake well before he opened the connecting door."

"Because he banged the furniture and knocked over a chair?" Christopher was so surprised by this revelation that he spoke his thoughts aloud. "But this was his dressing room. Surely he knew his way around his own rooms not to stumble about. Or had his valet let the fire die and not left him a taper?"

Mary thought his line of questioning too personal, but realized when he continued to frown that he was genuinely puzzled. She was grateful for his incomprehension. Yet, a little part of her wanted to blurt out how she truly felt: That he should shoulder some of the blame for her husband's drunkenness. In the months leading up to Sir Gerald's death, there were several occasions when the two men had stayed up late into the small hours, talking over their port. And if on those nights her husband had not drunk to excess, he would never have trespassed into her bedchamber, sweaty and stinking of spirits, demanding his marital rights with no regard to her feelings or her person.

But a moment's reflection and realization as to her position and his, Mary knew that while she could blame Christopher Bryce for his part in Sir Gerald's inebriation, she could not blame him for the degradation she had endured at the hands of her drunken husband. Her mother had told her bluntly the day of her wedding that it was her lot

in life to be an obedient wife. This meant accepting with good grace
her husband's carnal demands, whatever they happened to be, and
whenever he wished to avail himself. She must not complain. She must
do as she was told. And above all, she must hide her disgust. Mary had
no idea what her mother was talking about. Which was just as well.
On her wedding night and every subsequent night on which her
husband had *availed himself*, Mary had followed her mother's edicts,
even when Sir Gerald's demands were beyond what she was sure any
wife was expected to tolerate.

Her widowhood had been spent making that part of her married
life a distant memory. Yet here she was having to rake it up in an
attempt to convince Christopher Bryce she believed Sir Gerald's rooms
to be haunted. It helped that she was discussing the matter with him in
the steward's office, the reason she had come here, and not sent for him
to her sitting room; that setting would have been far too personal. She
certainly would not have confided in her neighbor, the bachelor
farmer. But in his role of steward, she knew that whatever he might
privately think of her fears, he would treat the matter, and her, with
respect. It was his duty to do so.

She would not have had the courage, or received the same treatment, had she voiced her suspicions to her mother, who would have
mocked her; her two younger brothers, who would have teased her; or
her Roxton cousins, all of whom would have smiled indulgently upon
her as if she were addle-brained. No one would have taken her
seriously.

"There was always a fire in Sir Gerald's dressing room, and plenty
of light. As you are well aware, Sir Gerald never skimped on wax."

Christopher was indeed well aware. Sir Gerald had spent a fortune
on the very best beeswax tapers. But he was still perplexed as to why
the Baronet would be stumbling about his own rooms, banging into
furniture at such a late hour, being bad-mannered and loud enough to
wake his wife in the process, like some drunken uncouth oaf returned
from *The Bear Inn*. And why would he come through to her rooms in
such an unfit state…

And then he knew.

Revelation hit him like an unexpected cuff across the ear. The
stinging shock momentarily robbed him of speech.

All those nights drinking… All those times he was confident he'd
left the Baronet sprawled out on the sofa in his book room, to sleep off
a bout of heavy drinking, to wake with a thudding head, a bad back
from an awkward night's sleep, and no recollection of the conversation
of the night before… Not once did Christopher think it a possibility

the man was not so drunk he was capable of staggering off to bother his wife with his amorous attentions.

He had been solely focused on Sir Gerald's loquacious confidences, intent on prizing from him a confession that he'd committed traitorous acts as a spy for the French or American rebels, or both. He'd never given Lady Mary a single thought—well, not then. Not because he hadn't wanted to, but because it was best for his sanity and his peace of mind not to do so. And he certainly did not allow his mind to cloud with thoughts of her while he drank with her husband. But now this…

She had no need to state the obvious, and he would not reveal to her that he fully understood. Best if he remain suitably blank-faced. So despite being revolted, wretched and furious with himself, for her benefit he managed to keep his expression and tone neutral.

"And when you decided you'd been woken by a—um—*ghost*, what did you do, my lady?"

Mary was so relieved he did not ask for further explanation about Sir Gerald's bumbling nocturnal wanderings that she said with a buoyancy in contrast to the trepidation and fear she had experienced at the time,

"I put my ear to the connecting door and listened for further noises. I wanted to be certain, so that I could tell you precisely what I heard."

"And what did you hear?"

Mary regarded him quizzically.

"I told you, Mr. Bryce. The banging of a door, and a chair being knocked over upon the first occasion, and the opening and closing of drawers on the second."

"Yes. Yes. Of course you did," Christopher apologized, mind still reeling with Sir Gerald's appalling behavior. "And you are certain you did not hear footfall when you had your ear to the door?"

"No. None. I am only stating the facts to you. I lack the imagination to make these things up! Which is why I am sure it must be the ghost of—"

"Does the connecting door have a bolt?"

"Yes. It's been bolted since Sir Gerald's death."

"Should've been bolted when he was alive," Christopher muttered through his teeth.

Instantly, he looked at Lady Mary to see if she had heard him. She had. The flush of heat to her face, and the widening of her eyes before she looked away, told him so. He went cold and glanced at his assistant. And sure enough, there was Timothy Deed, large ears wide open, and mouth at half-cock. So he, too, had caught Christopher's muttered wishful thinking. There was nowhere for him to climb in their estimation but up. But to save her the embarrassment of underscoring his verbal indiscretion he said, after clearing his throat of a sudden constriction,

"Best—best to keep the door bolted… as a precaution. To be safe."

"But… Mr. Bryce, what is the point of a bolt to a door? Such a device is surely superfluous. It won't stop an ethereal being from entering my room, will it? He could very well pass through the wall as a locked door."

"A specter may be able to perform such a feat, yes," Christopher conceded, suppressing a grin at her no-nonsense practicality which momentarily quelled any fear she may have had of a ghost entering her bedchamber. "But as this-this—*ghost*—hasn't passed through the wall into your bedchamber, but remained on the other side of the door, I doubt it intends to—"

"How can you be sure? And how do you know his intentions?"

Two questions Christopher could not answer. But he was certain that whatever was knocking chairs over and banging doors in Sir Gerald's dressing room, it could be any number of things, but an ethereal being it was not. He could have provided her with a myriad of alternatives to a ghost wreaking havoc in the dressing room, from a window left ajar by a forgetful servant, thus allowing in the elements and perhaps a bird, possibly an owl, a rodent or a squirrel was now trapped in the room. And there was another possibility—that the ghost was in fact an intruder of the flesh and blood variety—a disgruntled servant, perhaps, intent on thievery. A much more probable explanation, and one he intended to explore, but which he did not wish to confide in Lady Mary and cause her unnecessary worry. Hence his enquiry if the connecting door could be bolted.

And then he had a sudden puzzling thought.

"My lady, you do not say *it* but *he*, as if you know the identity of this ghost."

Lady Mary cocked her head and considered him as if he had lost his wits, and when he continued to look at her as if he was without sense, common or otherwise, she said with a catch of fear in her voice,

"Mr. Bryce, I have just explained matters to you in the plainest of terms. Who else could the ghost be? I do not know why Sir Gerald has suddenly appeared, but I can only think his spirit is unsettled and will only be at peace once he has found what he is looking for in his dressing room."

"Sir Gerald? You think—the ghost—You think *your late husband* is haunting this house?"

"Yes, Mr. Bryce, I do."

Christopher wasn't sure whether to burst out laughing or to offer suitable skeptical platitudes he hoped would quell her fear, so he said rather more gruffly than he intended,

"Why in the name of all that's sacred would Sir Gerald return from the dead, and for what?"

"If I knew, would I be asking you to find out? But I see by your expression that you think I am talking utter nonsense. So perhaps it would be for the best if I request the vicar's assistance. He at least will believe me and—"

"Please, my lady. I believe you. And seeking out the vicar may be what is required if we need to exorcise a ghost from this house. But perhaps, so as not to upset the rest of the household with talk of ghosts, you would like me to investigate first?"

"Yes, thank-you, I would," she replied with a sigh of relief. "I am sure if there is one person who can help Sir Gerald find what he is looking for it is you, Mr. Bryce."

He was glad she lacked a vivid imagination because the truth could turn out to be far more frightening than the ghost of a drunkard Sir Gerald. When she got to her feet and shook out her quilted petticoats, he scraped back his chair and stood, signaling for Mr. Deed to remain seated.

"I hope staying the night won't be too much of an inconvenience for you, and for your aunt," Lady Mary enquired politely. "But the sooner we know what Sir Gerald wants, the sooner he will be able to rest in peace."

"Yes, my lady. And no, it won't be an inconvenience. My aunt can bear with the loss of my company for one evening." Christopher adding dryly, "Best the ghost is placated as soon as possible. We don't want the servants fleeing to take up work in my cloth mills, now do we?"

"Most certainly not! How Mrs. Keble is to run this house without enough hands I—"

"My lady, that was my poor attempt at humor," Christopher interrupted quietly, unable to hide his grin at his ability to instantly rile her. "All current vacancies at my mills are filled."

"Oh? Ah! Yes. I apologize for not recognizing your wit. But that is good news, about your mills. For you, and for this house. I'm sure you haven't forgotten the Duke's secretary is due any day," she stumbled on when his grin widened and caused her cheeks to flush with heat. "And though he brings along his manservant, Mrs. Keble says his visits cause all manner of extra work for the kitchen and laundry maids, not to mention the men outdoors who are required to follow him upon his inspections further afield.”

“I'd not forgotten,” Christopher replied flatly. He considered Roxton's pompous secretary, Mr. Audley, a dead bore, and an overly officious interfering one at that. “How could I, when His Grace of Roxton's recent letter included a judicious reminder of his secretary's visit, even though his most humble servant also wrote to me, and the visit has been marked on the calendar for almost three months.”

Christopher sarcasm was lost on Mary who, suddenly remembering the letter from her ducal cousin, reached into her pocket to find it. She broke the seal with shaking fingers and sank back onto the chair to read. But before unfolding the single sheet of parchment she remembered her manners and looked up at the Squire.

“Excuse me, Mr. Bryce. His Grace's letter will contain news I've been waiting to—”

“Do not apologize. Read it.”

Mary smiled and nodded and dropped her gaze to the parchment. Christopher watched her. And Mr. Deed watched him. The Squire was so absorbed that when Mary finally looked up smiling, eyes moist, he was slow to respond. But his preoccupation went unnoticed because her thoughts were all for her cousins, the Duchess in particular. Such was her happiness and relief for the ducal couple that she included the Squire and his assistant in her joy and announced through her tears,

“The Duchess was safely delivered of her fifth child, and mother and infant are doing splendidly. Such a relief… Roxton writes with all the enthusiasm of a father whose fourth son might as well be his first! And I dare say if Otto had been a girl, he would've been just as pleased.”

“*Otto?*”

Christopher pulled a face and Mary smiled.

“Otto George Hesham. Otto after the Duchess's late and favorite brother,” Mary explained. “And George, I assume, for her father, Sir George Cavendish.”

“The poor mite! On both counts. I'm sorry, my lady, but even you must agree that Otto is a rather unfortunate Christian name for any child. As for bestowing the name of such a reprobate as Sir George Cavendish on a newborn, the Duke must have rocks in his head!”

“You are free and easy with your opinions today, Mr. Bryce,” Mary stated primly, again on her feet and hastily folding the letter. “Perhaps you forget that Sir George was not only the Duchess of Roxton's father but Sir Gerald's also, and Teddy's grandfather.”

“I do not need reminding, my lady,” Christopher said quietly. “He lived here in this house for a time when I was a boy, and I remember him well, very well. You, however, never met him, did you?"

"I did not have that pleasure, no. Now you will excuse me, it is almost time to change for dinner, and Teddy—"

"I apologize for disparaging the Duke's choice of names for his newborn son, my lady, but not for my remark about Sir George. Believe me, it is as well you never did have the—um—*pleasure*. Good day."

He inclined his head and said no more. When she turned to leave, he resumed his seat and took up the letter in front of him, but did not read, annoyed with himself for letting down his guard yet again, firstly about the Duke, and then about Sir George Cavendish.

Mary stood there a full five seconds, wondering what Christopher Bryce knew about Sir George Cavendish, such was his dark forbidding look, then decided it was not her business and best left alone. Not for the first time did she speculate about Mr. Christopher Bryce's history. The man was an enigma. A farmer and mill owner who had agreed to take two days out of his fortnight to act as steward of his neighbor's estate, was indeed a mystery. That he remained a bachelor at the age of forty, when his life experiences would have provided him with plenty of opportunity to find a wife, deepened her curiosity.

If not a wife, then why not a mistress? Men were permitted such indulgences in Polite Society. But she knew such behavior would not be tolerated in this provincial pocket of Gloucestershire. If the Squire did have a mistress—and why wouldn't he? He was, after all, an attractive man—she did not live nearby, but elsewhere, Cheltenham perhaps, or farther afield, in Bath. But as he rarely travelled further south than Stroud, and he shared his house in the next vale with an elderly aunt, this seemed unlikely... As to the many years he had spent on the Continent... Mary was intrigued. The only time she had enquired of Sir Gerald if their neighbor had ever mentioned his Continental wanderings, he had smugly replied that what he knew about Squire Bryce was not for the ears of his wife, or for that matter, any gently-bred female. He was sure her little ears would glow scarlet.

"Is there something else I may help you with, my lady?" Christopher asked tonelessly without lifting his gaze from the Duke of Roxton's elegant handwriting.

"N-no. Noth—Nothing," she replied, giving a start and mentally shaking herself out of a daydream of the Squire with a possible mistress in Bath and countless lovers left behind on the Continent. "As you will be staying well into the night, I will inform the housekeeper to set an extra cover for dinner—Teddy will enjoy your company—and to air the steward's bedchamber."

He looked up at her then. "Thank-you, my lady. That would be most welcome."

She nodded and he returned to his reading. Gathering up a handful of her petticoats she turned to leave when the door was flung wide, causing her to stagger back in surprise. It banged up against the wood paneling, the Squire's frock coat slipping off the peg and crumpling to the floor, as a large white-and-tan wire-haired hound bounded into the room. It had a dead pheasant clamped between its jaws, and left a trail of muddy paw prints in its wake.

Mary knew the dog. He belonged to Christopher, and was his constant companion. Teddy took the lurcher out with her into the fields and the wood at every opportunity. Yet, this knowledge did not stop Mary from retreating behind the chair she'd been sitting on. The prospect of her husband's ghost haunting his rooms scared her, but an unleashed dog held a deeper terror. And although she knew it was an irrational fear, she could not control or hide it. Everyone in her family loved dogs—that most faithful of animal companions—be they hunting dogs or lap dogs. And while her family tolerated her aversion, her mother did not. She refused to acknowledge any weakness in her children, and this despite knowing that as a small child, Mary had been mauled by one of the Countess's terriers. It had taken hold of her right hand and not let go. She still carried the scars from that encounter. Since then, instinctively she shied away from all dogs, regardless of their breed or size.

And so it was not something she could control when her breathing became quick and shallow. She scrambled to kneel upon the chair, hands tight about the back rail, as if this would somehow save her from being approached by Lorenzo.

Christopher's chin had lifted with the bang of the door. He saw his four-legged companion, saw Mary clambering onto the chair, and within a few strides had put himself between the chair and the lurcher before it could proudly offer up his bounty to her.

"I'm s-sorry," she stammered. "I know he's a good dog. It's just I c-can't—"

"One or two deep breaths and you'll soon be yourself again," he stated, glancing over his shoulder. "And you, my fine fellow," he added in a completely different tone, addressing the lurcher affectionately when it dropped the pheasant at the toe of his jockey boot, "have no manners. But I do appreciate the gift. Sit, Lorenzo! Now where's your partner in this enterprise, I wonder…"

No sooner had Lorenzo obeyed than into the room rushed a thin-shouldered girl with a heart-shaped face dusted in freckles and a long untidy braid of cherry-red hair. Theodora Charlotte Cavendish—Teddy to everyone except her grandmother, who insisted on calling her Theodora—was ten years old and a tomboy. She had a toothy grin and bright brown eyes. Notwithstanding the remarkable shade of red to her wavy hair, she resembled neither parent. This was a relief to her relatives, given her father was not handsome in any sense, but also a disappointment, because while her mother was not considered a great beauty, Lady Mary did resemble her cousin Antonia enough to be thought a pretty redhead.

And because Teddy was a tomboy, she wore a riding frock coat buttoned up over her bodice and chemise, and under her petticoats a pair of breeches, made especially for her by her doting mother. And these, along with a thick pair of knitted stockings were tucked into jockey boots, to ward off the cold, but mainly so she could climb trees and ride astride unencumbered and with her mother's pride intact.

Her boots were splashed with mud, her hem soaked, and her hands and face could do with a good scrubbing before dinner. But for all that, her mother and Christopher greeted her with welcoming smiles, not a word said about the state of her appearance. She instantly went up to the lurcher and threw her arms about his neck. For her affection, she received a lick across the chin.

"Clever Lorenzo! Good boy!" She looked up at the Squire. "Do you like the gift he brought you, Uncle Bryce? He was *very* well-behaved on our walk, until he came across Mr. Owens and his two hounds. They were driving birds out of the hedge at the back of Elwood's cider mill. There's a ditch as deep as a pond—Mama!? Here you are!"

She saw her mother when Christopher stepped aside but kept a leg close to his lurcher. She thought it odd she was kneeling upon a chair, but then realized why and scrambled to her feet, adding in a rush, "I'm sorry I let Lorenzo go on ahead. It was to surprise Uncle Bryce. I should've had him drop the bird in the kitchen. I didn't know you were here, Mama. I came in the back way on account of the mud—"

"You were not to know, Teddy," Mary interrupted with a smile as she got off the chair and brushed down her petticoats, a wary eye on Lorenzo who remained at his master's side and barely moved his head in response to her movement. She put an arm about her daughter and gently brushed the wisps of frizzy hair out of her eyes. "You'll just have enough time to wash and put on a change of clothes before dinner. The bodice and petticoats made for Uncle Dair's wedding—"

"But, Mama, I would much prefer to wear—"

"We have a guest at table tonight, and you could practice your very best table manners in your very best gown in preparation for your stay with Granny."

"Guest?" Teddy frowned. "But we never have guests."

"Mr. Bryce is to dine with us."

Teddy looked up swiftly and the frown between her brows cleared.

"Truly? Are you? Are you truly staying to dinner, Uncle Bryce?" When Christopher nodded, she clapped her hands and then asked her mother, "Is there a special reason, or is Uncle Bryce staying so he can catch the ghost?"

THREE

Startled, Mary and Christopher looked at one another. It was left to the steward's assistant, forgotten in his warm corner of the office, to break the silence.

"A ghost, Miss Teddy? Now who's been weavin' such tales to frighten young maidens?"

"I'm not frightened, Mr. Deed," the girl responded matter-of-factly, but she could hardly contain her excitement, brown eyes growing rounder. "And there *is* a ghost! It's haunting the kitchen. So Jane and Jenny say. They won't go into the pantry. Mrs. Keble says that it will be more than their lives are worth if they don't stop being silly hens and get about their business. But Jenny says nothing will make her go in there. And Jane says if she does, she'll faint and be of no use to anyone. So *nothing* is getting done, and Cook wanted to take off her cap and stamp on it, she was *that* angry. Mrs. Keble sent Luke into the pantry to bring out the jam jars for Jane and Jenny to count. They counted them twice. It was just as Jane said. Two jars of jam *are* missing—"

"I hope the ghost was good enough to take the lemon marmalade, and leave the orange," Christopher commented. "The lemon is far too bitter for my taste. Fruit picked too early is my guess."

"Lemon marmalade? Yes, it is rather bitter..." Mary said, then frowned up at Christopher. "How can you be concerned about the bitterness—" she began and was cut off by her daughter, who said with a giggle,

"You are a silly head sometimes, Uncle Bryce! Ghosts can't *taste* anything, can they?"

When Christopher made a face and tapped the side of his nose as if to say he was thinking the exact same thought, Teddy grinned, but Mary, who was still frowning, asked,

"Then why take the jam at all?"

"Mischief, so says Mrs. Keble," Teddy answered.

"It would be too much to hope that she also told the servants there is no ghost?" Christopher asked dryly.

"Yes, that would be too much," Teddy confirmed. "And Cook agreed with Mrs. Keble and said that she'd stake her life on it *there be no thieves at Abbeywood—*"

"There *are* no thieves," corrected her mother.

"My lady, I think Teddy was quoting Cook in her vernacular, were you not?"

The girl nodded her agreement with the Squire, then proceeded to mimic the cook's Cotswold speech. "Cook said *a body won't abide the notion there be thieves 'ere at Abbeywood, so thou be a ghost as what bin thieving them there jams, all to disturb yon peace.*" She shrugged and grinned. "So you see, there *must* be a ghost!"

"Your Uncle Dair would be impressed, but your grandmother appalled," Mary commented.

"Uncle Dair isn't afraid of any-*thing*," Teddy replied, and turned to Christopher saying proudly, "A war hero wouldn't be afraid of a ghost, would he?"

"No. He would not. But what I think your mother means is that your Uncle Dair, being a mimic himself, would enjoy your mimicry," Christopher explained, "but that your grandmother would not be pleased with you speaking in the tongue of your—um—*inferiors*."

"Inferiors?" Teddy didn't understand, and when neither Christopher nor Mary elaborated, she shrugged and stated without malice about her grandmother, the Countess of Strathsay, "Granny is appalled by every*thing* and every*one*."

"*That* is very true," Mary said on a sigh, more to herself than to those in the room, adding "I don't know why he—why a ghost would want to upset Cook."

She was unsettled by the thought of Sir Gerald's ghost not being confined to his dressing room. Which, when she thought about it, was a silly notion. Ghosts could go where they pleased. So it made her doubly relieved that the Squire was staying the night. With a wary eye on Lorenzo, whose gaze was following Teddy as she skipped and twirled about, and had sat up but then settled again at his master's feet, Mary put out a hand to her daughter.

That Teddy was incapable of remaining still reminded Mary of her eldest brother Alisdair. For his restlessness, and for staring out the window and not applying himself to his studies, he had been beaten by his tutors more times than she cared to count. Dair had always been happiest out-of-doors, and still was, and so was Teddy.

"We have disrupted Mr. Bryce's afternoon long enough with talk of a jam-stealing ghost. Perhaps while you're readying for dinner you can find a more suitable topic for dinner conversation—something Granny would approve. It will make for good practice for your visit with her at Cheltenham, which is only a few weeks away," she gently reminded her. "Don't you agree, Mr. Bryce?"

With this last sentence she directed a significant stare at Christopher, and was pleased when he was quick to agree. She was not pleased, however, when later, at the dining table after grace was said and with the parsnip soup and bread placed before them, he took up his soup spoon and asked Teddy casually,

"What else did Cook say about *a ghost as what bin thieving them jams?*"

Teddy eagerly gulped down the mouthful of soup and looked to her mother seated at the foot of the table for direction. Scrubbed clean until her chin and forehead gleamed, the girl's long, wavy red hair had been brushed free of tangles and held off her face by a blue satin hair band which matched the color of her silk petticoats and embroidered bodice. She wore new satin slippers and white stockings, and did her best to sit up straight, though the boning and the center busk of her bodice made slouching an impossibility.

As Lady Mary continued to eat her soup and made no comment, Teddy took this as a sign she was free to respond to the Squire's enquiry. She looked at Christopher, who sat across from her, and said earnestly,

"It likes pickles, too."

"Pickles? Does it? What type of pickles?"

"Type?" Teddy thought a moment. "Walnut. It's the walnut pickle that's missing."

"Walnut pickle? An excellent choice. Though I prefer Cook's pickled cucumbers. I'm glad it took the walnut and left the cucumber pickles."

Teddy giggled.

"It's a very thoughtful ghost then, isn't it, Uncle Bryce?"

"Very thoughtful—to me. But not to Cook, or Mrs. Keble, or Jane and Jenny. By the by, what sort of jam did it steal?"

"Strawberry jam. And a jar of marmalade."

"Do you think this ghost eats the walnut pickles with or without the strawberry jam, or perhaps with the marmalade?"

"Walnut pickles and strawberry jam eaten *together*?" Teddy pulled a face of revulsion. "*Faugh*! That would taste *awful*."

"Yes. But you said so yourself that ghosts can't taste, so how would it know?"

"Oh, Uncle Bryce, it doesn't need the sense of taste to steal—"

"Teddy. Young ladies and gentlemen do not use the word *faugh* at any time, and most certainly not at table," Mary lectured quietly. "Next time, please find a more polite word to express your disgust. And a more suitable topic for the dinner table, hopefully one that won't upset your grandmother. Now eat your soup before it is cold."

"Yes, Mama. Sorry, Mama," Teddy murmured, suitably chastened, and dropped her chin, but not before she caught Christopher's wink and they exchanged a smile.

The three diners finished their soup in silence. The only sounds were the tick of the clock on the mantel, the chink of silver spoons in porcelain bowls, and the heels of Teddy's satin slippers scuffing against the chair rail as she swung her stockinged legs back and forth. Her new petticoats and tidy hair might give her the semblance of the young miss, but the tomboy could not be suppressed, nor it seemed could the Squire's interest in discussing the ghost.

He, too, had made an effort with his appearance. Mary noticed this immediately when he came through to the hall via the servant's door, just before dinner was announced. His jockey boots were free of mud and were polished. His stock had been re-tied to fit snugly about his neck, and his tousle of curls scraped back and tied off with a neat satin bow. He wore his frock coat unbuttoned over his shirt and waist-coat. Cut to curve away from the torso to highlight the waistcoat beneath, on younger men, who wore fashionable embroidered waist-coats, the effect was most pleasing.

On middle-aged men such as her husband, such a cut drew unwanted attention to their expanding waistlines, and rarely did the silver or horn buttons of their waistcoats sit flat, often they did not do up at all. Sir Gerald, like many middle-aged men of means, carried a paunch, a trophy of a lifetime of good food, plenty of home-brewed cider and ale, and a sedentary lifestyle brought on by the success of their various ventures, whether mercantile, commercial, industrial, or agrarian.

Mr. Christopher Bryce, however, did not conform to type. Despite being middle-aged, he did not sport the quintessential paunch. In truth, he had the figure and bearing of a younger man. If not for the creases that came with age at the corners of his eyes and either side of his straight nose, he could easily have passed for a man many years his junior. A grave younger man to be sure, one who was austere with her, and with those he employed, and who kept very much to himself in social situations, but who was rarely, if ever, solemn when in the company of her daughter.

Mary caught his wink and the smile exchanged with Teddy and chose to be blind to it. Far from causing her concern that he was undermining her parental authority, she found the bond between them charming. Sir Gerald had been bitterly disappointed at having a daughter and not the longed-for son, and treated Teddy as an annoyance. Christopher Bryce, however, had never been dismissive or given the impression that because she was a girl, Teddy's life was worth less than had she been born male.

And so in this, too, the Squire was not archetypal. While the first families of the vale had expressed their condolences on Sir Gerald's lack of a son, and even offered Mary their heartfelt prayers she would deliver an heir with her next pregnancy, Christopher Bryce had never singled out Teddy's gender for comment. He treated her as he found her. She was simply Teddy. For this alone, Mary was prepared to tolerate his blunt, dictatorial dealings and his stubborn refusal to allow Teddy to visit her Roxton cousins.

As for Teddy spending time in his company, and he dining at their table, this too she welcomed, though her mother would've been horrified at such a social solecism. How very different had been her upbringing! The ingrained social dictates of her childhood had made her instinctively docile in the presence of her mother and her social superiors, and even at the age of thirty continued to influence her choices. Never a word had she spoken out of turn at the dinner table or in company when her mother was present, for fear of being ridiculed.

She was determined her daughter would have none of those fears and prejudices that had been instilled in her. Teddy's life would be different. So she was happy to let the Squire and her daughter banter back and forth like two tavern habitués, she consigned to interested spectator and societal referee. She was listening while they chatted between mouthfuls of baked trout and roasted meats with seasonal vegetables, a light in her violet eyes and a smile hovering just below her polite demeanor as hostess. Both had abided by her request and Christopher was listening to Teddy chatter about the escape and recapture of Will Bisley's prize sheep, which had given Cook, who was Will's cousin, *a month's mind of worry*. And then he returned the conversation to the ghost and the missing condiments. Mary wondered why. There had to be a good reason for him to do so. Christopher Bryce was not given to whimsy.

"Has our ghost purloined anything else from the pantry?" Christopher speculated as he refilled his wine glass. "Or was this his first and only visit to the kitchen?"

Teddy leaned forward and said with conspiratorial excitement, "It's not the first time! A loaf of bread was stolen. Not a whole loaf. Only what was left over from dinner. Cook was going to use it to make bread pudding."

"Bread?" asked Mary, and found herself ignored by her daughter and the Squire, though he did throw her a look.

"Anything else?" Christopher asked Teddy casually, sipping at his glass.

"Two bottles of elderflower wine. Luke said it was one, but Jane is certain it's two."

"*Two* bottles of elderflower wine?" Christopher repeated with awe and sat back. "Good!"

Teddy frowned. "Good? *Fau—*" She quickly swallowed back the vulgar exclamation, a glance at her mother, adding, "But you don't even like elderflower wine, Uncle Bryce."

"True. I hope the ghost takes *all* the elderflower wine. Better that than this fine Bordeaux we're drinking."

Mary was suddenly ill at ease. "I beg your pardon, Mr. Bryce. I should have asked... I thought—with you here for dinner—you would not mind me taking the liberty of having a bottle fetched."

"It was not meant as a criticism, my lady," Christopher stated quietly. "You may have wine with every meal, if that is your wish."

Teddy was curious. "Why must you ask Uncle Bryce's permission, Mama? It's our cellar."

Mary glanced at Christopher, then said,

"No, Teddy, it's not. Everything from the sugar spoon to the broom in the stables belongs to Sir Gerald's heir, your cousin—Sir John Cavendish. I've spoken to you before about him—about Jack," Lady Mary explained. "We live here with the permission of his guardian. And one day, when he is old enough to take on the management of Abbeywood, he will live here for part of the year, and no doubt the rest of the year in London."

"Can we stay here with Cousin Jack?"

As Christopher was sipping his wine and made no effort to

comment, Mary said, "I don't believe he would want that, Teddy. He'll bring his bride here, and I dare say by the time that day arrives, you'll be married, too, so you'll have a house of your own—"

"But I don't want to leave Abbeywood, *ever*. And I won't," Teddy stated flatly. "He can't make me! This is *my* home, *not* his. Besides, where will *you* live, Mama?"

"Me? Oh, I've not thought much about that, Teddy," Mary responded lightly, and smiled. "We don't need to worry yet. So many things can happen in a handful of years."

It was an untruth. She had thought of little else in her widowhood. But this was not the time or place to discuss her future, or her daughter's. So she was annoyed when Christopher made a blunt observation, and even more surprised by her daughter's response.

"Your mother is correct, Teddy. But if you reach the grand old age of one-and-twenty and remain unmarried, which I doubt, and Sir John has taken up residence here, I'm sure your Uncle Dair would welcome you at Fitzstuart Hall, if you wished to live there. Isn't that so, my lady?"

Teddy screwed up her mouth, freckled nose twitching in thought. And then she shook her head. "No. I don't want to live with Uncle Dair. I love him, but I want to stay here. Who would look after my chickens? And there is no Puzzlewood at Fitzstuart Hall. And you and mama let me ride *everywhere*. And what about Lorenzo, and you, Uncle Bryce, and Kate and Carlo and Silvia? How would I visit you all from so far away? No. I will stay here because it is the best place in the whole of England, isn't it, Uncle Bryce?"

"Yes... in the whole world," Christopher replied gently.

Mary smiled at Teddy, not at all surprised by her daughter's vehement championing of this picturesque pocket of England. She had fallen in love with the Cotswolds from the carriage window as a bride, catching glimpses of the patchwork of green rolling hills dotted with pockets of woodland and honey stone cottages clinging to the slopes. Sir Gerald had his driver take them through the local village, the inhabitants lined up outside their cottages on a hilly crooked lane, bobbing a curtsy or removing their hats, all eager to get a glimpse of their master's young wife.

"Yes. It is an idyll—even in the depths of winter. There isn't a more welcoming place in the kingdom I'd wish to be with you, Teddy. But you need not concern yourself about leaving here for many, many years," Mary assured her. "And even if you were to leave, even for a little while, say to go to school, you could return. Just as you do when you visit with Granny at Cheltenham. Mr. Bryce spent his childhood and youth here, just as you are doing, and then he went away for a time, but returned. Is that not so, Mr. Bryce?"

"Yes, my lady."

Teddy was unconvinced.

"Uncle Bryce came back because he could. He's a boy and his father left him Brycecomb. Girls don't inherit houses. Sir Gerald left us nothing but a great pile of debts. Granny said so. She said we are burdens, that girls are nothing but burdens on their male relatives."

Mary knew with depressing certainty her mother had expressed these opinions. She had heard them often enough. The Countess of Strathsay had been devastated when Mary, her firstborn, was not the son and heir the Earl of Strathsay needed, and she never let Mary forget her disappointment. For Mary, Teddy's birth was a blessing and compensation for a loveless marriage. Not for Teddy the hours she had spent sitting in stiff fabric and whale bone, a book balanced on her head to keep her spine and shoulders straight, no thought to her health or happiness.

Mary was determined Teddy's childhood would be different. So if climbing trees and riding astride and being outdoors all day made Teddy happy, then she, as her mother, would do her best to see that she could do those things. And the best place to do this was here, tucked away in the wilds of the Cotswolds, where they had few neighbors and fewer visitors, and no one could ridicule her for her mothering, or her daughter for being herself.

And now here was Teddy, slumped in her chair, as much as it was possible to slump in a boned corset, and with an expression of foreboding, so very different from the happy child she'd been while talking of a thieving ghost in the pantry, and all because her granny had unsettled her with talk of being made to leave Abbeywood. For the first time since she had dared mention the existence of a haunting, Mary wished the ghost would appear then and there to distract Teddy from needless worry.

The Squire seemed to have read her mind, because he eventually managed to steer the conversation back to the ghost, but not before offering Teddy reassurances of his own.

"Your father made me your legal guardian, Teddy. That means you cannot be taken from here without my permission. And your granny, or your cousin Jack, or your Uncle Dair cannot make me do what you don't want me to do. Does that make you feel better?"

Teddy nodded, but she did not appear completely convinced.

"Can Mama stay here, too?"

"Of course."

"Granny says when Mama finds a new husband, he will make her leave here."

Mary swallowed, not a look in Christopher's direction, made uneasy by such a question put to him, and in front of her. But she did not want to further unsettle her daughter with talk of leaving the only home she had known, so she said as casually as she could, hoping she sounded light-hearted,

"Dear me, Granny certainly had a bee buzzing near her ear when we last saw her, did she not?"

Teddy leaned in and said confidentially to Christopher, "Uncle Dair says that *all the time* about Granny." Then she settled against the chair back once more and said to her mother, "Granny told Uncle Dair you can't go on being a burden—and then told him to stop wearing the carpet to threads with his pacing. But he said that as the carpet belonged to him, he could walk it to threads if he wished. And then he took me riding, which put him in a better mood."

Mary extended her hand to her daughter, and when she placed her fingers in hers gave them a gentle squeeze.

"Teddy, Granny says the things she does because she worries about us, and wants everything to be just so. But sometimes—*most of the time*—when something or someone doesn't do what she expects, she becomes disagreeable. Particularly when her mind lacks occupation. Do you understand?"

"I think—*think* so… Granny has nothing better to do with her time than to fret and fuss over things that don't concern her, so Uncle Dair says."

"Yes. Yes, that's right."

"So you don't have to find a new husband?" she added eagerly.

Mary suppressed a sigh and smiled, picking up her wine glass and taking a sip so she could formulate a response. Ironically, in this case her mother was right. The Countess had badgered her from Buckinghamshire to Hampshire. Shut up in a carriage was the perfect place, and the journey to Dair's wedding the perfect opportunity, for her mother to give a lecture on duty, and tell her to stop being selfish and think of the family, and their good name, and Teddy's future. It was imperative she remarried. Two years in the wilds of Gloucestershire was time enough to mourn. And Mary was no longer a girl. Soon whatever beauty she possessed would fade altogether and no man would want her.

The Countess suggested that perhaps an older man who already had grown children would offer for her. And if she was exceedingly fortunate her new husband would be incapable of mounting her and merely want a companion for his old age. But this her mother doubted. Men were beasts, their carnal appetites fit only for…

Mary had stopped listening, though she resisted the urge to stare out at the scenery and kept her gaze firmly on her mother's tired features. For the hundredth, if not the thousandth time, she wondered what had possessed her father to marry such a bigoted creature. But her mother was right in one respect. She needed to do her duty to her family and to Teddy, and remarry. She knew she would only have to ask for Roxton's help and he would find her any number of possible bridegrooms for her consideration. She might be penniless, but she was still the daughter of an earl and the great-granddaughter of Charles the Second. And to the nobility, lineage counted for everything.

"Perhaps Jack won't want to come and live here, now we have a resident ghost?" Christopher suggested to lighten the mood and break the silence, gaze firmly on Teddy. He had not looked Mary's way since the girl had mentioned her mother needed to marry. "Particularly one intent on ransacking the pantry. Let's see…What has our incorporeal friend managed to take so far. Tell me if I leave anything off the list: Strawberry jam, walnut pickle, a jar of lemon marmalade, the remains of a loaf of bread, and *two* bottles of elderflower wine." When Teddy nodded he had listed all the items correctly, he added with satisfaction, "I'd say that's the beginnings of a feast, perhaps a picnic." He leaned in, a look left, then right, and whispered loudly, "Do you think this ghost will invite us to this picnic if we brought a wheel of Abbeywood's cheese and some cold cuts?"

Teddy hunched her shoulders, grinning and nodding vigorously.

"I suppose you would also like us to supply plates, knives, and napkins, too, Mr. Bryce?" Mary asked with a small smile, coming out of her abstraction and happy to join in a conversation which had once more turned to the absurd.

"Can we, Mama? And have a basket to put it all in!"

"A capital idea, Teddy," Christopher agreed, then added—the words out of his mouth before he'd given them careful consideration, "It's evident you have inherited not only your mother's autumnal loveliness, but also her generosity of spirit."

There followed a heavy pause in the conversation when nothing was said because too much had been said. It made for an awkward silence between the adults. Christopher's throat burned. Mary drew in breath, face inexplicably warm. Both made a conscious effort not to look at the other, and yet were more acutely aware of the other's presence than ever before. And both realized that something momentous had just occurred that could not now be ignored or undone.

FOUR

Autumnal loveliness...? From where had those feeble words sprung? And why those words? Could he not, after all these years, have chosen better? How had he allowed himself to be so unguarded—to blab like a Blue Coat schoolboy? He who had always been circumspect in her presence, sometimes to the point where it was best not to speak at all. Like the first time he had seen her. It was autumn, as it was now. The leaves had turned. No longer shades of green, they were vibrant yellows, oranges, and deep reds. Some had fallen. Others clung on, the pockets of forest dotted with fiery flashes against the fading light. He'd kept a dark red leaf from that day, because it was the same color as her glorious hair. He'd pressed it between the pages of the Bryce family Bible.

Sir Gerald had invited him to Abbeywood several months after his return from the Continent. Kate had just arrived and was knee deep in packing straw. But she would never have accompanied him had she, too, been invited. In truth, Kate would never again leave the safety and anonymity of Brycecomb Hall. And there, waiting in the Abbeywood Farm hall to greet him was the Lady Mary, hair dressed as it was now: One thick braid wound close to her head like a hair band, the rest coiled into netting at her nape.

He remembered that as he walked across the flagstones to greet her, his breathing slowed and the beat of his heart drummed in his ears, drowning out Sir Gerald's effusive introductions. And if her red-headed beauty affected his breathing and quickened his heart, her violet-blue eyes—the color of the wild harebell—caused him to forget his manners and stare openly. Later, thinking back on that moment, it was not so much their unusual color, but the way in which they darkened upon meeting him. That look, their silent exchange, lasted a few brief seconds, but he knew in that moment, as surely as he knew his name, that the Lady Mary Cavendish and he had made a lasting connection.

Neither had spoken of that first meeting since. It was as if it had never happened, and given the gulf in their disparate circumstances, that was for the best. She was the great-granddaughter of a Stuart king, and cousin once removed of the Duke of Roxton. He was a Cotswold squire with a past so base that had Sir Gerald an inkling of it, he would never have allowed Christopher into his house, least of all make his bow to the Lady Mary. All other considerations aside, there was the insurmountable fact she was married.

Yet, that first meeting, and the feelings it had awakened, remained just below the surface of their daily interactions: Suppressed. Simmering. Unsanctioned. Unforgettable. Undeniable. And now this…

How dare he make such a personal declaration. He had no right. He had placed her in an awkwardly embarrassing position. He was acting as the estate's steward, thus he was a servant, one rung above a housekeeper. And when he was not being steward, he was a simple squire of a small holding in the next vale. And when he wasn't farming, he was engaged in *trade*—a mill owner no less. What Christopher Bryce would never be was her social equal. The societal divide between them was so wide he might as well be on one side of the Atlantic and she on the other, and never the two should meet.

Society might accept into their ranks the daughter of a squire or a merchant if she married up into the nobility (though that would not stop the sniggers behind the poor girl's back), but it did not apply in the reverse. Daughters of the nobility did not marry down. That caused the type of scandal from which a female never made a recover, nor was her family ever able to remove the stain. Such base marriages were not unknown. There had been instances of elopements and clandestine matches, but such couplings caused scandal, heartache, and banishment. These wayward daughters of noblemen became the pariahs of their class. They might as well have leprosy. For Mary, such a match was unthinkable.

Mary's mother considered it enough of a humiliation Christopher

Bryce held her daughter's day-to-day living accountable to him, but for Sir Gerald to leave his only child, her granddaughter, the daughter of a lady, in the guardianship of such a man—that was a disgrace. And the yokel had the effrontery to deny a duke—Roxton no less—access to his own niece. Who did the upstart think he was?

Whipped up into an emotional frenzy by her mother's constant berating and her Roxton cousins' opposition to a stranger having the care of Teddy, Mary had agreed with them. She publically denounced Christopher, calling him a fiend and a brute. In front of her mother, her brother, the Duke of Roxton, and her cousin the Duchess of Kinross, she accused him of being uncompromisingly stubborn, cold-hearted, and high-handed. He kept her daughter a prisoner at Abbey-wood, and by virtue of her being Teddy's mother, kept her prisoner, too. She couldn't wait for Teddy to turn one-and-twenty. Or better still, to marry earlier, so that Mr. Christopher Bryce's guardianship would be at an end. And when Jack was of age, he would appoint a more fitting person to act as steward, and Mr. Bryce would return to his vale and his estate and remain there, no longer with any need to have anything to do with them or her, or with Abbeywood.

When she was calmer and away from her mother's malicious influence, away from her Roxton cousins—who were all so arrogantly self-assured of their place in the world—and she had returned to the tranquility of the vale with only her daughter for company, she regretted her outburst. Her accusations against Mr. Bryce were emotionally charged rants she wished she had never uttered.

Ideally she would have preferred the Duke of Roxton to be Teddy's guardian. He was, after all, Teddy's uncle. But if not the Duke, truth told, she was content to have Mr. Bryce, because Teddy loved her Uncle Bryce as much as she loved her true uncles, Mary's brothers Dair and Charles.

Tonight, Christopher Bryce sat at her table not as the steward, but as Squire Bryce, her neighbor and Teddy's legally appointed guardian. In these roles it was perfectly socially acceptable for him to do so, and until a few moments ago he had played his part well. In fact, in all the years they had known each other he had never faulted and strayed from the path of social formality in his dealings with her. And now, with one sentence, he had changed everything. She could never be comfortable in his company again…

"Mama isn't lovely, Uncle Bryce. She's beautiful," Teddy announced into the heavy silence as she scooped up a large helping of apple dumpling. "Uncle Dair says I'm certain to grow up to be just like her, but that I wasn't to tell because little brothers like to tease their elder sisters, not compliment them. I told Uncle Dair that he isn't little in the least, and that Mama and I keep no secrets. Granny said it's a crying shame I look like Mama with my frightful red hair and freckles because they will never change no matter how old I get or how much lemon juice is applied. So it's just as well I have powerful relatives to look after my interests... Sometimes, *most* times, I have no idea what Granny is talking about! But you like our red hair and you don't think the color frightful, do you, Uncle Bryce?"

"Yes, I do, and no, I don't," Christopher replied without hesitation, gaze fixed on Teddy. "You wouldn't be you with it any other way, would you?

"And Mama wouldn't be Mama. But I think you're fibbing when you say freckles are the ruby kisses left by fairies."

"Oh? But what a lovely notion!" Mary smiled, shaking off her pensiveness, determined to ignore and forget the Squire's unguarded compliment was ever uttered. "I've never heard freckles described in such a delightful way before."

"I cannot take the credit, my lady. A sprite said something similar in the bard's *Midsummer Night's Dream*, and I happened to remember it—"

"Because you like red hair and freckles," Teddy stated. "Mr. Shakespeare must've, too."

"Yes. Yes, something like that," Christopher murmured, and suddenly found the apple dumplings in front of him of intense interest.

"After pudding, Teddy and I usually retire to the parlor for a game of Goose, or she reads to me while I embroider." She looked at her daughter. "But perhaps today you would like to play at skittles in the hall?"

"May we? Will you play at skittles with us, Uncle Bryce?"

"Yes. I would like that," he replied. He set down his spoon and finally turned to look at Mary. "My lady, I crave your pardon for my earlier indiscreet admission. I did not mean to offend you, or make you uncomfortable. But—"

"It is of no importance, Mr. Bryce."

"—as it was a compliment, I will not retract it. I cannot."

Mary pushed back her chair and stood. Christopher and Teddy followed her lead. She placed her napkin on the table, brushed down the front of her damask gown, and only then did she look at the Squire. She lifted her chin slightly and said in an imperious manner her mother the Countess would've approved, "As you are a guest at my table, Mr. Bryce, I will accept your compliment. That is all I ever intend to say on the matter." She put out her hand for her daughter and said in an altogether different tone, "While the skittles are being readied, let's have our tea by the hall fire, shall we?"

They had tea and gingerbread biscuits in front of the main fireplace in the long hall, and played a round of Goose—because Uncle Bryce had stayed to dinner and three players were much better than two. And while they played the board game, two maids repositioned the larger of the two Turkey rugs up one end of the long room that had upon the paneled wall a row of paintings of lesser Cavendish ancestors. They then set out the nine wooden pins at this end of the rug and three wooden oblate balls at the other. One maid remained by the pins to set them upright when they were knocked down, while her companion was tasked with returning the wooden balls to the competitors.

Teddy and Christopher played three rounds, with Mary more than happy to be spectator and keep score. They won a game apiece, and on the third hand she saw Christopher deliberately turn his wrist, sending his ball wide of the mark of a pin he could easily have toppled. This allowed Teddy the chance to take the game, and as she was a tireless competitor and very much wanted to win, she took her time to size up the strike before pitching her ball. It toppled the remaining skittle and everyone in the hall applauded, Christopher making her a grandiloquent bow and conceding the game.

"You let her win," Mary stated some time later when she and Christopher were alone, Teddy fetched by her nurse to ready her for bed, and the intervening handful of hours allowing the couple to return to a semblance of easy formality.

"I gave her the chance to win. There is a difference."

Mary sat by the fire with her embroidery in her lap and her sewing box at her feet, attempting to thread a needle, while Christopher stood to one side of the enormous fireplace watching her and sipping a fresh cup of tea. Neither had spoken since Teddy had wished them a good night. Yet both were acutely aware of the other, which made threading the needle almost impossible, so she put her hands in her lap and looked up at him.

"Thank-you. And thank-you for making light of the ghost so she would not be afraid to go to her bed tonight."

"Ah. I should've realized you would be awake to my cunning plan."

"Not from the outset," she confessed. "But all that chatter about the ghost's culinary preferences was quite absurd and made me wonder…"

"And now, after hearing about the thefts from the pantry, do you believe it likely that it is a ghost who is making forays into the kitchen in search of food?"

"But… surely it could be a coincidence that I hear noises in Sir Gerald's rooms, and Cook announcing it must be a ghost not a thief who has stolen from the kitchen?"

"I do not believe it is a coincidence, or a ghost."

"Then what do you believe, Mr. Bryce?"

Christopher finished his tea, then put the teacup on its saucer and set both on the mantel.

"That whoever is in Sir Gerald's rooms is corporeal rather than ethereal, and that he is indeed a thief, but not just of condiments."

Mary sat up a little taller. Alarm registered in her voice. "A-a thief? There is a *thief* occupying Sir Gerald's rooms?"

Christopher thought it ironic she was more agitated at the prospect the intruder was a villain rather than a specter, but he managed to say without giving himself away,

"Yes, my lady. A hungry thief."

"Why?"

The side of his mouth twitched.

"Even thieves require sustenance."

"Dear me, you are witty today, Mr. Bryce," Mary retorted. "Why has a thief chosen to hide out in my husband's rooms of all the rooms in Abbeywood? There are other bedchambers, far from mine, that would serve him better. Particularly as he chooses to make enough noise in the middle of the night to wake me! Which surely defeats his purpose in hiding. Your supposition does not rule out the possibility that we have two intruders. The one in Sir Gerald's bedchamber being ethereal, and the one in the pantry most definitely possessing, at the very least, a human stomach!"

Christopher suppressed a chuckle, more at her indignation than her theorizing, and inclined his head. "That is a possibility, I grant you, my lady. But not plausible. As I said, I do not believe in coincidences.

But as to why this individual is a particularly noisy thief, I have no clearer idea than you."

That much was true. What he did not reveal was that he was very sure the thief had not chosen Sir Gerald's rooms at random. There was something of particular value in amongst Sir Gerald's personal possessions which the thief wanted, or been directed to find on behalf of persons unknown. Whatever the thief was searching for, Christopher wondered if it had something to do with Sir Gerald's involvement in a spy ring operating out of Stroud.

The Spymaster General was convinced Sir Gerald was the mastermind of this Stroud spy ring. Christopher was skeptical. Not that Sir Gerald was not capable of deviousness. He was. The man had deceived the local gentry, his wife, and his creditors that he possessed great wealth. He had also bragged to gentlemen of means and position within Gloucestershire that through his marriage to the daughter of an earl, and by reason of his birth as a member of the Cavendish family, he had important connections within government and political circles that would help advance the schemes and causes of the local squires.

On the strength of this Sir Gerald was "pricked" to be High Sheriff of Gloucestershire. An office he held with all the pomposity he could muster, so his neighbors had confided. And as the men of Gloucester possessed a legendary reticence, Sir Gerald as High Sheriff must have been insufferable. Which made Christopher wonder why they had suffered him at all.

The good people of Gloucester could not have known, as Christopher knew, that Sir Gerald's puffed up conceit was a cloud of hot air that hid a thunderstorm of lies. Sir Gerald was in debt up to his wig, and had been isolated from those within Polite Society with any political and social influence for many years. He could not get a well-shod heel inside the houses of his wife's noble connections, never mind their influential friends and relatives.

Which was why Shrewsbury believed Sir Gerald ripe for turning and betraying his country—he needed money and he needed to feel important. Spying for the French was a lucrative business, particularly now with Louis' government on the verge of openly declaring its support for the American rebels. But for all the hours Christopher had spent in Sir Gerald's company, he had only received the strongest impression that the Baronet was fiercely loyal to his King. Not only that, but Sir Gerald loathed the French with a passion bordering on mania, and this came from his hatred of his wife's half-French cousins, the Dukes of Roxton. Such was Sir Gerald's loathing of the Duke of

Roxton and his family that Christopher believed the man wanted to do everything in his power to bring about that family's downfall.

It was Christopher's belief—and he had told Shrewsbury as much —that if Sir Gerald was part of a spy ring, or had had anything to do with traitors to His Majesty's government, it was because he'd been duped into believing he was aiding the British cause, when in fact he was unwittingly helping the enemy. Sir Gerald did not have the brains to be a successful traitor, least of all the architect of an elaborate spy network. Shrewsbury charged Christopher with providing evidence to substantiate his accusations and in discovering just who had been Sir Gerald's contacts. Christopher also believed that one of those contacts was at that very moment holed up in Sir Gerald's private rooms enjoying Cook's walnut pickle.

All this he did not voice to Lady Mary, though he wished he could confide in her enough to allay her fears that Sir Gerald's ghost had not come back to haunt her. And if the pantry thief was a traitor in the pay of the French, he would deal with the villain expeditiously. But for now he turned the conversation away from ghosts and thieves and to a topic he was sure would divert her attention.

"May I ask what it is you are embroidering?"

Mary was startled by the question. No male who was not a close relative had ever shown enough polite interest to ask her such a question, her husband certainly had not, in all the years of their marriage. She was so delighted by it that she beamed.

"Oh! Yes! Yes, of course you may," she replied with genuine warmth. She held up the embroidery hoop by its lap stand so he could see her stitchery—the half-finished leaf, with its scrolls and swirls. "This is one of three acanthus leaves."

He peered closer. "And if I'm not mistaken, the yellow flower is a meadow buttercup, the white a strawberry flower, and you have a trail of fine ivy too."

"You know your flora in thread, Mr. Bryce!"

"Only when it is embroidered with such delicate care, my lady. But I also meant—what is the article you are embroidering?"

"When it is sewn up it will be an infant's christening cap."

"May I?"

He put out a hand and after she had secured the needle in the pink silk she gave him the embroidery hoop. Trailing the tips of his long fingers lightly above the stitchery, he inspected her handiwork, then stopped at the metallic twist of the unfinished acanthus leaf and looked up.

"Methinks this exquisite finery is not for just any infant."

"You are correct, Mr. Bryce. This cap will be for Cousin Duchess's baby, which is due in the new year."

"Cousin Duchess? Not the Duchess of Roxton's latest infant then?"

"No. Not for baby Otto. The Roxtons still use the cap I embroidered for the christening of Frederick—their first baby and their heir. They then decided to use it for their subsequent babies. It is something of which I am very proud," she added in an emphatic rush, as if she needed to elevate her handiwork above the mundane.

"And so you should be. You have a very fine hand, and the shading of your stitches is beyond compare."

"Oh! I thought—"

"That being male I would have little appreciation of the care and attention, and the fine worksmanship, not to mention love, which goes into such needlecraft?"

"Yes," she confessed guiltily, and blushed because she could not help herself and his words touched her deeply. "I always thought—privately of course—that I was a fair embroiderer, much better with a needle and thread than any of my nurses. But no one except family has ever said so. And I assumed their praise was more out of a sense of duty and politeness than because they considered my stitchery above the ordinary."

"You sell yourself short. To produce such fine floral designs, you not only need to have an expert technique with short and long stitches but also an understanding of tonal shade. You also need the ability to blend colors to give your creations the appearance of nature. Is that not so?"

She nodded, unable to articulate her astonishment at his knowledge of what she assumed was of interest and understood by her sex alone.

"Am I right in presuming you also sketched the pattern before you began?"

"Yes, of course. I draw all my own patterns."

"Then you are not only a skilled needlewoman, but an artist as well."

"A draughtsman rather than an artist. I can only reproduce what I see. I lack the imagination to conjure images."

"Then at least concede that you are able to draw well, too. And what you have drawn you then paint with your needle and thread."

"Paint with my needle and thread..." she repeated, and smiled with satisfaction at his description. "That is very true. Thank-you." She took back her embroidery hoop and set it on her lap. "May I presume then that you have seen a great deal of embroidery in your day?"

"Possibly more than any male alive, other than the handful who choose to do embroidery work themselves."

"You refer to artisans who do so in their line of work, for profit, not as I do, to pass the time and as gifts for family and friends."

"There is that, of course. But no, I mean gentlemen who stitch purely for relaxation."

Mary sat forward, disbelieving. "I beg your pardon. A gentleman *embroider*? I do not believe you!"

"Oh, but you must, my lady. I have seen them sitting at tambour frames and with ivory and wood embroidery hoops such as yours. A few even knit and crochet." When Mary continued to stare at him in open-mouthed disbelief, he added with a smile, "My aunt can verify my claims, and were her eyes not grown so weak, no doubt would agree with my assessment of your skill, too."

"And where did you and your aunt gain such wisdom in the art of embroidery?"

"Here and—um—there. But mostly there."

"On the Continent?"

"Yes."

"You must have inspected an inordinate amount of stitchery to make such claims about mine—if indeed you are sincere."

Her frown of incomprehension was so reminiscent of her daughter that he grinned. He was so eager to have her believe him genuine that again he let down his guard, this time about his past— the first time he had been so open about it since his return to this sleepy vale.

"Sincere? With you—always. And yes, you can believe me when I tell you I have inspected, evaluated, praised, remarked upon, and offered constructive criticism when asked to do so, on a great many pieces of embroidery. So I do know beautiful stitchery when I see it."

Mary smiled thinly. Sometimes she could surprise herself when she muttered audibly, tongue firmly in cheek, "All pieces done by your aunt, I am sure."

He laughed out loud at her quip.

"If only that were true! That would've saved me a great deal of time and effort. But I regret none of it," he added seriously. "For that path has led me here—and to you—"

"Mr. Bryce, whatever path you have chosen to take is of concern to no one but yourself," she interrupted, throat and cheeks stained a crimson to match her flaming braids. She dropped her chin. "It is certainly not my con—"

"—and to Teddy. I have no children of my own, but I at least have the privilege of acting as an uncle to Theodora, and for that I will always be thankful to you."

She looked up at him, all embarrassment extinguished at mention of her daughter.

"To me? It was Sir Gerald who made you Teddy's guardian, not I. And I should be thanking *you*, Mr. Bryce. I don't believe I have formally done so. And I must, for all you've done for her, for taking an interest in her, and that was remiss of me."

"There is no need, my lady. I enjoy Teddy's company for its own sake. She reminds me of what it is to be young and carefree. She finds joy in the everyday, and she has a deep love of the vale. We should all strive to be like her. Most of us lose sight of that as we age."

Mary sighed without realizing it. "Yes. And there are those who never see it at all, at any age."

His lips twitched. He almost smiled, but schooled his features to remain grave.

"Pardon me for saying so, my lady, but Sir Gerald had little time for anyone but himself. Self-absorption makes one blind to the myriad of possibilities that surround one."

Mary had not been thinking of her husband at all, but of her mother, and she agreed with him. But she did not say so. One of her brows arched in surprise. "Sir Gerald had plenty of time for you, Mr. Bryce."

Because he spent that time droning on about himself and his misfortunes, real and imagined, and I patiently listened to his self-absorbed ramblings because it was demanded of me, not because I wanted to, Christopher wanted to reply. Instead he said levelly, ignoring the criticism in her tone,

"We spent that time discussing our mutual agricultural interests, Sir Gerald's onerous duties as High Sherriff of Gloucestershire, and further afield, there is the Stroudwater Navigation canal project, of which Sir Gerald and I are both investors."

Mary's mouth set in a thin prim line and though she did not actually roll her eyes, Christopher was certain she was mentally doing just that. Her polite remark, intended to mask her boredom merely underscored it for him, and he could not prevent a burst of laughter when she stated,

"How fascinating. I see now why you both could not tear yourselves away from the port and the fireplace." Adding when he laughed, cheeks aflame, "You think I jest, Mr. Bryce?"

"May I speak freely, my lady?" When Mary nodded, suddenly wary, he added without emotion, "As one neighbor to another..."

"Yes. Of course."

"What I think is you are good at hiding your true self behind a veil of politeness. Why not say what you mean: That you're glad you were not subjected to the tedium of discussing wool yields, cloth embezzlement, the poor laws, and advanced canal construction."

"But that's not what I meant at all," Mary argued, indignant. When it was Christopher's turn to raise his brows, as if he needed convincing, she explained, "I would gladly discuss any or all those subjects if I were given the opportunity to know something more about them. I expect—no! That is not true. *I know* Sir Gerald considered me incapable of comprehending any erudite matter with any depth. And that is true because I had a woefully inadequate education, even by female standards. That became glaringly obvious to me when, being a little older than Teddy, I went to live with my Roxton cousins. The more time I spent in the company of Cousin Duchess, the more I realized just how ignorant I was."

"Cousin Duchess? The cousin who is due to deliver a noble heir in the new year?"

"Yes. The very same. She is my closest cousin, though she is some twenty years my senior. Yes, Mr. Bryce, your mental arithmetic is quite correct. She is to be a new mother at fifty. Though this is not her first pregnancy. She has two sons by her first marriage to the old Duke of Roxton."

"The present duke is her son?"

"Yes. I have a complicated family tree, do I not?" Mary replied with a smile at his surprise, adding, "I am glad of it, and for her. Her Grace had an unconventional upbringing—her father was a physician and as his only child was given a boy's education—it has given her the ability to converse on all manner of topics, and in three or four languages. She also reads Latin and Greek, and is never afraid to ask questions."

Christopher pulled a face.

"She's not a boorish female pedant, is she?" he asked, more to alleviate Mary's feelings of inadequacy than an indictment of a noblewoman he did not know, or, for that matter, any objection to a female receiving an adequate education.

"No. No. Not at all! In fact she is the most delightfully feminine creature alive. Your comment of striving to remain young at heart suits her perfectly. For she is so vivacious, kind-hearted, and stunningly beautiful that when I was a child, to be in her company was to be in the presence of a fairy godmother. The years I spent with the Roxtons were the most magical of my life."

"You lived with the old Duke and his duchess…?"

"When I was twelve years old, after my parents became permanently *estranged* and my father went to live in the Bahamas. Dair and Charlie were sent off to Harrow, and because my mother's health was so poorly it was thought best that she spend time away, adjusting to her—to her *new situation*. She went to live in Cheltenham for a time, where she was unknown. She grew to like the place and has returned there every year since, to great fanfare. Teddy tells me Granny is the Queen of Cheltenham society."

"Yes," Christopher said with an exaggerated sigh, hoping to make Mary smile. "Teddy told me that, too."

But Mary did not smile. She was made uncomfortable and said apologetically, "I suspect Teddy has told you a great many things that do not bear repeating."

"Oh, have no fear, my lady. What Teddy tells me remains in here," he said and tapped his temple. "It's not for me to repeat the Countess's many maxims—to anyone." When Mary's shoulders slumped and she looked fretful, he added gently, "It would not be wrong of me to assume that whereas Teddy would miss you dreadfully were you to be parted from each other, you did not have the same sense of loss when you were sent to live with the Roxtons?"

Mary took a deep breath and nodded. She would not dissemble, and as he was a very willing ear, and she in need of a confidant—later she was to wonder if tiredness had played its part in loosening her tongue—she said with uncharacteristic openness and more emotion than she intended,

"Mr. Bryce, those four years with Cousin Duchess and M'sieur le Duc d'Roxton were the happiest I've ever been. Time spent in their company opened my eyes to a way of life hitherto unknown to me, in every respect. Except for the birth of my daughter, I have not experienced such happiness since…"

Her voice trailed off, unsettled that it was so easy for her to express herself to him when she had never done so with Sir Gerald, most definitely not with her mother, and had rarely opened herself up to anyone else in her extended family. When she gave it a moment's thought, the only other person with whom she had conversed in such a free and easy manner was with the old Duke of Roxton, who had a way of listening without comment and without giving his thoughts away. Much as Christopher Bryce was doing now—watching her intently, but most definitely not giving away what he was thinking.

Just as Teddy was confident and never ridiculed by her Uncle Bryce, as a twelve-year-old she had prattled on all manner of topics, and the old Duke had listened as if her conversation were the most interesting he had ever heard. Of course now, thinking back on it, she marveled at her own naïve bravado, particularly with such an ancient and formidable aristocrat. There were even times when she would be chattering away and catch him glance across at Cousin Duchess, curled up in her favorite chair reading. The couple would exchange a smile, and she, a girl of twelve, had the supreme audacity to ask *him* if he was listening to *her*. The old Duke was never at a loss, though his gaze was all for his wife, and was able to recite the last sentence she had spoken. And then he would ask her to please continue, her conversation was most edifying. Of course she realized years later that he was being ironic, and that his enigmatic smile and the look in his eyes when he gazed upon his wife was one of love and utter devotion.

Her parents had never looked at each other in that way, and if they had ever been in love, it was before she was born. She had been raised in a household where her parents rarely communicated, such was the icy hatred between them. Nor had Sir Gerald looked upon her with love and devotion because he had not loved her. But then, to be fair to him, she had not loved him either. Theirs was an arranged marriage. She had accepted his offer so she could escape her mother's misery. Perhaps if the Roxtons had been in England and not in faraway Constantinople, she would not have felt the need to rush into marriage. She had desperately wanted to go with them on their Continental journey, and they had wanted her to. But her mother had pleaded with the old Duke that she could not bear being left alone and parted from her only daughter. Despite Mary's protestations, the old Duke let the Countess have her way. Before the year was out, Mary accepted an offer of marriage from Sir Gerald Cavendish.

She doubted anyone would ever look at her the way the old Duke of Roxton had looked upon Cousin Duchess. When he had died, part of her cousin's heart had died along with him. Yet her cousin had eventually remarried, and to a man who was just as in love and devoted to her, and now they were expecting their first child. And here she was a widow and turned thirty—never been in love; never known the love and devotion of one good and worthy man, least of all two; never shared a passionate kiss with any man, never mind experiencing the intimacy that only two people in love were capable of...

Please don't let my heart shrivel and die, my hope to wither away, my capacity to love be limited to my daughter.

Why, of a sudden, was she so wretchedly self-absorbed? Her mother lectured that she needed to think of Teddy's future. Her family's honor and pride demanded she make another arranged marriage.

Females of her station had a higher calling and a duty to their lineage. Passion was transitory; love faded. Love matches were for others—people of low birth, and mushrooms who had sprung from nowhere. She was of the nobility. She had royal Stuart blood in her veins. She was—

Repeating her mother's dictums verbatim… Oh God, was she becoming her mother? Please, dear God, no—

"My lady. Here. Take this…"

Mary blinked tears off her lashes and glanced down to find a white linen handkerchief scrunched in her fist. She wondered what she was supposed to do with it until she realized she still could not see clearly, that her sight was blinded by tears, and that those tears had run down her flushed face and dripped off her cheeks and onto her embroidery.

FIVE

Mary shot to her feet, hurriedly dabbing at her eyes and stained cheeks, mortified by her behavior. She forgot about the ivory embroidery hoop in her lap until the lap stand clattered to the floor. Christopher scooped it up and placed it atop of her sewing box by her chair. And when she just stood there with his damp handkerchief in her hand, and this the second time he had been obliged to give it to her, he gently took it from her and shoved it in a pocket of his frock coat.

"Forgive me, Mr. Bryce. I don't know what came over me," she managed to say in a steady voice. She swallowed and brushed down her quilted petticoats then clasped her hands in front of her a little too tightly. "It was inconsiderate and—"

"Please, my lady. There is no need to explain. Powerful memories sometimes overwhelm us—"

"I do not wish to discuss this any further," she said with an imperious sniff, and looked anywhere but up at him. "If you please, I am sure you have matters to attend to, and I must ready for bed. If you would tell me what it is you wish me to do. I would like to be of some assistance in the capture of this-this thief."

Christopher stared at her, lips pressed together in a thin line, and gave himself a moment to collect his thoughts. He knew their intimate informality was over, and he knew when to hold his tongue. He also knew how to wait, and wait, and wait. Had he not waited eight years already? Six without any hope at all, and then with the death of her husband, two years waiting for her to reflect on that moment when they had first met, and see that it was fate that had brought him to her.

Kate accused him of being maudlin. She had warned him that Lady Mary's stiff-necked pride and his would be the millstone around their necks that would see them drown before any happy resolution could be found to their predicament. Not that *Proud Mary*—as Kate teasingly called her—had any idea as to his feelings for her, did she? That too, did not bode well for the future. Kate knew the Roxtons and their milieu far better than he. He may have spent a decade brushing up against the padded silk shoulders of the Italian nobility, but he had not been Christopher Bryce of Brycecomb Hall there, had he? He had been known simply as "Cristoforo", and in his chosen vocation that was all that was asked of him.

The English nobility was different from that to be found abroad. In Italian society, handsome and accomplished men could occupy a particular position within a nobleman's household, no questions asked. Cristoforo was accepted because he was acknowledged by the husband, and catered to the wife. But here, here on English soil, the home of his birth, he would always be shaped by his family circumstances and provincial upbringing, regardless of how he had gone about reshaping his life and himself while in self-imposed exile on the Continent.

Christopher did not want to hear what Kate had to say, but he knew she was right. After all, had she not done the same with her own life? But she could not provide counsel where the Lady Mary was concerned. He understood Mary better than anyone, better than her family and her husband, better than Kate, who had yet to meet her, and most definitely better than the Countess of Strathsay.

He just had to persuade her to look at herself and her world differently—to divest herself of her noble societal armor and all the stifling dictates that required when she went out in Polite Society—to see that the Mary that lived here in the vale was the true Mary.

The true Mary took delight in her bee-keeping, her cheese-making, and her embroidery. She was a good and loyal wife, albeit to a conceited, pompous husband who did not deserve her devotion. The true Mary took long walks up and down dale and performed her responsibilities and duties as the wife of local landowner with dignity and commitment. She did not send others to do her bidding, but took it upon herself to visit the sick and infirm, the old, and the very young amongst her husband's tenants, taking them food baskets and listening to their stories and grievances as if she had all the time in the world.

The Mary he knew told her daughter how beautiful and clever she was, that she was capable of anything she put her mind to, and let her be her tomboy self. Teddy believed her mother, and so she was a happy, self-assured, contented child. At ten years of age, that's all that mattered. And what about Mary's own accomplishments and beauty? She was so self-effacing and so awkward about her red-haired prettiness that he had at first mistaken her self-consciousness for conceit. That is until one day she made an impulsive remark about her cousin and a mutual paternal grandmother with the flaming curls, both being so extraordinarily beautiful that she was considered the plain one in the family. He had huffed his disbelief. She was sincere, and thus affronted.

Kate had smiled and agreed with him, and his face had flushed crimson with embarrassment that he had allowed himself to be so publicly effusive about his feelings. But Kate understood. Though her failing eyesight meant she could not see his expression, the sincerity and the love in his voice rang out loud and clear. Yet, she worried time was running out for him, because it was running out for Mary. The Roxtons and the Strathsays would never allow Mary to remain a widow forever. She was still pretty, still fertile, and thus still marriageable, and so she was an asset to their political and societal advancement. They would marry her off to a nobleman who would take her and Teddy far away from the vale. He had best come up with a plan, and soon, or Mary and Teddy would be lost to him forever. If indeed he had any chance at all. Did he have a plan…?

"MR. BRYCE? YOUR PLAN?" MARY ASKED A SECOND TIME WHEN he did not respond but continued to stare down at her. "You must have some idea of what you intend to do to catch this thief, and I should know of it so that I may help."

"Yes, yes, I do, my lady," he said with a nod, mentally shaking himself free of Kate's well-intentioned advice for a future that seemed as probable as the cow jumping over the moon in Mother Goose's Melody! "Once I've secured both doors that permit access to and from Sir Gerald's rooms, and thus the intruder cannot escape via the servant door, or out into the corridor—

"—assuming it is a thief and not a ghost."

"Yes. Assuming it is a thief and not a ghost," he repeated patiently.

"I intend to wait until I hear movement in Sir Gerald's rooms. I will then surprise the thief by entering via the connecting door in your bedchamber, and take him by force."

Lady Mary's eyes widened. "Without any assistance? Should you not have several of the servants with you in case this thief attempts to overpower you?"

"And have these men wait with me in your bedchamber? No. I would not do that to you, my lady. And I would prefer the fewer who know about this thief, the better. Besides," he added, stepping back and spreading out his arms and turning slowly about so she had the full measure of him, "do I appear as if I am in need of their assistance?"

Mary looked him up and down with all the seriousness of one taking the measure of a prize stallion she was considering for purchase: The Squire was not tall but he was above average in height, his chest and shoulders wide, his calves solid, his feet long, and when he flexed his hands to make fists she was sure he could punch through walls with ease. For all his athleticism, he had a lean frame, and the fine nose and intelligent eyes of a patrician, not a brute by any means. She shook her head in agreement, and had to smile when he lifted his brows as if providing an exclamation point for his question.

"You will, unfortunately, have to abide the inconvenience of my company in your bedchamber," he apologized, the smile gone. "If there were another way…"

Mary lowered her lashes and hoped she wasn't blushing, though she felt the heat in her cheeks. She swallowed and managed to say evenly, meeting his gaze,

"It is a small inconvenience for the desired outcome, Mr. Bryce. I intend to spend the night on the chaise in my dressing room—"

"I would not deprive you of your bed, my lady. I—"

"Please do not concern yourself on my account," she interrupted brusquely to bring the discussion to an end. She flashed a smile she hoped showed she was unruffled. "I'm confident you will apprehend this thief as quickly as possible… And when you do, what do you intend to do with him?"

"Lock him up until such time as he can be handed over to the magistrate."

What he did not say was that while the thief was locked up, Christopher intended to discover for himself if the cur was in fact a spy, and if he was a spy, he would extract what information he could from the devil before handing him over to Shrewsbury's henchmen, who, in the guise of men working in the employ of the local magistrate, would bundle him away for interrogation by the Spymaster himself.

"Perhaps I can be of some assistance to you, Mr. Bryce?"

He suppressed his surprise behind a bland smile, and glanced her over, from heeled mules up to the little lace-edged cap snugly pinned to the crown of her head. She was all of two inches above five feet in height, with wrists that had the circumference of a broomstick. If not for a well-endowed décolletage contained in a boned corset that acted as a counterweight to the width of her hooped petticoats over her hips, she would have appeared as fragile as eggshell. How she thought she could be of help… But he did not want to dampen her enthusiasm or make her fearful by pointing out that every man but the arthritic-riddled Mr. Deed could easily overpower her with one hand about her neck. Instead he said seriously,

"Perhaps you can, my lady. But only after I have the scoundrel securely in hand. I will then call you through to Sir Gerald's dressing room to unlock the servant door on the stair leading down to the kitchen. You could also show the way with a candle, or have your maid—"

"No! I will do it. I intend to send Betsy to bed before your arrival. I do not want her frightened and screaming…" Her gaze flickered up to his eyes. "Or asking questions I have no wish to answer."

"Very wise, my lady," he responded evenly, knowing she was referring to having him, a male, in her bedchamber, and without explanation to her maid. His presence would set the servants gossiping, and beyond them to the village and wider community. If he knew anything of the acid-tongued Mrs. Keble's habits, she was the source of groundless rumors already circulating the vale about the Squire and the widowed Lady Mary. "Best, too, to go about your regular nightly routine so Betsy is not made suspicious."

Mary took a deep breath and nodded.

"If you would give me an hour, and then come up via the main staircase and along the corridor to my sitting room, I will leave the door ajar. There will be sufficient light for you to make your way from there into my bedchamber. The connecting doors are folded away, except for the door through to Sir Gerald's apartment, which, as I told you, is bolted, so you will have no trouble finding your way."

CHRISTOPHER PACED AT THE BASE OF THE GRAND STAIRCASE, checking and re-checking the time on his silver pocket watch to make certain the hour she had asked for had well and truly passed. And just as he put a booted foot on the first step, lighted taper in hand, the housekeeper emerged out of the darkness to ask that as he was staying the night did he want his hound with him in his usual room, or taken out to the stables?

His reply was more curt than usual, given his nerves at what he was about to do. He told her Lorenzo would be staying in his basket in his room. He had then enquired as to the whereabouts of Luke, who had been given charge of the hound until Christopher sent for him. Mrs. Keble did not know, but would find out. She then lingered, a significant sly glance at his booted foot on the step and then up the staircase, as if to say it was not a steward's business to be using those stairs.

Christopher dismissed her without explanation, then waited until she had disappeared through the servant door, which she did, slowly, and with a glance over her shoulder and a sly smile as she closed the door. He then went up the staircase two steps at a time. He had slid into Lady Mary's sitting room before he realized he hadn't taken a conscious breath since the first landing.

And the Lady Mary was right. He navigated her rooms with ease. Her bedchamber sitting room was surprisingly sparse of furniture, though he was sure there were pictures on the walls and that those walls were covered in pretty wallpaper that matched the curtains. What was not surprising was that it was cold and dark. There were no tapers lit and no fire in the grate. For a brief moment he felt guilt because it was his dictates about the need to economize on behalf of the estate which meant only those rooms occupied for most of the day or night were permitted wax, coal, or firewood, and even then the amount was allocated. The next room, which looked to be a dressing room, was dimly lit, but not by a fire in the grate, because that was bare, too. So the room was as cold as the sitting room.

His frown of preoccupation as to why the Lady Mary did not have a fire replaced his nervousness at being in her rooms. And so he failed to notice this room was occupied. He was halfway across the rug and headed for the bedchamber when he realized he was not alone. He spun about and froze. Lady Mary was seated before her dressing table. A small candelabra of four candles illuminated glass jars and various toiletry implements, and the looking glass. But she was turned away from her reflection, facing him, and was brushing her hair. She had brought the weight forward over her left shoulder. Holding the long thick mane about five inches from the ends, she was brushing it free of tangles.

His gaze followed the silver-backed bristled brush up and down when she resumed combing the silken red tresses in long, even strokes. He feared looking anywhere else. Yet, he caught a glimpse of her slim ankles in their white stockings, knew she wore a white night chemise with a little lace border along the hem, and that over this was a fur lined silk banyan with three-quarter sleeves and upturned fur cuffs. This dressing gown was open and hung loose from her shoulders. A white nightcap and several hair pins were by the candelabra on the dressing table.

When she saw him she was not at all nervous. She set aside the brush and scurried over in her bare feet without wrapping the banyan across her breasts. He swallowed hard and thought he might choke on his dry tongue.

"Mr. Bryce, you're here at last. Good," she hissed in a whisper. "I expected you ten minutes ago. Did you lose your way?"

He shook his head. Instead of asking if she had heard any noises coming from Sir Gerald's dressing room he swallowed again to loosen his tongue and rasped out rudely, "Do you have a fire in your bedchamber?"

Mary blinked up at him, momentarily distracted. "Fire?"

"There is no—there is no fire in the sitting room or here—here in your dressing room. Is—is there one in your bedchamber?"

"No. No there is not."

She frowned up at him, wondering why he would ask her such a question, and mistook the suppressed desire reflected in his dark eyes for one of disapproval, thinking he was expecting her to account for her use of every piece of coal and stick of firewood.

"You may decide on the household allocation of coal, Mr. Bryce," she stated, suddenly riled, "but once allocated, I may decide to do with my portion as I please, may I not?"

"Of—of course. I was only asking because—"

"Don't concern yourself. I do not waste my portion. Though why you would think I—"

"I am certain you would not do so, my lady. It was not meant as a criticism."

All the heat went out of her voice. "Oh? You don't? Then why did you ask?"

"Because the days are getting shorter and colder, and if you don't have a fire to take the chill from the room, particularly in here where you—where you—*dress*—and most definitely when you—when you —*bathe*—you'll find yourself with a bout of influenza."

"Under present arrangements I have a fire in here every third day."

"Every third day? And in the bedchamber…?"

She pressed her lips together then said without looking up at him, "I do not need a fire. The down coverlet and the curtains about the bed serve me well enough."

"Not in winter they won't!"

"I assure you I am more than comfortable. Besides, I am exceedingly warm-blooded so I can tolerate the cold better than most."

His gaze flickered over her, from stockinged bare feet on up the flimsy nightgown, and he would have been prepared to believe her, but for one important telling sign that she was definitely not as warm as she was trying to appear. Her nightgown was a translucent white cotton, and when his gaze lingered for the briefest of moments at her breasts it was evident she was far colder than she was prepared to admit. Again he found his throat unaccountably dry, but managed to say in an even tone,

"You must have a fire in here, and in your bedchamber, every day. Whatever you've done with your allocation of coal, you should make certain it is more fairly distributed so that your needs are met, too."

Mary's frown returned. Feeling compelled to justify her actions, a guilty petulance sounded in her voice.

"You will not persuade me to change my decision, Mr. Bryce. I assure you I am more than comfortable. If I am uncustomarily cold tonight, it is because I was waiting up for you, and now we are standing about conversing, when normally I am already snuggled up in my bed. And Betsy uses the bed warmer to take the chill off the sheets, so they at least are warm when I slip into them."

He had a sudden revelation. "You've given all your coal to Teddy, haven't you?"

"Yes. Of course. What did you think I had done with it? Sold it in exchange for silver twist, or-or a clutch of hair ribbons? I am not that frivolous, nor that silly, as the people of your station seem to think is the predominant condition for females of my birth—"

"You do not need to feel guilty. Or, as you rightly pointed out, justify yourself to me. But what I would say is you did not need to suffer inconvenience and discomfort either. If you had lowered your pride and come to me—"

She gasped, indignant. "My-my—*pride?*"

"—I would gladly have provided Teddy's rooms—and yours—with more coal and firewood."

"You—you would?"

He smiled thinly at her disbelief.

"I am strict but I am not unfair, nor am I cruel. I would not wish either of you to suffer cold or catch flu." His smile went awry. "And unlike the majority of *people of my station*—whatever you comprehend that to mean, steward or squire—I'm not predisposed to judging an entire strata of society on the wasteful frivolities and over-consumption of one vainglorious wastrel. Though I would willingly do so, if you were its shining exemplar."

"Mr. Bryce, I have asked you not to use my husband as—Oh!?" she added with surprise as she fully comprehended his final sentence. She breathed in and unconsciously took a step forward. "You would? I did not think you… I did not want you to think *me* a spendthrift. That I could *not* economize. I—we—Teddy and I—have been doing our best to—"

"Where are your mules, my lady?" he blurted out, startling himself by such an outburst. It was not what he had meant to say at all, but the nearness of her upended his thoughts.

Lady Mary was mystified. "My—*mules*…?"

"Yes. Yes, your mules. You should at least try to keep your toes warm by wearing shoes."

"Under normal circumstances I would. But, again, these circumstances are far from normal, are they? They clatter, particularly on the wooden floor. I thought that if you wanted to catch the thief you would need us to be as quiet as possible. If I were to wear my mules, and with you in your jockey boots, the thief would hear more than one pair of shoes in my bedchamber, and he may suspect we were up to something, and try to flee the scene—"

"Heaven forbid he should have such thoughts about us, my lady," Christopher scoffed, regaining mastery of himself and suppressing a crooked smile at her blunt naïvety.

Had she honestly given no thought to the appropriateness—or not —of him being in her rooms at this late hour, other than what her servants and this thief might think? He should be gratified she did not believe him capable of taking advantage of her, but he was also depressingly aware that this was because she had given him no thought at all, other than in his dual role of steward and neighbor. Just as she gave no thought to the horse in the stable that was to carry her to market, whether it be stallion or gelding, as long as it did the task assigned it.

That was just as well, because just now, when she had leaned in and lightly brushed up against the front of his frock coat, it could very well have been a branding iron that had seared right through his clothes to his chest. He had tensed, all his senses heightened by that barely-there touch of her full breasts brushing against him. And what he had done in response? He had just stood there like a block of wood, enduring the torture of her nearness without moving, spouting drivel about the whereabouts of her shoes, and without doing what he most wanted to do: Take her in his arms and kiss her.

"He could very easily jump out the window," Mary continued, her indignation so acute that she was unaware of the tightness in his jaw, or how he flexed his fingers, and she certainly did not hear his words. But she did notice when his expression of forbearance changed to one of confusion at her mention of the window. She smiled smugly. "Aha! You forgot about the tree, didn't you, Mr. Bryce?"

"Jump out the window?" Christopher repeated, suppressing his thoughts and frowning down at her. "The tree...?"

"The tree branches outside my bedchamber window extend across to Sir Gerald's dressing room window. It is a very sturdy old beech and easy to climb. Teddy has done so, and scared the life out of me by appearing at my window, waving at me from a branch. As you can imagine, I almost fell off my chair! But I did my best to smile and wave, because she looked so pleased with herself, I didn't have the heart to chastise her then and there."

"Of course you wouldn't," he replied with a smile. "Please continue, I'm interested in your theory."

"I came to this surprising conclusion while I was brushing my hair—this is the time when I reflect on my day, and sometimes thoughts come to me—trying to imagine how the thief, if it is not a ghost, was able to come and go from Sir Gerald's apartment with no one the wiser. He could not use the servant passage, he would be found out. And he could not use the main corridor because I have the key. And even if he picked that lock, he would still be taking an enormous risk of being seen. Besides, he seems to be most keen on the kitchen and obtaining food, so the servant door or the tree would be the most logical choice, don't you agree?"

Christopher crossed his arms and nodded. "Go on, my lady."

"Well... You mentioned in your office about the window in Sir Gerald's dressing room being left ajar and that this may have let in a bird or a squirrel, or something similar, and that was the noise I heard. But what if the window was closed but not latched, and nobody has checked to see if this is so since Sir Gerald's passing? It is easily accessible from the outside by someone shifting across the branch. And it would not take much strength to lift the sash and then climb inside onto the window seat."

Christopher stared at her, thinking over what she had just theorized, and then his face split into a grin and his eyes sparked with new knowledge. "Yes. By Jove, I think you're right! The window... Why didn't I think of that? Of course! He's been using the window to come and go whenever he jolly well pleases. You are clever."

"I am?" she replied wonderingly. No one had ever called her that before, ever.

There was such genuine warmth in his smile that she wondered what caused him to limit his smiles. Gone were the stern lines about his mouth, and he appeared far more approachable. Just as when he spoke with Teddy. But what she had not noticed then that she did now was just how exceedingly handsome he was when he was at his ease.

Though that was not strictly true. She, and every woman within a radius of fifty miles, was aware of Mr. Bryce's good looks. What she was determined to ignore, as she had upon their first introduction, were the feelings and sensations he stirred within her. So she forced herself to pay no heed to the pulse deep within her triggered by his smile, and which throbbed unbearably whenever she allowed herself outrageous thoughts of kissing him.

"I think... I do believe... I am now quite chilled," she muttered, and wrapping the fur lined banyan over her breasts and folding her arms, Mary brushed past Christopher with hunched shoulders and scurried into her bedchamber with head down.

SIX

Christopher followed her, bringing the candelabra with him, for he suspected the bedchamber was cold and dark. It was. The only light was provided by the full moon shining in through the undraped window, filtering through the branches of the old beech, illuminating the window seat and bare wooden floor. He put the candelabra on the bedside table and went to peer out the window.

Sure enough a strong central bough of the beech with its many branches extended from the dressing room across the front of this bedchamber window to the window of Sir Gerald's dressing room. It was thick enough to easily support the weight of a child, and he suspected also that of an agile adult capable of climbing without lingering to catch his breath or to admire the view of rolling hills.

He turned away from the window to the bed. The velvet curtains were pulled across on the side closest the window to ward off any drafts, but the covers remained untouched. And then he remembered Mary said she intended to sleep on the chaise in her dressing room. Now she was over by the connecting door with an ear to the panel listening for signs of life, ethereal or temporal, in Sir Gerald's dressing room.

Christopher lingered longer than was polite at the foot of the bed. He couldn't help himself. He was paralyzed by a frisson of memory. The ornately-carved mahogany bed posts, the velvet curtains, the quilted damask coverlet, and the bank of feather pillows, all served to send him hurtling back to a previous life, a life lived many hundreds of miles away in the Italian States, in many beds such as this, with many different women. A life he had left far behind and had no wish to revisit.

It was not that his other life was filled with unpleasant memories, far from it. He liked to think he had fulfilled his duties to the mutual satisfaction of all parties. And he had been good at what he did, very good. But his choice of employment—for want of a better word—had been thrust upon him by virtue of his poverty, and his non-existent self-esteem. He had sunk so low there was nowhere else to go, not even the gutter. So when he was approached to train to be a cicisbeo, he did not refuse. Within a year he was transformed and made his debut in the drawing room of a *Lucchesi Conte*. And so began his third life as a gentleman companion, and a spy for the English, where he bought and sold lies, told lies, and lived a lie.

And now here he was in an altogether different bedchamber, the bedchamber of the very lovely but very proper Lady Mary Cavendish, trying not to think of what had occurred in this bed between a husband and his wife.

It was not his business, and up until today he had not dwelt on it. That would not have been polite, or good for his sanity. He had only hoped that in the bedchamber, the conceited Sir Gerald was less self-interested and just as concerned for his wife's needs as his own. But now that he knew the man had had the ill-manners to come to her bed drunk, he could hazard a guess as to the rest—the Baronet had been just as selfish with his carnal wants as he was about everything else in his life. And that made his blood boil. With fists clenched to quell a rising anger, he turned his back on the bed and strode over to the door, where Mary had an ear pressed to a panel, listening for sounds in the next room. The sooner he was out of her bedchamber the better for his peace of mind.

He put up a hand to unbolt the door, the latch affixed surprisingly high on the frame—that's when Mary threw herself at him.

"No! Leave it!" she hissed, up on her toes, fingers clawing at his wrist to stop him sliding the bolt free. "You have no right—no right at all to touch that latch!"

There was no resistance from Christopher. He pushed the bolt back into place. But he did not move away, Mary standing between him and the door. He looked down at her, puzzled, and said calmly, "I was not about to open the door without your permission, just draw the bolt in readiness."

Embarrassed by her uncharacteristic outburst, she lowered her chin before mustering the courage to look up into his brown eyes. "Excuse me. Of course you would not do so without my consent. It's just—it's just that this door hasn't been opened in two years, and I—I made the decision to bolt it—I bolted it myself in fact—which gave me a certain satisfaction… So I should be the one to *un*bolt it."

Christopher wasn't sure what she meant by satisfaction, or why it was so important to her that she be the one to unbolt it, but glancing at the set of padded steps by the bed he seized on the only practical help he could provide.

"Would you like me to fetch the footstool so you can do the honors now?"

Mary didn't know why but his offer made her suddenly weepy. She sniffed and mentally castigated herself for being maudlin, hands tightly clasped in front of her. Perhaps it was the combination of being cold because she was in her stockinged feet in a room without a fire, and the fact the Squire stood so close she was pegged to the door, making her light-headed and hot. But it was that throb deep within her that pulsed to new life at his proximity which unsettled her equilibrium the most.

She was not one for allowing emotion to get the better of her. Sentiment and permitting the heart to rule the head were, according to her mother, signs of a weakness of character. Such behavior was beneath a noblewoman, who must set the example, *be* the example to those of lesser rank. Above all, one must not be an embarrassment, to oneself and one's husband. Well, no one could accuse her of being an embarrassment to Sir Gerald or her family in her ten years of marriage. Even now, as a widow, she was conscious of being in control of her emotions, and the situations in which she found herself, at all times… So why, of a sudden, was the Squire and his nearness making her feel ridiculously vulnerable?

"The footstool…?" Christopher repeated in the protracted silence between them. Adding when she looked up at him, "Why do you need it?"

"Footstool…?" Mary pushed aside her muddled emotions, frowning. "I thought that obvious. My height. Or should I say, lack of it. I am not tall enough to reach the bolt, even in heels."

"Ha! That will teach me to be obtuse! I meant: Why is the latch positioned out of your reach so that you need a footstool?"

"So that I could not reach it," she replied flatly.

He suppressed a grin at her customary candor but was still puzzled. "So you could not reach it…?"

"To be correct, there are two bolts. One here, the other over there on the door into my dressing room."

He looked over his shoulder, but as the dressing room door had been folded away, the bolt was hidden. The latch, however, was not, and the loop clearly visible attached to the door jamb, and at the same out-of-reach height as this one. He was mystified.

"I don't under—"

"Why would you?" Mary interrupted, cutting him off. "You were Sir Gerald's friend and neighbor, not his wife. Now if you would please step back so that I may have some air… I am a little dizzy…"

Christopher ignored her request. The reason for the bolts dawned on him. He was appalled.

"He—He *locked* you in here?"

Mary took a deep breath then spoke in the manner of her mother, as if lecturing a menial of limited intelligence.

"Mr. Bryce, I don't expect you to understand. But when I married Sir Gerald, I did so with the knowledge that I accepted him as my husband for better and for worse. I was determined to be a good wife in every respect… I am not a coward, and I do believe I carried out my wifely duties to the best of my abilities. Though why I am justifying myself to you, I know not! And now—now I am a widow and may keep one door open, just as I may keep this door bolted against thieves and-and ghosts and anyone else if I wish it. I have the choice. It is mine, and mine alone to make."

"Yes. Yes, of course it is," Christopher replied without hesitation, trying to mask his disgust at Sir Gerald's actions and ignoring her condescension because of the rising panic evident in her tone.

Discovering Sir Gerald came to his wife's rooms drunk was shocking enough—knowing he had bolted the door so she could not escape his amorous attentions was monstrous. He did not know what to say that would not sound trite, but he was spared a speech, the words remaining on his tongue when a thud from Sir Gerald's dressing room had Mary clutching his arm and staring at the door, eyes wide. They both quickly pressed an ear to the panel and huddled side by side, listening. A minute stretched to three and so did the silence.

How long they leant against the door waiting for a sound, later neither could recall. It was long enough for Mary's eyelids to droop, overcome with weariness despite the cold seeping into her bones. Christopher allowed himself to study her while he continued to listen for any sign of life from the now eerily quiet next room. His gaze swept over the abundance of curls, pulled over one shoulder to her waist in a blaze of fire-like color against the whiteness of her cotton nightdress. He had always been partial to redheads. In the northern Italian States, such beauties shone like beacons amongst the populace. They had dazzled him, drawn him in, and some had scorched him, much like a moth to flame. But this redhead before him was very different to the copper-headed sirens in Italy, who were attuned to the effect they had on men. He would wager all he owned that Lady Mary Cavendish was oblivious to the allure her fiery beauty had on men in general, and most particularly on him. She would have been shocked to learn of it, and to know that he was her moth, and she his flame.

While he was admiring her, he was thinking he should look out the window again, perhaps even open it to see if it was possible to discover if Sir Gerald's dressing room window was indeed open. For if the thief came and went via the tree, and the sash was up, there was the possibility he had gone out and had yet to return. But the best-laid plans often go awry, no matter how well-considered. Life had a way of throwing surprising opportunities in one's path, that once presented must be taken for fear they may never come again. This was Christopher's thinking when he seized his moment—and it had little to do with the bolted door. Later he was to wonder at his impudence.

He must have dozed off too, because Mary was shaking his arm, the light of triumph in her violet eyes.

"Mr. Bryce?! Did you not hear that?" she hissed. "It was most definitely furniture being moved about! A thud we might dismiss as anything, but not this! I don't know if it is a ghost or a thief in the next room, but at least now *you* know I didn't dream the whole thing up!"

When Christopher accepted her triumph by stepping back to sweep her a bow worthy of an Ottoman potentate, Mary responded by clamping a hand to her mouth to stop herself from laughing. She was so caught up in the moment, between nervousness and exhilaration at the prospect of discovering a ghost or catching a thief, that she impulsively moved into him and whispered,

"That was indeed a fitting acknowledgement. But as it was far from humble, I am left wondering if you are in truth mocking me, sir?"

"Mocking you, my lady? How could you think it?" he replied with a raise of one eyebrow.

"Oh, you are!" she breathed, feigning annoyance, and gave him a playful shove, as if to cast him aside as she was used to doing with her brothers, particularly Dair, when they teased her. "I know that look! I can't be fooled!"

He caught at her fingers and pressed her hand against his chest and she let him, regarding him with an enquiring smile at his impulsive gesture, but not the least affronted by it. He went to speak, but could not, and shook his head at his emotional weakness where she was concerned. For it was the first time she had let down her guard and shown him the true Mary, that playful side of her he knew existed—he had witnessed it many times in her exchanges with her daughter, but she had never been so with him—until now.

"Never would I... I could not... I want..." he muttered, unable to complete a sentence.

"Want, Mr. Bryce...?" she asked quietly, all playfulness banished. She had never seen him flustered, and certainly he was never lost for words with her or Teddy, whatever his natural reticence with others. "What is it that you want?"

Did she truly have no idea? The lack of guile in her expression gave him pause, wondering if he could say it. But he was no callow youth. And he had always known what to say to women; he was well versed in the art of flirtation. But those women and that world seemed a lifetime ago now. And with Mary flirtation would never do. He needed to be sincere. Finally, after an eternity of seconds, he said it.

"You. *You* are what I want."

"Me?"

"Yes."

She leaned in closer, drawn to his warmth, and looked up into his eyes, searching for any hint of insincerity. She was so close her breasts lightly brushed his chest, and with her chin tilted up and her nose level with his stock, she caught the peppery scent of his warm bare skin just below the ear at his unshaven jaw. It caused her to pause and breathe deeply. She was more surprised than shocked by her response, and dared to give herself up to this new and tantalizing experience.

Instinctively she knew the scent of him, pleasant and thoroughly masculine, was authentic. That it was the essence of him, not some bottled concoction. That even if he scrubbed and scrubbed, it would still be there. It was so intoxicating, and she so needful of it, that she closed her eyes to better breathe him in. And as time slowed and she let herself enjoy the moment, that certain something deep within her came to life and this time would not be quelled. Emotional control and being an example to others burst like a soap bubble. Her overwhelming desire was to press her body hard against him. And she, who had never kissed a man, or had the desire to do so, and had only ever shared a furtive fumbled kiss with her cousin Evelyn when they were both fourteen years old, wanted to kiss this man—desperately.

And then he did the most natural thing in the world. He gently took her face between his hands and kissed her.

It was a cautious, gentle kiss, but it was everything Mary had dreamed of and more. And she wanted more. She moved into him, mouth and body pressed to his, as her arms went up about his neck to hold on fast. She could not breathe. She thought her knees would buckle. Her mind began to swirl. Yet, for all that, she felt more alive than she had ever been.

He gathered her to him and slid a hand inside her banyan to the small of her back, fingers twisting up in her night dress, pulling it askew, exposing her bare legs above her knee-high stockings as he held her hard against him. And all the while he kept kissing her. And when his mouth opened on hers and she felt his tongue, she gasped and pulled back, but only for a moment, only long enough to look up into his eyes and to give him pause for thought: That she had never been kissed before now, not like this, not properly, possibly not ever.

He wondered if he had shocked her and should stop. There was certainly surprise in her eyes. He hesitated. He would not go on kissing her if that was not her wish. He should have been more tentative and paced himself. But as she was thirty years of age, he had expected her to have some experience of a passionate kiss. But her reaction suggested the opposite. Just one more reason to loathe the gauche Sir Gerald. He went to gently press his lips to her forehead before putting her away from him. This was not the time or place to make love to her. That could wait for another day... What had he been thinking? Certainly not with his brain...

But her moment of hesitation was but a moment. A new, altogether different light replaced her initial shock, sparked her lovely eyes, and sent color flooding across her cheeks. She went on tiptoe and murmured, pulling at the front of his waistcoat so that he stayed where he was and did not move away,

"More. I want more. I want—I want you, too."

He needed no further encouragement.

Whatever was happening, whatever it was in the next room was of supreme indifference.

He gathered her back up into his arms and she yielded her mouth to his. He had waited eight long years to kiss her, and she had waited a lifetime for just such a kiss. For how long they stayed this way, neither knew or cared. In the throes of an all-consuming passion, time and space became irrelevant. All that mattered was being in the moment, enjoying that moment, and for as long as possible. He, who had had more women in his past than he cared to count, had never wanted any woman as much as he wanted her. And she, who had never understood what it was to want a man carnally to the point of madness, wanted this man beyond reason. Soon excruciating need overwhelmed them both.

He was stripped out of his frock coat and she divested of her silk banyan and both articles were trampled underfoot as they staggered back towards the bed with little interruption to their heated kisses. In one swift and easy movement he lifted her into his arms, swung her about, and carried her to the four poster. And as they fell into the pillows and blissful ignorance of everything and everyone but themselves, Mary's stockinged toes clipped the edge of the silver candelabra Christopher had placed on the bedside table. The candelabra and its four tapers that were providing a pale light to the room toppled, then crashed to the floor. Still alight, the tapers flickered and the thin woolen Turkey rug caught fire and began to smolder.

It said much about the couple's complete preoccupation that the clang of heavy silverware and sudden darkness around them did not instantly register. And when it became apparent that something was amiss, but not precisely what, it was the strong odor of burning wool —which had the same acrid smell as burning feathers—that snapped them out of their unbridled fervor and had them falling apart and into action.

Christopher scrambled off the bed. He saw what was amiss and scooped up the candelabra and the four tapers, three of which were still alight, and set them to rights on the bedside table, and all without dripping wax on himself and burning his flesh. With the light restored, he turned and saw that there was a small black hole smoldering in the carpet. He quickly ground his heel into the carpet to stop the fire spreading.

"Damn! Damn and blast!" he growled.

He then swore under his breath and raked the disordered auburn curls out of his eyes. His swearing had nothing to do with the damaged rug and everything to do with the interruption. The tightness between his thighs was so uncomfortable that he took a deep breath and tried to regain mastery of himself. He adjusted his breeches but left his shirt tail untucked and hanging loose to provide some semblance of modesty. Straightening his crumpled waistcoat, he stared at the carpet, hands on slim hips, regaining his breath and wondering how he had allowed himself, a man of forty, to lose all sense of decorum. It was so unlike him. No doubt too many years of abstinence to count had played its part...

But he blamed Mary—for his celibacy and his lust. When he finally thought himself in control, he looked towards the bed, and the heat rushed back down between his thighs, and he briefly closed his eyes on a groan.

Mary had shifted onto her knees and was watching him. Her nightgown had slipped off one shoulder exposing a quantity of round alabaster breast, the edge of the lace collar taut and slicing across the dark pink tinge of areola. And with her glorious hair tumbled about her shoulders in messy abundance, her face flushed and mouth slightly parted, she was so yearningly beautiful his discomfort became excruciating. He fixed on her eyes—big violet eyes that blinked at him with incomprehension. She set his heart racing and his mind reeling.

Before he could say or do anything, she came to life and scampered across to the edge of the mattress and swung her stockinged legs over the side. When she attempted to slide her nightgown up onto her shoulder, while at the same time pulling it down over her bare thighs, she pitched forward and fell off the bed. It would have been comical had she not been in danger of hurting herself.

Christopher caught her before she fell flat on her face, scooped her up and set her on her feet. But he did not let her go.

"Steady, or you'll hurt more than your pride."

"Hurt? Hurt my-my—*pride?*" She stepped away, tossing the weight of her long hair over a shoulder, and glared up at him. "I don't know where you get your notions about—" She broke off, the acrid smell of singed wool assailing her nostrils. She grimaced, wrinkling up her little nose, before peering over his arm at the Turkey rug. "Oh no! It's ruined!"

He burst out laughing. "Oh, my darling, the carpet is the least of our worries!"

"Mr. Bryce! As I was saying: I don't know what you—"

"*Mr.* Bryce?" He pulled a face and gently brushed a long tangle of red curl away from her throat and over her shoulder. "Surely, here, in the privacy of your rooms, you may call me by my Christian name?"

"No, I may not. *Particularly* not here, here in my-my rooms."

He arched a brow.

"Not even after we shared a kiss?"

"No! It—it would not be right for me to call you—to call you —*Christopher.*"

His touch lingered at the base of throat, a finger lightly stroking the curve of her neck. "I have waited such a long time to hear you say it that I almost wish it was my true name—"

Mary pulled back out of his reach and looked up at him, momentarily diverted from her present predicament. "Christopher is not—is not *your name?*"

"It is not the name I was given at birth, the one I had for the first three months of my life, but Christopher is the only name I have ever answered to."

Inquisitiveness replaced her awkwardness and shock.

"Why don't you use your birth name?"

"Because that name is Cavendish."

"*Cavendish*? That's not a Christian name."

"Well, it is mine."

He'd never before disclosed that piece of his past to anyone, and never inked it anywhere. He had always used the name Christopher because it was what he had believed his name to be. That is until Sir George Cavendish willed him a substantial legacy in the name of Cavendish Bryce and his parents were left no option but to divulge the truth. A truth he was ignorant of and wanted no part of, and which sent him to the Continent searching for answers. But he wanted Mary to know the truth—all of it—and this was the first step.

He also knew family nomenclature was a requisite topic of conversation over tea and seedy cake for those not only related by birth or marriage to the nobility, but any family with pretensions to greatness. And the Cavendish family was one of the first families, and not only was Mary related by marriage to a branch of that illustrious family, her sister-in-law, the present Duchess of Roxton, was a Cavendish by birth. And how did he know this, and more, about Mary's relations? Kate was an expert on noble family lineages because she had once been part of that world, and thus still corresponded with many of the titled and influential. And because of her infirmity, it had become Christopher's task to read these letters to her, and so he knew a great deal about Mary's relatives and connections.

He couldn't help a smile at Mary's deepening frown, not surprised she would show interest, and be interested enough in the name of Cavendish to forget her embarrassment at what had just occurred between them. No doubt her mind was mapping an extensive family tree and trying to decide on which branch he sat.

"Were you given it because your mother's family are distantly related to the Cavendishs?"

"No. Not my mother's family." He scooped up her banyan, gave it a shake and held it open for her. "Best keep warm."

She allowed him to help her into the dressing gown, still preoccupied with this new-found information about his name. She did not wait for him to answer her question, and asked another as she turned to face him. "Is it because you are a distant cousin of Sir Gerald's?"

He adjusted the banyan to sit square on her shoulders, then took the left and right panels and crossed them over her breasts. "Cousin? No. And not that distant."

Unconsciously she pulled the banyan closer and folded her arms. "Then what do you mean, *not that distant?*"

He wondered how best to explain himself as he picked up his frock coat, which had also been left a crumpled heap on the carpet. He gave it a shake and brushed down the arms and the pocket flaps in the hopes of removing some of the creases. And when he shrugged it on, Mary was quick to help him find the second sleeve. She then did for him what he had done for her—adjust the set of the coat across his shoulders—as if it were the most natural thing in the world for her to do so. But her assistance with such a small domestic detail startled him. It was so unexpected, and yet offered him a presentiment of a future he had often dreamed of with her, that all he could do was mutter his thanks.

When she came back to stand before him and waited, silent and expectant, for his response, he finally found his voice again.

"I do have Cavendish blood. But the-the—*connection* is-is —*complicated...*"

"Complicated?"

"Yes. So complicated that it is a story for another day... And another day will see you have enough coal and firewood for both rooms."

At his mention of coal her preoccupation with his name vanished, replaced with indignation.

"If one kiss was all that was required for me to have a good fire in both rooms, it's a wonder you did not try to kiss me sooner!"

It was meant as a set-down. All it did was make Christopher chuckle deep in his throat.

"I wish I had. Eight years sooner—that day we were introduced downstairs in the hall. Kissing you was my first thought. The second you can guess..."

Mary frowned, not comprehending. "Second? Guess? What?"

He folded his arms and shook his head, grinning. "That's one of the particulars about you I adore. No chicanery whatsoever."

While he was speaking, Mary had finally understood his meaning about his second thought and blushed rosily. Not so much because he wanted to make love to her, but because, if she were truthful with herself, she now realized that the warm tingling throbbing somewhere deep inside her had first come to life upon meeting him. His second thought had been her first. She was so shocked by this admission that she disguised it with anger.

"I did not give you permission to-to—*adore* me, Mr. Bryce! I—I—"

"And yet you let me kiss you…?"

She pouted. "I did no such thing!"

He frowned and cocked his head. Inside he was still laughing. "No? You're right. Thinking back on it, you didn't, did you?"

"No! I did not!"

He tapped his mouth with a finger, his shoulders shaking with laughter. He found her embarrassed petulance adorable. "My dear Lady Mary, lower your voice or you may wake the ghost."

She pulled a face but did as he asked. "I knew you were just humoring me! I'll wager you don't believe there is even a thief, least of all a ghost!"

"But—I assure you, I—"

He said no more, swallowing the rest of the sentence whole when in the pause between words he heard the faintest of noises, not unlike the sound of scratching on wood. Mary heard it too, and she glanced at the door and back at Christopher.

"Did you hear—"

"Yes. Yes, I did," he interrupted in a whisper, all humor extinguished.

Together they crept up to the door as if it were a live thing ready to pounce on them, and put an ear to the panel. They had only a few moments to wait and then there was the same sound. Someone or something was scratching fingernails up and down the paneling. That Mary and Christopher both heard it was evident when they stared at one another, eyes wide and lips parted. Neither spoke, and both breathed shallow, as if not wanting to alert whatever it was on the other side to their presence. Though they also had the same thought— that their heated conversation, not to mention the candelabra hitting the floor, was more than enough of a disturbance to alert thief or specter alike.

And as they stared at one another, wondering if the noise would continue or perhaps something else might stir them into action, the unexpected happened. It was so utterly bone chillingly astonishing that they did not at first believe it to be real. And it wasn't. It just couldn't be.

A voice on the other side of the bolted door hissed through the paneling,

"Mary? Mary! Is that you?"

SEVEN

Time suspended. Mary and Christopher drew in a startled collective breath, stared at the door, then at each other, their respective expressions a mirror of the frozen shock the other was feeling. But neither was given the opportunity to speak when their shared moment was splintered by the voice on other side of the door, which whined,

"Mary, be a good girl and let me in. I'm chilled to m'marrow!"

Instead of doing as the voice ordered, Mary scuttled backwards, to get as far from the door as possible, until her foot caught in the fabric of her banyan and she stumbled back and came hard up against the bed. Face white, breathing quick and shallow, she slid to the floor. She was shaking from toes to ears and glared at Christopher.

"Now you *must* believe me! It is a ghost!"

"We'll know soon enough," he replied calmly, though he was uncharacteristically stunned that the specter or thief or whatever it was should address the Lady Mary with such familiarity.

He was torn between swiftly unlatching the bolt to discover once and for all if it was Sir Gerald's ghost or a thief, and dashing over to gather Mary into his arms to soothe away her tremors. But practicality won out and he decided on the former. Surely, she'd have no qualms who drew back the bolt now.

"No! Wait!" she hissed, and came to life and back to Christopher's side. She took a deep breath and squared her shoulders. "If we open the door, we open it together. I don't want Teddy thinking her mother a coward. Besides… I've just had a ridiculous thought… If ghosts can't taste strawberry jam, they certainly can't feel cold and be *chilled to the marrow*, can they?"

"Ha! Precisely!" Christopher grinned. "Just the sort of response Teddy would give! So, are you ready for me to open the door?"

Mary nodded, though she did swallow her apprehension down hard.

"Remember the strawberry jam," Christopher whispered as he slid back the bolt, then turned the handle.

Instinctively, Mary leaned in to his shoulder and stepped with him away from the door as he opened it into the bedchamber. For a moment neither of them moved, then Christopher took a peek first, Mary followed, both silent and remaining behind the door, as if it were a shield offering protection from whatever force came from deep within the dressing room across the threshold. But there was no sudden burst of light. No rush of cold air. And there was no noise. It was deathly quiet.

Sir Gerald's dressing room was in darkness. It was impossible to see beyond the first couple of feet. Off to their right was the faintest haze of candlelight. The window, if that was the means by which the thief had entered the room, was to the left, and as there was no breeze from that direction, or any other, Christopher assumed it to be closed tight and the curtains pulled against the night. So where was the owner of the voice? Could it belong to an ethereal being, as Mary suggested?

Both were mystified. Both were lulled into a false sense of relief that they had not been immediately confronted with a specter floating before them or a thief brandishing a weapon and barking demands.

"Wait. We need light," Christopher whispered. "I'll fetch a taper."

Mary nodded, and turned a shoulder to watch him step over to the bedside table for the candelabra. She turned back to face the open doorway, and that's when she saw it, looming large out of the blackness.

A figure draped all in white glided towards her. It made no sound on the floorboards and seemed to float. It held a single taper close to its chest, the harsh yellow light projecting upwards under its chin, illuminating a long, lean face from which unblinking eyes stared straight at her. Encircling its head was a halo of silver hair in wild disorder. It had an arm outstretched in its billowy white sleeve, and one crooked bony finger beckoned her.

Mary's gaze left the wild eyes and travelled the length of the outstretched arm to fix on that beckoning finger. Two fingers of the left hand, middle and ring, were stumps. Such a macabre sight had her transfixed. But far from turning and fleeing as the figure continued to approach, she remained in the doorway, rigid with fright. A small part of her was composed enough to want to shout out to Christopher that she had been right all along—here was proof a ghost was haunting Sir Gerald's dressing room! And curiosity kept her terror in check. The specter was most definitely not her dead husband. So who was it? And why was it inhabiting her husband's rooms? And how did it know her name? That was the most terrifying question of all. And then it spoke, and confirmed her worst fears.

"I must be a fright by the look on your sweet face. To appear without warning in this manner is unforgiveable, but a necessity, *ma chérie*. You'll understand once I explain. It was time to return."

"Explain? Return?" Mary repeated, nonplussed.

"Identify yourself, sir!" Christopher demanded, standing by Mary in the doorframe and holding aloft the candelabra to better inspect the draped figure.

"Mary knows who I am."

"Stay where you are!" Christopher ordered then glanced at Mary for answers.

But she stared at the figure and then up at Christopher and lifted her shoulders and shook her head as if to say she was clueless as to the specter's identity.

"*Mon Dieu*," muttered the figure. "I must indeed be a sorry sight if my dearest cousin can't recognize me…"

"Again I say identify yourself!"

The specter had halted at Christopher's command, but now it took a step closer, gaze fixed on Mary. To her surprise, and Christopher's, it chose to address her in French.

"*Chérie*, if I had been able to walk through your front door in the light of day, I would gladly have done so. Believe me, I am the last person upon this earth who wants to bring you pain and suffering. I had hoped—it was my heartfelt wish—that time and circumstance had not altered me to such a great extent that *you* would've forgotten me? But now… now, seeing your sweet face for the first time in seven years, a face that is as beautiful and loved as that last day we parted in Paris all those years ago, I fear I may have left my return too late…"

In the silence that followed, Christopher looked to Mary for an explanation but she ignored him and approached the figure, unafraid, and peered hard into its face.

Was this a specter or a man? It had a strong square jaw and cheekbones that were a little too prominent, as if he had not eaten a decent meal in months. A scar bisected the left eyebrow, narrowly missing the eye, and far from being pale, the skin on his face and hands was tanned a warm caramel, as if he had spent many years in warmer climes.

But it was only when she fixed on the blue eyes, blue eyes filled with sadness and apprehension, and the mouth that quivered into a hesitant smile, that Mary knew with certainty the spectre's identity. But recognition only deepened her confusion. Unwelcome tears welled up.

"Evelyn? *Eve*? Is it—is it truly you?"

"Ah, *ma chérie*... You *do* see me!" the specter cried out, opening wide its arms to embrace her.

"Stay back! Stay back I say!" Christopher demanded, brandishing the candelabra as if it were a sword.

Reason told Christopher here was flesh and blood dressed up in a nightshirt several sizes too large for its emaciated human frame. Yet, a tiny sliver of doubt had him wondering if indeed the supernatural was playing tricks on them when Mary covered her face with her hands, and then quickly dashed her eyes dry before exclaiming,

"How is it you are here? Why are you here? You're dead. You *died*. M'sieur le Duc received word—Your parents—we—*all of us*—mourned you! We still do. Evelyn, you've been dead to us for five long years."

"Yes, you did. And yes, I have been. I am sorry for it, but I have returned—returned from the dead—because I must make amends."

"Returned from the dead...?"

That's when Mary knew the figure before her had to be a ghost—the ghost of her long-lost cousin Evelyn Gaius Ffolkes, Viscount Vallentine and heir presumptive to the earldom of Stretham-Ely, whose tortured and bloated body was fished from the Riga River five years ago. There was a ring, a family heirloom, discovered on the right hand. With this proof sent the Duke, there was a funeral and an empty coffin interned in the Roxton mausoleum.

And only three months ago she had visited the mausoleum, on her most recent stay with her Roxton cousins to celebrate her brother's wedding. After the wedding breakfast, Mary and her cousin the Duchess had laid bouquets of white roses within the marble tomb, Mary placing a single white rose on Evelyn's empty casket with a prayer for his poor tortured soul, hoping it was finally at peace.

But now she was meant to believe that this "man" standing before her was her cousin returned to make amends? For what? she wondered. And why now? And why here, before her? He couldn't be flesh and blood, could he?! He had to be a ghost, didn't he?! It was all too much.

Overwhelmed and emotionally fraught, Mary took a shattering breath, her knees buckled and she crumpled to the floor.

"I NEVER FAINT. I'M NOT A FAINTER," MARY MUTTERED sluggishly.

"No. No, you're not," Christopher agreed, holding a tumbler of water. He had scooped her up before she hit the floor in a dead faint, then carried her back through to her bedchamber to place her gently on the bed. "I've never seen you faint, ever."

"No. No, you haven't…" She shifted to sit up, and he helped her, plumping the pillows at her back to make her comfortable before handing her the water. She sipped and met Christopher's gaze. "Is he—Evelyn's not a ghost, is he?" she asked rhetorically.

Christopher set the tumbler aside and took hold of her hands. She was trembling, and not from cold. It was shock. All he knew about the identity of the stranger in the overlarge nightshirt was that he said he was Mary's long lost cousin, a cousin Mary and her family thought was dead, and that his name appeared to be Evelyn.

Christopher was just as bewildered by this as Mary, but for her sake he kept his thoughts and opinions to himself. All he truly cared about was that she was not more troubled than she already was. He pressed her fingers, and when she looked into his eyes he could see she, like him, had a head full of questions, and was still trying to make sense of it all.

"No. Not a ghost," he replied, adding with a small smile he hoped would lighten her mood, "But your cousin is a thief, of sorts—of jam and pickles…"

Mary smiled, comforted by his placid voice and her cold fingers being warmed in his hands, which were surprisingly large and smooth. They sat there looking at each other for only a matter of seconds, as if they were the only two people in the room, speech unnecessary to communicate they were having the same thoughts—how much they had enjoyed their furtive passionate kiss, and how that one kiss had changed everything between them. Though in what way, neither was prepared to speculate for fear of ruining the moment. Then movement over Christopher's shoulder had Mary snatching back her fingers, and her face ripened with color.

Christopher got off the bed with a frown and pulled the coverlet up to keep her warm.

"I'll have Betsy fetch you a mug of warm milk—"

"Tea for me," Evelyn the ghost said buoyantly, brushing past Christopher to take his place on the bed with all the familiarity of one invited to do so. He said over his shoulder to the Squire, "And you fetch the milk and tea. No one must know I'm here." And with the expectation Christopher would immediately do his bidding, turned back to Mary and said with conspiratorial enjoyment, "Shall we have gossip with our tea and milk? I can provide one or two lumps of scandal, m'self, but I'm relying on you to tell me what's been happening in town. It will be like old times!"

He then let out such a raucous high-pitched laugh that Christopher winced. But Evelyn's peculiar affectation brought Mary to life, as if she was truly seeing him for the very first time, and she threw her arms about his neck, so overcome with emotion she could barely get the words out.

"Oh, Eve! Eve! It *is* you!"

"Of course it's me, *mon petit lapin*. Well, a shadow of me, but me nonetheless." He gently pulled out of her embrace, held her shoulders, and looked into her moist eyes. "No tears, Mary dear," he murmured, and kissed her forehead. "I beg you. Never from you…"

Mary smiled and nodded, and sniffed. Here was her dearest cousin, believed dead, returned! He was right, too. He was a shadow of his former self, ghost-like in his appearance, with a mane of wild hair turned to silver before its time. But his blue eyes were just as piercing, and the enigmatic smile, which always hid his true feelings—but not from her—was his and his alone.

They had been confidants in childhood. He, an only child, coddled and delicate and a brilliant musician. She, the only girl amongst a band of rough-and-tumble brothers and boy cousins, who was never included in their games and schemes. And being the same age, it was only natural they would be drawn to one another. And while the boys went off riding, hunting, shooting, or just roaming about the Treat estate, Mary remained indoors at her embroidery or watercolors, practicing at being a lady, because that's what the daughters of earls did, and because the boys did not want her. Evelyn, however, would double back and join her. They would hide out in one of the many unoccupied rooms in the palace-home of the Duke of Roxton, and there spend the day—Evelyn playing his viola, Mary with her embroidery, the first to hear and praise his compositions.

Such wonderfully carefree days were etched in her memory forever…

She put a hand to Evelyn's cheek, and traced the contours of his gaunt face, and with touch sprang tears, tears that blinded her sight and made her gulp down an overwhelming emotion that he was indeed flesh and blood and alive!

"Oh, Eve, why did you never send me word? Why did you not let your inconsolable parents know you were alive? How could you allow us to grieve so? All those years... all those tears..."

"Believe me, *ma chérie*, there were many, *many* times when I wanted to write. But... it was better this way. Better that no one know the truth. Best that I remain—*dead.*"

Mary was incredulous.

"Surely nothing can be so awful that you would prefer to be dead to your family—to me—to those who love you?"

Evelyn huffed and shrugged and threw up a hand. As it was the one with two mutilated fingers, it only served to underscore how low his life must have sunk that he preferred to be dead to his family. He looked away from her steady, tear-filled gaze and shook his head.

Mary held her breath, wondering if he was about to confide in her. But the moment passed, and he caught up her hand and kissed it, saying with a forced smile and a twinkle in his blue eyes,

"I'm home now. That's all that matters... Please, *ma chérie*, dry those beautiful eyes and be happy for me—for *us.*"

Mary nodded and smiled and quickly wiped her face with the back of her shaking hands and that's when Christopher stepped in and stuck out his handkerchief. She took it without looking at him. Possibly she had forgotten he was still in the room, her attention wholly focused on Evelyn.

"I *am* happy. And you are right. All that matters is that you are alive and have come home. It is—it is a dream come true!"

"Yes. A dream come true, *ma chérie*," Evelyn replied softly, taking the handkerchief and patting dry her wet cheeks.

Christopher wanted to rip the linen square from the interloper's fingers. Instead, he turned on a boot heel and left the room to fetch firewood, hot milk, and tea.

EIGHT

Evelyn's directive that his presence be kept a secret was ignored. Christopher was not a lackey, and Mary's cousin had no authority over him. What was the man doing here, at an isolated house miles from anywhere, hiding out, even from the servants? And why had he chosen to return from the dead here, and now? The timing of his miraculous reappearance could not have been worse. Christopher had finally let down his guard with the Lady Mary, and her response was everything he had hoped for. Yet, they had barely kissed, and he was given no time to explain his feelings, when they were interrupted by Evelyn. Christopher harbored this niggling worry that the man may have been listening through the wall, and timed his interruption. As to the evident cousinly affection between the pair, that bothered Christopher the most. But he did not possess an envious disposition, and so was pleased for Mary and her family that her cousin was indeed alive and well, and she so happy to see him.

He roused her sleeping maid, and by the time Betsy came into the kitchen, Christopher had stoked the slumbering fire into new life, put the kettle on the hob, prepared a tea tray, and taken the silver tea caddy from its locked cabinet. There was a matching silver teapot, strainer, and sugar bowl, but those had been packed away with the silver cutlery, plate, and goblets for Sir Jack Cavendish when he came of age. The Lady Mary was given use of the tea caddy and the second-best tea service of blue-and-white patterned Worcester. They had been part of her dowry, and upon marriage became her husband's property. And upon his death, along with everything else, it all became the property of his heir; Lady Mary had no claim to anything, because Sir Gerald had selfishly left her nothing.

Christopher thought it callous of Sir Gerald not to have willed to his wife at least the tea caddy and Worcester tea service, to say nothing of an income to live on. He wished he was at liberty to give it to her, not because they were expensive and ornate grandiose statements of her position in society, but because they had once belonged to her, and they were something personal for Teddy to inherit.

As he set out the teacup and saucer, milk jug, and sugar bowl, he had a flash of memory of the Lady Mary cheerfully showing her little daughter how to use the silver sugar tongs to drop a sliver into her milky tea without creating a splash. The little girl had a chubby hand about the tongs, and with patient guidance from her mother was able to select a little lump of sugar. And when it went plop in her milky tea, Teddy had giggled with delight and looked around at her mother for approval. Mary had smiled and kissed the top of her daughter's strawberry curls, telling her what a splendid job she had done with the tongs. Sir Gerald, who was present, merely grunted and crumpled his newspaper to his chest to accept a cup of tea from his wife, not a word of encouragement or acknowledgment for his little daughter's efforts. Evidence that Teddy had given the task her undivided attention showed in the tip of her tongue caught in the corner of her mouth. She still did that when concentrating on a task, be it saddling her horse, or writing without trailing her left hand in the ink and smudging it. It was a quirk inherited from her father, which made his unresponsiveness that much more deplorable.

And yet, had there been guests Sir Gerald wished to impress, Christopher knew the Baronet would have been overly effusive with his compliments and his largesse of tea and cake. In all his years at Abbeywood, Sir Gerald made no effort to know his plain-spoken neighbors, all of whom frowned on tea-drinking as the beverage of choice of city dwelling idlers with more money than sense; and in Sir Gerald's case, money as well as sense was lacking.

It was not surprising that in a county where cider was drunk, from laborer to master, tea and its associated paraphernalia were met with contemptuous scowls by yeoman farmers, and coveted sidelong glances by their wives. Derogatory opinion was declared loudly and proudly at a supper at which Christopher had been present. Everyone agreed excessive tea-drinking led to unnecessary waste and indolence. A certain baronet living among them was held up as the prime example of this. This baronet boasted of his connections to the aristocracy and kept tea in a silver caddy, for pity's sake!

It was only when Christopher coughed into his fist that the assembled company remembered too late that he was sitting there— possibly Sir Gerald's only friend in the world. Conversation came to a halt mid nod. With a shake of the head at the memory of those startled faces about the vicar's table, Christopher unlocked the tea caddy with a duplicate key he kept on a chain in his waistcoat pocket. Lady Mary carried the other on her chatelaine. It had not always been thus.

The two keys had once been in the keeping of the housekeeper to whom Sir Gerald had entrusted the making of his tea. Christopher had removed both keys from her almost immediately upon her master's death because Mrs. Keble had not only indulged herself by unlawfully taking tea from the caddy whenever she pleased, but there was the accusation—with no conclusive evidence, but Christopher believed it to be so—that she had profiteered by on-selling used tea leaves, and even tea dust, on market days to villagers. And the quantity of tea drunk by Sir Gerald meant that the quantity of used tea being sold by his housekeeper had provided Mrs. Keble with a hefty secondary income.

Inexplicably to Christopher, the woman had expected the quantity of tea supplied to the house to remain as it had been when Sir Gerald was alive, and that she would simply continue on with her illegal business venture unimpeded. So when Christopher confiscated the keys, gathered up all the silver and locked it away in a chest, and had all tea supplies brought directly to him, Mrs. Keble was incensed. He had hoped she would be offended enough to give notice of her own accord, or make some damning statement that would expose her illegal trading activities.

But Mrs. Keble proved more cunning than he had at first realized. When she could not seduce him with her charms, she tried to extort him, threatening to take her accusations to the Lady Mary. Her ladyship would be vastly interested to know that the Squire was paying for her ladyship's tea, clothing, and postal allowances out of his own pocket. It was all true, but how the housekeeper came to find this out, when he had managed to keep it from the Duke of Roxton, the estate's co-executor, was a mystery. He did not want Mary discovering he was her benefactor, or that she was a great deal poorer than she or her family realized.

Sir Gerald had left his wife and child destitute. There was no allowance. There was only debt, and so much of it that it was through Christopher's generosity in lending the estate a substantial sum, to be paid back over time through estate revenues from wool and grain sales, that the contents of the house and parcels of farming land were not immediately sold off to pay Sir Gerald's creditors.

Kate had accused him of allowing his heart to rule his head. There was no guarantee that, for his efforts on her behalf, the Lady Mary would ever look upon him as anything more than a neighbor. In fact, *Proud Mary* resented his high-handedness, particularly his intractability in allowing Teddy to visit her Roxton relatives. Christopher had abruptly terminated the conversation in an uncharacteristic temper, and words were said that should have been left unsaid. He had saved the estate, not only for Mary, but for her daughter, and for Sir Gerald's heir Jack. They were the innocent victims of a man for whom the seven deadly sins were a way of life. The consequences of such a life on others he did not need to elaborate, because Kate, as a former disciple of at least five of those sins, was only too well aware.

He had immediately asked for forgiveness for uttering such hurtful words, and she had readily given it. That did not make him feel less of a nidget, and it took him some time to forgive himself.

"UNCLE BRYCE, IS THE GHOST KEEPING YOU AWAKE, TOO?"

Christopher was brought out of his introspection by Teddy. She was standing in the kitchen doorway, a quilted banyan over her night-gown, lace night cap askew. Her sleepy nurse stood at her back with a candlestick, one hand lightly on the girl's shoulder for reassurance. She told her to go stand by the fire to keep warm, while she made her a mug of hot milk.

"Mr. Bryce has the milk on the table ready for us, see," she added brightly and went about filling a small saucepan with milk.

"Best heat all of it," Christopher said. "Betsy will be here directly." He did not need to add that the milk was for Lady Mary. He caught the nurse's significant sidelong glance at Teddy, alerting him that the child was unsettled, and he suspected she had woken from a bad dream, given she had mentioned the ghost. He acknowledged this with a slight lift of his brows, before taking a seat at the table.

He beckoned Teddy to him, saying with a smile, "Would you be disappointed if I told you there is no ghost?"

Teddy's small hand convulsed in his. "No ghost? Truly?"

"Truly."

"But… How-how can you be sure?"

Christopher heard her note of hesitant uncertainty and looked grave. He did not answer immediately. He wanted her to feel he had given the question serious thought. He was also surprised at the change in her since dinner, when she had laughed and teased him about a supposed ghost in the kitchen, and its liking for jam. The thought of a ghost haunting the house must have played on her mind while alone in the dark of her bedchamber; and who knew what else the maids and Cook had said in front of her about the ghost that she may only have remembered while falling asleep.

"Truth is, I can't be absolutely certain. Ghosts could be anywhere. Folk will tell you the Puzzlewood is haunted, but we ride through there often enough and have yet to come across a ghost—"

"But we go in daylight, Uncle Bryce. And ghosts only come out at night."

"Ah, yes, so they do. But not here, not in this house, day or night. No one has actually seen a ghost, they have only presumed there is one because they can't explain how some condiments went missing from the pantry."

Teddy moved in closer so she could whisper. Fear put a quaver in her voice. "Strawberry jam was Papa's favorite."

Christopher was startled. "Was it?"

Teddy nodded. "Yes. He kept it all to himself. No one else was to eat it. Not even Mama."

"I see." Christopher smiled. Privately, he seethed at such selfish behavior, which did not surprise him. It was typical of Sir Gerald. "But you and your mama prefer marmalade, so everyone had what they liked best, didn't they?"

"Yes. We did. But Mama and I like strawberry jam, too." She suddenly hunched her shoulders, and said in a conspiratorial whisper, leaning in to Christopher, "Cook let me have a spoon of it here in the kitchen. But I wasn't to tell Papa. And I didn't."

Christopher wondered where this conversation was going, and should not have been surprised by what Teddy said next, but he was, and could have kicked himself for not thinking of it sooner himself.

She looked over her thin shoulder, and there was Jane, come out of the scullery sleepy-eyed and tying her cap on straight to take over from Nurse, who was stirring the milk in the saucepan. Betsy, who had also appeared, had gone straight up to the fireplace to see to the hot water for the teapot. Satisfied she would not be overheard, she turned back to Christopher and said solemnly,

"I know it's bad manners to eavesdrop. Mama has told me to close my ears and try hard not to listen. But sometimes that is very difficult when the servants talk as if I'm not here at all."

"Yes, I understand your dilemma. Once something is heard it is very hard to *unhear* it."

Teddy nodded. "That's what I think, too. But I don't want to disappoint Mama. I can tell you what I can't forget, can't I, Uncle Bryce?"

Christopher smiled. "Yes. Whatever you like."

The girl nodded again, gave a little sigh, and confessed, "Cook says she would take an oath on her second son Timothy's grave that the ghost haunting the house *be the dead master*. That's Papa, isn't it? Cook says the missing strawberry jam is proof that it *doth be him*. She says his soul *be restless* and can't settle because of what he did—did to himself."

"Did to—*himself?*"

"Yes. Papa haunts the house because he can't find peace. And that's what ghosts are—the souls of dead people who must wander the earth until they make amends for their sins. Only then will they be allowed into heaven. Cook says any man that *doth take his own life* is not a Christian and should be buried at the crossroads. Sinners aren't buried in the churchyard. And sinners don't go to heaven. Cook said Papa *killed 'eself and that doth be a sin*, so Papa's grave should be at the crossroads. But Cook says he was given a Christian burial because he *not be common folk but a baronet*—"

"That's not true, Teddy. None of it," Christopher interrupted. "Your father's death was an accident. He died when he tripped and his musket discharged, and he shot himself. That is a sad fact, but it is fact nonetheless. Sir Gerald would never have killed himself." Of that he was thoroughly convinced; the man was an egotist and too much the coward to ever end his own life. "And the vicar would never have allowed your father to have a Christian burial, baronet or no, if he thought for one moment he had taken his own life. The Reverend Sanders answers to God, and to no one else."

"So Granny could not make the vicar bury Papa amongst Christians to save her good name, even though he did not deserve to be there?"

"She could try and persuade the vicar to do that," Christopher explained, keeping his features under control, though he wanted to smile at Teddy's naïve supposition the Countess of Strathsay was omnipotent. "But the Reverend Sanders would not do what is against his conscience, and what is against God's will. I am very sure that is what he told your grandmother; if indeed she approached him. Though I have no knowledge that she did."

Teddy gave a little sigh and smiled. The wrinkles of anxiety in her freckled brow disappeared.

"I'm glad. I like the Reverend Sanders."

"Me too."

"So the ghost is not Papa?"

"No. In fact there is no ghost."

Teddy looked disappointed and relieved at one and the same time. "But if there is no ghost, then who took Papa's jam and drank the elderflower wine?"

"A very good question. What if I told you the condiments and the wine were not stolen, but eaten by a very hungry visitor?"

Teddy's eyes widened. "A visitor? *Here*? But no one comes to visit us. Mama and I always have to do the visiting."

"Well this visitor is here to see your Mama, and to meet you."

"*Me?*"

"Yes. But unfortunately you will have to wait to meet him, possibly until dinner time tomorrow."

"Oh?" Teddy's shoulders slumped. "He won't be at breakfast?"

"I should think not. He's traveled a very long way so I doubt he will be up with the sun like the rest of us. Which is just as well because Kate is expecting us both to nuncheon. You don't want to disappoint her, do you?"

Teddy shook her head, then smiled and said confidentially, "I have a surprise for her."

"You do? Good. Kate likes surprises."

Teddy wanted to know more about the visitor. "Is the visitor a friend of Mama's?"

"Yes. I think he may even be a long-lost cousin."

Teddy was intrigued, and all the fears conjured up in the darkness of her bed about the ghost of her father visiting the house were vanquished by her curiosity.

"A long lost *cousin*? Does Granny know him?"

"I'm sure she must."

"And Uncle Dair and Uncle Charles, too?"

"I am certain your uncles have known this cousin for as many years as your Mama."

"So this cousin of Mama's is the hungry visitor we thought was a ghost?"

"Yes. A cousin who likes strawberry jam as much as your Papa."

Teddy let out a sigh of relief which Christopher ignored, and said, "Cook and Jane and Jennie, *and* Luke will be very pleased to hear there isn't a ghost after all."

It was then that a solid youth of medium height entered the kitchen via the walled vegetable garden. It was Luke and he carried a load of firewood. Christopher's faithful lurcher was at his heels. Seeing Lorenzo, his master had a sudden idea. He turned to Teddy and said, a glance at her nurse, who had come over to the table carrying a mug of hot milk, to ensure she was attentive,

"I wonder if you would do me the favor of taking care of Lorenzo tonight? Luke and I need to set some fires and—"

"Oh yes! Yes please!" Teddy interrupted excitedly, and dropped to her knees to give Lorenzo a hug about the throat when he nuzzled her hand. "He can sleep with me!"

"Now Miss Theodora, I don't be thinking it a wise choice to have that animal—" began Nurse and was cut off by Christopher.

"At the foot of your bed. Not under the covers. Or he will expect me to do likewise." He gave Nurse a curt nod, then stood and pushed the chair to the table, saying to Teddy as casually as he could because it was a fib, "Of course you do know ghosts don't care for dogs…?"

Teddy looked up swiftly from patting Lorenzo, eyes wide. "Truly? Are—are ghosts afraid of dogs?"

"They must be. I've not heard of a ghost haunting a house where a dog is present. Ah! Now what's this?" he added with a laugh, surprised when Teddy threw her arms about him and hugged him.

"Thank-you for letting Lorenzo stay with me," Teddy muttered, cheek pressed to his frock coat.

Christopher returned her hug, then went down on his haunches, took hold of her hand, and looked into her eyes.

"You'll always be safe with Lorenzo, and with me, Teddy. You know that, don't you?" When she nodded he gently flicked her cheek and said with a smile, "And you are doing me a favor by looking after him. Now off you go to bed, and be sure to drink all your milk. We'll be riding out early in the morning, and I have no doubts Lorenzo will have you awake before Nurse."

"Is that true about ghosts and dogs, sir?" Betsy asked in the silence that followed Teddy's departure. She poured boiling water over the tea leaves in the porcelain teapot, a glance exchanged with Jane, who was stoking the fire, and Luke, who had dumped the firewood in its box, both servants waiting further instructions from Christopher who remained by the table deep in thought.

"I have no idea…" Christopher answered, pulling himself out of his abstraction.

His thoughts had returned to the surprising turn of events upstairs, the kiss shared with Mary, followed by the unexpected appearance of her cousin. He sensed there was something between Mary and her cousin that ran deeper than cousinly ties of affection. It filled him with a dread that time was no longer on his side, and that this cousin could very well unseat his plans for the future, a future he had always dreamed of sharing with Mary. He wished it had been a ghost haunting the house. A ghost would've been the least of his worries.

CHRISTOPHER ASSURED THE SERVANTS THAT THE GHOST WAS IN fact a guest playing an elaborate prank. The gentleman in question was a cousin of the Lady Mary, and an eccentric. He went on to add that he wouldn't be at all surprised if he was weak-brained and childish, traits that were peculiar to particular individuals within the nobility. Pretending to be a ghost and haunting the pantry for food were surely evidence of that. Christopher assured them such antics would not be repeated. And they were not to worry the gentleman would again trespass into the servant areas of the house. The Lady Mary had him firmly in hand and he would comply with her wishes.

Jane nodded vigorously, eyes wide with new knowledge, happy to obey the Squire's directives. Neither she nor Betsy and Luke gave any indication they found Christopher's explanation implausible, or that they were surprised to discover the ghost was in fact a guest. Luke gave a grunt of understanding, which was all Christopher could hope for—it was as verbose as some men got in this pocket of England.

Luke followed Christopher up the back stairs, carrying firewood, and went along the passage to Sir Gerald's dressing room. After positioning several burning tapers to provide light, the lad set to work at the grate of a fireplace that had not been used in over two years. Christopher glanced about the silent stillness where all vestiges of occupation by its previous owner had been removed. The row of mahogany tallboys were covered with dust sheets, and on the opposite wall, the pegs in the paneling where frock coats, shirts, and other wearable paraphernalia were once left hanging to drop creases from garments and to air before wearing, seemed oddly out of place.

The dressing table was bare. Cleared of its crystal ointment jars, pomades, boar bristle brushes, gold snuffboxes, and etuis. Everything from silver shoe buckles to linen shirts, pairs of breeches in many fabrics, embellished waistcoats, and frock coats for every conceivable season and occasion, had been counted, cleaned, folded, grouped, and meticulously written up in ledgers. The personal effects of Sir Gerald Cavendish were then carefully packed away into chests, wardrobes, and boxes. This valuable inventory now belonged to Sir Jack Cavendish, who, when he came of age and claimed his inheritance, could do with his uncle's effects as he pleased. For now Christopher remained custodian.

Some of this painstaking work had been undone by Lady Mary's cousin. It was easy to see where he had disturbed the peace of this silent space. The dust sheet covering one of the lowboys had been thrown back and several of its drawers pulled out and left hanging on their hinges, contents ransacked. A chair moved from the dressing table left tracks in the light dust covering the floorboards where it had been dragged across to the chaise longue to be used as a makeshift table. On the padded seat was an opened jar of walnut pickle and the remnants of a fistful of bread. Crumbs surrounded the chair, and up against one leg were a couple of empty bottles of elderflower wine.

The dustsheet that once covered the chaise longue had been thrown back and the seat piled with clothes. As they appeared to have been layered in a particular manner, and formed a hollowed-out mound, it looked as if Mary's cousin had tunneled his way under this formation to try and keep himself warm at night.

The room was as cold as an icehouse, and the interloper would have found it impossible, in spite of the layers of clothing heaped upon him, to find any warmth. The corners of Christopher's mouth curved upwards. Good. He savored the image of Mary's cousin with teeth chattering and body convulsing with tremors of cold. The man should be made to feel uncomfortable. Christopher wondered how he could add to this discomfort to see him leave as soon as possible. Tomorrow, if he had his wish.

He left Luke at the grate and went through to Mary's bedchamber with the bucket of coals, firewood, and a lighted taper. He set to work at the fireplace, one ear to the conversation. Mary and her eccentric cousin were exactly where he had left them, sitting upon her bed, she against the bank of pillows, with her fur-lined banyan wrapped tight about her, and he facing her, with the quilted coverlet pulled up around his hunched shoulders. They were chattering away like two dear old friends reunited after years apart, which was precisely what they were. Except they were not two womenfolk in intimate conversation, but a man of indeterminate motives, and a widow who had, up until this night, never had any man other than her husband in her bedchamber, and now had kissed the one at the grate, and was sharing conversation in her bed with the other!

Christopher's mind reeled at this change in circumstances. All the more so because Mary was in such free and easy conversation punctuated by laughter that he was left to wonder if he knew her at all. More surprising still was that the conversation was conducted entirely in the French tongue.

But why should he be surprised? He knew she spoke French. All her Roxton relatives did. And he had heard Mary speak that foreign tongue with her daughter, as a teacher with her pupil, each sentence constructed and spoken with deliberation. But there had been none of the vivacity, spontaneity, and intimacy which she was exhibiting now conversing with her cousin. The French tongue gave her decidedly feminine voice a delicate timbre. And as he continued at the grate, waiting for the fire to take hold, his linguistic ear tuned to the language and their conversation, and his smile of appreciation dropped into a frown of concerned preoccupation.

NINE

Mary was incredulous. She sat up.

"An agent of the crown? *You?* A-a *spy?*"

"*Was* an agent of the crown, dearest. Firstly in the Italian States, then Istanbul, and for a few years in St. Petersburg. But as I told your brother, I'd grown weary of the game and all I wished to do was return home." When Mary blinked at him but made no comment it was Evelyn's turn to sit up. He put a hand to his mouth in surprise, blue eyes wide, and then laughed and grabbed for her hand across the embroidered coverlet. "Egad! I've let the pig out of the pen, haven't I? You had no notion Dair was an agent."

"A war hero, yes. But a spy, no," Mary confessed. "But the revelation does not surprise me. He was always one to treat his life cheaply, though he never did so with the lives of others. But I'm very sure he won't be doing that from now on. I sincerely hope that as a married man he will think twice about putting his life in danger—"

"*Dair*—married? Well! Well! I never cease to be amazed. Six months ago he was swaggering about the crooked lanes of Lisbon as a privateer, a girl under each arm. The sly dog!" Evelyn peered at Mary. "He's not got himself mixed up in something he can't get out of—or worse, settled for one of those icicle misses your mother would approve?"

"No. Not Dair. He's married the sweetest girl imaginable and means to become a gentleman farmer and manage the estate."

"Good—God! The man fell in love?!"

"He did, and fell hard. Rory is a delight."

"Is she?" Evelyn was skeptical. "I wonder what Shrewsbury will make of it—losing his two best agents in a matter of months…"

"I should think Lord Shrewsbury is well-pleased," Mary retorted good-naturedly, then couldn't help smiling cheekily. "After all, Dair married *his* granddaughter."

Evelyn snorted his surprise and laughed out loud at that. "Did he? Bloody hell! But how utterly fitting! I can't wait to congratulate him."

"I wish he was here for you to do so. My poor brother had one month of marriage and then was compelled to leave his bride and sail out to Barbados. A hurricane devastated the island. Most if not all its inhabitants, landowners and slaves alike, perished, Father amongst them. The family ring—the Strathsay Fire and Ice—was sent as proof he died along with his mistress, their children, and his slaves. The ring should have been enough, but Dair, Roxton, Mme la Duchesse, and of course Mama, want incontrovertible proof of Father's death—"

"Who can blame them?" Evelyn cut in, much subdued. "Dair cannot get on with his life without the surety of his inheritance." He shrugged and looked sheepish. "The last thing he needs is for your father to return from the dead. Not that I want your father dead," he added quickly, in case he had offended her. But he had not. Mary was remarkably composed, so he squeezed her hand and asked pensively, "You do not believe your father is dead, *ma chérie?*"

She shook her head, sniffed, but did not tear up.

"I do believe it, and seem to be the only one who is certain." She pressed her free hand to her breast. "I know, Eve. I know in my heart that Father died in that hurricane. I did not wish death upon him. But… for Dair. For Charles. For my mother. This is the only outcome that will secure their future happiness. Dair can inherit the title and begin his new life as the Earl of Strathsay with his bride. Charles can again hold his head high, no longer burdened with the shame of having a father who owned slaves. Never mind that he himself is charged with treason! And mother will finally have good reason to be miserable. Gray mourning will suit her austere personality perfectly."

"Dear me! No wonder Dair has gone full sail to the islands! But what of you, *ma chérie?* You say it is the only outcome for your brothers and your mother, but for you…?"

Mary let go of her cousin's hand and sat back against the bank of feather pillows and met his gaze. Her voice held a wisp of emotion. "I told you when we were children that for me, Father died the day he deserted his family, and I stand by that."

"I remember," Evelyn said quietly. "We were lying under the chandelier in M'sieur le Duc's saloon, like we always did. Do you remember? I believed you—literally. It was dear Maman who disabused me of that notion in her usual cryptic but ever so dramatic way, saying that the Earl was not in fact dead, but because he was a monster of the first order, he was dead to the family. I had no idea what she was talking about. Whoever did with her? Except perhaps *mon père*, who incidentally set me straight on that score, as he always did. Ah! *Mon père*," he murmured with a deep sigh. "I miss him so terribly much… But! We were not talking of my father, but yours," he added, rallying enough to smile.

"I would rather talk of yours," Mary replied quietly. "Your father was such a *gentle*man, Eve. Such a kind and loving soul. Such a good husband and fa—"

"Mary. No! Not yet." Evelyn's voice was strained but emphatic. Yet, he could not hide his anguish. "I cannot speak about—about *him*, or-or *them*—yet."

"Very well. But when you do, you can talk to me about anything you wish. I am here for you—always."

"Yes, I do know that. You always have been."

"Then tell me what brought you here."

"I thought it time to come home…"

"Silly! Not here, to England. *Here*, to Abbeywood, to me."

"I had a most illuminating conversation with your brother while in Lisbon," he replied, avoiding the question. "There was a great deal of family history to catch up on, not least that Roxton and Deb now have four brats—

"—five. I had their letter today announcing the arrival of little Otto."

"Otto?" Evelyn grinned. "How fitting! How many years have I been away?"

"Seven. Five of those without a word to any of us," she replied, keeping the recrimination from her tone

"Mary, I have a specific question I wish to put to you. Not tonight. Good God! I've given you enough of a shock as it is, turning up on your doorstep, back from the dead, without a word of warning. But I do want you to know I have spoken with Dair about your situation, and he knows I am sincere. But I—we—must wait until after I have met with Lord Shrewsbury. I had hoped he would be here already…?"

Mary tensed. She had been about to ask him what he could possibly have discussed with her brother that concerned her, but mention of England's Spymaster General turned her focus to more immediate and mundane concerns.

"Lord Shrewsbury? Here?! I cannot entertain Lord Shrewsbury,

Eve! I do not have the means. Nor do I have the servants, and half the house is shut up and in covers, and oh! I wish you had given me notice."

Evelyn laughingly shook his head. "My dear Mary, none of that will matter a jot to Shrewsbury, and it certainly doesn't matter to me—"

"Oh, but you are used to living hand-to-mouth, and in the most appalling of foreign places, but here, this is still my home. Mama would be horrified to think I was entertaining Lord Shrewsbury in such straightened circumstances. And I cannot invite our neighbors to dine because it is not within our means to do so, though I am sure his lordship will expect a dressed dinner every night and good company to sit down with him at table—"

"*Ma chérie*! Mary! *Listen*," Evelyn demanded gently and scrambled up the bed to sit beside her. He tenderly brushed a long loose curl from her flushed cheek, and looked into her eyes. "Set your mind at ease. Shrewsbury comes here for a private visit. There is no need for your neighbors to know. In fact, the less said about it the better. He may even use an alias, as I have done in the past, so as not to draw attention to himself. If certain persons were to discover he was here, or had been here, it would signal to our enemies that perhaps England's Spymaster General is not in complete control of the situation with France, with whom, I am afraid to say, we will be at war very soon. Though that piece of news is between us and no other—"

Mary stared at him, astounded. "You think any person here, in this out of the way place, has any notion of whom we are at war with now, least of all whom we are about to go to war with—"

"It may surprise you," Evelyn interjected patiently, "but your little corner of England is a veritable hotbed of intrigue, and that is one of the reasons for Shrewsbury's visit."

"Well, I know nothing of spies and spying, or about wars for that matter. Nobody tells me anything!" Mary grumbled. "But what I do know is that Lord Shrewsbury will expect a good dinner, regardless if it is in a private capacity, using an alias, or announcing his arrival with trumpets bellowing! And men cannot be agreeable, or discuss matters of importance, if they do not have a good dinner." She blushed and smiled when Evelyn laughed out loud. "Perhaps if the French and English sat down to dine matters would resolve themselves."

"Oh, my dear Mary! And I suppose the war in the American Colonies boils down to a good cup of tea—or the lack of one?" He kissed the back of her hand and said more sensibly, "There may be something in what you say… You always were the most levelheaded of us cousins."

Mary smiled. "By sensible you mean unimaginative—no! I won't allow you to think me anything else. It's true. I am sensible. Someone has to be. So I cannot deny I am relieved that his lordship is visiting in a private capacity. My resources are limited, and every penny is accounted for." She colored painfully, when admitting, "You need to understand that Sir Gerald left his estate burdened with unpaid accounts. Though Teddy and I still live under this roof, we do so with the good grace of the steward for the estate."

"I know that, *ma chérie*. Your brother told me. You will not be surprised when I tell you that I, like the rest of the family, believed Sir Gerald unworthy of you, in every respect. Why your mother promoted such a deplorable match—"

"He-he was a Cavendish, and Deborah his sister." Mary countered in a small voice.

"Yes. And she is the best of that lot! No doubt she takes after her mother. Their father Sir George was, by all accounts, a muckworm who littered the countryside with his by-blows."

Mary's brow wrinkled. "How—How do you know that, Eve? Sir George spent most of his time away from Abbeywood, in London. Sir Gerald said his father rarely came here."

"Indeed?" Evelyn shrugged and threw up a hand in dismissal. "Something I heard a long time ago… Let's consign it to gossip. But what I will say without hesitation is that the only worthy decision Sir Gerald ever made in his life was marrying you!"

"And he gave me Teddy."

"Ah yes! Your daughter." When Mary nodded, sudden tears in her eyes, he squeezed her fingers gently. "Let's have no more talk of debt and the dead. I may provide for my cousin and her daughter with whatever largesse I care to distribute. I am not beholden to a shabby steward. I'm surprised Roxton allows it."

"Under the terms of Sir Gerald's will, there is little he can do about it."

"That must be a thorn in his finger indeed for the illustrious Duke," Evelyn muttered dryly. He patted Mary's hand and said more audibly, "But I am here, and I will. This steward won't refuse me. I'll set him straight—"

Mary let out in involuntary giggle. "In that nightgown, I suppose?"

"Ha! I'll have you know my man and my clothes are only a day's ride behind me. But I was so very keen to see you I couldn't wait, so came on ahead. Ah! Your milk and my tea have arrived," he inter-

rupted, when Betsy put the tray with the tea things and Mary's mug of
hot milk on the bedside table and bobbed a clumsy curtsy for good
measure.

"Oh! Tea! Yes!" Mary said a little breathlessly and quickly gathered
the banyan about her and slid off the bed. She dismissed Betsy, saying
she would not be needed until morning, and without a word spoken
about her visitor.

Betsy curtsied again but did not depart immediately. After what
the Squire had mentioned in the kitchen, curiosity had the better of
her. She glanced at her ladyship's cousin and was shocked into immobility. It was not the gentleman's wild gray mane, or his beard, or even
his gaunt appearance that most caused alarm, but the fact he was
sitting cross-legged in the middle of her mistress's bed in a nightshirt as
if he had a right to be there. For a simple country girl who had never
been to a village larger than Bisley, and who was more than a little in
awe of her mistress as the daughter of an earl, to see a stranger who was
not her ladyship's husband making himself comfortable amongst the
pillows shocked her mute and motionless.

It said much about Mary's preoccupation, and the fact she expected
Betsy to do as she was bid no questions asked, that she went about
making Evelyn a cup of tea oblivious to her maid's mules being fixed to
the floorboards.

It was left to Christopher, who had remained by the fireplace, to
remind Betsy of her duty with a quiet word at her back. This merely
underscored the fact he, too, lingered in the bedchamber when he
should've departed as soon as the fire was well alight. Betsy made a
hurried curtsy and scurried away to fetch the extra bed linen and
coverlet for the chaise longue in Sir Gerald's sitting room. As for
Christopher, he was going nowhere while Evelyn remained in Mary's
bedchamber. He would see to it the connecting door was closed and
the bolt slid fast before he took himself off to the steward's sparse
bedchamber at the far end of the house.

CHRISTOPHER'S EXPRESSION PROVIDED A GLARING WINDOW TO
his thoughts, Evelyn remarking casually yet provokingly, as he lifted
the tea cup off its saucer, "Should I introduce myself, or will you do
the honors with your candelabra-wielding knight errant, *chérie?*"

It was only then that Mary realized Christopher was in the room.
She had disregarded his presence, thinking it one of the servants seeing

to the fire. Realizing it was Christopher upset her composure. This joyful reunion with Evelyn had allowed her to conveniently push to the back of her mind her earlier uncharacteristically impetuous behavior in sharing a passionate kiss with the Squire. What had she been thinking? What had led her to forget her upbringing and drop her defenses to fall into his arms like an over-eager, moonstruck schoolroom miss? She would never have done the unthinkable while married, so why as a respectable widow had she cast caution to the four winds? But that kiss… She had never experienced anything like it. The feelings and sensations aroused in her were so overwhelming she was overcome with acute embarrassment. She was flustered and unable to put together a coherent sentence. And for the first time in her life she ignored protocol and what was right, put her head down and bustled off to her dressing room mumbling,

"You need clothes to wear, Eve… I need my chatelaine… There is a key to a clothes press… "

Christopher turned to follow her but Evelyn stopped him with one hard sentence.

"You're not going anywhere, *Silvanus*. We need to talk."

TEN

"I am, sir," Christopher enunciated through his teeth as he turned to face the visitor, "Squire Bryce of Brycecomb Hall. And you are...?"

"Is that so?" Evelyn said with a casual insolence that grated on Christopher's ear. He ignored the question and sipped at his tea, unperturbed, and continued in the same light arrogant tone that carried an undercurrent of menace. "You may very well be Squire Bryce of Backwater Hall, but I am confident that in the service of your country you masquerade as the Roman god of forests and flocks... Silvanus is particularly apt, given your agricultural pursuits. By all means, if I am wrong, correct me."

When Christopher remained mute, Evelyn smiled his satisfaction and over the rim of his cup openly appraised the Squire. And had he measured Christopher by his provincial clothing alone he would've dismissed him as beneath his notice. But there were nuances to the man that caught Evelyn's attention. For when Christopher had scooped Mary up from her faint and then spoken to her while she recovered on her bed, Evelyn had been at leisure to observe them both, Christopher in particular. There was something arresting about the handsome face that made it memorable. Perhaps it was the man's eyes. They were intelligent and caring, and held a certain sad reticence. And then there was way the squire moved with a grace and ease usually exhibited on the polished parquetry of a society ballroom, not the muck of a country midden. As for his long fingers, they belonged at the keys of a pianoforte, or the strings of a viola, as Evelyn's once had, before his had been mutilated for double-crossing the Empress of all the Russias. But it was when he spoke that Evelyn was convinced he'd had the good fortune to stumble upon the very man he needed to seek out. For not only did the squire have a pleasingly mellow voice, the cadence was of one who had spent more time away from his roots than amongst them.

It helped enormously that Evelyn had the upper hand in this meeting, for he knew the name by which Shrewsbury's agent operated in this quarter of the country, and he knew enough about his background that when questioned, Christopher could only infer that he had received such information from Shrewsbury himself. It cost him nothing to use the operative's code name, and gained him everything when Christopher, by not denying the allegation, inadvertently identified himself.

"I say again: And you, sir, are…?" Christopher asked with an upward arrogant tilt of his square chin.

Evelyn put aside his teacup and hopped off the bed. He made a grand gesture of stretching out his arms left and right as he came towards him, and boomed in a baritone, "I am Apollo, God of the sun and music, thy worthy Silvanus!"

This announcement was accompanied by a high-pitched laugh which brought Christopher within one angry stride of Evelyn's chest. He wanted to think the man a fool, but one look into the piercing blue eyes and he knew the opposite was true. It cut through his irritation and he said with controlled anger, lowering his voice because he did not want Lady Mary to overhear them from her dressing room,

"Understand this: I am not one of Shrewsbury's automata, and I won't be yours, whoever you are—Lady Mary's long lost cousin, spy, or Shrewsbury's Machiavellian marionette!"

"So you *were* listening from your post by the fireplace, and thus are fluent in the French tongue? But of course you must be. And possibly speak it like a native, too. What an unusually accomplished Squire Backwater you are to be sure!"

"Well enough to know that you most unwisely, and unnecessarily, identified yourself and Lord Fitzstuart as spies to the Lady Mary."

"So my dear cousin has no idea that you, too, are a spy?"

Christopher gave a huff, but his response was delayed when Mary bustled through from her dressing room, holding aloft her chatelaine in one hand and a little brass key in the other. Her cheeks were slightly flushed and there was a sparkle in her violet eyes that softened Christopher's mouth. Both men took a step away from each other, and tried to appear as if they had not been in conversation. But they need not have worried, because she was preoccupied, and did her best not to look Christopher's way, saying to Evelyn,

"I was certain I had kept the key to Sir Gerald's dressing table in the enamel container attached here," rattling the chatelaine before dropping her hand, the chatelaine's gold chain, which was normally pinned to her bodice, wound securely round her wrist. "If you would give me but a moment, I will have the drawer opened and find the set of keys that open the trunks that have—" She stopped on a sudden thought and abruptly turned to Christopher and said without looking him directly in the eye, "Mr. Bryce, I presume you have no objection if I open the trunk storing Sir Gerald's wedding clothes, for I am very sure there are some garments packed away that would do for my cousin until his bags and his man arrive?"

"No objection, my lady. If I can be of assistance—"

"No! I need none. Thank-you," she stated, and without another word or look at either man, went through to Sir Gerald's dressing room where there was light and warmth for the first time in two years.

Christopher watched her go with her back very straight and chin up. It was the fact her cheeks were apple red and she could not meet his gaze that told him about her state of mind. She was thinking about their kiss, and thinking about it had made her uncomfortable in his presence. He wished her long-lost cousin a thousand miles away so he could follow her, explain to her his feelings, that they were heartfelt, and to kiss her again. Instead he turned to Evelyn and found him regarding him with a half-smile that set his teeth on edge.

"To answer your question: No, she does not know, because I am not a spy," he stated. "I agreed to do one task for the Spymaster General, and one task only: To discover if Sir Gerald was a traitor. The man was not. A conceited fool, yes. But not a traitor."

"Is that so?" Evelyn replied as if he did not believe him. "But surely the fact he passed on information to another, information the French were most interested in receiving for the American Patriots' cause, is an act of treason, and therefore he is a traitor?"

"Not if he believed he was helping the English cause in doing so. No."

"Helping the English cause in doing so?" Evelyn repeated with an affected start worthy of any stage actor. He put a hand to his chest. "I do not understand your meaning, Mr. Bryce of Backwater Hall—"

"It's *Brycecomb*," Christopher enunciated. "And you, sir, have a most irritating way of hiding your intelligence!"

Evelyn let out another of his piercing laughs. "*Mon Dieu!* You have the silver tongue of a lawyer, to be sure!" he exclaimed in French, before adding in English, and in an altogether different voice, as he stepped up to Christopher so as not to be overheard, "This is not the time or place for further discussion. Be assured, Shrewsbury will be here tomorrow, or the day after, and he—*we*—will expect your full assistance—"

"You can be certain of it. For that will be the end of my involvement in these cloak-and-dagger affairs, for I do not have the stomach for subterfuge."

Evelyn cocked his head, unperturbed by the squire's angry annoyance, and mused, "Do you not indeed? And yet I would've thought, given your history and your previous line of—er—*employment*, artifice would be second nature to a man of your—Steady on!" he snorted when Christopher snatched up a handful of his nightshirt, screwed it tightly in his fist, and jerked Evelyn to him.

"*For-why doth thee be an expert in t'art, wouldn't thou, laiking butty*," Christopher growled in a low Cotswolds burr that stripped him of thirty years and hurled him back to his origins. He let go of Evelyn with a contemptuous push.

A tense silence descended on the bedchamber, punctuated by the crackle of the burning logs, and the scrape and knock of drawers being opened and closed in the next room. And then Evelyn came to life, pulling at the front of his nightshirt, to shake out the twisted crease of Christopher's fingers in the linen, saying more to himself, but so he could be overheard,

"Tish! Tish! Gerry must've put on a bit of weight over the years! I mean he was pasty and paunchy to begin with, but this is—*frightful*."

Christopher frowned, breathing more steadily after his uncharacteristic outburst which left him angry with himself.

"The man over-ate like he over-spent: As if tomorrow would take care of his mounting debts, and his health; the consequences could go hang. Had he not accidentally shot himself, time would have seen his heart give out before his natural time."

"Poor Mary." Evelyn sighed mournfully. "She was wasted on such an oaf. The family never did like him." He looked at Christopher from under his lashes. "So shooting himself must've come as a relief to you...?"

"*What?*"

"Well. Let's face facts. Unless you force-fed him to death to speed up his demise, it could've taken another couple of years before his heart gave out. How long were you prepared to wait? Or are you as doggedly loyal and determined as your manly chin suggests?"

"I have no idea what you're—"

"Oh! I think you do, Silvanus!" Evelyn said as a teacher to a naughty school boy, waggling a finger at him. He tugged at the front of the nightshirt so it billowed out, and backed towards the bed as he did so, saying with the splutter of a laugh, "Good God! The man was grossly fat, corpulent, obese, however you want to phrase it, and you must have wondered when he would have a heart attack and put you out of *your* misery."

"I say again, sir. I have no idea what you're talking about, or where you are taking this absurd conversation. But if you think I ever thought—"

"Oh! I do! I do!" Evelyn announced, coming to a standstill up against the bed. He jerked his head over his shoulder at the mattress and put his tongue in his cheek before saying with a lewd, lopsided grin, "Gerry must've been a sweaty mess of lard, whichever side you care to butter it. I shudder at the thought of such a delicate beauty bedded by an uncouth mountain of corpulent fle—"

Christopher leapt to life and lunged for Evelyn. "Enough o'ye filthy maundering!"

With a yelp, Evelyn yanked up the nightshirt and jumped up onto the mattress, scrambling across it, laughing gleefully. "I knew it! I knew it!" he hissed loudly. "I knew it the first time I saw you look my cousin's way! Hey! Ho! Squire Backwater has *feelings* for the Lady Mary!"

"Mr. Bryce! Mr. Bryce?" It was Mary, calling from the next room.

Christopher had one boot up on the bed and a hand out to seize Evelyn, who was still laughing and jumping up and down on the mattress, not in any way frightened for his life, or that the straightness of his fine nose might be broken by the larger, more solid, and furious squire. At the sound of Mary's voice both men froze, as if they were two small boys caught out playing a game of *grandmother's footsteps*. They waited a moment to hear if she would add anything further to her call, or worse, come back into the bedchamber.

But when she did not, they both came to life again, Evelyn to drop to his knees amongst the pillows, chuckling, and Christopher, to hop down off the bed and brush at his frock coat, mortified at his school boy behavior. But what concerned and overwhelmed him was that this thin slip of a man, with the irritating laugh and bright blue eyes that saw too much, and who had been in his company for less time than it took him to pull on his boots, had peeled back his feelings for Mary like a scab to a never-healing wound and made them raw again.

"Off you trot to assist m'cousin, while I indulge in a second cup of tea and a snooze," Evelyn commanded with a nonchalant wave and a loud yawn. "It's damnably freezing in this house, and one night awake shivering is enough. But mind your manners. She's a lady by birth as well as reputation, and you her servant, regardless you may think yourself her knight errant. No! Don't speak! Lady Mary is waiting!"

Christopher stared at Evelyn as if he were truly mad. Inside he was still seething. He took a deep breath, swallowed, and said very low, "I don't care who you are—the King of Poland for all I know—or that you are her ladyship's cousin. Know this: If you ever make unguarded or crude remarks about her marriage again, I'll knock all your good teeth to the back of your throat. Understand?" When the silence stretched, Christopher took a step nearer the bed. "*Dost thou Majesty understand?*"

Evelyn settled amongst the pillows and plucked a long red hair from the front of his nightgown. He met Christopher's unblinking gaze, and then, after a moment, shrugged, and said with a pout that was at odds with the hard glitter to his eyes, "Perfectly, Squire Worthy."

With a curt nod, Christopher turned on a heel and disappeared into Sir Gerald's dressing room.

And there was Luke, holding aloft a taper to shed light on a large trunk he had pulled out from a neatly-arranged stack that had been under a dust sheet, but was now a disordered mess in the corner. Mary was bent over the closed trunk, bathed in the glow of candlelight. She was jiggling a key in the lock, long hair falling over one shoulder to the floor. She had never looked more beautiful, or more unobtainable.

<h1 style="text-align:center">ELEVEN</h1>

"Oh! Here you are, Mr. Bryce," Mary announced, surprised when he appeared beside her. She did not look up. "I seem to have got the key stuck in the lock."

"Let me look at it."

He crouched and she instantly straightened and stepped away, signaling for Luke to move closer to provide Christopher with more light. He worked at the lock for several moments in silence, before she said, as if he had asked her for an explanation,

"Evelyn and I are cousins. I believe we are both related to the fourth Duke of Roxton, who was Evelyn's great-grandfather, and my great-great grandfather. The present Duke is his first cousin, and my first cousin once removed."

"The key is wedged up into the mechanism," he replied as if she had not spoken. "It may take me a moment. I don't want to force it or the key could snap."

"It may not be the correct key. There were several in the drawer."

"That would make you second cousins once removed."

"Second cousins once removed? Oh? Yes. Yes, I believe you are right…" She peered over his shoulder, trying to see what he was doing. "He—Evelyn—he eloped with a girl the family considered most unsuitable—French. Daughter of a Farmer-General. She died in child-birth. She was very young and very pretty… Such a tragedy… News of her death was the last letter I received from him."

"It needs lubrication," Christopher stated and stood up. "Some lard should do the trick," he said to Luke and took the taper from him.

"Ask Jane." He put the candlestick on the trunk and waited for Luke to disappear through the servant door. "Let me see what other keys we have." When he turned, it was to find Mary staring at him. He smiled to himself when she quickly looked away. He watched her rummage through the dressing room drawer. "I am sorry about his wife."

"I wish my brother had told me Eve was alive. I cannot understand why he would keep such news to himself, and from the family."

"Perhaps he was ordered to do so?" he ventured. When she came away from the drawer holding several keys and waited for him to continue, he added, "He is a spy, and so is your cousin, and thus both are constrained to do as they are bid."

"That makes sense," she said, as if this had never occurred to her, finally meeting his gaze. "Dair is a risk taker and an excellent soldier." She had a sudden thought. "Perhaps Evelyn had to pretend to be dead for reasons of state?" She handed him the keys. "They are all labeled, but one is not."

"Thank-you. Yes, perhaps your cousin was given such orders," he agreed evenly, suppressing a smile at her earnestness. Quick appraisal of Cousin Evelyn told him the man did what was best for Evelyn and no other, reasons of state be damned, and that her cousin was most decidedly unlike her soldier-hero brother. But he kept this assessment to himself for now. "I am certain he will tell you what he can, eventually. Though… he may wish to keep the past in the past, and just get on with his future. Men who live by subterfuge have secrets that are best kept to themselves. You may not like what he has to tell you."

"The truth is always preferable to lies and dissimulation, Mr. Bryce."

"I beg to differ, my lady. The truth sometimes leads to disappointment and heartache, particularly if the recipient of such truths is ill-equipped to deal with a confessional. In that case, it would be best to leave the person in blissful ignorance."

"I helped him elope," she blurted out with a guilty blush.

Christopher was momentarily surprised, and wondered why she felt the need to tell him. Then he realized she had misconstrued his explanation as a criticism of her, and knew it was so when the response to his simple question was met with justification.

"Did you?" he asked smoothly.

"Yes. I did," Mary stated defiantly, thinking he did not believe her. "I am conventional and most definitely not a-a *dissenter*. I saw and heard enough cruel vitriol exchanged between my parents when I was young to wish away a lifetime of non-compliance. But that does not mean I will sit by idly, remain mute, or cower from what I believe to be right when called upon to add my voice, or act upon a worthy cause. To this day, my family have no notion that I aided in Evelyn's elopement. I helped Dominique—his bride-to-be—escape from her father's house to be with Evelyn. And I pawned my jewels so they had sufficient funds to see them across the border into Switzerland."

Christopher set the keys aside, having selected one he thought might be a better fit for the particular trunk. "That was admirable of you. But perhaps in this case, as it was a clandestine marriage not favored by either set of parents, it would have been wiser not to involve yourself?"

"There was no one else he could turn to. And I wanted to help. He is my cousin, and Dominique deserved that Eve should marry her."

Unconsciously, Christopher's gaze flickered to the open doorway into Mary's bedchamber, as if he expected her long-lost cousin to be leaning against the jamb with a defiant smirk. He was not. He met Mary's gaze.

"So it was not love. He ruined her." It was not a question and he was not surprised by her answer.

Mary nodded, eyes downcast. "Yes. And in the process ruined his friendship with Roxton and his wife, and was cast out by the family." She smiled weakly and shrugged. "To own a truth, I had nothing to fear from aiding and abetting Evelyn's unsanctioned marriage. As it so happened, Roxton—well, he wasn't the Duke then, but he is now— had just that week ordered my husband into exile for some unpardonable infringement. That meant I, too, was banished."

"Ah. I was unaware it was your ducal relative that had gone to such lengths to distance himself from Sir Gerald. I was told it was the other way round."

Mary's eyes widened. She knew immediately what he meant. "That Sir Gerald wished to distance himself from *my* family? Whatever for?"

Christopher hesitated, not because he did not want to tell her, but because he now realized that what Sir Gerald had confided in one of his late night drunken confessionals was in all probability untrue, or a version of the truth. He had no desire to upset Mary, but nor did he want to lie to her, so he said simply,

"He intimated that he disliked the—*attention* you received from the Duke—that it made him, and I presume you, uncomfortable."

Mary stared at him, transfixed. She became indignant.

"That I received—that he disliked—that I received—*attention* from-from *Roxton?*" When Christopher nodded she blushed. "But— that's *utter* nonsense. Cousin Julian—Roxton—has never looked at *any* woman sideways, least of all *me*. He is devoted to the Duchess. They are very much in love. Why would Sir Gerald make such a scurrilous accusation against my relative, and to you?"

Christopher took a moment to answer her.

"Let me assure you that he told me in the strictest confidence—

"That does not console me, Mr. Bryce. That he said it at all is most upsetting."

"Is it?"

"Yes! Very much so. Why would you think it would not be? Sir Gerald not only besmirched the Duke's good name, but mine, and I his wife. And he did so to-to *you*."

"I wonder what upsets you more, my lady?"

"It is a wonder that you believed him!"

"Pardon me for stating the obvious, but Sir Gerald set great store in his name, his noble connections, and yours. And I have exchanged enough correspondence with His Grace of Roxton, not to mention the visits here by his high-and mighty-secretary, to know something of the man behind the quill. I believed Sir Gerald because I knew it would take something monumental to wrest your husband from that ducal bosom."

Such was Mary's incredulous anger that she forgot her own good advice to keep her distance from the Squire, and came right up to him and looked into his eyes. "You have known me for as many years as you knew my husband, longer in fact, if we count these two years of my widowhood, and yet knowing me, you chose to besmirch my character by believing there was an immoral connection between me and a noble cousin whom I love and respect as a brother, as I do my own brothers."

"Such arrangements are not uncommon amongst the nobility."

"No, but they are also not as rife as some would believe. My father's deplorable conduct aside, the members of my family take their marriage vows *very* seriously."

Christopher's eyebrow raised of its own accord. "Indeed? Even the present Duke's esteemed parent?"

Mary rolled her eyes and huffed, as if this was such old news it was not worth her time to offer an explanation. But she humored him by asking flatly, "And what would you know of M'sieur le Duc d'Roxton, Mr. Bryce?"

Christopher put his hands behind his back. "That his sullied reputation was black enough to cast an ink stain across the map of Europe."

"Never sullied, Mr. Bryce. There you are wrong. Yes, he had mistresses aplenty and many casual liaisons, and yes, he did not care who knew about them, but M'sieur le Duc was a man of honor, in all things. And once he fell in love and married my cousin, his heart and his bed belonged very much and only to Mme la Duchesse. They were devoted. And if you think the son is anything like his father, then you are quite correct for the present duke is just as uxorious. If Sir Gerald intimated anything to the contrary, then he misled you, and that is unpardonable. I am sorry. Now, please, may we try the key one more time?" she added, and went to step past him. "I am suddenly weary, and it is very late, and Luke should have returned by now with the lard, should he not? Perhaps you need to find out what is keeping him?"

Christopher did not move.

"It was not Sir Gerald who told me about M'sieur le Duc, but my mother. She, like you, defended him, though not with quite the same passionate conviction. She also gave a good account of the son."

"A sensible woman. Perhaps you should've given her opinion its due consideration, Mr. Bryce."

"Yes. But in my defense I have never besmirched *your* character. Not for one moment did I believe you willingly submitted to Roxton's attentions, but that it was he who attempted to seduce you, and that's why Sir Gerald saw fit to cut the connection."

Mary was puzzled. "Why would he wish to seduce me?"

It was a simple question requiring a simple answer. He knew from her earlier responses, particularly to his kiss, that she was clueless to her inherent allure. Her lack of carnal awareness he blamed on Sir Gerald, which again made him wonder at the man's boorish behavior in the bedchamber, but he was not daunted by it. He knew that this same lack of awareness saw her and her long-lost cousin cozy up on her bed, and she think nothing of it. He also knew the only way forward was to be utterly truthful with her, however much she might be made uncomfortable. He had to hold to the belief that their kiss had opened her mind to possibilities, possibilities with him.

"Why? Because you are very beautiful and desirable."

Mary went white, and then her face flooded with the heat of embarrassment. She was fraught with uncertainty and confusion.

"*Me*? Beautiful and-and des-*desirable*?"

"Yes. I defy any man to say otherwise."

In all her thirty years, nothing and no one had prepared her for this. Her mother had only ever bemoaned her looks, loudly lamenting upon one occasion before a room full of tea-drinking ladies that she had been saddled with a daughter who was "a bran-faced, redheaded dolt". It did not help that her first cousin, the Duchess of Roxton and Kinross, was a celebrated beauty. And so at eighteen, she had supposed

Sir Gerald had offered for her because of her lineage and connections, and had disregarded her indifferent looks.

"You may not offer me such-such *hollow* compliments, Mr. Bryce!"

"We've had this conversation before. It's Christopher. And there is nothing hollow about my compliments. You are beautiful, and you are desirable. And that is the truth."

"But you said so yourself that if the truth leads to disappointment and heartache, then that truth is best left unsaid."

"Ha! That will teach me to be truthful," Christopher replied with a false heavy sigh of regret, though his lips twitched into a smile. But when Mary did not realize he was teasing her and kept wringing her hands, the smile died and he asked gently, "Will you tell me why such a compliment, no doubt told to you by others many times, is a cause for disappointment and heartache when uttered by me?"

Mary shook her head, unable to articulate in a few sentences an explanation that he would understand, and that would not deeply offend him. Her mother had preached the sermon enough times that it was forever etched in her mind—to people of birth, the gentry were little better than menials. A steward was to be ignored as a servant, and a squire, as a small landowner, required a begrudging nod of acknowledgment for his freehold existence, but conversation must be kept to inconsequentials such as the weather and the state of the roads. Compliments offered by social inferiors amounted to toad-eating flattery, and were to be avoided and discouraged, and could never be believed for their own sake.

But in the eight years she had known Christopher Bryce, he had never been insincere. In fact, he was quite the opposite. He was frank to the point of curtness. So she believed him when he said he thought her beautiful and desirable. So she reasoned she must be truthful with him, too.

"Mr. Bryce, I have never received such a compliment before, from any man."

His dark brows drew sharply together. "Never?" He was so incredulous he vocalized his thoughts. "But how is that possible?"

She was overjoyed by his heartfelt puzzlement and cemented his praise in sincerity. Meeting his gaze she was filled with a happiness she had never known before, one that left her giddy, as if she were on a swing and at its highest point in the air; her own heart beating rapidly.

She wanted to thank him, and had a sudden urge to gently brush back the dark auburn curls come loose from the riband at his nape, to rise up on tiptoe and press her lips to his mouth so the frown would clear from his brow. Perhaps he would then take her in his arms and kiss her as he had that first time, with ardor and with his tongue and—*No!*

She must stop this fanciful schoolroom-miss nonsense. She was thirty years old, not seventeen. Just because a handsome man found her attractive did not mean she should go all to pieces and lose a sense of perspective. There was no future with a squire in the wilds of the Cotswolds. Not that he had offered her one, just a kiss, and a furtive one at that. She was Lady Mary Fitzstuart Cavendish, and she must face the cold reality that she needed to remarry, and marry well. To do so, she must trade on her unsullied reputation and her connections and marry title and wealth, for she was penniless, and she had a daughter whose future depended on her.

She dropped her gaze on a shattering breath of reality, and when he just stood there, looking down at her, she panicked and blurted out,

"Don't you understand? You should not—*cannot*—give me such compliments. You have never done so before, and I wonder why of a sudden you would. Perhaps that is my fault, for asking you to come to my bedchamber because of my irrational fears there was a ghost. And seeing me in my night clothes inflamed your senses. And men cannot be blamed for their behavior when it is women who by their imprudent actions—"

"Don't talk rot, Mary!" he growled, the words out of his mouth before he had time to temper his anger. "I won't allow you to demean yourself, and me, or our feelings. I am not a beast, and you are not a wanton. Far from it. My intentions towards you have always been honorable. I admit that I had the bad manners to act the over-eager schoolboy and kiss you. But again, to be truthful, I was never more relieved when your cousin materialized as the resident ghost when he did. I told you I want you—I do. I want you in every way. I want to kiss you, for us to make love, but most of all I want—"

"You are quick to tell me what it is *you* want, Mr. Bryce," Mary interrupted, hoping indignation would silence him once and for all. "You kiss me, tell me you wish to make love with me, that you are sincere in your feelings, but you have not once asked what it is *I* want."

"I was so eager to let you know the sincerity of my feelings that I did not stop to think..." Christopher replied, instantly contrite. "Forgive me. More than anything, I want to know what it is you want."

Mary's anger instantly deflated because she was at a loss to answer her own question. She blinked her bafflement and he was forced to suppress a smile, though he did say with a hint of mischief,

"Please, take your time..."

That did rile her to say curtly, "As no member of my family, and certainly not my husband, has ever asked me what I want, you will have to forgive *me* if I am at a loss to give *you* an immediate response. But there is one thing I do know, Mr. Bryce, and that is you greatly unsettle me. So much so that I do not want to-to *feel* the way you make me feel. It puzzles and-and frightens me, and it is—"

Christopher cocked his head and folded his arms.

"And how *do* I make you feel, Mary?"

"I just told you! I don't know! I am-I am—confounded. *You* confound me! And I dare not dwell on my feelings, whatever they may be. Feelings do not lead anywhere. It is a path I cannot take—"

"But if we took that path *together*?"

Mary stared up at him, forlorn. "Oh, but don't you see? That is impossible. *Impossible.*"

"Nothing is impossible when two people are in love."

"In love...?" Mary blinked, and for some inexplicable reason she was overwhelmed with sadness. Tears welled up but she refused to let them fall. Her voice was a hoarse whisper. "You cannot say that. You do not know that."

"For my own part, yes, I do," he replied calmly, though his throat burned and he felt the need to swallow hard. "I am very sure I fell in love with you at first sight. No one was more surprised than I, at my age, to be struck down in this way. But it was not something I could control. And every day since has only strengthened that conviction, and my love for you. I never thought I would ever have the opportunity to tell you my feelings, because you were married. And I did not think it appropriate, or want to appear too eager, and tell you in the first year of your widowhood. But now, almost two years since Sir Gerald's death I hope that we—"

"Please. Please. Say no more!"

Christopher turned tack when she quickly wiped tears from her eyes and would not look at him.

"But surely you knew my feelings?"

Mary shook her head vigorously, eyes downcast. She did not know, but she had always hoped that it was true. And if she were honest with herself, she had dreamed of hearing his declaration. So why now that he had told her he loved her was she not ecstatic, but made utterly miserable? Was it because no one had ever confessed to loving her? Was it because she loved him in return but could never tell him so because their disparate situations meant they could never walk together that same path he spoke of? It was all too overwhelming and her head began to ache.

"My lady? Mary?" When she looked up at him and he was sure he had her attention, he took a step closer and said with a soft smile, "Please do not concern yourself further. I will not press you anymore tonight. You have had enough of an emotional upheaval, what with your cousin literally returning from the dead. I understand. I did the same thing myself to my parents—"

"You—you did?" Mary asked, temporarily emerging from her befuddlement.

"Returning after a long absence abroad requires adjustment by all parties," he replied without answering her question directly. "You both need time to become reacquainted. But I dare hope that in the not-too-distant future I may approach you again, and ask, most humbly, that if your feelings do align with mine, we might find a way to—"

"My lady?"

It was the housekeeper.

Startled, the couple sprung back from each other and looked away, first to the floor and then up and around, and finally turned to the servant door.

Mrs. Keble lingered just inside the doorway, Luke at her back. A secretive, almost knowing smile lifted the corners of her mouth. Christopher had no idea how long they had been standing there, and if they had been overheard. But when Mary brushed past him on a deep intake of breath and the housekeeper shot him a look of smug triumph, he knew she had had a box seat to his feelings.

"Oh! Thank goodness you're here, Mrs. Keble," Mary said, clearing her throat. "My cousin has just arrived in the night, and without his valet and baggage, so we must find him something to wear in the meantime. This trunk contains Sir Gerald's wedding clothes and I'm sure they would do until such time…"

Christopher stopped listening, ears humming with embarrassment and lost opportunity as he returned to the task of removing one key and substituting another before finally managing to open the trunk containing clothes that had not seen the light of day or night for ten years. He then moved aside so the two women could carefully unpack the trunk's contents. Mrs. Keble had brought with her the clothing ledger and set to marking off the clothes Mary selected for her cousin to wear. So it was only within a matter of minutes the equilibrium of the house returned to everyday normality. It was as if there had never been talk of a ghost, Christopher and Mary had never shared a kiss, and he had not confessed his feelings.

He heard without deciphering the words Lady Mary and Mrs. Keble's conversation about the preparations necessary for the arrival of further guests in the coming days. Bedchambers long since shut up needed airing, mattresses and rugs beaten, the dust wiped away, the furniture polished, and new tapers put in all the sconces. Chimney flues would need checking, the silver plate unlocked, and the best Sevres dinner set unpacked and used for the duration of the guests' stay.

As Abbeywood would be host to her cousin and Lord Shrewsbury was due any day, hired help would be required to ensure the comforts these noblemen and their entourage were used to. Lady Mary suggested several names of girls in the village who could be brought in to help in the kitchens and laundry. Christopher nodded his agreement. Mrs. Keble added that perhaps now was not the best time to dismiss the Blandfords, Old Jack, and young Tanner, who knew their respective positions within the household well, and would not need further instruction. Indeed Blandford could take on the role of butler for he had been underbutler in Sir Gerald's day. Lady Mary said Mrs. Keble's suggestion was an excellent one. Both women then turned to the Squire to have his assent. Christopher gave it without question or argument. He then excused himself and went off to the steward's room at the back of the house, where he lay down on the bed, exhausted. But he did not sleep.

TWELVE

The view of Brycecomb Hall from the ridge never failed to quiet Christopher's pulse and make him content. The Jacobean mansion of Guiting Yellow stone sat proud in manicured parkland that nestled at the foot of the escarpment. Undulating farmland crisscrossed with old hedgerows and dry stone walls stretched out beyond the estate's imposing gatehouse, dotted with woolly sheep, farms with the necessary cidermill house, and coppices of oak, maple, ash, elm, and beech. Slicing through this patchwork and running along one side of the estate's high dry stone walls was a meandering river with water as clear as polished glass. Weavers' stone cottages lined one side of the bank; behind them on the slope of the hill brightly-colored cloth on tenterhooks dried in the sun. A newly-built cloth mill, one of three in the district, and an old flour mill utilized the river's energy to drive large waterwheels, and all were owned by the enterprising squire of Brycecomb Hall.

Just on sunrise, when the mist still hung low to the valley floor, blanketing this magical landscape, only the turrets of Brycecomb Hall were visible above the clouds. Their finials pinpricked the morning sky, serving as a landlocked beacon that allowed travelers by horse and on foot to find their way. Christopher needed no such beacon, for the countryside was as familiar to him as the creases in his palms.

The estate had been home to Bryces since Henry Tudor's time, and the house with its mullioned windows, ornate gables, and fanciful turrets, built in the time of the first King Charles, was testament to the family's skill in surviving political upheaval, and shrewd management as squires of a thriving estate. Christopher had been born here, and it was here that he wished to spend the rest of his earthly existence.

He had grown up in the Jacobean manor house an only child of elderly parents, attending the local Blue Coat school with other lads from the village and surrounding farms considered bright enough to learn a little Greek and Latin with their reading, writing, and arithmetic. And then, against his wishes, he was sent faraway to Harrow, to mix with the sons of gentlemen. What made those years bearable was knowing he could return home at the end of each term. His parents wished him to go on to university, to round off his education as a gentleman, but all he ever wanted to do was learn estate management from his father, so that when the day came for him to follow in his footsteps, he would be the sort of squire to make his father proud. He never wanted to leave the vale again.

And then when Christopher was eighteen the local magistrate for this picturesque pocket of the Cotswolds, a baronet, cousin of a duke and a distant relation of his father, Sir George Cavendish, died. His death changed Christopher's life forever.

Sir George was not only a distant cousin of Squire Bryce, he was also his neighbor. The largest landowner in the district, his modestly-named estate of Abbeywood Farm shared a river boundary with Bryce lands on the valley floor.

Christopher had met Sir George upon several occasions, knew he had a couple of sons about his own age who lived mostly in London, and that he was on his third marriage to a lady who preferred London as well. But the Baronet enjoyed country life. Despite the greater part of his time being spent in far-off London, he never missed the annual Brycecomb shoot.

When Christopher was fifteen, Sir George invited the Bryce family to spend a few days at Abbeywood Farm. The Baronet had guests all the way from London to stay for a fortnight-long house party. His family remained in London, possibly because he had brought along his latest mistress. At first, Christopher's mother refused to accept the invitation. She was not about to spend time with such an immoral lot! Christopher's father told her she must, and to ignore these Londoners and their ways. They had to think of "the boy" and his future. His parents had a heated argument, their first.

His mother was miserable the entire visit, while his father did his best to be sociable and compensated for his wife's gloominess by his over-eagerness to please his host. At dinner one evening Sir George made a point of singling out "the boy". It wasn't until his father nudged him that Christopher realized Sir George was referring to him.

Sir George told him to get to his feet so everyone could take a good look at him. Reluctantly, Christopher did so and every dinner conversation stopped. Over the tops of pleated fans, and peering through raised quizzing glasses, the diners looked Christopher over as Sir George encouraged everyone to agree with him that "the boy" had grown into a fine lad, and done his parents proud.

Unused to such unwanted attention, and embarrassed by it, Christopher resumed his seat without leave to do so and returned to eating what was on his plate. His father nudged him again, apologizing to Sir George, but the Baronet waved away "the boy's" lack of manners, and ordered everyone to eat up. With dinner conversations picking up where they had left off, Christopher dared to look up from his plate, and noticed for the first time a fashionable London lady in blue silks seated directly opposite. He wasn't sure what it was about her that made him stare. She was beautiful, but not in the first flush of youth, and she was far too decorated with paint and silks to be thought anything but gaudy by a lad brought up around the scrubbed, fresh-faced females of the vale, whose Sunday-best gowns wouldn't be considered adequate for even the lowliest servant in this London lady's household. But Christopher had an innate sense that there was something special about her. He knew he was staring, but he could not help it. She smiled at him. He smiled back. But then her eyes filled with tears and he instantly dropped his gaze, awkward and ill at ease. He did not look her way again.

Much later, while the guests played cards, he wandered off and found himself in a gallery that had up on its walls paintings of illustrious Cavendish ancestors. Here he stumbled upon his mother and the fashionable London lady in heated argument. His mother was shaking her head. The fashionable London lady was pleading with her, gloved fingers tightly about the closed sticks of a fan. She was greatly upset. But his mother remained resolute. He had never seen her so determined and unyielding, and this to a woman who was clearly her social superior, and thus should be obeyed. He stood there, hesitating between going forward and running away. And then the two women sensed a presence, looked up, and saw him. The London lady's face lit up. She smiled. Grabbing a handful of her rich petticoats, she bustled forward to meet him. But his mother quickly had her by the arm, and stopped her. Another argument ensued. Embarrassed to witness such an emotional scene, Christopher fled.

His mother never mentioned the episode or the London lady again, and there were no further visits to Abbeywood Farm. He saw Sir George again, at the hunt, and in the village, but it was only a handful of times before the Baronet's death. He bequeathed Christopher the astounding sum of five thousand pounds. The bequest was a recent codicil to his will. Christopher was mystified, so were Sir George's heirs. Christopher's parents and his lawyers were not. With the codicil was a letter addressed to a Cavendish Bryce from Sir George. The letter contained life-altering news.

Christopher refused to believe the letter's contents. But his father confirmed it was true, and his mother wept. Christopher was not Christopher Bryce, son of Henry Christopher and Sophie Ellen Bryce, but Cavendish Bryce, natural son of Sir George Cavendish and the fashionable titled London lady who had sat across from him at dinner and with whom his mother had argued all those years ago. He now learned that she was also his mother's younger sister.

Christopher (he would not be known by his birth name) was told his natural mother was married to a titled naval officer. She conceived Sir George's child while her husband the Admiral Lord was at sea. This consequence meant there was no chance of passing the child off as belonging to her husband. To avoid scandal she spent the last months of her pregnancy, and gave birth to her baby, in the wilds of the Cotswolds, at the home of her sister Sophie and brother-in-law Henry.

Polite Society was none the wiser that her adultery had born rotten fruit. But Sir George was well aware he had a bastard son and pleased to have the boy growing up so near to his estate. Christopher's natural mother suckled her infant son for three months, then was compelled to give him up for good and return to London and her life there. Her understanding but obdurate husband, who knew all about his wife's adultery and the birth, was back from his tour of duty and was waiting to welcome her home.

Christopher's parents did their best to explain he was more fortunate than most by-blows. His aunt and uncle loved him as their own, and had adopted him. He would inherit Brycecomb Hall and be Squire Bryce. Sir George had taken an interest in his welfare and upon his death had made him a rich man. What more could he ask for, they wondered?

But what boy of eighteen who grows up thinking one thing only to be told another, who idolized the man he believed to be his father, and who loved the woman he thought had given birth to him, can take such news in his stride and move forward as if nothing untoward has happened?

Christopher's world fell apart.

He did not want to hear what his parents—who now were not his parents—had to say. He wanted nothing to do with this couple who had been complicit in covering up the affair and the birth of a bastard child, and who had lied to him his entire life. He was not a squire's son, and he was not the son of a baronet. He neither belonged to one world or the other. He no longer knew who he was. But one thing he did know—he was a bastard, the ill-begotten fruit of an illicit affair between two adulterers. And he well-remembered the vicar's Sunday sermon warning parishioners about the evils of fornication out of wedlock—that a bastard child, and the children of such an abhorrent being and their children's children to ten generations, were not entitled to enter the Kingdom of Heaven.

Christopher rejected his parents, and he rejected Sir George's legacy. He left the vale with a few pounds in his pocket, homeless and heartbroken.

His parents told those who enquired that their son was on the Grand Tour and would return in a couple of years, once he had seen a bit of the world. They did not hear from Christopher for four long winters, and then they had to content themselves with intermittent letters, and the knowledge he was alive and well. They presumed he was living the life of a young English gentleman abroad, visiting ruins, museums, and cathedrals, and in the company of other English travelers. Christopher let them think so.

The truth was something else entirely.

He preferred not to think about those first few years abroad, and what he had done to survive. But by the time he was regularly writing to his parents, he had transformed from squire's son to "Cristoforo", sought-after cicisbeo of many a married lady—skilled in the gentlemanly arts of deportment, dance, and agreeable conversation. He discovered he had an innate talent for music and took up playing the mandora, and also that he had an ear for languages. Where these gifts came from he knew not, though he suspected one or the other of his true parents to be musically and linguistically talented. And there was another talent he was certain they had blessed him with, and which the womanizing baronet would have been proud. His reputation as a considerate and accomplished lover saw him rise to the position of acknowledged cicisbeo of the Contessa Maddalena De Nobili, wife of one of the Republic of Lucca's foremost noblemen.

It was while part of the De Nobili triangle of husband, wife, and cicisbeo, that "Cristoforo" was recruited by England's Spymaster General to report on Lucca's first families. The Spymaster's agent in Florence assured Christopher his parents would never find out their son had stooped so low as to become the whore-companion of a married foreign lady. No matter the cicisbeo had a respected and recognized status in Italian society, it would never be understood by the English, and thus Christopher would never be considered anything other than a high-class male whore.

But as long as he provided regular reports to the Spymaster's Florentine agent, then the English government would be grateful and Christopher's life, however he chose to live it, could go on unimpeded. Christopher wanted no part of such subterfuge. But as the English agent bluntly told him, Christopher's entire life was one of subterfuge. And if he did not cooperate it would not only be his adoptive parents who suffered. The titled lady who had given birth to him would be publically shamed, and as a consequence her husband the Admiral would lose his commissions and influence with the Admiralty, not to mention that the scandal that ensued would see the couple pariahs of good society. As for Sir George's heirs, who knew nothing of the existence of a bastard half-brother, they, too, would also be shamed, shunned by their illustrious relative, the Duke of Devonshire, and outraged to think their father had left a fortune to a bastard. Christopher wouldn't want to be the cause of the disharmony and ruin of at least three good families, now would he? Christopher most certainly would not.

Then one day he received news from his mother that her sister, the woman who had given birth to him, was now a widow. Her ladyship had moved abroad for her health and was dividing her time between a villa in the seaside town of Leghorn, and as a regular guest of the British consul in Florence—and she wanted to meet him. The medieval walled town of Lucca was just thirty miles away from her new home. Christopher did nothing with this piece of news. As far as he was concerned, he only needed or wanted one mother, and she was living in the wilds of Gloucestershire.

It was two years later, and he had just turned twenty-nine, when Kate found him. It coincided with the end of his contract with the Conte and Contessa De Nobili, and so he left Lucca and went to live with her. They had a year together before news reached him that his mother had taken ill.

He returned to the vale in time to nurse his mother through the final stages of her illness. His father, now old, gray, and stooped, could not live without his "darling Sophie" and died within six months of his wife's passing. It was the physician's opinion—and the vicar and his good wife agreed—that the couple died happy and at peace knowing their son was determined to take on the responsibilities as Squire of Brycecomb Hall. With his parents' deaths, Christopher knew he never wanted to leave the vale again. This was home.

Having mourned his parents, he sent for Kate. With Kate came Fran, Carlo, and Silvia. Brycecomb Hall was once again a happy place, albeit one stuffed to the rafters with furnishings and decorative objects from abroad, the glorious aromas of Italian cooking, and a menagerie of domesticated animals and birds worthy of a guinea a visit.

TEDDY'S FIRST VISIT TO BRYCECOMB HALL WAS WITHOUT HER parents' knowledge. She was six. She followed Christopher home one morning on her cob. And on every visit since, she was met with the same enthusiastic and loving welcome, as if she had been away for years, not days, and her company was most dreadfully missed.

"Ah! You are taller every time I see you, *cara ragazza*!" Silvia exclaimed as she hugged Teddy to her ample bosom and kissed the top of her head. "And more beautiful, always more beautiful!"

"Don't smother the child, Silvia!" her husband complained good-naturedly. Ignoring his own advice, he pulled Teddy into a loving hug before letting her go and spinning her about. "Yes! Yes! Much taller, *sei una bella ragazza*! Silvia! Why are you standing there? Get the child something to eat. She's half-starved."

"*Sto bene, grazie, signori Mansi*," Teddy responded with a smile and an impromptu curtsy.

She looked about at Christopher to see if she had spoken the sentence correctly. He winked at her and Teddy was again hugged and kissed and complimented by the couple, until Christopher cut short the profuse greetings.

"I'm famished. What's for dinner?" he asked in Italian. "I hope it's farro followed by rabbit stew?"

"Of course! And *tortelli lucchesi*," Silvia responded smugly. "Always I make all your favorites after you've spent time away eating *insipido cibo inglese*."

"Silvia, you are forever my angel." Christopher kissed his fingertips, adding in English as Carlo helped him shrug out of his greatcoat, so that Teddy would understand the run of conversation, "Teddy has brought something special for her ladyship but perhaps she could first have a couple of your delicious chestnut biscuits and a milk coffee in the kitchen?"

Silvia and Carlo knew what he meant. He wanted a private word with Kate without the child present.

"*Sì*! But of course!" Silvia exclaimed, helping Teddy out of her cape and handing it off to Carlo.

She brushed down the sleeves of the girl's fitted wool jacket and gave her flushed cheek an affectionate pinch. "We find a bone for your furry brother, too, eh?" she said, referring to Lorenzo, who obediently remained on the straw matting just inside the door but whose ears were wide to the conversation. With her arm about Teddy, Silvia said to Christopher, because the tiredness in his eyes worried her, "That great lady over the hill she keeps you away for too long. You are tired. You need sleep—"

"Enough, Silvia!" Carlo demanded, shaking out Christopher's greatcoat, then hanging it on a peg behind the door next to Teddy's wool cape. "It is not our business if the widow she does not know a worthy man when he is standing before her."

"What kept me away was a ghost," Christopher said placidly, and huffed, thinking of Evelyn, befuddled by the man's intentions toward Mary. He grinned when the couple's eyes widened with fright. "Not a real ghost. And say nothing. The child had a nightmare last night about her father's ghost." Adding in English to Teddy, "Do you wish to give your surprise to Kate before or after dinner? You decide."

"After. When we have our coffee in the salon."

"Very well, in the salon with our coffee it is," Christopher replied gravely, suppressing a smile that though she was all seriousness, Teddy could not help punctuating her sentence by hunching her shoulders with delight. And then he found out why when she added in a rush,

"After you play the mandora for us!"

"Ah! Must I?"

Teddy nodded. "You must."

"Very well. But if I do, then you must dance the steps I taught you —Or have you forgotten them? It has been a week since you were here last."

"No! No! I've not forgotten, Uncle Bryce. I've been practicing with Mama."

Christopher's eyebrows rose. "With your mama? She knows I've been teaching you the minuet? And she's been practicing with you?"

Teddy nodded excitedly. "But Mama promised she would not say a word. She said she would indeed be surprised when the day came that I danced the minuet with you." Adding naively, "Mama said she found it astonishing."

"I do not doubt that," Christopher muttered.

"Silly! Not that you don't know how to dance, Uncle Bryce, because Mama said you carry yourself very well indeed," Teddy assured him quickly, thinking he did not believe her. "Mama was *astonished* you were teaching *me*."

"Ah! I see. Shall we ask Kate to play the mandora while we practice our steps together? Is that agreeable?" When Teddy nodded, he said with a smile, "Now you will have to excuse me for a little while."

"Take the child to the kitchen and feed her and her furry brother, I beg of you, Silvia!" Carlo insisted.

Silvia shrugged good naturedly and hugged Teddy to her again, kissed her temple, and said in English, "Come, little one, see what Silvia she has for you in the kitchen. And I will have Carlo bring you a very strong coffee," she said to Christopher with a sad shake of the head before throwing up her hands and walking off towards the kitchen hand in hand with Teddy, Lorenzo trotting beside her.

Carlo scurried after Christopher as he strode across the paneled great hall with its large hanging tapestries and enormous fireplace. "*Signore! Signore!*" he hissed in a loud whisper, which stopped Christopher at the base of the oak staircase. "*Signore*, the mistress, she is having one of her bad days. I thought you should know. Today, it is a very bad day, one of the worst in a very long time…"

Christopher glanced up the staircase to the gallery, then looked down at Carlo, frowning, "Anything in particular I should know about?"

Carlo stuck out his bottom lip with a frown. "Letters four—no five —of them. They arrived just hours after you left to stay over the hill with the great lady—"

"That was bad timing."

"Yes. Very bad timing. The mistress has counted every hour you've been gone. She does not like that more and more you desert her."

"Contrary to what she claims, I do not desert her. She knows, as do you all, that my stay at Abbeywood is for only two nights in the fortnight. And nothing has changed in two years. It is just that this time it was three nights, due to unforeseen circumstances."

"The ghost?"

"Yes. The ghost."

Carlo shrugged. "She will not believe it. Not this time. This time is very bad."

"Once I've read the letters to her she'll be more cheerful. Bring the large coffee pot and make it strong. And keep Teddy with you a little longer than usual. I had best make an effort to read her at least one entire letter before dinner."

Carlo bowed and clasped his hands in front of him. "*Sì, Signore*. It will be done! Teddy she can play at bocce with Carlo."

Christopher patted the older man's shoulder affectionately. "Thank-you. And, Carlo. Let Teddy win occasionally…"

"Ah! I do not need to let her win. She beats Carlo fair and square. On my honor!"

KATE WAS IN HER BEDCHAMBER, CURLED UP IN THE WINDOW seat, bathed in the light and warmth of autumn sunshine that filtered through the mullioned windows. She was still in the dressing stage, salt-and-pepper waist-length hair mussed and unpinned about her shoulders, unbrushed since she had risen earlier that morning. She had a fur-trimmed dressing jacket across her shoulders, but it was left untied, revealing a fitted velvet bodice and quilted petticoats of rich burgundy and silver thread.

Given her present frame of mind, he was surprised she had bothered to dress at all, and was not still in her nightgown and banyan. But for a woman who had spent her entire adult life in Society's public gaze, dressing and being dressed in the height of fashion made from the best textiles and prints money could buy, with hair adornments and embroidered shoes to match, was as natural to her as breathing. So this uncharacteristic slovenliness was alarming, and had no doubt exacerbated her understandable frustration and self-pity as she struggled to come to terms with her growing loss of sight.

While she was not entirely blind, she had lost her central field of vision, and in both eyes. She explained, it was as if a splotch of black ink had been dripped onto the iris, so that light and vision existed only in a slim band at the very edges of her sight. It meant she could no longer participate in those things she loved most, which were to write, read, and embroider.

One of her greatest joys had been corresponding with her multitude of friends, here in England and on the Continent, allowing her to keep abreast of the political and social whirl that was Polite Society, a society of which she had been very much a part until the death of her husband the Admiral and the loss of income from his sinecures. But even with his death and her move to the Continent due to her straightened circumstances, she was not a recluse, and was welcomed with open arms by the English community abroad. And then her loss of vision became worse.

That's when her quest to find Christopher became a frantic fight against time. She was determined to see him, to etch his handsome face in her mind's eye forevermore before the blackness robbed her of him altogether, and his smile and those brown eyes were lost to her forever.

And now here she was, a world away from the drawing rooms of Society, English and Italian, no longer able to see a person's facial features; where the face was, there was only darkness. Her only contact with the outside world was maintained through correspondence—which Christopher read aloud to her, and the letters she sent—dictated to her lady's companion, Fran, who wrote them on her behalf. But Fran was limited to writing in English and schoolgirl French. Most correspondence required a high degree of competence in the French language, which meant waiting for Christopher to have the free time to be her eyes and her scribe.

Carlo need not have warned Christopher, though he was grateful for the man's concern, because it did not require a mastermind to see what had brought on her latest bout of self-loathing. She might appear a study of serenity, staring unseeing out the window with her hands lightly in her lap, but the paper littering the room told a different story.

Pages from freshly-opened letters were strewn from four-poster to dressing table and across to the window seat. Parchment littered bed coverlet, Turkey rug, and window seat cushions. Wax seals had been broken or torn off, some pages were so heavily creased it was as if they had been scrunched into a tight ball and tossed away, only to be retrieved and hastily smoothed out again. Thankfully, none had been torn to shreds. That had happened in the past and Christopher with Fran's help had spent an evening reconstructing a letter from one of Kate's many faithful correspondents, a duchess no less.

Kate's selfless companion sat by the fire, crocheting, and as he crossed the room she looked up and went to speak, but he put a finger to his lips and also gestured for her to remain seated. Both exchanged a significant look, Fran going so far as to smile resignedly before rolling her eyes to the beamed ceiling, indication her mistress was in a particularly foul mood.

"I know you're there," Kate stated turning her head from the view. "That's the thing about blindness. When one sense starts to fail other senses become more acute." She tilted her cheek to receive his kiss, then resettled on the cushions, nose twitching. "You reek of horseflesh and manly sweat."

"Yes, I must. Thank-you for the reminder I need to bathe and change before dinner. But I came to you first. But if you would prefer I go—"

"No! Stay," she commanded, brushing the window seat clear of paper so he could sit beside her. "And it wasn't a criticism. I defy any female not to swoon at the scent of you. You're worth bottling."

Christopher did not immediately sit where directed. Instead he went on his haunches to collect the paper she had swept to the floor.

"Fran, be good enough to help me pick up the rest of these letters strewn like petals…"

"I've made you blush! I can hear it in your voice," Kate teased, adding sullenly, "I don't know why you've gone all coy since returning to England, when you are well aware of the effect you have on females, and had no conscience about using it to your advantage when it suited, too. English roses are no different to Italian blooms, y'know."

"Cristoforo had that effect on females. Christopher does not."

"Ballocks!"

Christopher laughed and straightened. He handed Fran a pile of paper to add to her own collection and returned to the window seat. "Feel a little better for the outburst?"

"Don't be facetious. Of course I don't feel better. But you're here now. Though it was yesterday I needed you most. But what are my needs, what is reading aloud a few letters penned to an old lady, when compared to the needs and wants of *Proud Mary*? No doubt she did not think to thank you for putting yourself at her disposal at a moment's notice? She just expects you to do her bidding. I wonder if she even knows you have a home of your own, people who care about you, need you here just as much—*more*—than she ever could or would—"

"You're being unreasonable and unfair."

Kate sat up tall. "Unreasonable? Unfair? *Me?*"

"Yes. She was most concerned you were not inconvenienced if I stayed an extra night, and—"

"Was she?" Kate shrugged a shoulder, not placated. "She worries needlessly about your *aunt.*"

"—you forget," he continued, ignoring her slur on the word *aunt*, "it was not Mary who made me Teddy's guardian, or appointed me steward of Abbeywood, it was her husband."

"Apart from marrying Mary, appointing you that child's guardian was Gerald's only worthy act as baronet. The despicable dullard was a sad disappointment to his father. His sniveling cowardice and unfortunate looks, the fault of his mother. You would've made an exemplary baronet—

"There is no point to this, Kate," Christopher interrupted evenly, stifling a sigh of exasperation. "Or to ruminating over the past and what might have been had the planets and stars aligned differently. We can only go on as we are now."

"Gerald only made you Teddy's guardian as a spiteful joke at Roxton's expense!"

This startled him. Her petulance was pushing her into uncharted waters, and he wondered where this sudden need for confession was heading. He thought about his response and said with all the patience he could muster,

"Yes. I think you're right. It was spite that drove him to appoint me and not the Duke, because he wanted retribution for being banished from the Roxton family fold. So what better revenge than to make his lowly and unwitting neighbor his daughter's guardian, and to stipulate she not be permitted to visit her mother's relatives. Still, the unintentional outcome of such a stipulation, to which I am certain Gerald never gave consideration, is that I consider it a privilege to be Teddy's guardian."

"How can you continue to be so philosophical? To be so forgiving? You always see the good rather than the bad. And as for patience!" Kate gave a snort of derision. "Well! You didn't get *that* from *me*."

"No," he replied, turning to the door as a wide-eyed Carlo tiptoed into the room carrying a tray of coffee things. "My parents instilled forbearance. A most necessary quality for a farmer. Fran, if you would do the honors with the coffee pot, I'll sort through the pages and hopefully be able to pull together at least one letter. And while I sip my coffee to keep me awake, I'll read to you," he said to Kate, who he noticed still had her fists clenched, "but only if you allow Fran to brush and arrange your hair so that it better complements your beautiful face."

"No small wonder why you were a celebrated cicisbeo. You always know what to say to a woman—in any situation!"

"Not *every* situation," Christopher replied pensively. "I never know what to say to Mary... That surprised me at first; to find myself tongue-tied in her presence. And then I realized it is because I love her, and so everything I say to her must have meaning. It is important I be sincere. Just as it is important that I am sincere with you because you do know that I love you, too—in a different way, you understand, but—"

"Oh, for God's sake! Just stop it! I *hate* it when you're being-being —*you*."

"My lady! No! I've held m'peace long enough!" Fran announced, roughly handling the coffee cups so that they clattered on the tray. "You can't go on berating Mr. Bryce in this way after all he's done for you. You love him, so why be cruel? I know you aren't intentionally unkind and unthinking, but—"

"It's none of your affair, Fran, and no one asked for your opinion. Go back to your corner and your crocheting and leave me to my-to my —*misery*."

"Dear me," Christopher muttered. "Fran, Silvia, and Carlo have all had a rough couple of days—"

"Rough couple of days? Fran, Silvia and-and *Carlo*? What would you know? What would they? I'm the wretched one, the blind fool who—"

"While they would never doubt they are your servants, I would hazard a guess that not even the pompous Sir Gerald, if he'd been blessed with such a faithful and selfless companion as Fran, who has been with you now for ten years, would order her to *go back to her corner...*"

There was a moment's conversational pause. Kate stared up at him, wishing with all her heart she could look upon his face, see the love in his damp brown eyes, eyes that were so very like his father's, and his fine straight nose, and his smile, which were all hers. She knew it the first time she gazed upon him. Not the momentous day they sat opposite at dinner when he was just a boy of fifteen, but the day of his birth, when she had finally held him in her arms, exhausted and overwhelmed, and had lied to herself that she would never, ever, let him be parted from her; she would die first. All memories now, his birth, that dinner, those eyes, his smile, her straight nose...

Now she relied on his voice to tell her what she needed to know, to calm and reassure her. There was never any derision or correction in his tone, just patience, copious amounts of patience. He was always so tolerant and forgiving of her, and all of it, however much he tried to hide it, underscored with the sadness of her predicament.

A smoldering log in the grate popped, cracked, and fell apart, and brought her hurtling back to the immediate present, to the sounds of Fran lifting the silver coffee pot and pouring the hot dark liquid into a small porcelain cup, and Christopher shuffling paper near to her, steady, constant, reassuring, and so necessary to her happiness...

"Oh God, why are you always forgiving? Why am I *continually* ungrateful?" she blurted out on a shuddering breath. "I so *hate* myself!"

Christopher flicked out the skirts of his frock coat and sat beside her. Taking hold of her hand, he was pleased when she did not pull away, even though she kept her face averted. He shifted on the cushion so when she did finally make the decision to look at him, it would be more comfortable for her to see him.

"Kate," he said quietly, pressing her fingers. "Kate. I told Mary my name."

At that she turned to face him, shocked.

"What? Your *birth* name?"

"Yes."

Kate was so disbelieving she had to say it out loud. "You told Mary that as an infant you were called Cavendish?"

"Yes. I thought it was time."

Kate burst into tears.

THIRTEEN

Sitting in the window seat in the sun with his arm about
her and she leaning against his shoulder, Christopher recounted the
previous night's surprising events, deliberately omitting the kiss. He
was interested in what Kate could tell him about Mary's long lost
cousin.

"Evelyn Ffolkes is a rascal," Kate stated as a fact, not as a judgment.
She sat up, which allowed Christopher to reach for his coffee cup.
"And he has the worst possible timing to return from the dead."

"An understatement, my dear!" Christopher said with a short
laugh, a picture in his mind's eye of Mary and her cousin huddled
together on her bed, so deep in conversation that they had forgotten
his presence. "But as Mary was delighted at the reunion, for her sake I
can't be angry with him. Annoyed. Frustrated. Suspicious of his
motives. Most definitely…" He sipped at his coffee, and took a
moment to savor the bitter sweetness of the warm, treacle-like liquid.
He hoped he would soon feel less tired. Bathed in the warmth of the
morning sun, he was reminded that he had slept very little the night
before. "So what can you tell me about Mary's rascal of a cousin?"

All Kate's aggravated self-pity had evaporated, along with her petu-
lant mood, knowing Christopher had taken the monumental step of
confiding in Mary about his birth. He may only have told her the
name she had given him as an infant, and nothing yet of his illegitimacy, but it was a beginning. There had been a time when Christopher
had refused to believe the facts, or to acknowledge her existence. That
changed in Italy, when she had sought him out. His own life experi-

ences had made him better able to deal with the truth, about himself, and about her. All she had ever wanted was to be part of his life, however small, and when the answer to her prayers came, it was almost too late.

This new and fascinating turn of events at Abbeywood now occupied her thoughts, and was enough to temper her interest in her correspondence, though Fran was dutifully sorting the discarded pages into their respective correct order and letters.

"I know *of him* through his mother's letters," Kate told Christopher. "Evelyn was a musical genius. Truly gifted, and not just because his mother said so. Others praised his compositions and his playing. But his mother worried his musical virtuosity would hamper his willingness to marry and provide her with grandchildren. And she considered his preferred occupation unfit for the nephew of a duke. She was a haughty creature, prone to the dramatic, the granddaughter of one duke and the sister of another, and not just any duke, but M'sieur le Duc d'Roxton—"

"Your old beau?"

"Yes," she replied evenly, and though there was no hint of disapproval in his tone, she still felt a modicum of unease discussing the lax behavior of her past, something that had never bothered her at the time. "My old beau, as you call him, wasn't old *then*. And just so you are aware, Roxton and I were lovers well before his marriage—"

"—and when he did eventually marry, this great rake reformed himself for his beautiful young wife. Yes, I remember you telling me about their love story—a fairy story of sorts. You and everyone else of their acquaintance could not have been happier for the couple. I have always been desirous of meeting the heroine of a fairy love story. Mme la Duchesse particularly, because you tell me Mary has a great look of her."

"It's what others have told me. I have yet to meet the Lady Mary Cavendish, though I knew her grandmother Augusta very well indeed." Kate gave a little shudder. "She, too, was a very beautiful woman, but with a heart of stone."

"You will meet Mary, and I hope soon. But you were telling me about Evelyn Ffolkes' mother, the sister of M'sieur le Duc d'Roxton...?"

But Kate wasn't to be distracted from her own history, saying in a rush, "Roxton and I were lovers on not one but two occasions—"

"It's perfectly all right for me not to know."

"—and it is the second occasion you—and Polite Society—know about because we never sought to hide our affair. Most noblemen with mistresses do not see the need to do so; their reportage in the newssheets is mundane in the extreme. But that first time we —*connected*—"

"Were lovers," Christopher stated and grinned. "You're not talking to Teddy, Kate. Perhaps you forget I am almost forty years old?"

Kate shook her head, smiling, but said seriously. "A woman never forgets the day she becomes a mother. Regardless of the circumstance. That day... It is as if it were yesterday for me... I still wish it was yesterday..."

Christopher's mouth dried raw at the sadness in her voice. He cleared his throat.

"Mary said the birth of her daughter was the happiest day of her life. I cannot imagine how she would've coped, if at all, had she been forced to give Teddy up at three months old."

"She wouldn't. I almost didn't. A supportive lover helped ease the pain—well, to at least distract me from my sadness. Naturally Roxton could not empathize with my situation, but he did sympathize. I don't know if he fully appreciated the depths of my sadness, but he saw the fragile creature that I was, and we managed to keep our affair private. He helped me see that, with a few adjustments, my life could go on tolerably well. And this at a time when my head was befuddled with thoughts of killing myself—"

"Kate!? Oh Lord! No! *Why?*"

She put out her hand, and when he took it, squeezed his fingers, her smile widening with happiness at his concern, and to show him such dark thoughts were well in the past.

"Roxton had this gift for putting everything into blunt perspective. Those who did not know him well, who did not understand his haughty arrogance, thought him callous and self-absorbed, which he was to a degree—why wouldn't he be? He was a duke, for God's sake! But he was not so arrogant with those he cared about. Far from it... He said if I killed myself I would never experience the joy and disillusionment that came with watching offspring grow. Did I not see I had the best of two worlds—the convenience of having my child raised by a loving family, who took on all the responsibility while I need have none. My life would remain blissfully unaffected. He was as ever sardonic. And infuriatingly right!"

She sighed, shook her head gently, and took a deep breath, as if putting those memories aside. Fran materialized at Christopher's shoulder, offering more coffee, and a cup for Kate, which he carefully placed in her hands, before saying casually,

"Mary also told me that the happiest time in her life were the years spent as a young girl living with M'sieur le Duc and Mme la Duchesse—"

"Oh yes! I'd forgotten about that." She took a sip of her coffee and teased him, saying with deceptive sweetness, "Cousin Evelyn's return from the dead truly could not have come at a more inconvenient time in your protracted courtship of the Lady Mary, if she has finally begun to share confidences about her past, dull as that no doubt is. I confidently predict—"

"Now, Kate, she—"

"—Teddy will be one-and-twenty before the two of you share your first kiss!"

"How quaint," he cut in dryly, hoping his abruptness did not give him away. "Tell me what you know about her time living with the Roxtons."

"I remember laughing out loud at a letter from Roxton complaining that with old age came the revelation that he was losing his edge. He had to concede that he was less terrifying than his reputation. That while he could still quell a servant or toady with one look, it was becoming increasingly difficult to do so with his sons and younger relatives." Kate gave a snort. "Of course his wife had never been taken in by his cold arrogance. And he wondered if her unconditional love over the years had turned him soft. I knew he was being rhetorical, for where Antonia was concerned, he was always emotional custard. In one of his letters he singled out Mary for special mention. He called her a flame that could not be extinguished. He said she had an insatiable curiosity and an unvanquished spirit that was woefully tiresome for an old aristocrat who was unused to having his omniscience questioned by a twelve-year-old brat. Truth told, he was secretly pleased, because the girl worshipped him. Much like Teddy worships you. Don't shake your head, because you know it's true!"

"All I've done is to try and provide Teddy with the best example I can of what a father should be, and my example is my father, who was the best of men. Whereas Gerald was a woefully inadequate parent. But who can blame him when his example was Sir George?"

"Your father was a most excellent man—and I do mean Henry, not George. You could not have wished for better parents, my boy. And I count my blessings in that respect, every day believe me—"

"Kate, I—"

"Teddy's exuberance and zest for life, her heart of gold, and her optimism are reminiscent of her mother as a young girl living with the Roxtons," Kate said, quick to shift the conversation away from Christopher's birth, because enough had been said on that painfully emotional topic for one day. "I hope nothing happens in her life to make that change."

"Not if I have any say in the matter. The last breath will leave my body before I permit her to marry a man like her father, because I don't doubt Gerald took the snuffer to Mary's exuberance and optimism. But we were talking about Mary's cousin," he said in a more even tone. "What else can you tell me about Mr. Evelyn Ffolkes?"

"For one thing he is not Mr. Ffolkes but Lord Vallentine, and heir-presumptive to the Stretham-Ely earldom—"

"*He's* an earl?" Christopher huffed. "But of course he would have to be, wouldn't he!"

Kate ignored Christopher's incredulous sarcasm.

"He will be, as soon as his identity is verified. The earldom has stood vacant for a number of years on the presumption Evelyn was dead, and because the next in line to inherit, a much older cousin, does not want the burden of the title, and so has refused it until the requisite seven years has elapsed to declare Evelyn officially dead. And now Evelyn has returned within the seven years, he can inherit what is rightfully his. It's all turned out rather neatly, wouldn't you say?"

"Roxton won't be able to contain his delight in having another noble cousin back in the family fold. And command Mary to join them all at Treat for a homecoming celebration."

"Ah. That could be more problematic."

"Problematic? In what way?"

She thrust out her coffee cup, which Christopher took and handed off to Fran, then settled back against the cushions, gathering her thoughts on past events, knowing Christopher was all rapt attention.

"There is the fact that Evelyn eloped with a wholly unsuitable bride, which sent him into exile from his family, and he hasn't been officially, as far as I am aware, welcomed home." Kate shrugged and mused, "I suppose his death meant there was no need to forgive him. His hasty marriage broke his mother's heart—"

"Yes. It must have. Mary told me a little about her cousin's elopement, and that it was she who helped him and his bride flee France."

"Did she? How enterprising of her, and uncommon, too, to go against the family's wishes.

"She said the girl deserved to be married."

"Yes. I dare say she did..."

"And I had assumed that if he is to inherit an earldom, Roxton would see his way past the slight done the family by his cousin's elopement, particularly after all this time, and the death of the wife."

"Oh, undoubtedly, except for one small but significant event that I am very sure even Mary has no notion about. She would not know that this was the second time he had attempted an elopement. The first was thwarted by M'sieur le Duc d'Roxton. You see, Evelyn attempted to run off with Deb Roxton when she was little more than a girl—"

"*What*? The present duchess?"

"Yes, the very same. The whole sordid business was quickly wallpapered over. Which is why I am skeptical of Mary's cousin receiving a warm reception from his Roxton relatives. You see why I call him a rascal."

"Indeed." Christopher did not tell her about Evelyn's spying activities for England's Spymaster General, or the threats he had made towards him, which he considered hollow at best, but pondering, he did voice niggling concerns about why Evelyn had chosen to show up at Abbeywood Farm, when he could just as easily have pounded on Brycecomb's door to get answers about Sir Gerald's spying activities,

"So is it a coincidence he has chosen to return from the dead at Abbeywood, an isolated farmhouse, where his closest cousin, a widow no less, just happens to reside, or are his motives rather more complicated?"

Kate was skeptical. "I doubt it's a coincidence, my boy." When Christopher ground his teeth and locked his jaw, she added, cementing his suspicions of an ulterior motive, "London and Society would have been a far more appropriate venue for him to announce his return, particularly for one with such a theatrical temperament."

"Theatrical temperament? Ha!" Christopher was thinking how the wild-haired Evelyn had announced his return dressed in Sir Gerald's large nightshirt, looking every bit a specter "The man oozes drama from every pore."

"I would have thought his best course of action to secure his claim on the Stretham-Ely earldom would be to make amends with his ducal cousin," Kate reasoned.

"So why is he here bothering Mary?" Christopher asked quietly.

A question he and Kate wanted answering, but which would have to wait for another day. Now Teddy was at the door waiting to be noticed. And when Christopher smiled and beckoned her forward, she ran across the room to be gathered up in Kate's embrace.

TEDDY'S VISITS ALWAYS PUT KATE IN A BETTER MOOD. SHE LOST her self-absorption and the frustration with her failing eyesight. With Teddy the focus of attention, Kate was more her old self. It was after dinner, and they were in the salon, replete from one of Silvia's delectable Italian meals. Kate and Teddy were playing at chess, Teddy moving the pieces for both of them, while Kate sat in state, fluttering a blonde lace fan across her low, square décolletage as if she were at the Opera. She was wearing one of her many velvet gowns, hair dressed and makeup skillfully applied by Fran, and looking every inch the wife of an Admiral Lord.

Earlier, when Carlo had served them coffee after dinner, Christopher had danced the minuet with Teddy as promised, Fran exclaiming she had never seen a finer dancer than Mr. Bryce. To which Kate had quipped neither had she, and then found herself pulled up out of her chair by Christopher to dance with him. It was Teddy's encouragement that saw her acquiesce. And with everyone settled again, and Christopher strumming his mandora, he nodded to Teddy it was a good time to present her gift.

"Oh, what's this, child?" Kate asked when Teddy placed a parcel in her lap.

She fingered the parcel, saw that it was tied up with a wide blue silk ribbon, possibly one of Teddy's hair ribbons, and smiled up at the girl who remained by the arm of her chair, wishing she could see the eager smile and bright eyes of the little heart-shaped face framed by an abundance of red hair.

"It's for you. Something to help you, and there's also something to help you know me better," Teddy said with barely contained excitement, and glanced at Christopher who smiled at her encouragingly.

"Does your Uncle Bryce know what it is?" Kate asked.

Teddy shook her head, then added quickly because the old lady was blind and probably hadn't seen her head move, "No. It's a surprise to him, too."

"Oh, good!" Kate said, tugging on the ribbon. "A surprise for all of us then."

"It's a surprise to everyone except my Uncle Dair," Teddy added, not as confident as before she had handed over her gift. "Because part of the gift is from him. The other part I made myself. You'll see! I mean—"

"Yes, I will," Kate cut in and opened out the cloth wrapping.

Inside the parcel was a polished, brass-handled magnifying glass, which was of no use to Kate whatsoever, given her sight was not *failing*, it had *failed*. But of course it was the gesture that mattered. She held it up and pretended to look through the lens and smiled and thanked Teddy, presenting her cheek to the girl to kiss.

"Thank-you, my darling. It is the perfect thing for old tired eyes to read newsprint. And I am very sure that soon your Uncle Bryce will have use of it too, because he is—"

"Now, Kate! I hope you're not suggesting I'm getting old?" Christopher said with mock offence. "No! No one answer that."

But Teddy was the only one not smiling. She glanced up at Christopher, troubled, but as he continued to smile down at her, she had the confidence to turn back to Kate and confess in a rush,

"Uncle Dair was *very* sure a magnifying glass would help a person with poor sight. That's why he gave it to me to give to you. I tried to tell him that not all blind people are the same, that it was different for you, but Granny was there and she said it is bad-mannered to contra —*contradict* your elders. But Granny doesn't know you and neither does Uncle Dair. And I didn't want to disappoint him because it was a very generous gift, wasn't it?" She tucked her hand inside Kate's fingers and said near her ear, "I know the magnifying glass can't help you. I'm sorry."

Kate put a hand to Teddy's cheek and drew her closer to kiss it.

"I know you do, child. And it is a very fine magnifying glass, and a lovely gesture by your Uncle Dair. We won't tell him otherwise, and you will thank him from me next time you see him. Promise?"

"Promise."

"Ah! I see there you have another surprise for Kate, Teddy," Christopher announced, peering over Kate's shoulder into the unwrapped parcel, and hoping to divert everyone to the second gift.

"Mama helped me," Teddy said proudly, watching Kate unfold and then run her fingers over a piece of embroidered cloth. "But she only did so with the cutting out and sewing up of the edges. It's a pocket, but it's a special pocket. Shall I show you?"

"Please do," said Kate, and held up the pocket.

Christopher laid aside his mandora and with Fran moved to the front of Kate's chair to better to see the pear-shaped piece of cloth. It was indeed a pocket, with two long lengths of twill sewn to each side of the narrowest end, and which, when wrapped around the waist and tied, sat the pocket, slit side out, on the wearer's flank over her under-petticoats, but concealed under her gown. Either side of the slit was embroidered with a trail of vine leaves and flowers. The stitchery was very fine, but Christopher could see the workmanship was not up to Mary's standard. Still it was a lovely piece, and many hours had gone into its construction and embellishment.

"What a fine pocket it is, Teddy," Christopher complimented. "Perfect for Kate's handkerchief, etui, and the key to her tea caddy. What do you think, Fran?"

"That Miss Teddy has a fine needle indeed, Mr. Bryce," Fran said, a smile at the girl. "And that her ladyship will never again lose her handkerchief!"

"Oh, but you haven't seen it all!" Teddy exclaimed, all worry about the inappropriateness of the magnifying glass vanishing as she turned the pocket slit-side down to show the reverse, which was also embroidered, and where she had also stitched her initials in the corner. "I did this side all myself with no help from Mama!" she said with pride, and looked about at Fran and Christopher before turning to Kate. "This is me," she said, and taking hold of Kate's hand guided the tips of the old lady's fingers over the surface of her needlework. "Now you can see me. Do you like it?"

Kate's fingertips trailed over every bump in the embroidery, and at first it made no sense to her, though she tried hard to know what it was she was touching. And then Teddy explained it to her as she guided her fingers over the fabric once more, and then she understood.

"Uncle Bryce said that you can't see my freckles or my smile, but that you can see my red hair. So I've stitched a face, with eyes, nose, and mouth, and red hair. But this face is my face because it is covered in little knots of red thread. Those are my freckles. And if you trace your finger along the curve of these stitches here, you can feel my smile. See? I mean, can you feel them, Kate?"

When Kate nodded but did not speak, and neither did Christopher or Fran, Teddy wondered if there was something the matter with this gift. They were all staring at the pocket and her embroidery efforts as if there was something wrong with it, or it wasn't what they expected, and no one was saying a word. She began to suspect it was a silly idea, even though her mother had assured her Kate would love it and think her gift very thoughtful. But now Teddy wasn't so sure her mother was right. And when Kate clapped a hand to her mouth and her shoulders began to shake, Teddy was convinced stitching her portrait onto the pocket was the worst possible thing she could have done. That is until Christopher put an arm about her shoulders and dropped a kiss on her hair and said she was the cleverest girl he knew. And then Fran pulled her into a hug, tears in her eyes, saying she was a sweet, dear child who had made her ladyship very happy. Teddy was somewhat reassured by their praise, but it wasn't until Kate had dried her eyes and given her cheek a kiss that she felt entirely reassured.

"I shall treasure it always, my darling," Kate told her with a watery smile. "And it will now be my favorite pocket of all. I think what I shall keep in it are your letters, and when Uncle Bryce reads them aloud I can feel you with me by tracing your smile and your-your freckles—"

"Yes, that's what I thought too, because I'm off to Cheltenham to visit Granny very soon." Teddy frowned and screwed up her nose. "I just wish I'd made two pockets with faces—"

"So I could wear one, too?" Christopher suggested eagerly, but with a perfectly neutral expression. He scooped up Kate's gift and held the pocket to his hip, embroidered face out. "See, it suits me perfectly."

This made Teddy give a start and then laugh out loud, and Christopher played to her laughter by twirling about and then bowing to her, pocket still held in place. Her giggling and his play-acting considerably lightened the mood in the room.

"What are you doing with Teddy's gift, you naughty boy?" Kate demanded good-humouredly.

"Being silly!" Teddy told her. "Boys don't wear pockets, Uncle Bryce. You know they don't."

"They certainly do not!" Kate agreed with a laugh.

"I could start a fashion—"

"Start a riot, more belike," Kate muttered. "Now return my gift at once."

Christopher handed the pocket to Teddy, who gave it to Kate, and asked, "Why two pockets, if one is not for me?"

"The other was for Mama, to cheer her up because Granny doesn't want her at Cheltenham this year. Granny said as I'm now ten, it's high time I visited her by myself, and that Mama is to stay away. And Granny wants me to come to her two weeks earlier than our usual time. I know Mama is not very happy to be left behind, but she did put a brave face on it all the same, and said how fortunate I was to have Granny all to myself this visit."

"Then we shall have to see if we can accommodate Lady Strathsay's wishes," Christopher said, knowing Mary would do her best to hide her disappointment from her daughter, and wondering how he could delay Teddy's visit without Mary incurring the Countess's wrath. "Though I may not be able to spare the time to take you to Cheltenham early, as there is a meeting of the shareholders of the Stroud-water Navigation—"

"Oh, but you won't be put out in the least, Uncle Bryce, because Granny is sending someone special to fetch me in a big carriage."

"Someone special in a big carriage! Dear me, how your granny does spoil you, Teddy," Kate cooed with heavy sarcasm that was lost on a ten-year-old, but which garnered a stifled smirk from Christopher, who knew Kate's scathing opinion of the stiff-necked Countess of Strathsay.

But he was left wondering why Mary had not told him of her mother's diktat. He knew a letter had arrived from the Countess two days ago—he had given it to Mary. Yet she had not said a word as to its surprising contents. Perhaps she did not know how best to tell him she would not be going to Cheltenham this year, and that he also would not be needed. After all, he had always escorted their carriage on horseback, to and from the spa town, parting ways once he saw the carriage safely to the Countess's door. And yet now it seemed he, too, was being excluded by the Countess. Though if this was her stratagem, it was doomed to failure. He had every intention of accompanying this big unknown carriage and its occupants as far as the Countess's rented townhouse; he would be failing in his duty as a guardian to do anything less.

Who this special someone could be, what constituted a "big carriage", and when both were due to arrive at Abbeywood, Christopher, to his great surprise, was to have answers the very next day.

FOURTEEN

There was not one but two large traveling carriages in the forecourt of the stable yard at Abbeywood. Had it been anywhere else in the kingdom, the undersides and the wheels of both would have been splashed with enough mud to prove the general consensus that the roads in this part of England, if rutted tracks could be designated as such, were the worst in the kingdom. But it was not mud but lime that coated the carriages, from roads that were mostly deeply-rutted tracks that wound their way up the steep sides of hills, and then descended to valley floors in the same treacherous manner. It was a fair estimation that carriages, wagons, and even those on horseback had the slowest traveling times in England, too. It was as well the landscape was picturesque enough to provide diversion from an incommodious journey at any time of year and at every season, except perhaps when there was a downpour when neither rider, traveler, nor beast of burden could see five feet in front of their noses.

The carriages had been uncoupled, and the sticky lime was being quickly washed away, so as to prevent burns to the varnish. And as the luggage was off the roof, Christopher estimated the travelers had come in at dusk the night before. Which was just as well because it would have given them, their coachmen and outriders, and their horses the night to recover from the day before. Regardless of the distance since the last change of horses, be it five miles or ten, travel in the Cotswolds required a good deal of fortitude and forbearance.

These two qualities Christopher was having to draw on heavily, since receiving a note at first light that he was to present himself at Abbeywood after breakfast. Mr. Philip Audley, His Grace of Roxton's secretary demanded his immediate presence. Luke had delivered the note, and by the pull to his mouth and the look in his eye, the young footman was unhappy with the upheaval caused by the arrival of titled city folk, not least the inconvenience to himself of having to share his room with one or more of the servants attached to these noble masters.

Christopher dismounted in the cobbled yard just outside the stables, and gave the reins to Luke, who silently led both horses through to the stalls. Everywhere there was activity. Stable boys and the visiting outriders were down to the business of feeding, watering, and grooming a stable full of horses, while the local farrier was making the rounds, checking horseshoes. Christopher found the farm's head stableman in conversation with one of the visiting coachmen. The stableman assured the Squire everything and everyone was being well looked after; horses, outriders, and coachmen had places to sleep, and had been fed and watered. Christopher gave him permission to allocate the men three quarts of cider at suppertime, and to call in a couple of the village lads to lend a hand with mucking out the stables, cleaning the harnesses and tack, and readying the carriages for their onwards journey in—how many days?

The visiting coachman offered the information Christopher was seeking. His lordship was breaking his journey here at Abbeywood for a further two nights, and then continuing on to his final destination— the spa town of Cheltenham.

Christopher then spent a few minutes in conversation about the visitors' journey through the vale, and then reluctantly headed indoors to the steward's office. He hoped not to find Mr. Audley waiting him. That was wishful thinking. So was the thought the officious secretary had discovered an ounce of intelligent humility since his previous visit.

"You've finally managed to join us, Mr. Bryce," His Grace of Roxton's secretary announced, stating the obvious with just that note of sour superiority in his tone to set Christopher's teeth on edge.

Christopher glanced at Timothy Deed, who was seated at his usual place at the end of the desk, but such was the height of the pile of ledgers in front of him that he was only visible from the eyes up. But that was all that was needed for Christopher to witness the little man's beetle brows lift and then contract inwards, giving expression to his thoughts, which split Christopher's face into a grin. He wondered for how many hours Timothy had already endured the presence of the pompous Philip Audley.

"Is there something that has amused you that you wish to share with us?" Philip Audley asked with such excessive politeness it was meant as a put down.

"Not with you, Mr. Audley. How was your journey? Pleasant?"

The Squire's uncharacteristic small talk puzzled the secretary, diverting him from his thoughts, which was Christopher's object.

"What? My journey? What about my journey?"

"With two carriages out in the yard, I may presume your backside was afforded the luxury of velvet upholstery…?"

"My-my—*backside*? I don't under—"

Mr. Deed snorted into the ledgers.

"Your rump—"

"I know what a backside is!" The secretary shook himself, as if trying to rid a bad taste in the mouth. "I always forget how blunt you men of the provinces are. No doubt you do not think it the height of bad manners to mention particular parts of the anatomy in their most base form, but those of us who reside in more civilized counties and amongst more civilized persons—"

"Are you inferring the Lady Mary is uncivilized, Mr. Audley? And her ladyship the daughter of such a stickler for correct form as the Countess of Strathsay. For shame."

"I was making no such disparaging claims about her ladyship!"

"Good. I don't want you to even presume to know her. So you were saying about your backside…?"

Timothy Deed quickly clapped a hand to his mouth to suppress a second snort of laughter. But as Christopher kept a perfectly neutral expression the secretary assumed the Squire was merely being provincial, so said with a sniff, elevating his chin out of his linen stock,

"Naturally I was given a seat inside, in the first carriage, with his lordship and her ladyship. Which was right and proper for His Grace of Roxton's representative."

"What a high treat for the other occupants of the carriage to have your good self as a traveling companion. All the same, I prefer the saddle and fresh air. And the other representatives of his lordship and her ladyship…?" Christopher asked, knowing the secretary had a penchant for social irrelevancies that elevated his status above the ordinary. "They were relegated to the second carriage—naturally?"

"Lady Fitzstuart's lady's maid traveled with us, there being only room enough for Lord Shrewsbury's valet, my man, and Lord Vallentine's valet in the second carriage on account of the extra baggage when we stopped to take up Lord Vallentine's man at *The Two Greyhounds*," Philip Audley explained, as if these arrangements were of keen interest to everyone.

Christopher nodded gravely. As it so happened this was one time he was interested in the secretary's fondness for social minutiae. He had the information he required without asking directly for it. He now not only knew the Spymaster General Lord Shrewsbury was a visitor, but that he had been accompanied by his granddaughter, Lady Fitzstuart, wife of Lady Mary's brother, Major Lord Fitzstuart. He looked forward to meeting both, the prospect of being shut away with Audley for hours when he could be making their acquaintance deciding him to make his poor assistant his sacrificial lamb to Audley's administrative inanities.

"If you have everything you need, Mr. Audley, I'll leave you in Mr. Deed's capable hands."

"No! No, I do not have everything. Far from it! His Grace has sent me with a list of questions. And I have questions of my own, and you, Mr. Bryce, are required to answer them to my satisfaction. So I insist you remain here until I have executed my duty to my employer, and you have executed yours as steward. Do I make myself understood, sir?"

Timothy Deed looked from the thin-lipped secretary to his employer, and knew who was going to win this battle of wills before it began. Mr. Bryce always did, even if the secretary believed himself the victor. The squire had not removed his greatcoat, nor had he come further into the office, but stood just inside the room with the door left ajar, all signals of his intentions. Mr. Deed smiled to himself and lowered his eyes to the level of the top ledger, ears wide open, as ever.

"Perfectly, Mr. Audley. But why the urgency?" Christopher asked evenly, hiding his surprise at the secretary's note of desperation that lingered just below the surface of his haughtiness. "As we have the pleasure of your annotatable observations for the entire week, I am certain His Grace's questions can wait for later in the day, or tomorrow?"

It was not unusual for Christopher to bait the little man in his neat bob wig and immaculate austere clothing, and it usually took several hours, sometimes a day, before the secretary riled. And even then Audley was so single-minded and dull to his purpose that he often mistook Christopher's goading responses as the answers of a dullard, and thus would repeat his questions in a louder voice, as if the Squire was also hard of hearing. This invariably led to Christopher reverting to monosyllabic responses just to get the interview over with as quickly as possible. But not today. Mr. Philip Audley was rattled from the outset, and this intrigued Christopher.

"Regretfully, I am unable to stay the full week. I have business—that is to say, *His Grace* has business elsewhere—"

"Elsewhere? Where else? There is nothing within twenty miles of Abbeywood that would be of interest to the Duke, surely?"

"Sir! You are not party to His Grace's thoughts, or his business dealings, so you cannot know that—"

"That is correct. But I do know this area, and this is my dominion, not his. And thus if the Duke has business here, I have a right to know about it."

The secretary's mouth worked for several seconds but no words issued forth. Unable to supply a response, he snatched up his appointment diary which lay open on the desk where he had been seated, and stared down at his own handwriting without being able to read it. He mumbled a response, something about a meeting in Stroud with an individual Christopher had never heard of on a topic the secretary could not elaborate on, because it was in a sealed letter for this individual's perusal only, saying after clearing his throat, "If you would hand over the key to the tea caddy, I will see that it is passed on to Mrs. Keble."

Christopher frowned at this sudden change in the conversation and puzzled by the request. The secretary had uttered it as if it was the most natural thing in the world, which it was not, and all three in the steward's office knew it.

"Key to the tea caddy? What possible interest could you have in that key?"

"I do not have an interest in it, Mr. Bryce!" snapped the secretary. "Mrs. Keble requires the key, and thus you will supply—"

"No. I will not. Mrs. Keble has no right to fill your ear with her complaints or her requests."

"She didn't! I mean, it's not a-a complaint. Tea is needed by the guests—"

"Lady Mary has a key, and only she is authorized to use it. Mrs. Keble knows this, has known it for two years, and so have you. Now, if that is all your immediate wants unsatisfied, Mr. Deed can be of assistance to—"

"Mr. Bryce, as His Grace's representative, you will hand over that key or—"

Christopher took a stride toward the secretary, who instinctively retreated behind the desk, appointment book up to his chest as if it were a shield.

"Or what, Mr. Audley? You will wrest it from me? I think not. If it makes you feel less the earthworm, were His Grace the most noble Duke of Roxton standing before me with the same request, I would give him the same response." Christopher smiled thinly. "Though perhaps I would be a little more *polite*. Mr. Deed! If you need me in the next little while, you will find me in the walled garden, where I do believe the Lady Mary is presently taking the air."

On that pronouncement, Christopher turned, the skirts of his heavy greatcoat swishing against his booted legs, and left them, the secretary with his mouth at half-cock and Mr. Deed rising up on his arthritic knees from behind the mountain of ledgers and straining to hear voices beyond the window with its view of the walled garden. Only two gardeners were in line of sight, and he could not hear them, least of all see or hear her ladyship. The steward's assistant resumed his chair, wondering for the umpteenth time at the Squire's omniscience where the Lady Mary was concerned.

Mary was indeed taking the air, strolling the gravel path that was parallel to the south wall, where a long-established Jalap trailed a trellis affixed to the dry stones and which was top-heavy with red blossoms. In this part of the enclosed garden there was a hot house and an orchard of orange, peach, and apricot trees. On the opposite side of the path were beds of fragrant pale pink phlox, cornflower blue asters, and lavender blue daisies. Everywhere was autumn color and scent.

Beyond these flower beds were Mary's beehives, and farther afield, the large vegetable and herb gardens that supplied the house with produce, the plots running all the way to the bakery and cidermill house at the back of the kitchen. Four gardeners were working the plots, while two maids gathered produce into wicker baskets for Cook. Another maid was busy at the chicken coop fetching eggs. The dairy was just on the other side of a low dividing wall, a short walk through a gate.

And while this area of the estate had as many servants going about their daily tasks as those inside the house, the gardens gave Mary a sense of tranquility that indoors never could. This was a space Sir Gerald never visited because he considered it the realm of his servants, and not one for a gentleman to inhabit. Not even a walk in the formal garden, with its hedgerows and topiary could entice him. If he was not in his book room, the dining room, or bed, he was out hunting, shooting, or riding his dominion as lord of the manor.

And so Mary was left in peace to do as she pleased with the herb, vegetable, and flower beds, the formal walks, her bees, the chickens, and the dairy. And it was here within the high stone walls where she always found a spot, in the sun or shade, depending on the season, to sit and read her letters uninterrupted.

She had brought her visitor out to this part of the garden, not only because this was her favorite private space, but because it was level ground, and closest the house, and so an easy walk. But mainly they had come outdoors because she sensed her sister-in-law had something of importance to share with her she did not wish the others to overhear. She wondered if it was news from Barbados, from her brother about their father, but she did not speculate. In fact she could hardly think at all, or believe her sister-in-law had made the journey to Abbeywood.

It had been just on dusk the previous evening when Mrs. Keble surprised her with the news two carriages had turned in through the gates. Evelyn, newly shaved and groomed and looking less the specter and more himself, jumped up from his chair by the fire, where they had been enjoying a game of chess, not at all surprised. He announced that Lord Shrewsbury had finally arrived, and about time too. And while help had been hired from the village, Cook's requests for provisions fulfilled, and the guest bedrooms aired, dusted, and made ready, so that Mary felt Abbeywood was ready to welcome visitors, no thought had been given that a guest might not be able to take the stairs to the first landing, and an allotted bedchamber.

Mary had been mortified to be unable to provide Lady Fitzstuart with a bed downstairs. But as the guests were only staying three nights, and she had her grandfather's arm to lean upon, the young Lady Fitzstuart smiled sweetly that it was no inconvenience at all, and she meant it. Rory only wished her husband was with her, and not in the Caribbean. He could have carried her upstairs with ease, as he had done that first month of their marriage when they had stayed at Fitzstuart Hall, ancestral home of the earls of Strathsay. She was hopeful the commissioned flying chair would be installed in her new home by the time he returned.

Everyone made suitable murmurings of agreement, not wishing to upset a young woman who had been a bride less than two months when her new husband was forced to leave her for an extended period.

And no one wished to speculate aloud on when Major Lord Fitzstuart was likely to return. Though Lord Shrewsbury did answer the question that was on everyone's minds, and that was there was no news as no letters had yet been received from the Major, and in deference to the ladies, Lord Shrewsbury changed the topic of conversation.

It was only after Teddy said her good-nights to the assembled company and she went with her mother to the base of the stairs where her nurse waited that she asked in a concerned whisper about Lady Fitzstuart's pronounced limp, and why she relied on a walking stick to get about. She wondered if her new aunt had suffered an injury, to which Mary explained that Uncle Dair's wife had been born with a crooked foot, but that such a minor inconvenience did not diminish her kind and gentle nature or her beauty, did it? Teddy agreed that Aunt Rory, as Lady Fitzstuart had asked Teddy to call her, was as pretty and as delicate as one of Granny's precious porcelain figurines.

And now Teddy's Aunt Rory was using her walking stick and leaning lightly on Mary's arm, enjoying a stroll amongst the flower beds in the bracing morning air. Both ladies were wearing short coats with wool shawls draped across their shoulders, soft kid gloves, and had half-boots under their quilted petticoats.

"You must be disappointed not to be accompanying us to Cheltenham this year, my lady."

"Mary. I will always be Mary, and you will always be Rory. You are married to my brother, which now makes us sisters." Mary smiled and placed her hand over Rory's. "I've never had a sister before, and I am so very pleased that I have one now."

"Nor I! And though I love my brother very much, there were times when I wished for a sister to confide in—about those little things brothers—men—can have no notion about. But with not even a mother to turn to, poor Harvel had to listen, he had no choice." Rory glanced at Mary, adding with a light touch, "You were more fortunate, having a mother to offer a willing ear."

"I wish that were true," Mary stated bluntly, but without rancor. "And you must think so, too, or you would not have said so. But I am also very sure that as you are as wise as you are beautiful, you have the full measure of my mother, even in the short time you've come to know her. And what you don't know or understand about her, Dair would have confided in you."

"Yes. He did. I should not have pretended otherwise. Forgive me."

"There is nothing to forgive. You were being polite, or trying not to offend my feelings. But we Fitzstuarts have ever been blunt—at the very least, bruisingly truthful. Sometimes people mistake us for unfeeling. But *that* could not be further from the truth. I do believe our sad childhood made my brothers and me susceptible to bruising. And that is why you, who know my brother and love him very much, tried to spare my feelings." Mary smiled at some memory, lavender eyes bright, and added wryly, "Dair responded to the hurt by using his fists; Charles retreated into his books; and I...? I remained silent and biddable—a coward's way, I suppose, but at least my opinion and my feelings remained my own." Mary stopped and faced Rory. "Now it is you who must forgive me. I *am* feeling a little bruised because my mother does not want me at Cheltenham. At any other time—and I know you will not think me an undutiful daughter for saying so—her command that I stay away would be cause for relief, if it were not that I must send Teddy alone. It won't be the first time we have been parted. I have had to leave her here with her nurse on numerous occasions on my husband's orders, and then there was the time she could not join us at Treat for your wedding... But I would not deny Teddy a visit to her Granny. And I am more reconciled to the separation because you are taking her."

"Oh, I knew we were destined to be good friends as well as sisters when Alisdair confided we share the same peculiarity for brutal honesty!" Rory replied with a bright smile. "I had thought him being ironic, but now I see your brother does know you. And I am very glad Lady Strathsay asked Grand to stop in to take up Teddy and bring her to Cheltenham, for it has enabled us to be better acquainted, and for me to meet Teddy at her home. Although I confess that I do know a little about your daughter from Alisdair, who is a very proud uncle. It seems he and his niece share a love of being out-of-doors. Though I do wonder how she will hold up confined to a townhouse with only her grandmother for company..."

"That bothers me, too," Mary ruminated, then added, suppressing unwanted fears and forcing herself to be bright, "I'm sure my mother will take her out and about. Lady Strathsay does like to be seen. And Teddy does know how to behave, particularly when dressed in a boned bodice and hoops. But is there a particular reason you are required to be in Cheltenham?" she continued, deftly changing the conversation because talk of her mother always had the power to unsettle her. They resumed their stroll. "I hope you are not visiting the town because your grandfather is feeling poorly—or indeed you are unwell?"

"Oh no! We—Grand and I—are very well indeed. My brother and his wife are staying there for Silla's health. There is nothing intrinsically wrong with her. Being pregnant is a perfectly natural state, and the physicians say her pregnancy is progressing well. It's just that Silla has become even more... *particular* in her wants and needs. And Harvel wishes to please her, and do everything he can to ensure she has the best of everything, but in doing so he is wearing himself thin. So Grand and I want to cheer him up. And to be candid, I could do with the distraction, even if it is listening to Silla's demands and unreasonable fears."

"Yes. I understand—about your brother's anxieties, and yours... particularly yours, as I know how desperately you must want news of Dair. Have you had *any* word since learning of his safe arrival?" When Rory shook her head, Mary said with a forced practiced confidence she hoped hid her anxiety, "Another more detailed letter will come, and soon. Dair was never a prolific letter writer at any time, but he will write to you before any other because he loves you so very much."

Rory nodded vigorously, chin tucked in and gaze to the gravel path. Mary could not see her face, the peak of her sister-in-law's bonnet obstructing her view. And when she remained mute Mary suspected she was crying.

"Oh dear, I have upset you, and that was not my intent!"

Rory lifted her chin to allow Mary to see her expression, and far from being upset Rory was smiling from ear to ear, and there was such a light in her clear blue eyes that Mary blinked. But there was no time for her to think at the possible reason for Rory's radiance, though later she was to wonder at her own thickheadedness.

"Oh, Mary, I am so happy! I did want to write, but to have the opportunity to tell you in person, and for you to be the first to know is so much the better! I've not told a soul, not Grand, or Harvel, or Godmother Duchess, and most definitely not Silla, because she is still annoyed with me for stealing the candlelight for myself in marrying Alisdair."

"Lady Grasby is a self-absorbed silly widgeon of a woman," Mary stated, annoyed, the words out of her mouth before she could stop herself. "Oh, Rory, I—"

"I agree with you. So does Grand, and Harvel. But we must live with her as best we can. That she is finally breeding—and one hopes it is an heir—has gone a long way in placating my grandfather's nerves when in her company. He hopes for a boy—we all do—to secure the earldom beyond Harvel."

"Yes. That is most important. And I do hope for Lord Shrewsbury's peace of mind it is a boy—But I interrupted you. You were saying I am the first to know...?"

Rory giggled at Mary's look of studious inquiry and obvious lack of insight to what she was alluding. But she quickly stifled her exuberance because she did not want to appear smug, and said levelly,

"I do believe I will not tell Alisdair until he returns, because as much as my news will make him so very happy, he will worry needlessly about me. And he has enough to worry him in Barbados. Besides, as there is nothing he can do from such a great distance, what is the point of such worry? But husbands cannot help themselves, can they?" Rory leaned in to Mary, as if not wishing to be overheard, and said with a grin, "I know I am being selfishly mischievous, but I do want to wait to surprise him upon his return, so that I may see his expression for myself. Mary. Oh, Mary. Can you not guess? I am *enceinte*."

Mary's shocked surprise told Rory what she had suspected, that her sister-in-law had not an inkling as to her news. But Mary's shock was instantly replaced with happiness. She hugged Rory to her, so overjoyed she blinked instant tears off her lashes. Rory told her the answer to the all-important question without needing to be asked.

"I am fourteen weeks pregnant, so I am as sure as I can be that baby is here to stay."

"Dair will be thrilled! And I am honored you chose to confide in me first."

"I hope you will be doubly honored because I dearly want you to be godmother to our baby—"

Mary gasped. "Truly? Me? Godmother?"

Rory nodded. "Of course. I know it is what Alisdair would want, too. Please. You must say yes."

"Oh, I do! I do!"

Rory smiled and kissed Mary's flushed cheek. "Good. I'm glad that's settled. I do want our baby to have a godmother as lovely as mine own, for Godmother Duchess is the best godmother I could ever have hoped for. And I know you are just as loving and kind and wise as she."

When Mary had mastery of her voice—for she found her sister-in-law's words overwhelmingly touching—she thanked her, then asked, "Won't your family be disappointed not to be party to your wonderful news as soon as possible?"

"I mean to tell them," Rory explained. "But after our stay with Harvel and Silla."

"You feel Lady Grasby will resent you stepping into her candlelight once more?"

"Oh, you do indeed understand," Rory said with a smile of relief. "I somehow knew you would. And while Grand and my brother will be thrilled at my news, they will fuss at me, in the nicest possible way, as if somehow pregnancy will interfere with my-my ability to-to —*walk*. And while Silla likes such coddling, I do not."

"And Cousin Duchess…?"

"I shall write to her, and to the Roxtons once I have told my family, which I shall do on the last day of our Cheltenham stay. But there is one person I must tell when I make my happy news generally known, and as soon as possible, or she will feel forever slighted. I hope you can advise me how I can do this with the least fuss…"

"You are referring to my mother."

"Yes. Lady Strathsay must be told. But I fear with depressing certainty that once my pregnancy is made known to her, I will not hear the end of her good advice. You will not be offended, Mary dearest, when I tell you Her Ladyship is the source of much unwanted advice since I married her son."

Mary gave a sigh, and spying the bench under a rose arbor just up ahead, she took Rory there and sat with her.

"Do you truly want my guidance?" she asked her sister-in-law.

"Very much so."

"Then I will give it freely, and without prejudice. On no account tell my mother your wonderful news while you're in Cheltenham," Mary said bluntly. "You are right to worry. Once she knows about your pregnancy her advice, such as it is, will not stop. I apologise for painting such a bleak picture, but you must trust me in this. And until Dair is safely home, I would advise returning to live under your grand-father's roof, where you will be most comfortable. I would say use your need to cultivate your precious pineapples as the reason for returning to Talbot House, but my mother will dismiss that as mere fancy. So use the excuse that Talbot House has a flying chair. Which, when you come to think on it, is not an excuse at all but will become a necessity as your baby grows and thus so will the pressure on your ankles. And a very pregnant woman is never completely steady on her feet, and so cannot climb up and down the stairs with ease, never mind that you require a walking stick to do so. If you were to take a fall, none of us would ever forgive ourselves, and my mother would become even more abhorrent."

"That is an excellent idea," Rory agreed. "I don't need to stretch the truth even the tiniest bit, and Harvel will love having me at home. Particularly when his baby arrives, as I am very sure Silla will not breastfeed her infant, but hand it off to Nurse as soon as it starts to fuss. Which will allow me the opportunity to spend time with my niece or nephew, as I have very little idea about babies in general." She glanced at Mary and asked quietly, "Was Lady Strathsay any comfort to you when you were pregnant with Teddy?"

Mary gave a little shudder. "No. My mother was full of advice and when I needed her support the most, when I wished to breastfeed my infant, she added her voice to Sir Gerald's opposition, saying that as I had the misfortune to give birth to a daughter when my husband was badly in need of a son, the least I could do was not inconvenience him longer than was necessary. Breastfeeding would only delay matters, and that I had a duty to fall pregnant again as soon as possible."

Rory was appalled, but she had to ask the question anyway. "And did you?"

"Did I?" Mary asked, coming out of her preoccupation. "I was younger than you, and much more naïve. In fact I think I was quite stupid. Or, at the very least, ignorant and quite malleable."

"You were only doing your wifely duty, what you thought would please your husband, and your mother."

Mary smiled and touched Rory's hand. "Yes. You *are* much wiser than I ever was at your age. And as everyone knows I failed my husband by remaining barren for the rest of our marriage. I never had another baby, though I miscarried very early on in the pregnancy that came soon after I had Teddy. The physician was of the opinion there was a chance I might not conceive again, and I did not." She paused on a sigh, then quickly shook her mind free of such melancholy thoughts to say brightly, "But you, my dear sister, are clever and determined, and would never let yourself be persuaded, even if it was your husband putting such demands on you. But Dair is nothing like Sir Gerald, and your marriage nothing like mine. Yours is a happy marriage, and you will both be wonderfully loving parents."

"Thank-you, and for your confidence in us. And I ought not worry myself needlessly about not knowing the first thing about babies because Alisdair is a much better parent than his father ever was. He's so good and patient with Jamie, that I am very sure he will teach me, or, at the very least, make me less nervous handling an infant. Oh! Oh, dear! I have upset you," Rory announced apologetically when Mary sat up, back ramrod straight, with lips pressed firmly together. "Should I not have mentioned Jamie? Is he not generally spoken about in the family? I had thought—as his sister—and we are being private here in the garden, you would not object. If you could see Alisdair with Jamie, and with Jamie's half-brothers; they all adore your brother, and with Jamie's baby brother he knows precisely what to do, how to hold him, and to comfort him, that he makes it seem effortless. He is such a natural father—"

"I do not need convincing on that score, Rory," Mary interrupted quietly, a frown between her brows, and did her best to articulate her thoughts. "My brother is a loving uncle to Teddy, and has a natural way with children. I commend him for doing his best to be a good father to Jamie, when most men in similar circumstances, and at such a young age, would not acknowledge their base offspring, least of all go out of their way to be part of the mother's family. And what I have heard of the Banks family from Cousin Duchess, and observing the grandparents at your wedding breakfast, the boy is being brought up in a decent and loving home... It's just that Dair has never discussed Jamie with me. I wonder if that was because Sir Gerald was condemnatory at Dair's openness at having a natural son? Both my husband and my mother considered the Banks family as beneath their notice. So I cannot blame my brother when he was unaware of my thoughts; I never spoke up in my own defense, so why would I do so for him? Which is why I wonder what he must think of me. Am I making myself understood?"

Rory cocked her head and thought a moment, then smiled. "Yes. I think I do. Dair is a little in awe of you, y'know."

This revelation made Mary burst out laughing.

"Truly? Dair in awe of—*me*? But how can that be? I am a mouse and he, he is a lion!"

"But even mice can frighten the largest and most ferocious creatures into submission. Not that he is scared of you, but he admires your self-possession."

"My—*self-possession*?" Mary was incredulous of this quality in herself, but believed what Rory told her. "Dear me! I had no idea. What strange creatures we are. Sadly, we have not communicated our feelings, or admiration for one another, as sometimes happens with brothers and sisters, particularly those who have not lived together since a young age. I was twelve, Dair ten, and Charles eight, when we left our communal schoolroom at Fitzstuart Hall. The boys went off to Harrow, and I went to live at Treat with my cousins." She smiled and pressed Rory's gloved hands. "But since becoming a widow, I am learning to be better at expressing my own thoughts and opinions, as I have done just now to you about my own mother and my husband, something I would never have dared say aloud when I was married, thinking it disloyal to them both."

"May I ask that as your mother advised you against putting Teddy to your breast, did Lady Fitzstuart not breastfeed any of her children?"

"What? My mother suckle an infant?" Mary gave an unladylike snort that saw Rory grin. "Please do not let her lecture you otherwise, if it is your wish to breastfeed. If ever I was fortunate to remarry and have another child, I would do as I pleased—"

"—and breastfeed?"

"Most certainly. Is it not the most natural thing in the world for a mother to want to feed her own infant?"

Rory let out a little sigh of relief and her shoulders dropped. "Oh, good. I'm so glad we are in accord because though Silla won't do so, and others like her employ wet nurses, I could not. I dearly want to suckle my infant."

"Then you must, and not let anyone persuade you otherwise. Dair will certainly support your decision. I just pray he returns before the happy event, and I am sure he will," Mary added in a rush when, for the first time since they had come out into the garden, Rory's smile wavered and she looked worried. "Our mother had little to do with us until we were out of swaddling and making our first steps. But I understand why. She was continually pregnant for the first four years of her marriage, and loathed every minute," she continued, to divert Rory's thoughts from speculating on when her husband might return from Barbados. "Though none of her pregnancies were especially uncomfortable in themselves. And when we as infants progressed from the nursery, where she rarely visited, and were handed on to governesses and tutors, she would sweep into the schoolroom, to inspect our letters, to listen to us recite, but most of all to ensure we were being taught the manners and bearing of noble children. We were all terrified of her derision, Charles most of all. Poor Charlie wet his skirts twice when he failed to add his sums up quickly enough and she called him a dunderheaded disappointment."

Mary chuckled at a vivid memory that suddenly popped into her mind's eye. Not of poor Charlie, but of Dair.

"One day Dair climbed out the window when told our mother was on her way. He was only about seven at the time. I so wished to follow him, but of course I did not. He stayed out there the entire time she was in the schoolroom, all of us pretending ignorance as to his whereabouts. She never suspected he was on the window ledge. Why would she, when it was snowing outside? It wasn't fear that drove him to risk his neck on a precarious second floor window ledge, because, as you know, my brother is fearless. It was dislike. Can you imagine—I'm certain you can!—he preferred to freeze or break his leg than listen to our mother pontificate about the duties and responsibilities of an heir to an earldom? He was only a little boy, wanting to play at being knights with his brother, to climb trees, and ride his favorite pony.

None of us had any idea what an earldom was, least of all want Dair to have one!"

"He would have hated to be lectured, and to be stuck in a school-room even more!"

"Yes. He did. And it took two hipbaths full of hot water to thaw him out enough for him to declare that he would do it all again, though next time he would jump off the ledge too, because even sitting out there with snow falling all around him, with his teeth chattering and toes turning blue, he could still hear the drone of our mother's voice. Charlie laughed, and so did I. Poor Dair!"

Despite the enormity of the Countess of Strathsay's hardhearted treatment of her children, Mary and Rory found themselves laughing, so much so that when their reverie was interrupted, it took both of them a few moments to pull themselves together. Both women dabbed tears from their eyes and quickly shoved their handkerchiefs into pockets, before looking up to see who had joined them in the garden. The sun made them squint, and thus their visitor remained in silhouette, and not immediately recognizable. They rose up off the bench to greet him, he quickly realizing their difficulty when both women put a gloved hand up to shield their eyes from the sunlight. So he moved further into the arbor and the shade, and they joined him there.

Mary smiled up at Christopher and took a step closer to speak to him, and introduce her sister-in-law to the Squire. Rory did not smile, nor did she respond to the introduction. She had a gloved hand tight about the handle of her walking stick, as if she needed more than the usual propping up. And it was not from fatigue but because she had suffered a jolt of recognition so acute it left her speechless. She blinked, thinking herself mistaken. But she was not. But how could this be? Here before her was a gentleman with a head of auburn curls and a pair of damp brown eyes that were as familiar to her as if they were her own. And yet she had never met him before in all her two-and-twenty years. He was most definitely a stranger. But she knew who he was.

As certain as she was that her name was Aurora Christina Talbot Fitzstuart, she knew that this gentleman in conversation with Lady Mary was a close relation of the Duchess of Roxton—cousin or brother, and nothing further removed than that—the resemblance was too striking. Deb Roxton and this man had the same hair, and his eyes were her eyes.

Both the Duchess's brothers were deceased. One, the Lady Mary's husband Sir Gerald, had looked nothing like his sister. The other, a musician, had died many years ago in Paris, and so Rory had never met him and had no idea as to his visage. But here was a third brother, of

that she was convinced. Which left Rory wondering if Deb Roxton
even knew of the existence of Mr. Bryce of Brycecomb Hall. More startling, if it were possible, was that this marked resemblance must have
been staring Lady Mary in the face for several years at least, and yet
how had she remained oblivious to the connection?

Rory could not wait to make Mr. Bryce's better acquaintance.

FIFTEEN

"You are fortunate to live in such a picturesque part of the kingdom, Mr. Bryce," Rory said with a smile when the Squire had straightened from his bow. "And not only the rolling countryside in all its autumn splendor, but the quaint cottages in their small garden plots and lined up along the village lanes are as pleasing to the eye as the manor houses. I wondered why this was, and it came to me that it must be because no matter their size or shape, every home is built from the same distinctive pineapple-colored stone."

"Pineapple colored? I've not heard our local stone compared to such an exotic fruit before, my lady. You mean of course the flesh of the fruit?"

Rory dimpled. "I do indeed! Lady Mary will tell you, I am a little obsessed with the cultivation of the pineapple. Naturally, the color yellow is my favorite."

Christopher's gaze swept over her from white blonde hair threaded with yellow silk ribbons, to the little pineapple-shaped crocheted bag hanging from her gloved wrist. He brought his gaze back to her clear blue eyes with a smile.

"If I may be so bold, the color suits you very well indeed."

"Why, thank-you, Mr. Bryce," Rory responded with a quick curtsy, and shot a look at Mary whose cheeks had gained spots of color, and who had not once looked up at the Squire since making the necessary introductions; nor had he looked at her. "And I shall be bold in my reply, for I am pleased to make the acquaintance of Teddy's Uncle

Bryce. At supper last night, she spoke of little else but you and her visit to your house. Is that not so, my lady?"

"Y-yes. That is true. Teddy loves visiting Brycecomb Hall."

"Visiting and eating the best food in the whole wide world, is how she expressed it to me," Rory enthused. "I cannot recall what dishes in particular, but they were all Italian in origin, and to me, if not to my grandfather and Lord Vallentine, who have lived abroad, just as exotic as my pineapples."

"Ah! Nothing is quite as exotic as the pineapple, my lady," Christopher replied with a smile. "But what I will say, if I may be permitted to be so bold, is that like you with your pineapples, I am a little obsessed, too—with all things Italian. But most particularly with the food. Which is why I have always equated the yellow of the Cotswold stone, not with pineapples, but with the golden yellow pasta eaten in Lucca. And the secret as to why the pasta is such a golden yellow, so my Italian cook tells me, is in the flour, which contains eggs."

"How fascinating," Rory replied with genuine enthusiasm.

She liked the Squire, and understood why her little niece spoke of him with such affection. He had a sincere smile, and there was a kindness in his eyes. Though she detected a hint of sadness in them, too. But what interested her at that moment was the interaction—or lack thereof—between her sister-in-law and the Squire. It was as if they were going out of their way to ignore one another, and this Rory found *very* interesting indeed. Being romantically minded, she decided to test an idea forming in her head, and attempted to draw Mary into the conversation by saying with a practiced lightness,

"Do you enjoy this golden yellow pa—*pasta* as much as Teddy, Mary?"

"I've yet to try it, so I cannot comment."

"Yet to try it? You've not tasted it, *ever?*" Rory was surprised but she over-emphasized this with a dramatic gasp and a look at Mr. Bryce. "Has not Mr. Bryce, and if not Mr. Bryce then Teddy, been able to tempt you with his Italian cook's golden yellow pasta dishes?"

Rory was not as opaque as she supposed because Mary had a sneaking suspicion her sister-in-law was goading her into making an unguarded remark. Rory's smile was almost smug, as if she had discovered something quite by accident and only she knew about it. Mary hoped that this something was not her undeniable yet befuddled feelings for the Squire, feelings which had kept her awake half the night. She was ashamed to admit that instead of directing her thoughts to Evelyn's return from the dead and what this would mean for the family, she was consumed by that kiss and if Christopher Bryce would ever want to kiss her again.

"That can easily be rectified by accepting the invitation to Brycecomb Hall, my lady," Christopher replied, intruding on Mary's thoughts and before she could think of something non-committal and polite to say by way of reply. "That invitation has been outstanding now for—how many years…?"

Mary flushed scarlet, as if the Squire was privy to her thoughts, and so far forgot present company to say under her breath, "You know perfectly well why I've been unable to accept such an invitation. Sir Gerald, and your aunt—"

Christopher held her gaze.

"I do believe it was my aunt who extended the invitation."

"Which Sir Gerald declined on my behalf!"

Christopher put up an eyebrow, as if punctuating his point when he said evenly, "Surely that was well over two years ago now…?"

Mary continued to look up at him, aware Rory was all wide-eyed attention at her side, and fumbled to find an adequate response that would not sound ungrateful, yet knowing she had been thoughtless in allowing the old lady's invitation to lapse without an adequate excuse to do so. For some reason she had assumed that in permitting Teddy to visit Brycecomb Hall whenever she wished negated her responsibility as a neighbor to make the visit herself. Why, when she was conscientious about her responsibilities with tenants, and with the neighbors in the immediate vicinity of Abbeywood Farm, had she failed to make the journey cross-country to call at Brycecomb? She had no response, and the more she thought about it, the more miserable she became at her thoughtlessness and avoidance of her duty.

The silence stretched long enough for Christopher to be annoyed with himself for putting Mary on the spot, and so said to Rory by way of explanation and hoping to end Mary's misery,

"My aunt lives in seclusion and rarely has visitors. While she is in generally good health, her eyesight is failing her and, as I am sure you can appreciate, her increasing disability sometimes gets the better of her and she makes for poor company."

"Yes, I can appreciate her frustration," Rory stated without rancor. "Until she accepts the way things are and not the way things ought to be, she will remain unhappy."

"Oh good gracious, my lady, I did not mean—I wasn't referring—" Christopher interrupted, mortified, face drained of natural color to think he had inadvertently made reference to Rory's lameness, when that was the furthest thought from his mind. "I meant *appreciate* in a

general sense, never thinking in a thousand thoughts of your—" He
stopped himself and made Rory a formal bow. "Accept my apology, my
lady. I would never presume to know you so well as to make comment,
or—"

"Please, Mr. Bryce, you do not need to apologize," Rory replied
with a smile and a gloved hand to his sleeve. "I knew what you meant,
and I did not construe your remark in any other way than what you
intended. And to be perfectly truthful, I am glad it is out in the open
between us. I do not mind in the least to talk of my infirmity. I was
lame from birth, so have never known any other condition. But for
your aunt, who was born with perfect sight, the loss is the greater, and
thus it is understandable she is suffering, and her moods interchange-
able. No doubt Teddy's visits offer her some respite and diversion from
her gloomy thoughts.

"And now, Mr. Bryce," she added with a smile and extending her
hand, a glance at Mary, "you must forgive me if I return indoors. I
have walked enough for one morning. But I do hope to see you again
very soon. There was talk at the breakfast table that if the rain holds off
tomorrow, making a day of it with a picnic. I should like to see more
of your beautiful countryside. My grandfather suggested we take in a
visit to one of your mills, with your permission, of course. He—Lord
Shrewsbury—and Lord Vallentine, were most enthusiastic at the
prospect of inspecting a cloth mill. For neither of them, nor I, have
been inside one. Grand tells me such mills are the latest marvels of
modern manufactory. And as I have a turn for the scientific and the
mechanical, I should very much like to see how such places harness the
power of water." She gave a tinkle of laughter. "My husband says my
insatiable curiosity is one of my most endearing qualities—No, you
stay, dear sister," she said to Mary when her sister-in-law made motions
to join her. "You and Mr. Bryce no doubt have much to discuss, not
least the arrangements for the picnic."

Before either of them could comment to the contrary, Rory turned
and walked off, surprising herself at her ability to rattle on without
pause, and all because she had made another startling discovery that
was, if that were possible, more astonishing than Mr. Bryce's uncanny
resemblance to the Duchess of Roxton. And that was that the Squire
and her sister-in-law were in love. She did not doubt this for a
moment.

Rory prided herself on being an exceptional observer of human
nature. Her infirmity meant being ignored for the greater part of her
young life when attending social functions, because she could not
dance. And because she could not dance, she had plenty of opportu-

nity and time to sit watching people. And from watching she learnt a great deal about her fellows, from their nuances, whether they were happy, sad, confused, affronted, proud, and above all, if they were in love.

And while she was convinced the Squire was in love with Lady Mary and knew it, and that her sister-in-law shared the Squire's feelings, she wondered if Mary had yet made that admission to herself. In the Squire's company she had a shyness bordering on awkwardness, and when she spoke to him she was unable to meet his eye. As for him, he might make the effort to appear unaffected in Mary's presence, but Rory saw the look in his brown eyes when he gazed upon her sister-in-law.

She paused at an intersection of paths, and before taking the one that led into the house and out of the line of sight of the couple, she stopped and glanced over her shoulder. And there was the Squire adjusting Mary's shawl. He had stooped to pick it up when it slipped down Mary's back to trail on the ground, and then fussed with its arrangement so that it would not slip again. And when Mary turned and tilted her chin up at him, they were so close Rory held her breath in expectation of them sharing a kiss; happy to have her intuition about the couple confirmed. But the moment of intimacy was but a second, and the kiss was left unfulfilled when a servant appeared out from behind an arbor and came straight up to them. Mary instantly turned away, head in her shoulder, and took a few steps to put space between them. And he, slower to react and still caught in the moment, let his gaze linger longer than was polite on Mary, only coming to his senses when the servant repeated his message. Rory's smile broadened at the Squire's distraction but it fell away when, having been directed to the morning parlor, she heard her grandfather say enthusiastically to Lord Vallentine,

"Can't say I'm surprised. You're no fool. Neither is she. You've both got pedigrees as long as my arm, so the match will be well-received by everyone. Not least Roxton, who'll sigh with relief he don't have to find her a husband; she's too young to remain a widow. I hope it seals the breach between you, too. Well, you're both family, and you are his closest cousin when all's said and done. And family counts for everything with Roxton." He gripped Evelyn's hand and shook it vigorously. "Heed my words, m'boy—marriage to the Lady Mary is the best decision you've ever made. Congratulations."

By the time Christopher was ushered into the morning parlor, the two noblemen were alone again, Rory having been fetched by Teddy to see what she had packed in her trunk for her stay with her grandmother in Cheltenham. A servant was set at the double doors so the three men would not be disturbed, and when Christopher declined a cup of tea or coffee, Lord Shrewsbury came straight to the point.

"So, Squire Bryce of Brycecomb Hall, Lord Vallentine tells me he would trust you with his life. That's high praise indeed, given the two of you only met t'other night. But you've always presented as a loyal servant of the Crown, so I'm inclined to agree with him. That means I trust you, and trusting you means what I say in this room remains here, between us. Lives—many lives, perhaps thousands of lives—depend upon it. Your own fine neck into the bargain. Do I make myself clear, sir?"

"As clear as a cloudless blue sky, my lord," Christopher replied evenly. "Though why Lord Vallentine should trust me I know not, because I have yet to form a firm opinion of him."

"Ha!" Shrewsbury looked to Evelyn. "You were right. Boorishly truthful."

Evelyn sipped at his cup of tea before saying nonchalantly, "Which is why we'll trust him." His blue eyes looked the squire up and down, and then he said something that stunned Christopher. "And because, as you said so yourself, sir, family counts for everything and our squire is family—of sorts..."

Christopher was slow to respond because he was marveling at the transformation of Abbeywood's resident ghost. Gone was the mane of wild gray hair, which had been tamed with pomade and tied back off Evelyn's clean-shaven face with a big white satin bow. Without a beard, the nobleman's face was even leaner, if that were possible, his nose longer, and his chin heavier. And now that his body was no longer lost in the folds of one of Sir Gerald's large nightshirts, but fitted in a suit of gray velvet trimmed in silver thread, it became apparent there was not an ounce of fat on the lean frame. If there was one phrase to sum up Evelyn, Lord Vallentine, it was sartorially elegant.

"I beg your pardon?" Christopher replied, coming out of his preoccupation to finally hear Evelyn's words about family. "I have no idea what you—"

"Oh don't try to deny it! Not after I've just praised your bluntness to our Spymaster General." Evelyn scoffed. "Besides, you're easy to read. You're shocked, not by the facts, but that I would know about your parentage at all."

"Know?"

Evelyn threw up a lace-ruffled hand. "Have it your way. Though perhaps I should give you the benefit of the doubt, living remote as you do from society and never having met the legitimate members spawned by your sire. Except, of course, for dull Gerry, who for all his puffed-out-chest-pride at being a Cavendish looked nothing like 'em. He was the spit of his frumpish mother. Whereas you—ah! No one can deny you're Cavendish spawn." When Christopher's hands clenched, he sat up, blue eyes sparkling with triumph. "So you *do* know I'm talking about *your* family connection to—"

Christopher cut him off and addressed the old man, "What has this conversation to do with the Crown, my lord?"

"Come now, Mr. Bryce, there is no cause for offence," Lord Shrewsbury stated with a patronizing smile. "His lordship voiced the connection with the best of possible intentions. Your base parentage, while unfortunate, is not something that hindered you in the past, while you were living abroad, or here in this rural pocket of England. Indeed, from what I'm told, you've made the most of your rural roots. Huzzah to that, I say! And you are to be commended for remaining within your own sphere, and not, as many of your bastard brethren have tried and failed, to toady up to illustrious relatives to own to a connection that cannot be yours by right."

"If you sent for me to insult me, then this conversation is at an end," Christopher stated. "I would rather waste my time listening to Mr. Audley's strictures than converse about people I know not the first thing about."

"Don't *you* insult *my* intelligence!" Shrewsbury cut in coldly. "I *know* all about you. *Everything.* I was best friends with Sir George—your sire. I also knew your mother—intimately." He held Christopher's gaze and dared to smirk. "Aye, biblically. If you didn't have a great look of a Cavendish, I'd claim you as one of my by-blows. So let's not mince words, or facts. You may not be acquainted with the Duchess of Roxton personally but you cannot deny the connection. You are related by blood, however polluted. She is your half-sister. And because you are related, and because she is married to the premier duke in the kingdom, and because blood connection, family, loyalty to kin, is everything, you will assist us in our endeavors to ensure her duke's honor and reputation are not compromised, and she not distressed. Do I make myself understood?"

If the Spymaster General hoped to intimidate Christopher he was to be disappointed. He may have been able to unsettle him with such bully-boy tactics and mention of his bastard blood when Christopher was much younger and less sure of himself, but not today. And this was not London, and he was not a member of Shrewsbury's club or social circle; nor did he care to be.

Here in the vale no one had ever seen a duke, least of all met one in the flesh, and none could claim to be kin to one, however diluted the blood connection. And it was the good opinion and respect of these people that Christopher cared about. Being a benevolent land-lord and a fair employer to those who toiled on his lands and worked in his mills was almost as important to him as the three females in his life whom he loved: Kate, Mary, and Teddy. He owed no man his alle-giance except his sovereign. His connection by blood to noble men and women he had never met was of little consequence. It only mattered if it mattered to his mother. And it only mattered if Mary and her daughter were affected by anything that caused the Roxtons, and thus them, the slightest distress.

"You think because I have a tainted blood connection to the Roxtons that is enough for me to want to help maintain the Duke's unsullied reputation?" Christopher jerked his head in Evelyn's direc-tion. "He may trust me with his life, but he seems to have misread my nature if he advised you I could be threatened or appealed to comply, all because the Duchess and I share the same despicable sire."

"I did warn his lordship you would not yield on such grounds," Evelyn said on a sigh, not the least offended by Christopher's blunt-ness. He sat up and set aside his tea cup on its saucer. "I was all for leaving you out of our deliberations, because when all is said and done you're as stiff-necked as Roxton. Nothing but honor and truth and doing what is right will persuade my noble cousin, and you hold to the same damnably high principles." He pondered for a moment. "I wonder if such ingrained and stubborn virtue is a consequence of having been sired by unprincipled lotharios? Wanting to compensate for an arrogant and unscrupulous father's sins and all that… M'sieur le Duc de Roxton, my uncle, was the most insufferably arrogant nobleman to strut the noble stage, and a prize stallion until my sweet aunt reined him in. As for Sir George, by all accounts he knew how to satisfy a woman between the sheets."

"Is there a point to these vulgar family reminiscences?" Christopher cut in brusquely.

"What I said to his lordship is that in order to have you fall in with our plans, we need to appeal to your baser instincts," Evelyn contin-ued, as if Christopher had not interrupted him. He wandered over to where Christopher stood just inside the door, and lifted his chin to look him in the eye to say, very low, "You'll offer us your assistance if only because you're ears over toes in love—*and lust*—with Cousin

Mary. You've wanted to bed her for years—possibly since the first time you clapped eyes on her curvaceous loveliness. But your honor, and the esteem in which you hold her—which is only right and proper—forbids you from touching a flaming hair on her head—or anywhere else." When Christopher turned brick red, he smiled smugly. "There. You see. I *do* know you."

Evelyn then walked away and propped himself on the window seat, crossing his legs and adding in an audible drawl to once again include Shrewsbury in the conversation, "You won't want to upset the Lady Mary. And she will be, *very*, if any scandal, any accusations of an untrue or cruel or shocking nature are attached to the Duke, a man she respects immensely. And any scandal that affects the Duke will affect his wife, and his mother, too. Mme la Duchesse is expecting a happy event in the new year—God! I almost fell off m'chair when Mary confided that piece of startling news—and at her age, pregnancy is very dangerous for mother and infant. A scandal involving her son will cause her unnecessary worry and there is a chance she could miscarry—"

"Yes! All right! All right!" Christopher interrupted, exasperated by Evelyn's theatrical persuasion. "You have my attention and my cooperation. Just tell me what is you want of me and be done with it!"

Evelyn smiled thinly and addressed Shrewsbury. "See. He will help us. Or, at the very least, not get in the way of what you propose."

"And what do you propose, my lord?" Christopher asked.

"Shouldn't your first question be, of what does the Duke of Roxton stand accused?" Evelyn countered.

"Does it matter? My opinion is of little consequence to the desired outcome." When Evelyn pouted and pulled a face, Christopher added with a sigh of exasperation, "Very well. I'll humor you. Of what does the Duke stand accused?"

SIXTEEN

Christopher was scathing in his incredulous disbelief.

"Treason? *Roxton?* Never. I might not know the nobleman personally, and I'll be honest, I've not found much to like about him. Admire, yes. But not like. Having had dealings with him these past two years or more, I've a measure of the man through his correspondence, and letters written by his relatives to my—to Kate. And there is one thing the Duke is *not*, it is a traitor to his King and country."

"And yet his relative, and the brother of one of my most dedicated agents, is a traitor and fled to France before we could capture him! So it is not outside the realms of possibility," said Shrewsbury. "But you are right to be dismissive. The Duke is no more a traitor to his country than am I. Yet, on the face of it, and because of what he stands accused, there are those within Society who will believe the accusation should it surface. And not only believe it, but his political opponents will demand a trial at the very least. No matter it will be conducted by his peers. All of it will be written up in the newssheets, the damage done. The mob is ever cruel and indiscriminate. But such a scenario I cannot allow."

"But a trial would absolve the Duke of guilt," reasoned Christopher. "And having a measure of the man I'd think he'd welcome the opportunity to publically declare his innocence, and bring those who malign him to justice."

"Yes," Shrewsbury agreed, grinding his teeth. "It's just that sort of pompous pig-headed posturing I'd expect from Roxton, and what must be avoided at all costs."

Christopher looked to Evelyn to see his reaction, but as that nobleman remained obediently mute, and thus by lack of reply must agree with the Spymaster General, curiosity got the better of him.

"So if Roxton is not a traitor, and yet could be accused of treason, what or who has seen fit to cast blame his way? Or is it a case of being caught up in something not of his making? After all," Christopher added with a wry smile, "you once thought Sir Gerald capable of spying for the French, when in fact he thought he was assisting the English. The man was an imbecile—"

"—and your brother. His existence must've been a daily source of injury to your pride, to have had such a dunderhead inherit the title *and* be married to Lady Mary," Evelyn taunted Christopher.

Before Christopher could respond Shrewsbury said, "You are correct, Mr. Bryce. A case of being caught up in something not of his making. But whereas Sir Gerald was idiotic enough to believe the pig swill fed him—making a contribution to the war effort against the American rebels by passing on information to the French, Roxton is not an idiot. Far from it. He is one of the most intelligent men I have ever met. His fault lies in being too trusting with those closest to him. I, on the other hand, trust no one—well, not implicitly. Except my granddaughter. She is the white to my black."

"Lady Fitzstuart is an estimable young woman of whom you must be very proud," Christopher said, and when the silence stretched glanced at Evelyn, who put up his shoulders at the old man's continued introspection.

"Yes. She is. And that likeable rogue she married had best get himself back here *subito*!" Shrewsbury grumbled with uncharacteristic candor. "Up and leaving his bride like that... Whoever heard the like! And she such a sweet natured creature... But she'll suffer it for as long as she must because she loves him. Ugh! What do I know! Mr. Bryce? Have you managed to ascertain who among us is the traitor?"

"Here? At Abbeywood?"

"Yes. Here at Abbeywood! Where else?" Shrewsbury demanded with misdirected anger.

Shrewsbury wished Rory had never married. In his darkest, most private moments he wished her husband dead so she would be free again, to live with him always. But as soon as he had these thoughts he hated himself because he loved Rory more than anything on this earth, and he wanted her to be happy. And she was happiest with Dair. And the man loved her body and soul. And were she to be made a widow she would literally wither and die. And he would die alongside her if that happened. So he prayed every day for her husband's safe return, and he never prayed for anything.

"You can't think I came all this way for the pleasure of Lady Mary's company, or yours?" he said harshly, forcing down his dark thoughts to glare at Christopher without seeing him. He took a deep breath and waited for the Squire to come into focus before adding in a more even tone, "You have a good head on your shoulders. I've read your reports about dim-witted Gerry. Made for some entertaining reading. So I know you can think. But perhaps you're a bit too like His Grace of Roxton and inclined to trust a fellow rather than believe him capable of deceit, pure and simple. Unlike Roxton's cousin here," he added, a nod at Evelyn, "who looks as if he couldn't curdle milk, when in fact he'd wring a cat's neck to get at the cream if required. Isn't that so, my lord?"

"Just so, my lord. And I have the battle scars to prove my cold-blooded loyalty."

Shrewsbury chuckled when Evelyn held up his mutilated hand and then ran one of his finger stumps down along the scar that bisected the corner of his left eyebrow, narrowly missing his eye, as if to emphasize to what lengths he had gone in the service of the Spymaster General. He ended the display of fealty by making the old man an exaggerated bow.

"All for King and country… Shall I put Silvanus out of his misery as to the identity of the traitor amongst us?"

"No! No! Let him have his guess. I want confirmation of his intelligence, and yours."

Christopher frowned at Evelyn. "You know who it is?"

"Most certainly. In the words of our Spymaster General: You can't think I came all this way for the pleasure of Lady Mary's company, or yours." He grinned. "That ain't strictly true. I did come to see Mary, but on an altogether unrelated matter… So, Silvanus, who amongst us is the traitor, and why?"

Christopher wanted to shake the nobleman free of his superciliousness, and he wanted an end to this ridiculous parlor game amongst spies. As if he didn't have enough to get on with without this intrusion into his day. Roxton's pedantic nose-in-the-air secretary must be wondering at his whereabouts.

"Philip Audley," he said flatly, mentally kicking himself for not reaching this conclusion sooner. "He's the traitor, and if I were a betting man, I'd lay odds he's serving two masters—one English, and the other French."

Evelyn and Shrewsbury threw each other a surprised glance, then stared at Christopher in such astonishment that he knew he was right. They were so surprised neither spoke, so he explained placidly,

"If you recall I did cast suspicion the secretary's way some time ago. I said the man had opportunity and means, but I was unsure as to his motives. And thus I dismissed my suspicions as unfounded. I also believed my judgment clouded by my intense dislike of the man. I should've stuck to my instincts. But hindsight is a wonderful thing, isn't it, my lord? Sir Gerald once confided in me—and I passed this piece of news on to you—that he hoped by working closely with your agent, an agent he never named to me, he would be singled out for special mention. He gloated that he was sure that his work for the government would see him recognized as some sort of master spy, and that this would somehow show up the Duke of Roxton as incompetent in his ignorance of state matters. I had no idea what he meant then; I thought it was the wine talking. But I do now. Sir Gerald was working closely with Philip Audley under His Grace's noble nose, and he found the deception and petty backroom maneuverings exhilarating. May I ask how you discovered Audley was a spy for the French?"

"He began his career as an agent of the crown. And I did not discover it. I knew one of my agents was a traitorous dog but I had no conclusive proof as to the man's identity," Lord Shrewsbury replied frankly.

"But if Audley started out as one of your agents, then he was placed in the Duke's household to spy on him?" Christopher frowned, not liking the idea. "But is not the Duke one of your closest friends?"

Shrewsbury brushed aside Christopher's moral outrage on the Duke's behalf.

"Every man has his price and his Achilles heel. Roxton's mother is French. And his father's mother was too. That gives him a certain sympathy for the Bourbons. I had to make certain that sympathy was never exercised to our King's detriment."

"So Audley was sending you reports on Roxton and his family?"

"Just as you were spying on Sir Gerald and his family," Shrewsbury countered with a thin smile.

"In my defense, you were blackmailing me to be your eyes and ears. How did Audley give himself away?"

"He didn't. Lord Vallentine supplied me with the name of the traitor through channels of his own while an agent abroad."

Christopher put up his brows at Evelyn. "You were an agent for two masters," he stated as fact and without judgment.

"Yes. When needs must," Evelyn confessed. He gave a lopsided smile that was more grimace than grin. "No doubt you can appreciate that difficult circumstances often dictate a course of action that, were we here at home, we would never contemplate entertaining."

Christopher inclined his head in understanding, thinking of his time as a cicisbeo, and knowing by his smile and the glint in his eye that it was to this life Evelyn was referring. Of course he knew. Shrewsbury would have confided in him that Christopher was co-opted to spy on his Italian masters by the English consul in Florence, who was one of Shrewsbury's minions. But neither nobleman mentioned this out loud, and Evelyn said, by way of offering further explanation about the secretary's double dealings,

"Audley let Gerry believe they were feeding the French false estimates of English troop numbers and supplies to mislead the American rebels. When, in truth, the numbers were very real. It was a double bluff, in fact. And it was effective because the French had their own inside agent who was verifying the information sent by Audley via Sir Gerald."

"The inside agent working for the French, and Audley's accomplice, is the Duke's cousin Charles Fitzstuart, is it not? As younger brother of the war hero Dair Fitzstuart, he was never suspected of treasonous activity."

"Just so. But how do you know this?" Lord Shrewsbury asked.

"What you mean to say is how would I, a squire living in this backwater, know when Society has no idea that one of the Duke's relatives—your granddaughter's brother-in-law in fact—is a traitor?" Christopher asked smoothly. "Oh don't fear your blindfold of deceit has somehow slipped from the eyes of Society. I'm sure most of the populace believe the pap it's fed, that Mr. Fitzstuart is in Paris as part of an English delegation sent to negotiate a last-minute treaty with the French, in the hopes of preventing war between our two nations. But I have my own, very reliable, sources. I'm sure you haven't forgotten that Kate is a regular correspondent with many within social and government circles. And there is the fact I was here when the Lady Mary received the disturbing news of her brother's flight to Paris with the daughter of the Duke of Kinross."

"No doubt you offered your broad shoulder to cry on," Evelyn quipped.

Christopher ignored him. And so did Shrewsbury when he urged him to continue.

"I cannot yet fault your précis, Mr. Bryce. Would you like to hazard a guess as to Audley's methods?"

"I should think that self-evident—well, it is now. As the Duke's secretary he had access to all sorts of correspondence that crossed the desk of his noble employer. I'm sure he can sign the Duke's fist as well as his master. And Roxton trusted him, never dreaming the man was a spy, least of all a traitor. And when his secretary came here for his quarterly visits under the auspices of the Duke as co-guardian of the estate, to view the accounts, to question my running of the estate, Audley, with the aid of the gullible Sir Gerald, made contact with a local spy ring."

Shrewsbury crossed his arms and put up his chin. "And what makes you think there's a spy ring operating out of here, of all places?"

Christopher did not hesitate in his response. "Why not? If I were the French and wanted to find a way of smuggling sensitive information on England's war effort across the channel, what better way than through the auspices of an innocuous trade route? A great deal of fine cloth, in particular the Stroudwater scarlet, is sent from Stroud to the Levant. The East India Company handles the shipments from port, but from here, the bolts are transported via bullock team. And Stroud is also at the crossroads of the ancient trackway for cattle crossing over from Wales into England, and beyond to London markets. But my money is on the cloth trade. Notes, letters, and the like, rolled up securely in cloth, no one the wiser, certainly not customs officials, except those who know which ships and which bolts to search."

"There may be something in that, Squire Bryce, and it is something I intend to investigate further. It could also prove useful to us as a way of passing on misinformation to our French and American enemies."

"But it's not the method by which Audley had Sir Gerald send the French sensitive documents, is it?" Christopher asked, curious to know more.

"No. Charles Fitzstuart wrote coded letters to an aunt living in Paris which were intercepted by an American agent. And Sir Gerald had an accomplice here in this house to whom he entrusted the documents, which were written up on scraps of paper then secreted in *billet doux* hidden in the lining of—"

Christopher drew in an audible breath. "Mrs. Keble!"

"—of the woman's stays. Yes. The housekeeper, Mrs. Keble," Lord Shrewsbury confirmed.

"Lord, I've been a fool!" Christopher stated with an annoyed huff. He ran a hand over his mouth. "Audley was always making a nuisance of himself with pedantic requests and nit-picking quibbles over amounts in the ledgers, all guaranteed to make certain I avoided his company as much as possible. That was clever of him. I was not looking over his shoulder, and he had time to meet and plan and go about his activities without rousing suspicion."

"Don't be too hard on yourself, Bryce," the old man said good-humouredly. "Audley is a master of the game. He fooled the Duke, and he had me fooled, too. He fooled Sir Gerald, but that was no great effort. If it weren't for Vallentine here, Roxton's secretary may very well have continued passing on sensitive intelligence for the rest of the war. As for Mrs. Keble, greed was her downfall. She attempted to blackmail Audley with what she knew about his activities. He called her bluff and reported her to my department."

"I presume she found out about Audley's activities through her association with Sir Gerald?" Christopher asked

"Association? *Association*? Ha! You have a moral turn of phrase, Silvanus!" Evelyn sneered. "Gerry was rutting his housekeeper every chance he got, according to Audley. Lucky, Gerry, I say," he added with a smirk. "Mrs. Keble's a comely wench worth the tupping. And lucky for Mary her housekeeper was willing to be mounted by such a sweaty tub of lard. Gave her some reprieve—"

"Are you always this vulgar?" Christopher complained, then put up a hand. "No. Don't answer." And said before Evelyn could respond, "I presume you have a plan for taking Audley and Mrs. Keble into custody as soon as is possible?"

"Into custody?" Shrewsbury repeated, a quick look at Evelyn. "Er, yes. Yes! I do! Reason I called you in here. I want this handled as expeditiously as possible, with least fuss and without causing our ladies any distress. And it goes without saying, but I'll say it anyway, with Audley none the wiser we are on to him."

"So, unless you have any objections, which I know you won't because you want Audley out of your sight as much as we do, the plan is for all of us—Audley included—to picnic tomorrow at one of your cloth mills," Evelyn stuck in. "I'm told these manufactories are not only architectural and mechanical wonders, but that you own a mill with one of the largest waterwheel-driven turbines in all England—fascinating! A high treat for everyone! And the girl child tells me it's not far from here, if we take the path through a Puzzlewood. Enchanting! So nothing too arduous for the ladies, and something for them and the girl child to look forward to."

"Teddy. Her name is Teddy," Christopher enunciated.

"Teddy? I thought it was Theodora?" Evelyn replied with feigned vagueness.

"It is, but she doesn't like to be called that. And so no one does."

"Dear me, how you take your duties as guardian seriously, Silvanus," Evelyn drawled. "I dare say as a bachelor you'd consider a ten-year-old girl child a burden you could well do without, so you'll be relieved to know she'll soon be off your hands."

"She's not a burden and—" Christopher frowned. "What do you mean *she'll soon be off my hands?*"

"You haven't asked why he did it," Evelyn said smoothly to deflect a response to Christopher's question. "You told us the what and the wherefore, but *why* did Audley turn traitor d'you think?"

Christopher threw up a hand. "Any number of reasons," he said dismissively, not wanting to be diverted from Evelyn's throw-away line about Teddy. "As Teddy's guardian, you owe me an explanation as to why you would make such a statement regarding her welfare."

"All in good time, Mr. Bryce," Shrewsbury advised. "But not now. Now we must join the ladies in the hall." He nodded to the maid who had popped her head into the room to signal nuncheon was ready to be served. And when she disappeared, he turned to Christopher with a clap of his hands in satisfaction. "Catching traitors always gives me an appetite! Not a word to anyone, and you're to continue on treating Audley as if nothing is amiss."

"And the housekeeper?" Christopher asked as he followed the two nobleman across the room.

"She'll be under guard the moment we set out for the picnic. There are still a few questions she is required to answer."

"A pity you won't let me—um—*interrogate* her, sir."

"Ha! I can imagine your interrogation methods of pretty females!" Shrewsbury replied, with a deep chuckle at Evelyn's insinuation. "And if I were twenty years younger, you'd be left with second helpings… Sorry, m'boy. Not this time. Though I hate to deny you a prime piece of rump, you'd be missed if you didn't attend the picnic, not least by dear Lady Mary."

Christopher rolled his eyes at the vulgar repartee and bit down on his tongue to stop himself from commenting. But it was enough to deflect his thoughts from Teddy and ask,

"So why did Audley risk all to betray his country?"

The two noblemen stopped just inside the doorway and turned as one to look at Christopher. Shrewsbury said matter-of-factly,

"Audley is the second son of a second son, so there was never any likelihood of him inheriting the grand pile or the title. But his uncle sent him to Eton, which gave him an inflated sense of his self-worth. And after Cambridge, with no funds and limited prospects, this same uncle forced him to accept the position of secretary, first to an Admiral of the Fleet, and then his association with Charles Fitzstuart secured him the position with Roxton."

"Association?" Christopher asked.

"Audley and Fitzstuart were up at Cambridge together."

"Charles Fitzstuart *recruited* Audley to the American cause?"

Shrewsbury shook his head at Christopher's astonishment, but it was Evelyn who answered the question.

"The other way round, Silvanus."

Christopher was more confused than ever. "Audley's a *revolutionary?*"

"No. He's a greedy opportunist," Lord Shrewsbury spat out. "He no more cares for the rebels than he does the King's men. What he cares about is filling his coffers with French livres."

"Charlie's motives are rather more sound," said Evelyn. "He has *ideals*. Audley, as his lordship rightly pointed out, is a snot-nosed, arrogant opportunist and he managed to deceive us all, not least his friend and fellow traitor Charles Fitzstuart, his employer in ermine the Duke, and dear old gullible Gerry."

"The blackguard will soon have his comeuppance," Shrewsbury said, grinding his teeth with satisfaction. "For the moment we must break our bread with the scoundrel, avoid getting indigestion, and pretend all's right with the world. And tomorrow it will be!"

He turned on a heel and went out into the corridor to the great hall, Evelyn and Christopher following up behind.

Christopher wasn't as confident as the Spymaster. In fact he had a deep foreboding that the picnic and the visit to his cloth mill was just a ruse to hide a more sinister intent on the part of the Earl and his willing sidekick Lord Vallentine. If Lord Vallentine was interested in the workings of a cloth mill, Christopher would swallow his tricorne whole!

But as the next day proved crisp and bright without a hint of rain, Christopher pushed any misgivings away as he welcomed the picnic party from Abbeywood Farm to the Brycecomb cloth mill. Everyone, from the Spymaster to the servants accompanying the wagon carrying carpets, furniture, and food stuffs for the picnic, were in high spirits to have this autumn day out in the sunshine. But what made Christopher forget Audley was that one of the party was the Lady Mary. As soon as she was helped to dismount from her mare, she broke from the group and came straight up to him, emerald-green velvet riding skirts caught up over one arm. Her smile was radiant, and it was all for him.

SEVENTEEN

"Isn't the weather glorious for our picnic?" Mary announced, tilting her chin to look up at Christopher from under the poke of her straw bonnet. "I'm so pleased to find you here, Mr. Bryce."

"And I am pleased you found me, my lady." Christopher made her a formal bow, but was unable to hide his grin; her smile was infectious. He was standing forward of a select group of his mill workers, all neatly turned out to greet the noble visitors come to inspect their place of work, a first for the mill. He frowned, pretending puzzlement. "Where else did you expect to find me?"

"When you did not arrive at Abbeywood this morning, I wondered if perhaps you'd been kept away—that your aunt might be unwell?" she replied without a second's hesitation and unaware he was teasing her. "But I should've realized you would meet us here. Today you are Squire Bryce, are you not?"

"Today and every day I am Squire Bryce. It's just that there are some days in the fortnight when I take on the role of your steward."

"Yes. Yes, of course. Of course," Lady Mary responded, disconcerted by his smile and the twinkle in his eye, and her own inane responses. What a singularly stupid remark to make: *Today you are Squire Bryce!*? Of course he was!

She quickly dropped her chin before looking out beyond the mill workers to the imposing edifice behind them, mentally chastising herself for her inability to tell him what she was truly thinking. Perhaps she was flustered because here she was, for the first time, out of her milieu and firmly in his? That could account for it…

What she should have said, what she *ought* to have said, was that today he was dressed, not as Abbeywood's steward in disheveled coat and neckcloth, but as the proud owner of a mill and as a man of consequence. She could see he had made an effort with his appearance and attire, and he was all the more handsome for the endeavor. The dark suit of fine wool, the polished boots, hair tamed under a black felt tricorne, and with his white neckcloth neatly tied in a fashionable knot under his shaved square chin, he was the epitome of the prosperous gentleman. And if his clothes by their cut and color showed a restraint in proclaiming this prosperity, his magnificent home, this mill and its environs, and the surrounding farmland were all beacons to Squire Bryce's industry and innovation as the largest employer in the vale, and so Lord Shrewsbury had proclaimed not twenty minutes earlier, when the picnic party had emerged out of the darkness of the Puzzlewood forest into the sunshine of the valley floor, and found themselves in a picturesque vale.

Teddy pointed out the sprawling Jacobean mansion of golden yellow stone set in parkland to her mother, and said this was where Uncle Bryce, Kate, Carlo, and Sylvia lived, and wasn't it just like a home in a fairy story with its coiled chimney stacks and glistening windows? Mary had nodded her agreement, speechless, thinking the mansion had to be the finest house in the Cotswolds, if not in all of Gloucestershire.

Lord Shrewsbury announced that such a magnificent stone building, and the evidence of industry that dotted the landscape surrounding it, were tangible testament to the prosperity and entrepreneurial spirit of the ordinary man, and what could be achieved in an economy unfettered by tyrannical kings, ending his declaration with his remark about the squire's industry and innovation.

The Duke's secretary had responded, with no disrespect intended toward his lordship, by declaring the mill, the tall gabled weavers' cottages, and the rows of tenter racks littering the slope behind the mill —the evidence of the industry and innovation of which his lordship spoke—as a blight on an otherwise agrarian landscape worth painting in oils. That had the land belonged to his noble employer the Duke, such ugliness as factories and workers' cottages would never see the light of day. Evelyn had countered by saying Audley was an intellectual hypocrite, jealous of his fellow common man who had the motivation to get his hands dirty with industry, something a secretary with more brains than ballocks would never do out of principle.

Audley had started to stutter a refute, and Evelyn had taunted the secretary further. A debate broke out between the three men on the merits, or lack thereof, of allowing the lower orders to accumulate more wealth than their betters, a debate Teddy did not understand, and one that upset her because she saw it as an attack on her Uncle Bryce. Mary was quick to reassure her the gentlemen meant no offense and diverted her by asking if she knew the purpose of the peculiar frames—the tenter racks—hanging with cloth that covered the hill behind the mill.

And when her grandfather did not take the hint to desist with his monologue on the necessary evil of merchant princes to ensure the prosperity of the kingdom, Rory interrupted him with an observation about the hot houses visible over the wall in the garden of the main house. That perhaps Mr. Bryce might permit her to speak to his head gardener about his techniques to grow fruit in a valley that was sure to see low-hanging cloud and thus frost most mornings of the year. What did Grand think…?

And so the picnic party—the horses with their riders and the wagon loaded with assorted picnic paraphernalia—continued on to the cloth mill in subdued silence, crossing a delightful stone bridge to a bridle path that followed the fast-flowing river, and which took them right up to the entrance gates of the mill.

With Lady Mary by his side, Christopher stepped forward to welcome the rest of the picnic party, who had dismounted and were making their way towards him. The wagon continued along the bridle path, directed by one of Christopher's workers to a picturesque spot by the river that afforded shade and easy access to water to boil for tea.

While the Abbeywood servants went about the business of organizing the picnic, Christopher's guests assembled by the mill's double front doors, eager to have the mysteries of cloth manufacturing explained to them. Those workers given the privilege of meeting the noble visitors doffed their caps and bobbed curtsies of welcome when introduced. Before entering the building, Christopher pointed out the features in the mill's landscape, so that his guests would have some understanding of its layout, and how harnessing the power of the river was vital in operating the mill's machinery.

The building which housed the machinery was itself almost as magnificent as its owner's mansion. Less than a year old and box-like in construction, it too was of local yellow stone. Five stories high, it had rows of large windows on each floor, to allow in as much light as possible, with even larger windows set into the gabled roof. It was set back from the river and connected to it via a canal that diverted the water from a curved weir. Some three hundred yards in length, the canal was fitted with sluice gates to control the flow of water that went directly under the mill, where, unseen from outside, the fast-flowing water dropped onto a giant waterwheel. The turn of this mighty wheel generated the power necessary to move the gears, line shafting, and belt drives throughout each floor to run the mill's machinery.

Teddy asked where the water went after turning the wheel. And Christopher praised her for such a thoughtful question, telling everyone that after powering the waterwheel, the water was discharged into another canal to rejoin the river. He then pointed downstream, and all heads turned in that direction, where some five hundred yards away, steep-gabled weavers' cottages lined the right bank. The river then continued on its way, disappearing behind a wide bend to meander through the undulating patchwork of tilled fields, pastures of grazing sheep, and herds of dairy cows, all belonging to Squire Bryce.

Christopher had then followed up with a short précis of the specialist processes involved in the manufacture of wool into yarn and then cloth. He explained how these steps were all interconnected, with no one process more important than another. It was the same with those who worked for him. They relied on each other, and ultimately they relied on him, so that by all of them working together, they were able to achieve commercial success and share in the prosperity of their manufacturing endeavors.

With the workers gravely nodding, and the guests even more eager to inspect the mill, Christopher first apologized if his over-enthusiasm for his manufacturing endeavors caught his guests unawares, but he assured them that they would not be bored by anything they saw inside the factory. Everyone agreed, and then he turned to offer his crooked arm to Lady Mary to escort her indoors. But she balked, and not because she did not want to give him her arm, but because protocol demanded otherwise.

"Mr. Bryce, Lady Fitzstuart, as my brother's wife, has precedence," she said quietly, leaning into him so that only he would hear. "I am the daughter of an earl, but she is the wife of the heir to that earldom. It is she who has the privilege of your arm upon this occasion."

"Thank-you, my lady," he replied. "I would not wish to cause offense." And before turning to seek Rory out, said at her ear, "I mean no disrespect to her, but I wish it were otherwise, for surely you know —you must—that I want to offer my arm to you alone."

Mary looked up into his brown eyes and saw that he was sincere.

She swallowed and smiled. "Yes. Yes, I do know that *now*, and—and nothing would please me more."

He smiled and winked. "Oh, I do believe I could please you more, if you would let me—Lady Fitzstuart!" he announced audibly, turning away and taking a stride toward Rory, crooked arm at the ready. "If you would do me the great honor of allowing me to be your escort…"

Mary was left reeling by the underlying insinuation of that wink and accompanying comment. So it took her a few moments to react when he turned away from her, to realize her cousin Evelyn was beside her. She had no idea for how long, she had been so caught up in the moment with the Squire, and hoped he had not heard their exchange.

But Evelyn did not need to hear the words spoken to understand the meaning behind their conversation. The couple's closeness, their whispered conversation, and Christopher's wink all combined to give Evelyn a fair idea of how matters stood between them. It reinforced what he had surmised the night he had appeared before them and they thought him a ghost. But whereas he was confident of knowing Christopher's feelings for his cousin, he was not, until that moment, convinced that those feelings were reciprocated. He needed no further persuasion, and when he offered his arm to Mary without comment, he smiled to himself to see that she was still distracted enough to allow her gaze to follow the Squire as he took Rory through into the mill, the two of them in easy conversation.

No sooner was the picnic party inside the mill than Evelyn disengaged from the group. He kept Mary back near the stairwell that went down one flight to where the waterwheel was housed, and where the sound of rushing water could be heard just below their feet.

Everyone else had moved forward to gather around Christopher, who, with the aid of the master of the factory, explained the inner workings of the machinery that filled this and the two floors above. Called a waterframe and invented by a Mr. Arkwright, this technological marvel was far superior at spinning thread than a man or woman could do with a single spindle, and was capable of spinning 96 strands of yarn at once. At this, the guests oohed and aahed at the stationary machinery and the silent operators who stood to attention down the center aisle of the floor.

Christopher explained that to allow the factory's master to be heard over the clatter of the machinery, and to save the hearing of his visitors, all the waterframes on this level had been stopped. He encouraged everyone to walk freely about the factory floor to inspect the machinery, and when they were satisfied and ready to move on he would take them to the floors above to see the waterframes and their operators in action.

With the visitors suitably occupied, Evelyn spoke with Mary without fear of being overheard, and without drawing attention to their inattentiveness. Yet, he still chose to converse with her in French, lest there were any ears wide open to their conversation. He came straight to the point because he could see she was not pleased with him for removing her from the group, and was still distracted, but he needed for her to listen to him for what he had to say affected both their futures.

"*Ma chérie*, I'm going away. Mary? Mary, are you listening? I am leaving here today."

Mary tore her gaze from the picnic party. He had gained her undivided attention. "Leaving? But you've only just arrived, Eve. Why?"

"State business—"

"—as an agent of the crown? I thought you were no longer a spy."

He did not confirm or deny her presumption.

"I must carry out this last action before I can cast off my irredeemable past and move into my future."

"Very well. Then you must. But when will you return?"

"Here? I won't—"

"Not return?" Mary's violet eyes widened with anxiousness. "You're not returning to Abbeywood?"

Evelyn smiled, more attuned to her feelings than even she realized. He tested his assumption by saying rudely, "To Abbeywood? Why would I want to return to this Godforsaken part of the Kingdom, peopled by ignorant yokels—"

"It's not Godforsaken! And he is not—they are not ignorant," Mary said hotly, and was suddenly flustered by her slip of the tongue. She lowered her voice. "Don't you see the beauty that surrounds us here in the vale? There is a peace and a-a—*harmony* that exists nowhere else. And even if you cannot appreciate being in nature, this mill is surely testament to the willingness of those who live here to want to better their lives by embracing such manufacturing marvels. How then can you call them ignorant yokels?"

Evelyn ignored her slip, though he was not surprised by it. And though he wore a neutral if slightly skeptical expression, he teased her mercilessly.

"Oh how quickly you forget, *ma belle cousine*! But I have not. When Gerry was alive you couldn't wait to turn your back on this rural idyll, and flee to London at every opportunity. There was no talk of beauty or harmony in this place *then*. And yet I return after five years in the wilderness abroad to find you fallen in love with a picturesque pocket you could not wait to escape! Ah! But I think perhaps that has less to do with the scenery and more to do with the company."

"Yes! Yes you are right," Mary agreed, so outraged she completely misconstrued to whom he was alluding. "It *was* the company, and you know, *you know* what my—what my—*marriage*—was like, if you can call such servitude that! Is it any wonder I wished to flee, to get away."

"Ah! But it was not odious Gerry I was talking about, *chérie*."

Mary faltered and blinked. "Not Gerald? I don't understand..."

Eve's eyes lit up and he grinned. "Don't you? I'm sure he—Squire Backwater—does."

"Don't call him that!" she retorted, too annoyed to be embarrassed by his insinuation.

Evelyn leaned a silken shoulder against the white-washed brick wall, tongue firmly in cheek and eyebrows raised. "So what would you have me call your squire, *ma chérie*?"

"He's not *my* Squire. He's Teddy's guardian, and has only ever had her best interests at heart. And he gives generously of his time to Abbeywood as its steward, when it is now obvious to me, coming here, that his time would be better spent at his mills, and on his own lands amongst his own people. Yet he finds the time to balance Gerald's account books, which are in such a deplorable state it is a wonder Teddy and I haven't been forced to sell the clothes off our backs to feed ourselves."

"Have you ever wondered why that is?"

"What? Why we still have clothing?"

"Yes. You told me you refused the generous allowance Roxton offered you when you were made a widow. So where does your pin money and your clothing allowance come from if not from your relatives?"

"I don't require an allowance. I am an excellent seamstress, and altered and remade my clothing several times over. Besides, it is rare that I go into society these days to need a new gown—"

"Every beautiful woman needs a new gown... Squire Back—Bryce would agree with me. I'm certain if you ask him he'd supply you with any number of gowns, if he isn't doing so already."

Mary gasped.

"*If he isn't doing so already?*" she repeated. "Evelyn! I don't understand you today. In point of fact, you are deliberately going out of your way to goad me! As to why you are rude to Mr. Bryce at every opportunity—"

"I am jealous."

"Jealous? *Jealous* of-of—*Mr. Bryce?*"

"He's damnably handsome and clever. And here in this particular rural pocket, he is sovereign. His workers defer to him as if he were Louis XIV come amongst them. That is no small wonder, as the effortless ease in which he carries himself sets him apart from his fellows. And then there is the small fact he has a visage worthy of marble, which has females dangling at his cuffs, you included, *chérie*. No! Don't shake your head. I've seen the way you look at him, even if you cannot."

"Eve, I—"

"But he can only be Louis here, amongst his villagers. He'd never flourish in London, not because he don't look or could act the part, but because he can never be one of us. Whatever drop of noble blood courses through his veins, it is a dilution of the real thing and forever polluted."

"Diluted? Polluted? I do not understand. How is he these things? What do you know about him that I have not discovered in the eight years he has been my neighbor?"

Evelyn flicked her cheek. "You truly do not comprehend, do you? You are blind to what I saw the moment I clapped eyes on him. But that is because you are without guile, *ma chérie*. You take people as you find them, believe what they tell you. I wish I could be like you. Not that I think he cares the snap of two fingers about his ignoble bloodline. But you, *ma chérie*, you do indeed need to care. You are the daughter of Lord Fitzstuart and great-granddaughter of King Charlie—"

"I assure you I am keenly aware of what I owe my name and my lineage—my mother's letters are a constant reminder, and the fact I must think of Teddy and our future and marry again," Mary stated woodenly, keeping tight rein on her emotions and hoping the color in her face and the shake in her fingers were infinitesimally small compared to the pounding in her head and heart. "To tell you a truth, there is little else I do think about, given I have now turned thirty, which means my prospects of marrying again are diminishing daily."

"*Ma chérie*—Mary—I came to Abbeywood with one object in mind, only to find myself confronted with *him*. And if I were not going away immediately after our delightful picnic in the shadow of this entrepreneurial edifice, I'd have wished for nothing better than to have this conversation alone with you in your charming sitting room. But time is not on my side. What I want you to do while I'm gone is contemplate a future with—"

"Contemplate a future?"

"—with me."

"Eve?!" Mary's eyes widened and her lips parted. Finally she found her voice. "What is it you are asking me?"

"Oh, I think you know very well what it is I am asking you. But I've no wish to declare my intentions here, in these industrial surroundings, and in the presence of Squire Worthy. So I will not descend onto bended knee until my return in a month's time. And so, my dearest Mary, I am giving you a month's reprieve so that you may think seriously about the offer I wish to make you and what it will mean for us both. I hope that you will see, as I do, that it is the right choice, the most logical choice, for two cousins whose families are closely bound, and who have known each other from the cradle. But," he added with a shrug, "if in a month's time when I do ask you and you refuse the honor, I will know it is for the very best of reasons, and I will accept your decision."

Mary's eyes filled with tears and her heart began to beat harder as a great weight lifted from her shoulders at the prospect of marriage to her cousin. Her mother would be delirious with happiness, and so would her extended family. She would not be marrying just any man but heir designate to an earldom, and that meant she would be a countess. She could once again enter Society's drawing rooms with her head held high. She would be welcomed with open arms to all manner of balls, routs, and soirees. She would sit at the finest tables, dress in the finest silks and brocades, and have at her disposal carriages, sedans, houses, and servants galore. Evelyn was wealthy, and he was generous. She and Teddy would never want for anything ever again. Her daughter would have an earl for a stepfather, and a dowry befitting her mother's elevated station, and when the time came for her to marry, there would be no shortage of eligible suitors. Marriage to Evelyn would solve all their problems.

And then just as quickly as the weight rose up, it dropped like a stone back on her shoulders. But it did not stay there, it pressed down further still to settle on her chest. Without knowing why, a great sadness washed over her. She should have been ecstatically happy to receive a marriage proposal from her closest cousin, whom she had loved since a girl. It was a dream come true. Wasn't it? Why then was she miserable? She was wretched and eaten up with guilt, and it mystified her to the point of bringing on a sudden sick headache.

Desolate, she looked past Evelyn, out across the factory floor to where Teddy, Lord Shrewsbury, Rory Fitzstuart, Mr. Philip Audley, and the factory master were now assembled at the foot of the second stairwell in anticipation of inspecting the upper levels of the mill.

There seemed to be some discussion, and it centered around Rory. Mary realized her sister-in-law was offering to remain behind, her infirmity preventing her from taking the stairs as well as everyone else, and her slow progress aided by her walking stick would only hold up proceedings. Her grandfather was having none of her self-deprecation, and then a solution presented itself that had Mary quickly drying her eyes and smiling. Of course! While the others went on ahead, Teddy scrambling up the stairs with the factory master, Mr. Philip Audley one step behind them, and followed by Lord Shrewsbury carrying Rory's cane, Christopher Bryce effortlessly scooped up Rory into his arms. And with her comfortably situated, Christopher turned to follow the rest of the party upstairs.

But with one booted foot on the first step, he chanced to look over his shoulder, across the room and at her. His gaze remained steady and his handsome features were expressionless, so that she had no window into his thoughts. But she knew he must think her behavior unforgivably rude. And he had every right, and she did not blame him. She and Evelyn had the arrogance to engage in a private conversation and show no interest in his manufacturing venture, when it was obvious to anyone with eyes that the mill was a source of great pride. She had hurt him, she knew it, and she had a great desire to go after him, to explain, to ask his forgiveness, and to apologize for their behavior.

But she did none of those things. For when his gaze locked on hers, even though it was for the briefest of moments, and neither said a word or showed by a look what the other was thinking, she made an astonishing discovery. She was so startled by it that it sucked the air from her lungs and sent her giddy. She leaned back against the wall to stop herself pitching forward, her knees giving way and unsteady on her feet. She was so light-headed she thought she might faint. She knew she would not make it across the room without swaying. But there was one thing of which she was definite. As confidently as she knew Monday followed Sunday, she realized beyond any doubt that she was deeply and unutterably in love, and with the wrong man.

EIGHTEEN

Of all the places and times too numerous to count that they had been in each other's company, it took this place, a woolen mill, and a marriage proposal from another, for Mary to come to the astonishing realization she was in love, and had always been in love with Mr. Christopher Bryce.

From their very first introduction, when he had come to call on her husband, he had stirred within her an indefinable something which niggled and hungered inside her and would not let go. She had done her best to suppress this feeling with every fiber of her being, because she was married. And because she was married, and because her mother had taught her this from a young girl, she believed that to desire a man who was not her husband was wicked, and in a married woman who was a mother, it was also unnatural and abhorrent.

But her mother's dictum on female desire and marriage left her confused and troubled. For time spent living with her cousin the Duchess of Roxton had shown her a different world, one that contradicted every dictate her mother uttered. She had witnessed the playfulness that existed between the Duke and Duchess, how unselfconscious they were before family. They often held hands, shared a tender kiss, and could sit for hours together, comfortable in each other's company without saying a word. Above all, they were always kind to one another. It was obvious, even to a girl of Mary's tender years, that the ducal couple were deeply in love.

But in her marriage to Sir Gerald she had experienced none of these things, leaving her so emotionally and physically cold that she thought herself incapable of enjoying intimacy, and wondering if she was at all desirable. And while her husband was alive she found it effortless to suppress her natural inclinations and feelings.

When she was made a widow she continued along the same path, consumed with her uncertain future, and blind to all possibilities where love and all physical expression of love were concerned. So accustomed was she to the Squire's presence at Abbeywood that she failed to see him in any other light, any feelings she had for him long ago buried and unlikely ever to surface from the depths of her unresponsive heart.

And then they had shared that kiss in her bedchamber, reigniting the spark of desire she had first felt on that first meeting. And now, in this moment, as she watched Christopher turn and disappear up the stairwell carrying Rory, she knew beyond doubt that she loved him. And she knew that he loved her. He had told her so, but now she believed him. Such thoughts made her tingle with happiness. She wanted to go to him, to tell him, for him to know that his love was reciprocated a hundred times over. And then, from somewhere far off beyond her thoughts she heard a voice calling to her, and the warmth that came with loving and knowing she was loved drained away, leaving her cold and overcome with an inexplicable bewilderment and a palpable turmoil.

And with awareness came veracity. What was the point of telling Christopher she loved him when she was not free to act upon her feelings? She must and would accept Evelyn's marriage proposal. She could not, in good conscience, refuse Evelyn, and the honor done her. It was the right decision for her future, and Teddy's. She was expected to marry well, and a man from within her own social sphere. Evelyn and she were well-suited. They came from the same family and social strata. They shared a history, and they loved one another. It would be the match of the season!

And so she knew that in a month's time, when Evelyn asked her to become his wife, she would accept him, despite knowing that the love she had for him was quite different from the feelings she had for Christopher. The love for her cousin was safe, secure, and predictable. She knew exactly what to expect. What she felt for Christopher was something else entirely, leaving her bewildered, breathless, and floating in a raging sea of unforeseen possibilities.

And with veracity came honesty. She knew with depressing certainty she was her mother's daughter. The Countess's voice infiltrated her jumbled thoughts, pontificating on the subject of marriage: There could be no future for the son of a local squire and the daughter of an earl. Everyone knew that a female horse bred with a male donkey produced a jackass, a pariah that was neither a horse nor a donkey. The daughter of a squire might marry up into the nobility, but the daughters of the nobility did not marry down.

So it was with a heavy heart and a soul-deep sadness that she made the decision it was best for the peace of mind of all concerned not to act upon her feelings. And so she had come full circle. She was left numb and unresponsive. It took her several moments before she realized it was Evelyn who owned the voice that was calling to her, and that he was not far off at all.

He was still beside her, and he was asking if she was well, and did she wish to follow the others upstairs to see the rest of the mill? She shook her head. She would prefer to sit quietly for a moment on the step. And so he sat with her.

"Give me your fan, *ma chérie*," he ordered gently. When she unconsciously pulled it from a pocket tied beneath her skirts he took it, flicked it open and fluttered it like a woman. He fanned cool air across her flushed face, and when he had her attention, said quietly, "This month I am away is my gift to you to live it as you please."

"A gift?" Mary blinked at him, not understanding, yet he knew he had her complete attention.

"Yes. I may present as self-absorbed as Narcissus, but as an agent of the crown I am well trained in deception and knowing when someone is being deceitful. I can ferret out a person's innermost feelings, their secret desires that can be leveraged against them." He stopped fluttering the fan and smiled gently. "I am not blind, nor do I lack feeling. I see that the Squire stirs your blood, and that is no bad thing—Mary! Do not shake your head or turn your head away. Look at me!" When she met his gaze openly he said with a straightforwardness that shocked her, "If you do not satisfy yourself as to your feelings for this man, then you will always wonder, and that will be detrimental to both of us. I want a wife who is loyal in deed and thought. I also want a wife who knows something of the marriage bed. I never was one to prize virginity. Sexual inexperience is tedious in the extreme."

"But—I have a child! How can you—"

"Gerry was a pig. I would wager he never thought of your needs, and only satisfied himself. That is not making love. In its simplest form it is a bestial mounting for the purposes of procreation; at its most selfish, self-satisfaction of male carnal need."

"Please, Eve. I do not want—How can you talk to me about such th—"

"Because I was just like him—well, perhaps not as disgusting and definitely not as repulsive, but when I was much younger I only cared for my music. I did not care the snap of two fingers for the needs of the women I bedded. Not even Dominique."

"Oh, Eve! But she was your wife!"

"And you were gluttonous Gerry's wife. And thus I rest my case. But since poor Dominique's death I have had a vast experience of women. I am very sure my cavorting would turn your glorious hair white from shock. But I do not regret, need, or want to satisfy my curiosity further where other women are concerned. But you, *ma chérie*, have no experience whatsoever of what it is to make love and—"

"But surely, as my husband, it would be your place to-to make me understand—*to know*—what it is to make love?"

"But that still leaves us with the dilemma of your unsatisfied lust for Squire Worthy—"

"Eve! I-I—How can you know—" Mary began to stutter, cheeks drained of color.

"Which is why I am gifting you this month. You deserve to know how it is to be made love to, to enjoy the experience of making love. You need to expunge the memory of what you suffered at the hands of your brute of a husband. Besides, given your Squire's fascinating past in the Italian states, I am confident he'll do all in his power to prove himself an ideal lover."

Mary stared at Evelyn wonderingly. "And you would be content with such arrangement?"

"If at the end of the month your—um—*curiosity* is well and truly satisfied, and you accept my proposal of marriage, then such an arrangement will have benefits for us both."

"And what of him? He is such an honorable man... I cannot imagine he will agree."

At that Evelyn threw back his head and laughed. Mary did not see what there was to amuse him.

"Oh he's made a most successful transformation to Squire Worthy, to be sure. None here in this backwater has the imagination to think him anything else than what he presents to the world. And I have no doubts that this is how he wishes to spend the rest of his dull days. But that does not negate his past as a much sought-after cicisbeo—"

Mary wrinkled her little nose. "Cic—*cicisbeo*? What is this cicisbeo? And how do you know this about him? Did you spy on him when he lived abroad?"

"Ah! I have said too much. That is for you to ask him." He playfully tapped Mary under the chin with her fan, then handed it back to her and got to his feet. Helping her up, he said with a smile, "And if he esteems you as much as I think he does, and because he is tediously principled, he will want to confess all. You must remember that if you ask, you may receive a response that makes you wish you had not! Now let us rejoin the picnic party before our companions cast us adrift completely!"

W‍HEN M‍ARY AND E‍VELYN REJOINED THE OTHERS, THEY WERE congregated at the base of the staircase, and a considerable discussion was taking place on descending to the lower floor to inspect the workings of the waterwheel.

Christopher warned them not to be startled by the thunderous noise. That this was perfectly ordinary and was made by the rushing water as it was funneled along a narrow canal to drop onto the waterwheel, the weight of the falling water driving the wheel's blades and forcing it to turn. He stressed that the deafening noise was so great that it made it impossible to converse; even shouting at one another at close quarters was useless. He said it was exceedingly important for them all to follow direction, to not wander, and to do precisely as he instructed. Above all, they must be vigilant of each other at all times. He said this with a smile at Teddy, who was listening to him intently, eyes wide and mouth at half-cock. When she nodded her obedience, he winked at her, then proceeded to tell the group he hoped that the noise and his instructions would not reduce their enjoyment or wonder of Mr. Smeaton's marvelous waterwheel.

Everyone readied to descend the stairs, Teddy holding Christopher's hand, and Rory happy to take her grandfather's arm and use her walking stick to steady herself as there were only a dozen or so steps and these she could manage quite easily. But Lord Shrewsbury surprised them, and everyone paused and looked at him when he said gravely,

"I think it best if the ladies and the child remain here. I'm concerned about the noise, that it will be too great for female sensibilities. In light of what Mr. Bryce cautioned about not being able to hear or speak above the din, what if one of you were to faint, it could be impossible to summon help. Don't you agree, Vallentine?"

"Couldn't agree more, my lord! There's a frightful racket already coming up through the floorboards that I do not wonder the noise below will be monstrously bad for female nerves."

"But—Grand!" Rory whispered, astonished. "How can you think me so weak as to faint at the sound of a waterwheel?" She squeezed his forearm. "You must know how much I have longed to see one in operation, particularly the work of Mr. Smeaton." She appealed to Christopher. "Mr. Bryce, Mr. Smeaton is this country's foremost *civil* engineer, is he not? And best known for his tower at Eddystone Rocks."

"That is so, my lady," Christopher agreed, impressed by Rory's knowledge. "The lighthouse was indeed designed by him, and has since saved many ships and lives." He smiled at her, then said to her grandfather, "My lord, I specifically chose Mr. Smeaton to design and have built this waterwheel under our feet because I believe his to be the best and most efficient power device known today. In fact, for his research into the mechanics of waterwheels and windmills he was awarded the Copley Medal. Anyone with a keen interest in the scientific would not want to miss the opportunity to see for themselves Smeaton's wheel in operation."

"There, Grand! Mr. Bryce has one of the best—if not *the* best— waterwheels in the country! And we saw on the floors above how it powers all those waterframes to spin yarn so much the quicker than can be done by one woman at her spinning wheel. How many yarns more per frame, Mr. Bryce?"

"Ninety-six or a little more, my lady."

"Is that not an astonishing number, Grand? Such a waterwheel must be a marvel indeed! So you see why I cannot miss this opportunity to view it at firsthand."

Lord Shrewsbury patted her hand with a smile, and looked to be wavering in his decision, when Mr. Philip Audley added his voice to the argument, as if he were part of the discussion and had been personally appealed to.

"My dear Lady Fitzstuart," said the Duke of Roxton's secretary, with a patronizing smile and a sigh of resignation, even going so far as to shake his head at her slightly. "What is the viewing of a waterwheel when compared to your health and safety? I humbly add my entreaties to Lord Shrewsbury's, that he is in the right in this. I fear any machinery that has the power to drive such noisome contraptions and at such speed must be as loud as the loudest thunderclap. And does not a thunderclap cause one to jump in fright?" He sniffed in the direction of Christopher without looking at him, and his nostrils pinched with disdain, before he looked about and addressed the others. "It behooves us, does it not, to show some Christian charity and forgive Mr. Bryce his insensitivity in suggesting that the ladies descend into what would for them equate to the pits of hell, to view such an alarming device. For surely such a suggestion demonstrates a marked lack of sensibility and an ignorance of the delicate sensibilities possessed by a female belonging to a station far above his own. He forgets, being as he is surrounded by females of farming stock, bred up from the cradle, much like mules, to labor long and hard. Such women share the dull sensibilities of their masters; no noise is too great to cause them a fright. And no doubt that is the reason they are well-suited to this mercantile enterprise. But we who have spent our entire lives esteeming the fragile beauty and delicacy of those of the highest rank, of which you, my dear Lady Fitzstuart and my dear Lady Mary are at its apex, know very well how you should be treated, and would never suffer you to be exposed to such unpleasantness. And I can say with confidence that my esteemed employer, His Grace of Roxton, would most certainly agree with me in this."

He ended with a confident smile and a bow to each.

The immediate response to this convoluted and derisory speech was one of awed silence. Everyone was still digesting the secretary's words and wondering what to offer by way of reply to the man's overt condescension, not to mention gall, at the complete lack of manners and blatant insolence directed at their host, when, to the collective amazement, a spirited rebuttal came, not from Rory, or her grandfather, or the Squire, but from the Lady Mary. And such was her outrage that she was oblivious to her passionate defense of the Squire, but he was not, nor was anyone else.

This Mary, the Lady Mary Cavendish who always chose her words carefully, who stood ramrod straight, who was aloof and haughty with those unknown to her, and when in the presence of her mother never escaped her shadow. This same Mary now stepped out of that shadow, words tumbling forth, hands gesticulating, and violet eyes bright, damp, and fierce. This Mary was a revelation to all, but not to Evelyn, nor to Christopher. It would have surprised both men to know they shared a private satisfaction—Evelyn because he had seen glimpses of this Mary while they were growing up together and so knew she still existed somewhere within her; and Christopher because he always believed that just below her haughty exterior was this Mary just waiting to burst forth and be recognized—his true Mary.

"Who are you, sir, to dare to presume to know me or my sister, Lady Fitzstuart?" Mary enunciated, voice trembling with controlled anger. And with every word uttered, her voice grew in strength and confidence, and no one spoke and everyone kept their gaze upon her. "Who are you to belittle Mr. Bryce? You come here as my cousin Roxton's representative, and we have tolerated you at Abbeywood for years only because you are the Duke's instrument. But you have forgotten that simple premise in your conceit. My cousin would never, not in a hundred lifetimes, scorn the labors of his tenants who work from daylight to dusk on his behalf, and who strive to make a life for themselves. He is modest and intelligent enough to know what he owes them, and they him. And they esteem him all the more because of it. Just as Mr. Bryce appreciates his mill workers and is a fair and just master.

"But you, Mr. Audley, are so arrogant as to dismiss him and the good, hard-working people of this vale, when it is such people to whom you should be grateful. Have you never given a thought to who makes your clothes, prepares your food, supplies the paper and quills and ink you use as His Grace's secretary? Are those good people so beneath your notice merely because they are of common birth? I tend to my beehives, feed my hens, and collect their eggs. I churn butter and turn cheese wheels. These are necessary tasks for a working farm. They also require the use of my hands, these *fine hands* which you think are fit only to embroider and play a pianoforte because I am a lady. And yet you deem such farming skills as I engage in as only worthy of the wives and daughters of farming stock you insultingly called *mules*?! Am I too then a mule, Mr. Audley? No! Do not speak. I have no time for your fawning platitudes.

"I am very proud to have contributed to Abbeywood's production. And if I were to own to a truth, I have gained far greater satisfaction living and working—yes, *working*, Mr. Audley—here in the vale amongst its people than all the parading about in fine silks in Society drawing rooms! Nor would my cousin ever treat Mr. Bryce with such condescension as you presume to do, sir! You think because I have kept quiet all these years, that I approve of your despicable behavior? You think I do not see, hear, *feel* how you've done your best to make his tenure as steward unwelcoming and demeaning at every turn? He has only ever wanted Abbeywood to thrive so that my nephew will have an inheritance worth having; something my husband never spent an ounce of thought on. Indeed, I am very sure Sir Gerald was intent on running the estate dry so Jack would have nothing. And yet in a mere two years Mr. Bryce has managed to give my nephew, a boy who is not even his relative, a future worth having.

"And you know this, Mr. Audley. It stares you in the face every time you draw up a chair to inspect the ledgers Mr. Bryce and his assistant Mr. Deed so carefully prepare. You have pored over every plus and minus, every calculation hoping upon hope to find a fault in their accounting. And that is not because you care one jot for the estate. You may even crave His Grace's praise for your exertions on his behalf, but I am convinced now more than ever that your petty-minded behavior is governed by a bitter and discontented disposition. You could have been so much better than you are if you had only been humble and taken pride in your achievements, and we would have thought the more of you for that."

She took a deep breath and put up her chin, gaze still very much on the red-faced secretary, and held her hands lightly in front of her and squared her shoulders.

"I will be writing to His Grace to have you relieved from your obligations at Abbeywood. My cousin can appoint another in your place, though I think that, too, unnecessary, and will tell him so. Now signal to me that you have understood all I have said, then apologize to Mr. Bryce. Then you may leave us for some quiet reflection by the mill pond until nuncheon is ready."

The secretary quickly made her an obedient bow, eyes downcast, but when he hesitated to turn to Christopher to do the same, Shrewsbury growled at him to get on with it. He muttered a clipped apology to the Squire, bowed, and strode from the millhouse without making eye contact with anyone. Evelyn followed him to the door and momentarily blocked his exit.

"Quite right of you to slink off with your tail between your legs. But don't go far. Shrewsbury and I have a few questions that require answers."

Philip Audley looked up into Evelyn's blue eyes, and there was no contrition in his look or in his voice. In fact there was a hint of menace in his tone, and gone was all semblance of patronizing humility.

"Rest assured, my lord, I will not go far. I have my own questions to bring to that discussion. Now if you will get out of my way. I find I cannot breathe in air thick with patrician self-righteousness."

Evelyn slapped his back. "Good. Soon you won't have to!" and threw back his head with a harsh laugh and stepped away from the door with an exaggerated bow of leave, unnerving the secretary, which was Evelyn's intent.

Mary watched them, and not hearing their harsh whispered exchange, she smiled at her cousin's theatrics, then sighed as if with relief. She was surprised by the wave of calm that settled on her after such an uncharacteristic outburst. At the very least she expected to be ill at ease. But she was not. And as the slighted secretary disappeared outside, into the room stepped her lady's maid who, with a nod in her direction, let Mary know that nuncheon was ready to be served. So she turned to her daughter, who was regarding her quizzically, unsure if her mother was still angry. It did not escape her notice that twice Teddy had glanced at Christopher, as if requiring his reassurance all was still right with her world. This only deepened Mary's feelings. For surely, to her daughter here was the only man who had ever truly been a father to her.

When Mary put out her hand with a smile, Teddy eagerly took hold of her fingers. She then pulled her into her arms, turned to Rory and said,

"Would you be exceedingly disappointed if I asked you to contain your curiosity until after we eat? I am very sure a respite and refreshment will revive you—everyone," she added glancing about the small space, careful not to indicate to anyone else she was making a veiled reference to Rory's pregnancy. "Once we're fortified, we'll be able to give our full attention to Smeaton's waterwheel. What say you, Teddy? Shall we share some of Cook's special strawberry jam with our guests?"

"Strawberry? Truly?"

"Yes, and the walnut pickle, because I know it is Lord Vallentine's particular favorite."

She glanced over Teddy's head at Evelyn, who now stood beside the Squire, and resisted the urge to look at Christopher, smiling at her cousin when he put up his brows in acknowledgment of her veiled reminder he had stolen that particular pickle from the pantry as a ghost.

"And the pickled cucumbers?" asked Teddy. "Did you remember the pickled cucumbers, because they're Uncle Bryce's favorite."

Mary looked down into Teddy's upturned smiling face and kissed her forehead.

"Yes! I remembered. He told us at dinner. And yes, I had Cook pack a bottle of those too."

Teddy grinned and hunched her shoulders, much more herself since her mother's uncharacteristic angry outburst. She looked over at Christopher to see his reaction, but he was not given the opportunity to respond because Evelyn elbowed him in the ribs to get his attention.

"Pickled cucumbers, Silvanus?" he purred and pulled a face. "Glad the walnut pickle is all mine. She will be too, in a month's time. And yet I do like to offer my opposition a sporting chance. Makes the getting and keeping that much more worthwhile. After nuncheon, before you start boring on about waterwheels, let's you and I take a stroll. You'll want to hear what I propose, believe me."

NINETEEN

"HERE WE ARE, TAKING THAT STROLL. SO WHAT IS IT YOU WANT?"

Christopher stopped by the first sluice gate, turned and looked back the way they had come, along the path that followed the canal carrying rushing water away from the millhouse. He and Evelyn were distant enough from the picnic party not to be overheard, but still within line of sight to keep an eye on the guests, and the servants attending to them. And while the picnic party sat in state around a table heavy with silver, porcelain, and a banquet fit for any lord's great hall, the mill workers, cottage spinners, and their families were enjoying a modest feast of their own down by the stream.

His workers appreciated the few hours' rest and recreation out-of-doors, and the lamb stew, bread, parsnip cakes, and cider he'd provided, but what they most valued was this opportunity to observe the nobility at such close quarters. The village on market days was as far as most had ventured in their lives. So the vicar and his good wife, and the local squires and their families were as high up the social ladder as any of them had seen, and then only from afar. Not even the Lady Mary Cavendish, who everyone knew was the most titled lady in the vale, had ever crossed to this side of the Puzzlewood. So to discover she was as pretty as commonly reported, with bright, glossy red hair the same color as flame, was not very tall, and had a fine delicate nose and large eyes, was very satisfactory indeed.

In fact watching her and her noble companions at the picnic table was a high treat that Christopher knew would be talked about for weeks, if not months to come, and be stamped in the collective memory forever. Grandparents would tell their grandchildren about the time gentlemen and ladies with skin as white and as clean as fresh snow, and everyone dressed in richly embroidered velvets and silks, came to picnic at the mill. The ladies with dyed ostrich plumes in their broad-brimmed silk straw hats, smiling behind fluttering fans, and the gentlemen with lace at their wrists using silver knife and fork, and drinking from goblets that were instantly refilled by servants who ran around catering to their every whim.

It was a lovely idyll and worthy of oils. The warmth of the sun bathed the autumnal colors of the woods on the hills behind them in a golden glow, the noble grouping picnicking by the stream so out of context to their surroundings that they could be mistaken for elfin lords and faerie queens come out of hiding to dine. But with gray clouds rolling in from the northeast, Christopher predicted rain before the light began to fade to dusk. And he had yet to take the guests on a tour of the waterwheel before their return to Abbeywood, a journey which would be at least an hour longer because it was uphill. And if the rain came, the tracks would turn to slush, and if night fell, the journey would be impossible.

So Evelyn needing a private word with him only added to Christopher's anxiousness. He really had no wish to hear what Mary's cousin had to say, nor could he guess what it could be about, though he wondered if it had to do with Philip Audley's impending incarceration for treason, and wanting his cooperation for some scheme to take the secretary into custody. That said, looking over at the man seated across from Lord Shrewsbury enjoying a glass of wine and a second pear tart, Audley either had no idea he'd been found out, or was exceedingly arrogant in his belief he had outsmarted even England's Spymaster General, and become complacent. Christopher believed Audley guilty of the latter.

So what did Evelyn want with him? he wondered, managing to temper his apprehension and face his lordship without giving away his thoughts. And then Evelyn confounded him.

"Look at 'em," Evelyn said, leaning his shoulder blades up against the timber bulkhead of the sluice gate and lifting his long chin in direction of the picnic party. "Two of the prettiest flowers in the kingdom and thank God neither is a gormless ornament. But then m'cousin Dair wouldn't have married anything less than a rare jewel. And Lady Fitzstuart is about as rare as they come. As for our ruby, well, we're partial, ain't we? Ha! I always knew there was fire under that ice! Can't possess hair like that and not have a passionate nature. She—"

"Listen, Vallentine or Stretham-Ely, or whatever it is you call your-self—Apollo will do! If you've brought me out here to wax lyrical about your cousin and what she means to you, then I'll stop you there. Those are rain clouds, and the ladies would like to see Smeaton's water-wheel before—"

"She gave quite a speech, didn't she?" Evelyn continued as if Christopher hadn't spoken.

"Yes... Yes, she did."

"The sort of speech a Parliamentarian gives in the House when they believe wholeheartedly in what they're saying, one full of convic-tion tinged with aggrieved indignation. I'm so pleased I was there to hear it. I always knew she had it in her but it still surprised me. She has more in common with her cousin—my Tante Antonia—than she real-izes. If only she would embrace Tante Antonia's exuberance... I thought that too much to ask after ten years living with Gerry. Of course my first thought was that she would never have made such an impassioned speech if Gerry were still alive. He was overbearing, figu-ratively and literally, and her mother..." Evelyn shuddered. "Colder than a reptile. But my second thought was that my first thought was wrong. My guess is that eventually, even if Gerry had lived, Mary would've found a way to chip her way out of the ice block those two had encased her in. But that would not have helped her, or you, would it? Because you're one of those damnably principled fellows like our cousin Roxton. The two of you would get along splendidly. Possibly be wary on first meeting and think the other an arrogant prude, and you'd both be right!"

"You've never given a direct response in your life, have you?"

Evelyn laughed in his annoying high-pitched way.

"What would be the fun in that? I do so like to prod and poke the metaphorical wound of unconsummated love. It's just a pity I can no longer play my viola at the same time as I pontificate. Makes for a dramatic accompaniment to one's feelings! I used to, y'know. Prance about in high heels, viola under m'chin, providing endless entertain-ment and wet eyes for my audience—mostly women, but there were my fellow musicians who appreciated my compositions. Light as meringue, but delicious nonetheless." He sighed heavily. "Sadly, those heady days are behind me, as are my two fingers!" He laughed again and shook his head. "But let's not get maudlin on *my* behalf. I'm here to talk about *you* and m'cousin—"

"I certainly won't discuss the Lady Mary with you."

Evelyn gave Christopher a friendly punch in the shoulder. "Do shelve that stubborn streak and shut up, Squire Backwater. The rain is coming and I've something to say."

"And you haven't yet?"

"Touché. Now be quiet and listen. And I will be succinct for your benefit, because I fear it is the only way you will comprehend what it is I am offering you." He glanced up at Christopher and seeing he had his full attention, continued. "I said in the millhouse Mary is to be mine in a month's time. You cannot have failed to comprehend what I meant by that, surely? But just in case you are incredulous, or think me capable of acting the scoundrel with m'own cousin, let me assure you I mean to ask her to marry me. I am confident she will accept my offer. I may be a bit tatty around the edges these days, and I am missing partial digits, but I'm still quite a catch. I come with an earldom and a great pile of stone somewhere up north. Could marry a pretty little virgin straight out of the schoolroom—and plenty of mamas would sacrifice their daughters for a title and pedigree like mine—if that was my wish, but it isn't. So you can lift that ugly frown back up off your manly chest. Virgins don't interest me. Mary does. And I know she interests you, too, Silvanus—mightily interests you, and has done for years, is my guess. So. Tell me: What are you going to do about it?"

"About it? About *what*?"

Evelyn threw a hand in the air and rolled his eyes. "This perfectly wonderful marriage proposal of mine to make Mary my countess, that's what."

Christopher drew in a breath and swallowed. It was the only visible sign of emotion he allowed himself to this life-crushing news.

Of course. This was no surprise. But to hear it said out loud... That made it fixed. It also made perfect sense. Two noble cousins. Two childhood friends—secret sweethearts—married to others and now free to marry one another. A romantically fitting outcome. Why did he think it would be any different? He always knew Mary had to remarry, and marry well. But a little part of him, even if it was only the size of his smallest toe, believed in the possibility that when she did, it would be for love, and to him. He loved her. She loved him. It had been left unsaid between them and yet *he* knew, and so did *she*. It was a feeling, a sense, which was always with him. And so he had allowed himself to dream of asking her, and in his dream she always said yes. It was that simple.

But now...

That dream was but a daydream, and would remain so. It was for the best. And best to know sooner rather than later. Best to get on with life. He had so much to do. Perhaps he would take Kate on holiday to the seaside, let her feel the salt air in her hair and on her skin, the sand under feet. She always did love the sea...

Mary was to marry her cousin in a month... She would become the Countess of Stretham-Ely and leave the vale to live anywhere but here...

Mentally he turned away to face the wall, gut tightening and head pounding, and curled himself into a ball. And then the wall collapsed, leaving him in pitch black. Was he still curled on the floor, or was he floating? All he knew was that he was surrounded by nothingness. He felt nothing. He thought nothing. There was nothing left for him to say, or do, or want, or need. Ever. He wondered if he were going mad. He knew he was numb...

With supreme effort of will he forced his body to respond. And while he mentally remained in this emotionless void, spinning in blackness, he managed to make his limbs obey to make Evelyn a formal bow. And when he straightened and met the nobleman's gaze, he made certain he did not blink or look away, but stayed staring into his icy blue eyes. And then from somewhere far off he heard his own voice echoing in his ears, flat and detached and cold. And all he wanted to do was howl his despair at the moon.

"I wish you happy, my lord. She deserves—she deserves to be happy—to be your countess. Thank-you for—for telling me here, away from—away from—If you'll excuse me, I must see to the mill—"

"No! No you don't!" Evelyn grabbed his coat sleeve. "Don't walk away from me, Silvanus! I'm not done with you."

Christopher swayed and stared at the fingers holding fast to his arm, not knowing what he was supposed to do. But there was one thing he knew he wanted, and knew he had power over, and that was to put distance between him and this man, and fast, before he did something he regretted. The only thought that kept him in check was knowing that as they stood on higher ground at the sluice gate, he was in full view not only of his workers and their families, but also of those seated about the table. Mary sat facing him, and Teddy was down by the stream watching the village children cast lines into the water. And both could see him and Lord Vallentine seemingly in congenial conversation.

He jerked his mind and his arm free.

"But I'm done with you, my lord. And I've offered you my felicitations. Now I must return to my guests."

Evelyn blocked Christopher's exit. With both arms outstretched and palms flat on the top of the sluice gate frame, there was nowhere for Christopher to go unless he turned away and crossed to the bank.

But that would leave him on the wrong side of the canal. He had to get past Evelyn, and he did not want to knock him out of the way for fear of him toppling over and into the fast-flowing water; he would surely drown. So he waited, a glance down at the rushing water beneath their boots.

"I've not asked her—yet," Evelyn told him. "She knows my intentions. She has a month to think it over. But then," he added, sticking out his bottom lip, "she is free to refuse me, if that is her wish."

That did bring Christopher hurtling out of the abyss of numbed despair to huff with incredulous anger,

"Refuse to marry you? Her closest cousin? Whom she has known since her childhood? You're offering her safety, security, wealth, and the title of countess. Oh, and a marriage vastly different from her first. Refuse you? Ha! I think not! She's been too well-trained, bred up from the cradle to know her own worth and yours. If you think for one moment she'll not accept a marriage proposal from you, then you're battered on the inside as well as out! It's a noble family alliance everyone will whole heartedly embrace. Her witch of a mother will be in seventh heaven. That should at least put a stop to her badgering; and not soon enough! And whatever your past indiscretions, they'll be forgiven. Roxton will slap your back with a hearty congratulations. Bravo! You'll be the hero of the hour."

Evelyn rolled his eyes and looked sheepish. "I know. I know. Burden of family expectation fulfilled and all that."

Christopher stepped up to him menacingly. "You'd best be doing this for the right reasons, Apollo, or so help me I'll—"

"—break every bone in my noble body? Rattle m'bone box? Call me out?" Far from cowering, Evelyn eyed him up and down with a smirk. "I dare say you'd like to do all three. But fortunately for me we are not social equals. So a duel ain't on the cards, is it? Besides, I didn't bring you out here to goad you with the news of our impending engagement, but, as I told you earlier in our full and frank discussion, to give you fair warning and fair play"

"*Fair play?* This isn't some sort of game! I won't be drawn in to satisfy some perverse amusement."

It was Evelyn's turn to huff. "Won't you? And I thought you were in love with M—"

"Of course I'm in love with her! You know I'm in love with her. I have been for eight *excruciating* years. And now you've goaded me into finally saying it out loud. Bravo, my lord!"

Evelyn regarded Christopher coolly and enunciated, "So I say again, Silvanus: What are you going to do about it?"

Christopher threw a hand into the air. He wanted to look out across the stream to the picnic party, to see if Mary was still there. Instead, he stared down at the rushing water. He wasn't given to dramatic gestures, and up until a moment ago, he would not have thought himself capable of a heated outburst either. Other people—Kate—behaved in such a fashion; he was always pragmatic and phlegmatic to a fault. His father said to be a good farmer required patience; to know how to wait, and with good grace. But not today. And, so it seemed, not where his feelings for Mary were concerned. With the internal void of nothingness threatening to swallow him up, he took a deep breath, wanting this conversation over with, and said quietly, "What would you have me do about it?"

"Ah! Now that's more like it! I'll tell you what I told Mary. I'm going away for a month. Some unfinished business for Shrewsbury. What happens while I'm away is of supreme indifference to me. It's what happens once I return that is most important. So I'm contracting you to look after her while I'm gone. You'll be her cicesbeo—"

"I'll be her *what*?"

"Oh do listen! The rain is coming. You know very well what I'm talking about."

"I will not take on such a role with her!"

"Whyever not? You did it often enough in Lucca. Half a dozen times in fact."

"That was completely different. There can be no comparison."

"That's true. Mary doesn't have an understanding elderly husband to make up a threesome at cards, or to fund your lifestyle, or turn a blind eye when his much-younger wife spends the night with her lover. And poor Mary is vastly more under-experienced in the bedroom than were your previous contracted lovers."

"Never!"

"And we won't commit anything to paper, not in this country. People wouldn't understand. What is a perfectly acceptable arrangement in Lucca is considered sordid in the extreme here. Fellows here are emasculated by such an arrangement, but not I! So, Silvanus, it will be a gentleman's verbal agreement. But in every other respect, I'm perfectly amenable to such an arrangement."

"You *are* battered in the brain if you think I'll agree to it!"

Evelyn feigned surprise. "But why would you refuse? I'm giving you permission to be my future wife's lover—for you to have unlimited access to her person for four weeks. This is the woman who has kept you throbbing for release for eight years—you did use the word *excruciating*—and you're going to decline such a golden opportunity? You're the one with gruel for brains, Silvanus! Dear me, you never balked at a contract in the past—"

"That was different! *I* was different! *She* is different!"

"Yes. Love changes everything, doesn't it? More's the pity…" Evelyn looked Christopher up and down, smiled and said flippantly, his tone at odds with the hard glint in his eye, "Then do it for love, Silvanus. Make her happy for four weeks. Give her some of that vast carnal experience you acquired as the kept lover of other men's wives. Give her a wicked past. Something to make her blush and smile once in a while when she's sitting at her stitchery, the countess of my pile up north."

"She'd never agree to such an arrangement! She—"

"—doesn't have to know. But what she does know is that I'm not opposed to her having a brief, torrid affair—with you. I've given her permission."

"How magnanimous of you!"

Evelyn sighed and waved a hand, "I thought so."

Christopher had second thoughts about throwing him into the canal. His eyes narrowed. "Why are you doing this? Why are you torturing me? Or should I ask the obvious: What's in it for you?"

"I do want her to be happy. But you're right to be suspicious. I'm not altruistic. As far as I'm concerned you can keep your physical frustrations bottled until you pop. But when Mary chooses to marry me, then I'll have her all to myself, body and soul." His mouth twitched. "And she'll know a thing or two about making love, thanks to you. Which means her mind won't wander to what might have been—with you. She'll know, and it won't matter a jot to me, or to her."

"No."

Evelyn let out a small sigh of resignation and pushed himself away from the wooden cross post of the sluice gate and stood tall. He brushed his hands, and after pulling on the lace at both his wrists he looked up at Christopher. He saw the stubbornness in the hard clench to the strong jaw. But then he chanced to look into the Squire's damp brown eyes—eyes that reminded him of Deborah Roxton—and they were a window to a different story. Here was conflict, desolation, and uncertainty writ large, indication the Squire was experiencing an internal moral struggle of epic proportions. So Evelyn appealed to him in a way he knew would allow Christopher to seriously consider the proposal he was offering him.

"Very well. Have it your way," he said, with a shrug of feigned indifference. "You still have a month. A month to accomplish what you haven't been able to in the eight years you've known each other.

You have a month to convince her you're the better man and she should marry you."

Evelyn then turned and walked back to join the picnic party. Christopher, a few paces behind, crossed to the mill where his millwright was waiting to speak with him. Neither man spoke of their conversation again, to anyone.

CHRISTOPHER WAS ABLE TO GIVE HIS GUESTS A TOUR OF THE waterwheel and have them all safely on their way well before the rainclouds rolled in to darken the sky, and which sent the villagers rushing to collect the cloth off the tenters to bring indoors before the heavens opened.

The wagon loaded with picnic things and those servants from Abbeywood who had accompanied it set off for home just as the picnic party re-entered the mill to see Smeaton's waterwheel in action.

The ladies, far from being disconcerted by the noise, were exhilarated, though they did clap their hands over their ears at the thunderous racket of rushing water as it fell onto the blades of the gigantic wooden wheel, driving it ever forward. No one spoke. No one would be heard had they tried. And when signaled to do so by Mr. Bryce, everyone returned to the upper floor, happy and satisfied that their visit to his mill was now complete, and a wonderful time was had by all. Rory waylaid the millwright and was deep in discussion about the natural powers of water and wind to turn various wheels and the subsequent generation of energy until her grandfather gently reminded her about the prospect of the entire party being soaked to their skins if they did not set off at once.

After much leave-taking and thanks, Teddy giving her Uncle Bryce a big hug because she was off on her month's stay with Granny at Cheltenham at first light, the ladies and Teddy set off for home accompanied by two of the farm's stablehands. Evelyn, Lord Shrewsbury, and Mr. Audley remained behind, the Spymaster giving the excuse that he had Crown business to discuss with the Squire, and so neither lady asked any further questions and went off none the wiser. The gentlemen would catch them up at the Puzzlewood.

But no sooner had the horses disappeared from view, the gentlemen waiting patiently for the ladies to be out of sight, than Philip Audley turned to Lord Shrewsbury and said with a condescending smile and his habitual sniff of disdain at Christopher,

"I can only assume you asked that I remain behind because this business with Mr. Bryce concerns Abbeywood. And no one knows the estate better than I—"

"Or its housekeeper!" Evelyn interrupted with a snort.

The secretary blinked. "I beg your pardon, my lord?"

Evelyn dug in a frock coat pocket and pulled out a small ceramic cylinder. This he dangled before Audley's gaze. "Recognize this?"

"No. But it looks to be a billet doux, my lord."

"Give the man a *macaron*."

It was Lord Shrewsbury's turn to snort. He shook his head and said to Evelyn, "He's cooler than an icebox in January, ain't he!"

"And where he's going it's all fire and brimstone, so he'll need plenty of ice," Evelyn quipped.

"If you have no further use of my time, I have work to get on with," Christopher stated, interrupting the private reverie between the Spymaster General and his subordinate.

"Eh? Not interested in seeing the thorn in your side get his come-uppance?" Shrewsbury asked, disappointed.

Christopher eyed the secretary, who stood ramrod straight and had yet to break a sweat. The man looked untouchable and unimpeachable. He had been subjected to this man's petty-minded arrogance time and again, all in the name of his ducal employer, and knew that had the secretary been the duke, he'd have been an overbearing tyrant, most particularly with his servants. He was also an opportunist and a suspected traitor to his King and country. If that were true, he deserved everything and more that Shrewsbury had planned for him. Yet, Christopher had no wish to see him suffer, or to watch his humiliation, so he shook his head.

"No."

"Very well. But we require your full cooperation. Your mill is requisitioned for Crown business—"

"*The mill?* Whatever for? I have workers, and—"

Evelyn interrupted Christopher with a dismissive wave. "Hold onto your cloth, Squire. Just for tonight. And just the lower floor." He forced a grin. "Your tour of Smeaton's waterwheel was most illuminating. I was skeptical at first, but his lordship was in the right. No one can hear you scream down there—"

"*Scream?*" interrupted the secretary but was ignored.

"You planned this from the off!" Christopher growled.

"Yes. We did," Evelyn replied with a smug smile. "But we also managed to give the ladies a lovely day out, did we not, my lord?"

"That we did. Ah! And here's your escort, Audley!"

The secretary looked over his shoulder. Two burly men stood in the doorway of the mill, and at Shrewsbury's beckoning stepped out into the light and came forward. At their backs were two more men of equal size. The secretary stared at the Spymaster General.

"I don't understand. *My* escort?"

"Your game's up, Mendacius," Evelyn said near the secretary's ear. "Best to come quietly. Best not to make a scene. Mrs. Keble did and she was dealt with, and it wasn't pretty—"

"Mrs. Keble? Dealt with? Wasn't *pretty*?" Philip Audley's eyes went wide and then his face lost color. He looked wildly about, at Shrewsbury, at Evelyn, at the two men who now stood at his back, and then finally he looked to Christopher and surprised everyone by appealing to him.

"Bryce! You cannot believe—This is outrageous! You know who I am. I am the Duke's secretary. I cannot be touched. They cannot touch me! You cannot allow this—"

"For the first time in your life, Audley, show some humility. And for God's sake, tell the truth."

With that Christopher turned on a boot heel and strode off in direction of his house, and despite the scuffles and sounds of struggle he left behind, he did not look back.

TWENTY

FIVE DAYS CAME AND WENT BEFORE MARY ENQUIRED OF THE steward's assistant if he had received any communication from Mr. Bryce. Mr. Deed had not. Two more days went by—two days that Christopher usually spent at Abbeywood, and this time did not. In two years he had never missed a day. Mary again summoned Mr. Deed to her drawing room. The little man was as mystified as she as to the Squire's absence.

She went for a stroll in the garden, woolen shawl tight about her shoulders, then sat at her escritoire to write the Squire a short note, one she had formulated in her head while out in the bracing fresh air. She wondered if his aunt was unwell, or he himself had taken ill. Though she thought the latter unlikely; he was as strong and as healthy as a prize stallion on race day, and she had never known him to be ill a day in his life. She enquired when he might next be at Abbeywood as she wished to discuss certain particulars concerning a visit to Treat after Christmas; her cousin the Duchess was due to deliver her baby in the new year.

With the letter written and the ink dry, she asked for Luke. But then she had second thoughts about sending it and was about to dismiss Luke when the youth startled her.

"M'lady, the master said if thou was to ask, I was to show ye."

"Ask? Ask you what, Luke?"

"'Bout the master's whereabouts. 'Bout where Mr. Bryce he be."

Mary sat up. She hoped she wasn't blushing.

"You know where he is?"

Luke nodded.

"And he asked that you take me to him?"

Luke nodded again.

Mary drew in a deep breath then stood, decided.

"Then take me."

Luke hesitated. And that made Mary anxious.

"What is it? He's not ill is he?"

The youth shook his head.

"No, m'lady. But thee rides to yon Puzzle, and then be a walk—a long walk—through the *vorest*. Thy ladyship will need thy boots and cape."

BOOTED AND CAPED, WITH THE HOOD UP OVER HER HAIR, MARY sat sidesaddle on her mount while Luke walked the mare deep into the Puzzlewood. About halfway in, he had Mary dismount. Leaving the mare tethered, he took her off the well-worn path, via a secret track that was no secret at all because it was used by journeymen, poachers, and travellers who walked the length of the Cotswolds. Particular markings on tree trunks showed the route. And while Mary had little idea of where she was in relation to the broader landscape, the canopy of entangled branches high above allowing for only filtered light, she felt the gradient rise under her boots and the angle of the trees change so that she knew they were walking along the ridge.

And then the canopy gave way to milky blue sky and she was on a rocky outcrop with the cool breeze chafing her cheeks, and looking out over the valley floor. Below her was Brycecomb Hall in all its honey-comb-colored glory, and to the left, the mill and its weavers' cottages, and running through both the river twisted and curled like a loose hair ribbon dropped from the head of a giantess.

Luke waited until Mary turned from the view, then led her down a winding path and back under cover of the wood. They were now descending into the vale. More than once she gave her gloved hand into the youth's firm grasp to help her around a particularly rocky outcrop of limestone, or over fallen trees, or across the smooth stepping stones that spanned fast-flowing rivulets. All done in silence and with only the sound of disturbed leaf litter under their feet, and the bubble of water over rocks, the forest eerily quiet of birdlife, flown to warmer climes for the onset of winter.

And then after what seemed like hours, but was less than one, the forest opened out into a small clearing. And on the edge of the clearing set back from the stream was a gamekeeper's cottage, its chimney smoking. But it was no ordinary cottage, for though it was built from the same yellow stone as the local cottages, this one had a columned façade, reminding Mary of an Italianate folly, a gentleman's whimsy found in the parklands of many a great house. Treat had a few such buildings scattered about its extensive grounds, so too did her childhood home of Fitzstuart Hall. But the folly was of passing interest, for by the stream, angling rod dangling out over the water, was the Squire in shirt sleeves and boots, faithful hound by his side.

"My lady."

"Mr. Bryce."

Christopher had set aside his angling rod, but had not moved from his spot on the bank. Mary came up to him, but halted a few feet away. Both were acutely aware of the other, but also that they were not alone, and the silence stretched. And then Lorenzo sat up, ears pricked. The movement was enough for Mary to take her eyes from Christopher and frown at his four-legged companion, gloved hands tightly held in front of her.

Her uneasiness gave Christopher an excuse to move, and he turned to Luke who was shuffling his feet, gaze respectfully on the moss under his shoes.

"Luke. Take Lorenzo home, and give this to Carlo for her ladyship's companion."

Christopher held out a letter which he'd taken from his waistcoat pocket. It was not sealed and did not need to be. Luke could not read. Carlo could not read English. It would be left to Fran to inform her mistress he would be gone for a few days, maybe longer. Though he had added a line for Fran's eyes only, that if he was urgently required Luke knew where to find him.

The youth took the letter and had Lorenzo to heel when he hesitated, a swift glance at Mary. "Will thee be takin' 'er ladyship 'ome?"

"When she wishes to return. In the meantime, you know what to say."

"Aye. I'll not let thee down, master."

Mary watched Luke, with Lorenzo trotting beside him, disappear back into the wood, then turned to focus on Christopher. Carefully removing the hood of her cape back off her hair and settling it on her shoulders she asked,

"What is he to say?"

Christopher closed the gap between them and smiled down at her. "Nothing. He is to say nothing."

"Oh!" Mary smiled up at him, but then tilted her chin in enquiry. "Why have you stayed away from Abbeywood since the picnic?"

"Why has it taken you this long to want to find me?"

"I didn't—I mean, I didn't know you were here. I thought—I thought you may have taken ill, or your aunt had, or-or perhaps after what I said at the mill you were displeased—that I may have embarrassed you."

"You think too much, my lady."

Mary nodded and sighed in resignation at the truth in his words. "Yes. I do." She met his gaze. "So why, if not for the reasons I stated, have you stayed away?"

"Because, my lady—Mary," he murmured, taking her face gently between his hands and lowering his mouth to within an inch of hers, "I am on the cusp of madness. All I think about is kissing you."

"You do? And so it is with me," she breathed in surprise, and in expectation of receiving his kiss went on tiptoe, hands pressed to the front of his wool waistcoat to steady herself. "And if you do not kiss me," she confessed shyly as she yielded her mouth, "I *will* go mad."

When they came up for air, she was disorientated and disconcerted because he had been the one to break off their heated kiss. He desperately wanted to go on kissing her, to scoop her up and carry her into the cottage and there, on the bed, make unbridled passionate love; to indulge in the kind of lovemaking where conscious thought and physical need were as one, where inhibition is cast to the winds, and where they would lie naked and exhausted amongst a tangle of limbs and bedding, utterly satiated.

That moment would come, he did not doubt it, but not yet, not until he was certain she was ready to be his, body and soul. And if he were truthful with himself, he was more than a little apprehensive at the prospect of initiating her into lovemaking. For he was convinced she had never made love. Ten years married to a selfish, self-satisfied pig of a man who locked her into her bedchamber could only have left her fearful and with an abhorrence of the sex act.

While for him, who had only bedded experienced women, lovemaking had always been uncomplicated, though it had at times bordered on the mechanical. So much so that once he left Lucca and closed that chapter of his life, he had not made love since. Not until

Mary had his physical appetite returned, only for it to be suppressed because she was married and thus unobtainable. He had wanted to make love to her for so many years now it was a dream rather than a possibility. And now that the dream was to be fulfilled, making love took on a whole new significance. It would be very different with Mary. He loved Mary beyond reason. And so the thought of bedding her threatened to overwhelm and cripple him. For his own sake as well as hers he needed to take matters slowly, with every action and reaction between them deliberate. There would be nothing perfunctory about making love with Mary.

Thus he released her, stepped away and smiled. Taking hold of her hand, he pushed back the edge of her glove to expose the white bare flesh of her wrist, and here he kissed her before straightening and smiling into her eyes. He kept hold of her hand.

"Come. Let me show you my humble lodgings."

"The cottage was here before my father turned it into his angling lodge," Christopher explained, standing on the shallow steps that led up to the front door. "The estate's gamekeeper lived here for a time, and then, after my grandfather made his discoveries, he built the gamekeeper another cottage on the other side of the wood, and kept this for himself. But it was my father who added the front colonnade to give the structure an Italianate appearance, built on a third room and altered the foundations to allow for the heating mechanism."

"Discoveries?"

"My father was an antiquarian, and a collector of Roman artifacts. His father before him discovered the remains of a Roman villa just behind this cottage. Which no doubt sparked my father's interest in all things Roman. There are coins, pots, and various implements up at the Hall. They are all drawn and catalogued—"

"By your father?"

Christopher shook his head, then grinned at a memory.

"No. My father was a poor draughtsman. My mother was the artist in the family. He co-opted her—co-opted us both—into his passion for antiquities. She faithfully and diligently made drawings of all his finds, and even had the patience to allow me to sketch with her."

"You had a happy childhood."

It was a statement Christopher readily agreed with. "I did. They both loved me very much, as you do Teddy. And they were a well-matched couple. Some of their happiest memories were here at the cottage…"

"Cousin Duchess would be vastly interested in your father's collection," Mary said, when the silence stretched between them. "She reads the Roman and Greek writers in their own tongue, and I've no doubts could date the coins, too."

"Then when Her Grace visits, I will be sure to show her the collection," Christopher quipped, putting this fanciful notion in the same basket as the existence of fairy folk and elves. "The locals mistook what was left of the Roman villa as the ruins of an ancient fairy kingdom—"

"Fairy kingdom?"

"Yes. And with no other source of knowledge but their own folklore, why would they think otherwise?" Christopher reasoned. "It made perfect sense to them. But my grandfather had his men—those who were not superstitious of upsetting the fairies—clear the site. What they discovered was not a tiny set of buildings built by fairy folk, but the remains of a Roman villa, with colonnades and many rooms. Most of the stone had been removed, no doubt used elsewhere, but the outline of stones and a mosaic tiled floor remained, with the terracotta pots and some coins. Would you like to see where it is?"

"Oh, yes, please! I have never seen a Roman villa, though I have visited Bath on several occasions, which I'm sure your father told you was occupied by the Romans. Did your grandfather ever visit Bath?" she asked, knowing she was prattling, all because he had taken hold of her hand again, and this simple gesture had the power to flood her with happiness. "The King's bath is fed by a thermal spring, and one can taste the waters. But it tastes quite foul and there is an odor to it— Oh! But of course you would know this," she added, suddenly self-conscious. "You lived in the Italian States—"

"Which does not necessarily mean I know the first thing about the Romans," he countered mildly. "But yes, I do," he added with a smile over his shoulder as he guided her through a wooden gate which was set in an archway heavy with an entangled ancient rose vine. "My father's collection of coins fascinated me and set me on that path. As did this ruin, and the thermal spring. Here is where the foundations are, but the mosaic floor is—"

"But there is nothing here," Mary interrupted, disappointed, staring at a small rectangular clearing that was bare but for a covering of autumn leaves. She had expected ancient carved stones or foundations at the very least.

"It is still all there, but my father had the site covered to protect the foundations from weather and pilfering."

"And the mosaic tiles?"

"Ah! I'll show you those in a moment. But first come see the source of our very own thermal spring. And there is also a bathing pool."

"Bathing pool? Was that built by the Romans, too?"

He shook his head. "No. It is a natural phenomenon. It's where the hot waters of the spring spill into the stream… Here! Here's the source."

He pulled aside a curtain of entangled roots and vine, clinging to a large piece of jutting rock that was part of the escarpment just beyond the furthest point of the outline of the villa. Here was a small pond. Though this pond was very different from any Mary had seen before, because steam rose from its surface and she did not doubt the water was very hot, possibly boiling. She tugged off a glove and held her hand over the water, fascinated that such intense heat radiated out of the earth without the need for fire to heat it. She flinched as her palm smarted in the steam, and quickly drew back, but not quickly enough for Christopher, who caught her about the waist and lifted her up and away, thinking she had burned herself.

"Show me!" he demanded, grabbing her wrist and turning over her hand to inspect her palm. His sigh of relief was audible. "Thank God. I'd never forgive myself had you burned yourself! Your hand would not recover from such an injury…" Relieved, he did the most natural thing in the world and pressed his lips to the center of her palm. "You are the most precious thing in the world to me."

"I am?" Mary said wonderingly.

"Yes. You are. But surely you knew that?"

"I have never been that to anyone before."

He smiled. "You are—to Teddy."

"Oh, yes, to Teddy. But she is my daughter and I her mother. Between mother and child that is a given."

"It is. My mother made a habit of telling me how much I was wanted. But what of your own mother?"

Mary swallowed and looked away. "No. Not to my mother."

"I should not have said—"

"It is perfectly all right, Mr.—Christopher. It is the truth. If I'd been a boy, I would be the heir, and it would've meant one less pregnancy for her to endure." It was her turn to smile. "I'm glad your mother felt the same way about you as I do about Teddy."

"Yes. Yes, they both felt that way. Which made the situation all the more heartbreaking—"

"Heartbreaking?"

"Let me show you why I brought you here," he said, deftly

changing the subject. "My grandfather believed that this hot spring was used first by the Saxons, and then the Romans, possibly as a place of worship to their pagan gods."

"So the building your grandfather uncovered could've been a temple perhaps?"

"He thought so. But just as the temple was left to ruin, so too the spring silted up and was lost. My grandfather uncovered it, but it was my father who harnessed the thermal properties to heat the cottage. He built a weir and a pump, then had laid a series of pipes. Here is the pump and this valve can shut off the flow of water in summer, diverting it through that larger pipe straight to the stream. But for most of the year the hot water flows through these series of parallel pipes that run under the foundations of the cottage, heating the floor and in turn the interior. The pipes then carry the water to the stream where it discharges into a pool, another weir built by my father.

"Come," he said, taking hold of her hand and leading her back through the arbor-covered gate, past the cottage, and downstream past where his angling rod still lay propped on the wicker fishing basket that held his lures. "Here's the pool. The hot water is released underwater, and by the time it reaches the weir it's still hot, but not scalding. The icy water of the stream helps to dilute the heat and make it a pleasant temperature for bathing."

He went down on his haunches and dabbled the tips of his fingers in the pool, and invited Mary to do likewise. She did, and smiled up at him.

"Oh! It is the temperature of bathwater! How ingenious of your father and grandfather! Such enterprising gentlemen. I see now where you inherited your entrepreneurial spirit and interest in all things mechanical. They would have been proud of your cloth mills and approved of Smeaton's waterwheel very much."

Christopher gave a bark of harsh laughter and shook his head. "I wish they were alive to hear you say so. But my mother would argue that my insatiable curiosity, not to mention stubbornness to want to solve what I perceive as a problem, are traits singular to *her*. But yes, my love of tinkering with the mechanical and my interest in Roman antiquity was most certainly instilled in me by Squire Bryce senior. Who, by the way, was Henry Christopher—"

"Which is why you were known as Christopher and not by your birth name Cavendish? Couldn't your parents decide by which name you should be known?"

"Something like that," he answered. "Now let me show you the cottage and the mosaic."

Mary followed him back to the cottage, a frown between her brows, for this was the second time he had changed the subject when the conversation turned to the personal, most particularly about his parents. Her brow cleared and so did her thoughts when he sat on the bench under the portico outside the front door and removed his jockey boots. She watched him set them aside and then wriggle his toes in their black stockings. For some unfathomable reason this simple action had the power to ripen her cheeks with embarrassment. She mentally upbraided herself for such a ridiculous reaction to an equally innocuous action as looking upon a man's unshod feet. She could only suppose it was because it was not every day, in fact not *any* day, that a man removed his shoes in female company. It was in fact a deeply intimate act, as intimate as what was occurring now when she sat beside him on the bench and he went down on bended knee before her and unlaced her half-boots, and removed them for her.

He then opened the front door, and held it wide for her to enter before him. She stood there a moment and looked out across the clearing to the stream, and further afield to the forest of autumn colors. She had no idea why she was hesitating, but subconsciously knew that by entering the cottage her life would be changed forever.

Christopher continued to wait. He did not have to speak. She saw in his soft smile that he was asking her to trust him. She did. She smiled back, took the hand he held out to her, and stepped into the warmth of the cottage. He closed the door, drew the latch, and shut out the world. They were now alone, to do as they pleased, and that pleased them greatly.

TWENTY-ONE

"Oh! It's warm! The floor is warm."

Mary's astonishment and delight had Christopher grinning. His grin widened, if that were possible, when she lifted her petticoats to look down at the stone flagging and her toes wriggling in their white clocked stockings. She smiled up at him.

"It is magical! And I would have thought it magic at work had you not shown me the thermal spring and the pipes laid by your father." She unbuttoned her cape and he took it from her and hung it on a peg on the wall beside his frock coat. "Oh, he is clever!" She walked about the room, wholly focused on the warmth under her feet. "All the floor is warm. And that has in turn made the room warm. You could stay snug in here all winter long without the need for firewood or coal, or a bed warmer. Even if you were snowed in for months and months you would never be cold."

"Yes. But you forget one all important ingredient to ensure we can last out the entire winter." When she stood still and looked at him enquiringly, he laughed. "I suppose it must be a male preoccupation, and for those who do the cooking and thus think about food as much as men do. *Not* thinking about food is a luxury few can afford."

Mary appeared disgruntled. "I may not be able to cook but I do know how to prepare a menu—"

"—and keep bees, collect eggs, and turn cheese wheels."

"Now you are making fun of me!"

"No. Not at all. I was being playful with you. There is a difference."

Mary pondered that for a moment, then conceded, "Yes, of course

you were. Forgive me. It's just that I-I do not know how to be-to be
—*playful*. We were discouraged as children from exhibiting such
frivolity. My mother thought it vulgar and beneath the children of an
earl to show such-such—spirit. Though I must admit my brother Dair
has always been a rogue in spite of our mother. He never listened to a
word she said. And I do know playfulness when I see it," she added
earnestly, and blushed because he was regarding her with an understanding smile. "Cousin Duchess is the most playful person I know."

Christopher gasped dramatically and put a hand to his chest in
mock horror. "But she, my lady, is a duchess, and so can do as she
pleases."

Mary giggled. "So you have met my mother!"

"I would like to."

Mary's smile died. "I would not like you to meet her."

"Why?"

Mary regarded him forlornly. He had the loveliest smile, and the
kindest eyes, and she was quite sure he was the most caring person she
had ever met. All she wanted to do was kiss him and to have done with
talk of her mother. Talk of her mother was a reminder of what was to
come, and she did not want to think of the future, she only wanted to
think of the here and now, with him.

"Because she is not a nice person and you are."

"Thank-you. Though I would still like to meet her one day."

"Let's not talk about her, not here."

"As you wish."

For the first time since entering the cottage she noticed her
surroundings, and was diverted sufficiently to push her mother and the
future she had mapped out for herself to the back of her mind and
look about her. There was a small, rustic dining table that had upon it
a branch of candles and two chairs drawn up to it. It was in the
furthest corner, and opposite was a bed with a high mattress set into
the wall, much in the French manner. It was nestled head to toe in a
niche, but the curtains that could be pulled together from either end
for privacy were not heavy velvet to keep out the cold, but of a
diaphanous blue silk that allowed for light and, if lying in bed, to see
out the window with its view of the stream. A large chest, a small
bookcase, and a wingchair completed the furniture. There was no fireplace, but with a heated floor, none was necessary.

"Sorry to harp on about food, but I'm rather famished and there is
stew…"

"I'm hungry too."

Mary followed Christopher into the next room and found herself in a kitchen well-equipped for its compact size, complete with fireplace stove, work bench, shelves holding various containers and the necessary implements for cooking all manner of dishes, and a sink next to a door that led outside, she assumed to a kitchen garden and the wood pile. A heavy pot suspended over the coal fire was being kept warm, and when Christopher carefully lifted the lid to stir the contents, a burst of delicious mingled cooking aromas permeated the air and made Mary realize she had not eaten since first light, and then only a slice of bread and butter. And the preceding few days she had lost her appetite with the worry of the decision she was to make about her future, and with thoughts consumed with Christopher.

And now here she was in his cottage kitchen, watching him prepare their dinner.

"Is there anything I may do?"

"Set the table? You'll find cutlery and goblets in that cupboard over there. And a cloth for the table, and napkins. And there is a loaf of fresh bread in that terracotta pot by the sink. Oh, and wine, but that's in the next room. Which reminds me, I must show you the mosaic before we sit. But first, taste this and tell me if it needs more salt, or perhaps a pinch of pepper?"

He held up a ladle over the pot with his hand underneath and she gingerly took a sip of the rich broth, then ate the small morsel of meat. She let the flavors linger on her tongue, surprised by their intensity and richness, and how much flavor was in such a small bite. The taste was oddly familiar and yet delightfully different.

"What is this?"

"*Stufato di coniglio con carote e cipolle* or you may know it better as *ragoût de lapin aux carottes et oignons.*"

"*De lapin*—rabbit…? Rabbit stew with onions and carrots? But I cannot distinguish the herbs you've used. But it does not need salt or pepper. It is perfect as it is."

"Good. Silvia will be pleased. I followed her recipe as best as I could remember. As for the herbs and spices, that's a secret between Silvia, me, and the pot." He dropped the ladle back into the stew and replaced the lid. "Let me show you the mosaic and then we'll eat."

"And you made this rabbit stew all on your own?"

"And trapped the rabbit too, if you want details from first principles."

"Is this Silvia one and the same that Teddy has told me about—the wife of Carlo?"

"Yes. The very same. Silvia is my Italian cook-housekeeper. I brought her and her husband Carlo with me when I returned from

Italy with my—aunt. They had been in her employ before they were in mine."

Mary watched as he took a taper from the candelabra on the work bench, pulled back the heavy curtain that separated the kitchen from the third room, and disappeared inside. When she did not immediately follow, he poked his head back into the kitchen.

"This is where the wine is kept. And so is the mosaic. You will find the floor a little chilly."

The temperature of the floor in this third room was in marked contrast to the rest of the cottage. It was cold, but the temperature was forgotten when Christopher held the candle low over the floor. The entire area but for the outer perimeter on three sides was covered in tiny geometric tiles of yellows, browns, reds, and blacks. When viewed in its entirety, the tiles depicted the head of a woman, possibly a goddess. Along the fourth wall the mosaic disappeared under the stone work, and orientating herself, Mary suspected that this wall had been built over part of the foundations of the villa. Christopher confirmed her suspicions.

"My father wanted to preserve the mosaics, but he also wanted to enjoy them. So this was his compromise. Instead of re-burying the entire villa, he left this section of the floor exposed and preserved it from the weather by adding this third room to the cottage. In this way he could come here and enjoy it whenever he pleased. It is also used as a cold room for storing wine and provisions.

"Do you intend to keep the villa buried? It seems a shame to lock away something so beautiful, when there are others, scholars and the like, who would appreciate the opportunity to study it. You never know but this site could be just as important as the one in Bath, particularly because it has this natural thermal spring. And the Romans were fond of such springs as places of worship."

"For someone who professes to have had a woeful education, you do know more than you think about Roman antiquity! Here, this decanted bottle of red will complement the stew nicely."

"I was an excellent listener," Mary said proudly, following Christopher back into the kitchen. She collected up the forks and spoons, covers, and linen. "And Cousin Duchess and the Duke often discussed Roman history—and the different scholars in particular. Of course I had no idea what they were talking about, but I did listen, and it improved my French."

Christopher ladled a large helping of stew into two bowls. "They always spoke in French?"

"Except on Tuesdays. Tuesdays they spoke exclusively in Italian."

"So you can speak the Italian tongue?" Christopher asked her in the language of Dante.

"*Poco*—But not enough to converse with your servants."

Christopher carried the bowls into the main room and set them on the table Mary had set. He then returned with the decanter and half-filled her goblet. Before sitting he raised his to her and looked into her eyes.

"Welcome to my humble cottage, my la—"

"Mary," she interrupted with a smile, raising her glass. "Here it will always be Mary. And you will always be Christopher. Shall I say grace?"

In spite of himself, Christopher felt the color rise in his cheeks at the soft pronouncement of his name, nodded, and quickly took his seat. After grace they ate in companionable silence for a time, Mary only making comment on the deliciousness of Silvia's secret recipe rabbit stew, before asking conversationally,

"Will you tell me something of your life abroad?"

Christopher paused in pulling a chunk of bread from the loaf and looked across at her.

"Anything. But first will you answer a question that I have been eager to ask you since your arrival?"

"Of course."

"Have you finished the embroidery work on the christening cap for your cousin's baby?"

Mary peered at him as if he had a fever. "Is that truly your question or are you being playful again?"

He shook his head with a laugh. "That truly is my question."

She sat back with a self-satisfied smile. "I have indeed. And sewn it up to my satisfaction so that all that is needed is for me to attach the silk ribbon ties. Teddy says it is my finest work yet."

"I do not doubt it. Teddy has a discerning eye. Your cousin will be delighted. A very fitting gift for a ducal baby, and one the parents will cherish. It is sure to become a family heirloom. I hope you'll show me before sending it off to your cousin."

"I would be very happy to. Which puts me in mind of a question I have for you regarding Teddy and the christening…"

Christopher looked up from sopping up the last vestiges of stew from his bowl with a chunk of bread and waited for her to continue.

"I intend to be at the christening of Cousin Duchess's baby, and I want Teddy to accompany me. Cousin Duchess is my closest cousin. She was a second mother to me—indeed was a better mother to me than my own. And it is not every day a duchess gives birth to an heir, and even rarer that this duchess, who is a duchess twice over, will be the mother of two ducal houses. That in itself is cause for celebration. But what I most want is for Teddy to have some contact with my Roxton family; to see what they mean to her mother. Is that such an impossible request?

"No."

"Oh?" Mary sat forward. "Then you will not oppose Teddy coming with me?"

Christopher refilled her wine goblet. His gaze did not leave her for a moment.

"Why would I? She should be there with you on such an important occasion. But have you ever thought to ask Teddy her wishes? And need I remind you that Teddy was to accompany you to her Uncle Dair's wedding at Treat. I gave my permission for her to attend that momentous event. Your brother is her favorite uncle. It was illness which kept her from that happy day, not I."

"Thank-you, I do not need reminding. And it was a sad disappointment to us all when she was taken ill. But at the time I was more concerned for her health than her attendance at Dair's wedding—"

"And still you went, leaving her in the care of her nurse, and managed to get yourself held up by highwaymen into the bargain."

Mary gaped at him.

"I left her because the physician assured me she had turned a corner in her illness. I would never have done so had she still been feverish. But I knew you were coming into Buckinghamshire to fetch her, so that put my mind at rest. And if the truth be told, it was *you* she most wanted when she was ill." Mary screwed up her little nose. "What has the hold-up of our carriage by ruffians got to do with anything?"

"You could have been injured—worse! Molested. Shot. Killed. And where would that have left Teddy and-and—me! If you'd waited but a day I could've escorted your carriage into Hampshire, and seen you safely to Treat. But no, you go off alone, with only your mother as company. Two vulnerable females with no male protector, in fact no protection whatsoever."

"Mother would not hear of waiting. We had already been delayed by Teddy's illness."

"You should have insisted."

"Yes. I should have."

"When you and Teddy go anywhere, do I not ride with your carriage as far as I'm able?"

"Yes, you do," she replied in the same quiet tone.

She said this with a small smile, one she could not suppress because his guarded anger for her welfare was of immense interest. Because now he put her in mind of it, he had always accompanied them on their travels, be it to Bath, or further afield when she went to Treat. He had become so much a part of the fabric of her life and Teddy's, much like her most devoted servants, that she had taken him and his service for granted. But at least with her lady's maid and Teddy's nurse she had always shown gratitude, and they were paid well. Christopher received no payment, and if she had thanked him it was in a perfunctory manner, because she had considered his presence as an interference at best, at worst a strain on her liberty. She had not until now considered an alternative: That he cared for her and wanted to keep her safe. She was mortified. He had every right to his anger, but that anger and concern left her with a deep sense of contentment, which had brought out the smile. Yet, her smile fell away, troubled by something he had said earlier about Teddy's wishes.

When he returned to the table, having cleared it of their evening meal and in its place set down a coffee pot and two mugs, she asked bluntly,

"What did you mean *have I thought to ask Teddy what she wants?*"

He looked up from pouring out the coffee and remained silent until he had set a mug before her, with the sugar bowl, a small earthenware creamer, and a spoon. He then sat again.

"Precisely that. Have you ever asked Teddy if she wishes to visit your Roxton relatives?"

"No. Just as my mother never asked me. She goes where I go—well, she did unless her father said otherwise. Just as you have placed restrictions on her movements, so did he."

"Ah, but I was only carrying out *her* wishes, not mine. "

"Carrying out her wishes?" Mary was incredulous.

"Yes. And, pardon my bluntness, but Sir Gerald imposed restrictions out of spite. He used you and Teddy as a means to have his revenge on the Duke of Roxton for exiling him."

"I know that well enough, Mr.—Christopher!" Mary stated, annoyed. "But there was not much I could do about it, was there? If you want the truth, I blame Roxton as much as I do my husband for my banishment from my family. In exiling Sir Gerald, he exiled me, and he ought to have thought about the consequences before making his decree. But what is done cannot be undone. So please tell me how it is you are carrying out my daughter's wishes?"

Christopher sipped at his coffee and then set the mug down and stared at it a good five seconds before replying.

"Sir Gerald filled her head with all sorts of nonsense, as he did mine—about Roxton. You remember me telling you the reason he told me he was banished from the ducal family fold was because he had discovered the Duke making up to you—"

"Yes, I remember that well enough not to be reminded, thank-you," Mary replied, blushing scarlet. "And I disabused you of that accusation."

"You did. And before you dash coffee in my face, you will remember that I never believed you complicit. And you rightly corrected me about the Duke and his devotion to his duchess."

"And Teddy? What nonsense did Sir Gerald tell his daughter about my cousins?"

"You must remember that Teddy is just a child—"

"*Christopher*. You are speaking to her *mother*."

"Which is why I am hesitating to tell you. Anyone else would laugh off such a tale as ludicrous. But you will believe me because you know of what your husband was capable, and because you can trust me."

Mary put her hand out across the table. "I do. In everything."

Christopher smiled thinly. At any other time her confidence in him would have been gratifying, but what he had to tell her was not, so he took hold of her hand, looked into her violet eyes, and said calmly,

"You know that when a small child is told a tale by an adult, particularly a parent, and that tale is told often enough, it does not matter how fanciful it is, the authority behind the tale lends an authenticity to it that is never questioned. I had hoped she would outgrow the notion—at the very least seek reassurance from you that it was not true. I could offer Teddy reassurance, but as I have never met the Duke, my reassurances were somewhat hollow to her. And as much as I wanted her to approach you, to ask you if there was any truth to the tale, she made me promise not to tell you."

"Why? Teddy and I have never kept secrets."

"She kept this one, because her father also told her as part of the tale that you had been bewitched by the ogre and thus could not be relied upon to tell her the truth in this instance."

"Ogre? Bewitched?" Mary's fingers convulsed in his. "What dreadful notion did that man put in my daughter's head? Surely it can be no worse than what he intimated to you about Roxton and me?"

"It is no worse, but is the more despicable because Teddy is an impressionable child, and his daughter. And he did not tell her this tale once, but on several occasions to reinforce her fear."

"Fear? Of my cousins?"

"Of the Duke in particular. Teddy thinks—she *believes*—the Duke capable of magic and that he is an ogre living in the guise of a noble-man. That her father discovered the truth, which is why he was banished to his estate. And that this ogre put a spell on you that cannot be broken. That it is this spell that compels you to visit your Roxton relatives."

"Oh, but this is such babble!" Mary blurted out before she could stop herself.

"It is. But Teddy believes it to be true."

"Of course she does. It was her Papa who told her. Horrid, odious man!"

She looked up from where their fingers were entwined, shocked to have voiced aloud her private thoughts when she had never before been publically disloyal *because good wives, daughters of earls, conducted them-selves differently*. But again, that was her mother's voice, and she was done with listening to that inner voice, particularly with Christopher. She wanted to be open and honest and *herself* with him, especially here in the cottage.

"He was—all those things I just called him," she stated firmly. "Sir Gerald was not only odious and horrid, he was cruel and utterly self-centered. In every way."

Christopher knew she was referring not only to Sir Gerald's conduct towards his only child but also how he treated her as a wife, but chose to ignore this for the time being, saying, "He warned Teddy that if she ever went to Treat, the ogre duke would lock her up in one of his towers and she would never see you again."

"Good—God! I didn't think it possible to loathe him more, but I do now," she muttered, and withdrawing her hand from his pushed back her chair and stood.

She needed to walk, to pace off her anger and resentment. This she did in front of the bed niche, arms hugging her sides. Christopher watched and waited for her to speak; he could see by her mulish expression she had more to say, and did, stopping in mid-step and turning to face him.

"Do you think it a possibility she made herself sick in Bucking-hamshire so she had an excuse not to go to Treat and Dair's wedding?"

"I do."

"You know she hates being cooped up, that she prefers being outside. She is so like her Uncle Dair. To think if she went to Treat she would end up in a tower dungeon... monster! She must've been terrified."

"She was certainly greatly relieved when I arrived to take her home."

Mary briefly covered her face with her hands, then let them drop to her sides, hands clenched into fists. "Why did I not see her fear? How could I have allowed him to fix in her head such gross untruths? How could he have used his own daughter so fiendishly?"

"You said so yourself. He was self-centered. He cared for nothing but his own wants, and to the detriment of all else, his wife and daughter included."

"Her life was to be so very different from mine. I was determined. Her days were to be filled with love and laughter and hope, and he— and he—*ruined* that for her."

"You cannot think that," he said, taking Mary in his arms and holding her close because she was crying. He let her, and only when she was still did he speak. "She is loved, and you have given her a wonderful childhood. There are not many children, least of all girls, who are permitted to roam the countryside at will. You understand her needs, that she must be at liberty to be outdoors, to ride, to play with the village children, to call at Brycecomb Hall whenever she pleases. You have no idea how welcome her visits are; they brighten up my mother's otherwise lonely days, so much so that she and the rest of the household are in good spirits for at least three days afterwards. And for me, the best part is I've been allowed to share in her life. I have you to thank for that."

Mary took a shattering breath and nodded. But she did not look up at him but rested her damp cheek on his chest and said on a deep sigh, "Every night in my prayers I thank God that you are part of her life, for if anyone has been a father to her, it is you."

Christopher kissed the top of her head, then took her damp face between his hands and smiled into her violet eyes.

"Thank-you. Now dry your cheeks and we will think no more about Sir Gerald, or ogres, or even Teddy tonight. It is too late in the day for me to take you angling, or for you to bathe in the warm waters of the stream, so we must amuse ourselves as best we can here in the warmth of the cottage. Shall I play for you?"

"Play?"

"My mandora—a type of lute. I learned to play in Lucca."

"Oh yes! I should like that very much. But I fear I may be a very poor audience tonight. Your stew, the wine, and a head full of unwelcome thoughts have made me sleepy."

"Then I shall play you to sleep." He saw her glance at the bed and managed to say evenly, "There is a pitcher and basin, soap, towel, and toothpowder by the sink. While I was clearing away our dinner and making the coffee, I filled the pitcher with hot water, which should be tepid by now. Unfortunately I cannot provide you with a hairbrush, but there is a comb. And you can wear this over your chemise," he added, holding out a brocade garment he had taken from the large chest up against one wall, and which Mary now noticed had leaning beside it the many stringed instrument Christopher called a mandora. "It's one of my banyans, so you'll have to fold back the sleeves. Do you need assistance with your lacings?"

"My-my lacings?" Mary repeated, taken aback to be asked such a question, and in such a straightforward manner. No man had ever asked her that, or had ever helped her unlace her stays. But she immediately castigated herself for her shocked response. He was only being helpful and she had every intention of spending the night with him, so it was ridiculous to be scandalized. "You're thirty not thirteen! Take stock and show some mettle you ridiculous creature!" she muttered under her breath, grabbed the banyan and sailed into the kitchen, saying over her shoulder, "No, thank-you! I'll manage!"

When she returned, the bedcovers had been turned down and the diaphanous curtains pulled across the front of the bed. Only two candles in their holders were alight, one on the table, the other on the chest by Christopher, who sat cross-legged in the shadows on the opposite side of the room in the wingchair, and who was lightly strumming the strings of the mandora. He had been playing since she had disappeared into the kitchen to undress, wash, and uncoil her braids. She was now in her chemise and stockings and wearing Christopher's brocade banyan, which trailed on the floor, her hair in one long thick braid down her back, tied off with a ribbon.

When he did not look up but continued to concentrate on his fingers plucking at the strings, she scurried across to the bed and there shrugged off the banyan and quickly put it over a chair back. But when she attempted to get into bed, she found she could not find where the curtains parted and spent several seconds in panic until she lifted the hem of the curtain high enough to duck under it. She then scrambled up onto the mattress and pulled the covers up to her chin. She lay so stiff and still she was oblivious to her surroundings, only that she was in a strange bed in a cottage on the edge of the Puzzlewood, and with a man who was not her husband or her lover, and who seemed content to remain on the other side of the room strumming a lute.

But as she listened to his gentle plucking of the strings, her shoulders relaxed; so too did her fingers gripping the coverlet, and her head sank into the soft down of the pillow. The music was low and melodic and very soothing. She became aware, too, of the scent of lavender mixed with another floral essence—roses perhaps? It was infused into the bed linen. It too calmed her. Soon her whole body went limp, her eyelids drooped, and turning her head on the pillow, she drifted into a deep sleep.

CHRISTOPHER KEPT AN EYE ON HER, QUICK TO LOOK AWAY WHEN she glanced over at him to see if he was watching her failed attempts to find where the curtains parted. He congratulated himself on keeping his expression neutral, though inside he was laughing out loud. He was sure his shoulders were shaking of their own accord. He found her prudery adorable, but for fear of offending her would never dare acknowledge her failed attempts to maintain a sense of decorum in what must be for her the most bizarre of circumstances.

He was mindful that they were at a most delicate stage in their growing intimacy, and he would not for the world sabotage its progress by upsetting the equilibrium so far achieved between them. He was still unclear as to her treatment at the hands of her boorish husband, and thus he would err on the side of caution. And if there was one thing he discovered about himself in the years he spent abroad, and most particularly when employed as a cicisbeo, it was that he had boundless reserves of patience; Mary would let him know in her own way and in her own good time what it was she wanted from him, and he was comfortable with that. He would then be able to accommodate her needs without asking, but not tonight.

She was asleep, and he was tired, too. So he continued to strum the strings of the mandora for a little while longer, then retrieved a Witney blanket from the chest, pulled it up over himself in the wingchair, and went to sleep. When he was shaken awake, his first thought was that he had not slept at all, but the remaining notches in the guttering candle told him more than two hours had elapsed since he had curled up in the chair.

Mary was standing before him in her chemise and stockings. He wondered if she was sleep walking, or in her half-waking state was disorientated and confused by the unfamiliar surroundings. She rocked gently from side to side, mussed hair falling across her face and down her back, the plait unraveled, the ribbon lost somewhere in the bedclothes. The silk drawstring of her chemise had come loose, widening the neckline enough to allow a billowy sleeve to slip from her left shoulder, exposing the creamy whiteness of her décolletage and one plump and perfect breast.

If Christopher had been half-asleep, he was wide-awake now gazing on her ethereal loveliness in the soft glow of candlelight. He threw off the blanket, intending to wrap it around her then put her back to bed, convinced she had no idea where she was. So he was surprised when she shook her head and stopped him just as he was about to arrange the folded blanket about her shoulders. She pulled it from his fingers and dropped it onto the wingchair.

"Come to bed," she demanded drowsily, taking hold of his hand. "I need you to keep me warm."

He did not hesitate to do as commanded.

TWENTY-TWO

MARY WOKE IN CHRISTOPHER'S ARMS, HE STILL IN HIS SHIRT AND breeches under the coverlet. It was before dawn, so she snuggled in, delighting in the warmth of him pressed up against her back and curved around her bottom and down her thighs. He shared her pillow, face lost in the tangle of her hair, and with an arm outstretched across the curve of her body, he had taken possession of the silken knot that kept her stocking up over her knee and there found anchorage while he slept.

WHEN SHE NEXT OPENED HER EYES SHE WAS ALONE AND IT WAS late morning. The window shutters were wide, allowing daylight to flood the cottage and to fill with the sounds of the forest, of autumn leaves rustling in the breeze and—whistling? Now that came from the next room. It had her sitting up and brushing the hair from her face. And then Christopher padded in from the kitchen carrying two mugs of tea. He set these on the table, pulled aside the diaphanous curtains, and handed her a mug. He then propped himself on the mattress at the foot of the bed. He was in his shirt sleeves without his waistcoat or his stock, the shirt left unbuttoned and gaping wide at the throat. But his face was freshly shaved and his hair slickly pulled back, as if he'd been for a swim. He confirmed this when he said, after sipping at his tea,

"You'll have to excuse me if I smell of an excess of sandalwood soap. The trade-off with having a constant supply of boiling water from a thermal spring is that it comes with a mineralized scent. Not as offensive as the waters at Bath, because the stream dilutes the effect, but I fear it is still there…"

She sipped at her tea, then looked up at him in surprise. It had nothing to do with the mineralized waters. He lifted an eyebrow and said it for her.

"After eight years, it would be remiss of me if I did not know how you take your tea."

"In ten years of marriage, Sir Gerald never made the effort to know that or anything else about me. But let's not talk about him—" She sipped at her tea again and wondered aloud, "Does sandalwood truly mask the mineral scent? I can't smell either."

"That's because you are so very faraway…"

"Would you care for me to assure you one way or the other?" she asked blandly, though the light in her eyes gave away her effort to be playful.

He lifted his chin, exposing his throat, and tilted his head in invitation. "If you would be so kind, I'd be much obliged…"

She took another sip of her tea, then set aside the mug and scrambled over the tumble of bedclothes to kneel beside him. With a hand to his shoulder to steady herself, she leaned in to sniff at his throat. And as she did so, she closed her eyes and allowed her other senses to become subordinate. Breathing deeply, she caught the hint of sandalwood and of bergamot. But there was something else, something not found in the soap or a scent carefully concocted by a perfumer. It was definitely not malodorous, and the absence of any mineral smell whatsoever made her suspicious his intent all along was to have her in intimate proximity. She didn't care about his intent. All she cared about was breathing in the essence of him, a pleasing and thoroughly masculine peppery tang—the very same authentic scent that had threatened to overwhelm her senses in her bedroom when they had set out to catch a ghost.

That episode seemed a lifetime ago now, but then as now, the pulse deep within her woke and would not be quelled. She swayed and felt her knees buckle, and then her eyes opened under heavy lids as he steadied her, hands to her waist, his mug having been quickly thrust to the flagstones.

There was a moment, perhaps not more than two, when they stared at one another in breathless anticipation. And in the next, inhibition and reticence gave way to need. If the scent of him was thoroughly intoxicating to her, having his hands to the curve of her waist was enough to send a ripple of longing pulsating through his every nerve. This most tantalizing of female curves was the bridge between the soft roundness of her exquisite breasts above and the flare of her hips and sweet wetness to be had between her thighs below. And the only barrier to pleasuring this luscious creature's warm feminine flesh was a chemise of the finest cotton, and that was no barrier at all.

He was done with exercising restraint. He had been exercising restraint with her in thought and deed for so long now he had begun to wonder if he was more monk than man. He pulled her towards him, hands gliding over her hips to find anchorage splayed about the curve of her firm bottom, she responding by pressing herself to his hard leanness, arms around his back to hold on tight. Locked together they indulged in a passionate kiss that soon had them scrambling along the bed until they were hard up against the padded headboard. With nowhere else to go, and gripped by an acute urgency—or was it relief? —to finally be able to slake a lust that had simmered for years, they were soon in a frenzy of undressing. With clothing consigned to the floor, they tumbled naked amongst the pillows and bedcovers, a tangle of heated flesh and feverish kissing, and gave themselves up to overwhelming need.

Her kisses were no less hungry than his. Her caresses just as intimate. But when her touch strayed between his legs to explore the hard length of him, he forced himself to deny such a pleasurable torture for fear that, after so many years of abstinence, he would be unable to prolong his release to match hers. He was not so caught in the moment that he'd lost all perspective. His overriding desire was for her to enjoy making love, and with him. His own needs were secondary, for he knew that when she tumbled off into blissful oblivion, so too would he.

He gently and reluctantly withdrew from her touch, sliding down the bed, kisses progressing from her mouth to suckle at her breast as he caressed her curves. And when he lightly stroked the pulse between her thighs, she gasped in surprise but did not make him stop. Instead, her hand found his, and together they found a rhythm that sent her beyond reason. And when he judged her to be close to the precipice of climax, he permitted his tongue the ultimate indulgence. But this sensual extravagance was his undoing, and hers. For despite her hunger for release, her mind froze, and then so too did her body. Such was her panic that she pushed him off and scrambled away, dragging the coverlet with her to cover her nakedness. She sat back against the headboard, shaking, unfulfilled, mind and body in turmoil. Hugging her stockinged knees, she turned away to face the window, profile hidden by a tumbled mane of red hair.

He sat up, stunned. He had gone too far too soon. Of course he had. She had never enjoyed a sensual kiss before that night in her bedchamber. And here he was introducing her to the carnal pleasures of oral stimulation without a second thought. Her reaction left him in no doubts that she had not known of its existence before now. He wondered if she had been indulged in anything more perfunctory than the mechanics of copulation. And that had him speculating if she had ever found fulfilment, with or without her husband's involvement. Knowing the sort of upbringing she'd had at the hands of a cold-hearted and unemotional parent, it was too much to expect that a conversation between mother and daughter about the marriage bed had ever taken place. And knowing her husband to be vainglorious, any pleasure while making love would have been self-serving and most definitely not mutual.

Regarding Mary now as she stared out the window, all he wanted to do was take her in his arms and reassure her that her reaction and lack of experience was nothing of which to be ashamed. Sexual ignorance amongst aristocratic wives was not unusual; in fact, in many polite circles it was encouraged. So were the selfish needs of noble husbands. In this way the arrogant ignorance of the husband was never challenged, and thus he need not concern himself with satisfying his wife's needs. And then there was the occasional husband who did care about his wife's pleasure, in and out of the bedchamber, but being unable for whatever reason to cater to her needs, he willingly accepted into his household a gentleman who could. And Christopher knew this, because for nine years he had been that gentleman, and in four separate noble households.

He did not take Mary in his arms, nor did he voice his thoughts. He remained at the other end of the bed, coverlet covering his aching manhood, and waited for Mary to break the silence; he could see she was itching to do so. Her mortification was no surprise, but what she ultimately confessed appalled him.

She finally looked away from the window and threw at him, "I know what you must be thinking!"

"Do you? I doubt it. But please tell me."

"You're thinking that for a woman of my age I am pathetically ignorant."

"Not pathetic. That you were deliberately kept in ignorance is hardly your fault. Nor is it a particularly unusual circumstance."

"Meaning?"

"There are women who go their entire lives never knowing intimacy of any kind, least of all physical enjoyment with a lover."

"You mean those women who live their lives in a convent? Nuns?"

He gave a bark of laughter which he quickly stifled for fear she thought him insincere.

"Well, yes, there are those women. They take a vow of chastity by choice. But I was referring to females of your social standing. Wives of noblemen whose husbands prefer to keep them in ignorance for one reason or another, but usually because they are selfish."

"I was told that only men need to satisfy their carnal appetites. That women do not. That to have such-such—*urges* is undignified and bestial, and that only whores and prostitutes indulge in such behavior. Wives—good wives—keep their thoughts pure and their bodies for procreation."

Christopher knew it had to have been the Countess who had filled her daughter's head with utter nonsense, but he did not say so because he could see she had more to say as she had dropped her knees and was regarding him with such earnestness he dared not smile or interrupt.

"But I instinctively knew such an argument was flawed, for why do some couples marry for love and remain in love if they are not compatible in every way? My cousin married a duke who had the reputation of being a great libertine before he met her. And yet, upon marriage he became a devoted husband and father. They loved each other deeply and found pleasure in each other's company, so it seemed only natural to assume they enjoyed making love for its own sake." She shrugged, a blush to her cheeks. "Even as a girl of fifteen I knew there had to be a good reason why the sex act is called *making love*."

"Clever—for a young girl to reason that out for herself, and against the absurd dictates drummed into her by a woman who clearly had never *made love*."

"Oh my mother wasn't the one who told me good wives keep their thoughts pure and their bodies for procreation. I'm sure she believed it though. No, my mother was far more prescriptive. She loathed the sex act. And I know this because when my parents' marriage became intolerable and my father abandoned us, it was my nurse who confided the reason. I did not understand at the time what she meant, but I never forgot what she told me… And later, when I married, I wondered if indeed I was like her."

"You are nothing like that woman!" Christopher growled.

Mary smiled, and comforted by his angry denial she inched further down the bed to be nearer to him, and asked curiously, "But you have never met her, so how do you know?"

"I don't know her, but I know you."

"Oh! But… just now… My reaction—my idiotic reaction to-to—"

"It was not idiotic. It was an instinctive response to a new and very different experience. And if you do not like it, then I will never—"

"Oh, I never meant you to think that. It may have appeared that way because of my ignorance, but to tell a truth—" She blushed and glanced away before looking at him through her lashes with a shy smile. "—I liked it rather too well. I was most surprised you would indulge me in such a selfless way—"

"Selfless? Believe me, pleasuring you is not selfless. It gives me great satisfaction to make you happy. That is what *making love* is all about— pleasuring each other; satisfying each other; making each other happy."

Mary came closer still and put out her hand to him, which he willingly took in a firm clasp.

"Then it is only fair that you show me how I may pleasure you in return."

He kissed her fingers and smiled into her eyes. "If that is your wish."

She stared into his damp brown eyes and she saw only love and understanding and it brought tears to her eyes. "I want to make love with you—for us to make love—very much."

"That makes two of us. But all in good time. Now we should dress and have breakfast. I thought we'd eat down by the stream. I caught and prepared us a trout, which is best cooked out-of-doors—"

"He—Sir Gerald—he was the one who told me only whores and prostitutes indulge in bestial behavior," she confessed in a rush, gaze locked on his. "He said that for me to be a good wife I must remain still. He said I must not move or turn about, and that I must take my thoughts elsewhere while he availed himself of my body. I was not to speak, or call out, or offer any resistance. He said it was his right as my husband to take me how and when he liked. He said his only interest in being in my bedchamber was the business of getting me with child. He never undressed before me. He never asked me to remove my nightgown. He never kissed me or touched me in a way that made me feel anything but a means to an end."

She swallowed and gave a little sigh, fingers convulsing in his. But he remained mute for he could see she was not finished. So he kept his gaze steady, on her eyes, and he did not flinch or show emotion. Outwardly he was as calm as the most tranquil lake; inside he was a raging sea of anger, disbelief, and wretchedness on her behalf.

"He would bolt both doors—but I had nowhere to run," she continued mildly, relating what had happened to her as if it had happened to someone else. "And he only approached the bed once my back was to him. He would then lift my nightgown and cover me as a stallion does a mare. When he was done, he would thank me, unbolt both doors, and leave. Dear God! *Thank me*, as if I had offered him a cup of tea! Every visit was the same. In ten years of marriage, not even when he was drunk, did he take me in any other way. I *hated* that man.

"But what could I do? I was married to him for better or worse. I was his wife, and as my husband, he was within his rights to come to my bedchamber whenever he pleased, and in whatever state he cared to. And as obedience had been drummed into me since a child, I did not question any of it. But instinctively I knew that the way in which he conducted himself in the bedchamber was not—was not—*usual*, even between couples in arranged marriages. But I was too ashamed to confide in anyone. And so I tried not to think about it, ever, even when it was happening. And I never want to think or talk about his visits ever again!"

She paused, as if expecting some response from him. But Christopher could hardly breathe, least of all put a coherent sentence together, and when he did manage to cobble a few words they were uttered in a hoarse whisper, his throat as raw as his emotions.

"I—I don't—I don't doubt—doubt that. We'll—we'll never speak of it again—unless you want to."

"Good. And I won't," she stated emphatically, and feeling more confident now she had confided in him, she continued, her confession becoming indignant. "It was easy to let my natural feeling and inclinations die inside me, to not expect to be loved, because I had never been loved by my mother, so why would my husband be any different? She told me outright that she resented the fact I had not been born male. My birth, she is convinced, was the cause of all her subsequent troubles with my father. She may never have loved me, but I love Teddy with all my heart. So I knew with Teddy's birth I could not be entirely like her. Teddy is Sir Gerald's only saving grace. To think such a sweet, dear child was conceived in such a cold, calculating, and *unfeeling* way breaks my heart. But at least I do know I have a heart! That I have her at all is the only good and wholesome thing to ever come from my marriage. *The only one.* If not for Teddy, I truly believe that any love I had to give would have shriveled up long ago. And if not for you, I may never have believed myself capable of being the object of desire. But you do desire me, don't you—"

"Very much. I don't think I have ever desired a woman as I desire you, Mary."

She snatched up his fingers and pressed them to her hot cheek before kissing the back of his hand.

"And I you…" She sniffed back tears, then surprised him by giving a tinkle of laughter. "And not in a hundred years—*not ever*—would I have believed it possible that I would find myself in a cottage, *naked in bed*, with the handsome squire of Brycecombe Hall!"

"Handsome? Am I?"

Mary gave him a playful shove. "Oh, *you know* you are! You *know* all the females, young and old, within a twenty-mile radius go weak at the knees and become simpering misses every time they see you!"

He put up an eyebrow. "Only twenty miles?"

She grabbed the nearest pillow and flung it at him; he caught it, and then adroitly pulled her into his arms. Gently brushing the hair out of her face, he enquired,

"And do I make your knees go weak, Mary?"

She settled in his embrace. "Every time I see you. Do you doubt it? But I've never been a simpering miss with you."

He chuckled. "No. You were—*you are*—never that. Which is just as well, or I might not like you half as much." He pinched her chin. "That's a lie. I could not love you more…"

She kissed his mouth then, and after a few moments pulled away, and he let her go. She hopped down off the bed, scooped up her chemise from amongst the pile of clothes, and wiggled into it. He dared not blink for fear he might be dreaming, and if he blinked, she'd be gone. His overwhelming desire was to pull her back into bed and make love to her, but remembering her harrowing confession cooled his ardor quicker than a pitcher of ice water. All in good time, and that time was not now. A rumble of hunger told him his stomach agreed with him.

"Breakfast?" he asked casually as he followed her lead and pulled on his drawers. When she did not immediately answer he turned, still holding his shirt, and found her staring fixedly at him. "Don't go all weak at the knees on me now," he teased, and winked. "Unless you want me to *carry* you outdoors to our breakfast spot."

She shook herself free of the mesmerizing sight of him naked, all lean muscular masculine lines and all hers, and tilted her nose with a sniff she hoped masked her own desire.

"My knees are perfectly strong enough to carry me to breakfast, where we will converse on all manner of topics over your splendidly cooked trout. And then I want you to show me how to fish, for I have never been angling before. And if there are any more ruins to explore, I should like to see those, too. And then perhaps I might bathe in your warm stream. After that, I am quite willing to go all weak at the knees, for I very much want to make love with you."

CHRISTOPHER OPENED ONE EYE AND FOUND MARY SITTING UP IN bed beside him with the coverlet drawn back. She was admiring him. She was so absorbed that she failed to notice he was awake until he pulled the coverlet from her fingers and up over his nakedness.

"I can't sleep with you watching me," he said drowsily.

"Can't you? Then tell me what you've been doing this past half hour if not sleeping?"

"You've been watching me for *half an hour*?"

She giggled guiltily and snuggled down beside him. "I like to look at you—most particularly when you're asleep—and naked."

He shifted to put an arm about her and held her against him.

"I like to look at you, too, but there is one thing I like doing with you even more."

"Oh? Only one?" she asked with feigned disappointment.

He was not fooled. Her physical response spoke volumes. She squirmed against him in impish anticipation of his riposte. And when he did not answer immediately, she squirmed even more. And then he turned within their embrace, first to face her, and then to roll onto his back bringing her with him, so that she ended up on top of him, which had her giggling even harder. She pretended to struggle but he was not to be dissuaded, and very soon she was straddling him, her mane of red hair falling about her in wild disorder and tickling his face.

She sat up and smiled down at him, and he smiled up at her, and in that single moment he marveled at how five short days alone together had changed their relationship forever. It was as if they had been friends and lovers for years, so comfortable and unselfconscious were they with each other. It was how he had dreamed of it being, and how he hoped their life would continue once they returned to the world beyond this cottage in the woods.

He did not want to speculate on an alternative, for if he allowed his mind to wander, there was that shadow, that big black cloud that loomed over them, of the very real possibility their time alone together was finite; that this idyll was a prelude to the rest of her life with another; that this Mary, the real Mary, *his Mary* would be taken from him forever.

"Are you going to tell me what this one thing is," she murmured, leaning forward to kiss him. "Or shall I hazard a guess?"

He came out of his introspection and returned her kiss with a grin. "What would be the amusement in just telling you? Guess."

"Very well. Challenge accepted." She leaned further in to whisper at his ear, her soft purr on his neck heightening all his senses. "But perhaps I would prefer to show you…" She slid down the length of his torso, lithe as a cat, and hovered over him. There was a decided twinkle of mischief in her eye. "Your answer, it seems, is staring me in the face."

"You cheeky strumpet!" he retorted lovingly. "He is too well-pleased with himself and can wait!"

And in one easy movement he sat up, rolled over, and slid her beneath him, she again gasping and giggling and making a feeble attempt at resistance. She was now the one lying amongst the bedcovers, looking up at him. And it was his turn to whisper near her ear.

"If you must know, you wanton baggage, it's tea—making you a cup of tea. But that too can wait…"

And as she had done, he slid down the length of her curves, lithe as a cat, and she drew breath deep in her throat. He did not hover.

He had tidied the cottage, made a pot of tea, and toasted the last of the bread by the time she returned from bathing in the warm waters of the weir. She found him sitting under the portico waiting for her. It was midday, and it was the first time they had stepped outside the cottage in over a day.

She had wound a plait about her head to keep her untidy mane from her face, and was wearing the petticoats, bodice, and half-boots she had arrived in. The hems were stained with mud and water, the bodice crumpled, and the half-boots scuffed. She was not wearing her stays. A week ago he could never have imagined the Lady Mary Cavendish would allow herself to go about in public so unkempt. It would have been unthinkable to her. Yet, watching her come across the path towards him, she had never looked more beautiful in her dishevelment. There was something about her that went beyond the superficial —the regal way she carried herself, upright and correct at all times. It was a glow, yes, a glow of contentment, and one of confidence. That was it! She looked confident and content, and it radiated. He smiled to himself as he sipped his tea, at the small part he had played in her new-found self-assurance and happiness.

She took the mug and the slice of toast he offered her, kissed him in thanks, and they sat in companionable silence looking out at the red and gold autumn view of ducks waddling on the bank by the stream, and in the patches of golden and white ragwort. And then she caught him completely unawares by asking a question that surprised him and made him jerk his mug so violently away from his mouth mid sip that tea splashed the front of his shirt.

"What is a-a *cicis—bo*?"

TWENTY-THREE

"A cicisbeo?" he repeated, pronouncing the word correctly as he concentrated on wiping his shirt front free of tea before it was too badly stained; this also helped hide his surprise at her question. *Where had that come from?* He didn't have a long wait to find out.

"Oh, is that how you say it? And you were one—one of these cicisbeo—?"

"The plural is cicisbei."

"Evelyn told me you were one of these cicisbei while you lived abroad?"

Christopher sipped at what was left of his tea. He wondered when mention of her noble cousin would intrude on their time together. And the man had had the gall to tell her about his past! Or at the very least intimate at it to pique her curiosity enough to ask. So be it. He had intended to tell her anyway, but not so soon, not here at the cottage. So much for best-laid plans. He finished off a corner of toast then said to delay the inevitable,

"I'll need to get in fresh supplies if we are staying here a little longer."

"You want to leave?"

He heard her anxiousness and shook his head.

"No. I'd stay here with you forever if that were possible. But we need food, and perhaps you'd like a change of clothes? That's if you wish to stay…?"

"I do. Teddy won't be home for another fortnight, and Evelyn said I have a month to—"

She stopped herself. She did not want to think about the future. She did not want to think beyond being here with Christopher. And she wouldn't, not yet. So she returned to her original question, hoping to divert the conversation and her thoughts back to the here and now.

But for Christopher, her question was anything but about the here and now.

"And were you a cicisbeo?"

"Yes."

"Will you tell me about it?"

"I had intended to do so, just not yet. But now that you have asked… What did your cousin tell you?"

"Nothing much beyond the word. Though he did say you were sought after, which I assume means you were expert in whatever these cicisbei do—" She paused when Christopher laughed harshly, but when he did not comment further, added quietly, "He also said you would tell me if I asked, but that I should be careful what I wish for. And by that I can only assume whatever you did in this capacity is not for the eyes and ears of a lady…?"

"Not an English lady, that's certain. The English have little understanding of such an arrangement, and never will. But the Italians are far more pragmatic, and as it is an accepted practice amongst the aristocracies of the Italian states and principalities, the position of cicisbeo is, if not highly regarded by all, a fact of life. As such there is no shortage of young gentlemen applying for the position within a noble household."

"And while you were living in the Italian states you applied and were given this position?" Mary asked, trying to understand what he was telling her.

"Ah, my path to such an official post was different from most. I need to take you back to my first couple of years away from the vale. I was eighteen and abroad, and without any income or friends to call on who could help me. Not that I would've asked for help at that time in my life… I fell on hard times, and that required I earn my keep. To be truthful, I was not myself. I'd been given some unwelcome news—shocking to me—that made me run away from home. And I let this news dictate my state of mind. You must remember, I was very young, so thinking or acting rationally was beyond my capabilities. As a consequence, I was quite stupidly self-destructive. To be blunt: I accepted an arrangement with a woman who fed and clothed me in exchange for certain favors—"

"You were her lover?"

"That is a polite way of putting it. I was her lover, and then there were others. Soon she was providing my—*services*—to other women—"

"How old were you when you embarked on this most interesting career?"

"Eighteen."

"*Eighteen*? You were just a-a boy!"

"Was I? Yes, I suppose I was. But I'd left the boy behind, here at home. And by the time I'd turned twenty, I'd slept—if I can use that euphemism—in so many beds I stopped counting. And I was paid for the privilege."

Mary gasped, the full import of what he was confiding in her finally dawning. Her violet eyes went round and she could barely comprehend the full extent of this revelation.

"I never—I never knew such a—such a *vocation* existed. Females turn to prostitution for any number of reasons and give their bodies to men for pecuniary gain—but men? Are there truly men who are—who do—" She looked to him for direction. "Is there an equivalent word?"

"There are several. Gallant. Varlet. Petticoat pensioner. To name three," he said mildly. "To bring this sordid little episode to its apex, when I was about twenty, I came to the attention of a noblewoman. Yes, she hired me as her *gallant*, but then she took a fancy to me, and convinced her husband to sponsor me as—"

"—a petticoat pensioner?"

Christopher laughed out loud. "Oh, my darling, you say it so politely. As if I were being hired to be her dancing instructor or her pianoforte teacher! But no, not as her paid whore, lover, gallant, call it what you will, but as her cicisbeo. A high honor indeed."

"Is it?"

"Yes. And highly unusual for a foreigner to be elevated to such a position. It is usual for noble couples to select a young nobleman from among their peers. But as this noblewoman, and more importantly her husband, were aristocrats—he a Conte and member of the governing council—an exception was made. Though I was to receive intensive training before I took up the post officially."

"Training? I do not understand. What sort of training? In the bedchamber?"

Christopher heard the underlying bafflement in her question and he smiled to himself and explained patiently, "No. Not the bedchamber. A cicisbeo is much more than a woman's lover. He performs many ceremonial functions so that the bedchamber almost becomes secondary. I had a series of tutors and was trained in deportment, swordsmanship, dance, musicianship, the art of conversation, and language. I had to reach a certain level of expertise before I could go into society as the Contessa's male companion. But I was not a complete country bumpkin, and I was a quick learner. I could fence, knew a few rudimentary dances, and while I wasn't the most diligent student at Harrow, I was no fool either."

"Harrow?" Mary repeated, grasping for something with which she was familiar. "My brothers went to Harrow."

"Yes. Dair and Charles were many years behind me."

She frowned. "You never told me you were sent to Harrow."

He smiled. "You never asked. Perhaps now that you do," he said teasingly to lighten her mood, "it makes me a more acceptable lover to her ladyship?"

But Mary was not to be placated or diverted from her line of enquiry.

"Don't be silly, Christopher! So while you were being schooled in the art of being a gentleman companion, you were also bedding this woman?"

"That was part of the arrangement."

"And her husband knew and was comfortable with this —*arrangement*?"

"I could not have been his wife's cicisbeo without his consent and signature to the contract."

"Indeed! A written contract? How civilized to be sure."

But he was not fooled by her cool civility. It was a veneer, and thin at best. With every revelation he offered about his past, there were imperceptible changes in her posture until she was sitting ramrod straight with her hands lightly in her lap and chin parallel to the ground. It was the attitude she adopted with him as steward, when he was called to her drawing room to give an account of his actions. It was her shield of indifference, brought out to protect herself from circumstances and feelings beyond her control. But he was having none of it. Not now. Not when they had come so far and were on such intimate terms. As he seemed unable to tease her into a better frame of mind, he tried a more direct approach.

"Mary. Darling. You do realize my life as a cicisbeo was literally another lifetime ago. And that since then I have had a decade here at home as Squire Bryce."

"And you accepted a contractual arrangement with this couple, who took you in and groomed you to be the wife's lover?" Mary stated slowly, ignoring his comment as she tried to make sense of it all. "And once you had learned the finer arts of your-of your—*vocation*—you went out into society together, and everyone knew you were this noblewoman's paid lover."

"A cicisbeo is more than a lover. As I told you the position is more akin to a close male companion. To call it anything less is to denigrate an arrangement between a husband, his wife, and her lover that is a long-held custom amongst the Italian nobility. It is so widespread it is part of the fabric of their life. When invitations are sent out for balls and parties and nights at the opera, all three—husband, wife, and cicisbeo—receive a formal invitation each, and all three attend together. No one raises an eyebrow of surprise or dissent. And everyone is civilized and respectful of such an arrangement."

"Oh, I am very sure more than a few eyebrows were raised at you, and there were a fair share of sudden weak knees among their females!" Mary threw at him, all semblance of placid enquiry evaporating. "I hope your contract was for many years' duration, or what a waste of good tutoring!"

"Mary, the Contessa was not my only contract."

She sat up even taller. "You were a cicisbeo for more than one lady?"

"Not concurrently. A contract is exclusive but they are only binding for two years, sometimes three at most."

"How many contracts did you fulfill?"

"In ten years? Four."

"Four? You were the official lover, companion, call it what you will, to four different noblewomen?"

"Yes." When her hands balled into fists in her lap, he said quietly but firmly, "I have already confessed to a past littered with lovers, and yet you are most offended that I was a cicisbeo to four noblewomen in particular. But as a member of Polite Society, you are surely aware that English noblemen have illicit affairs, set up mistresses, and live an almost separate life from their lawful wife."

"But that is different! *They* are different! *You* are different!"

He completely misconstrued her meaning and said with a frown of puzzlement at her distress,

"How so? An Englishman's promiscuity is not condemned. Indeed, he is lauded for his sexual prowess and domestic dexterity. And yet because in Italian Society it is the wife who takes a lover with her husband's consent, such an arrangement is condemned by ignorant Englishmen?"

"Oh, what do I care about the carnal habits of my peers, or of the Italians for that matter!" Mary threw at him dismissively. "I'm not blind to what goes on around me. I have a brother who has an illegitimate child—a sweet boy—and even my mother acknowledges his existence because in her mind he is a symbol of her son's virility. Woe betide if her daughter were to ever take a lover—"

"A bit late in the day to worry about her good opinion now," Christopher muttered with a roll of his eyes.

"Touché!" she retorted, and startled him by pulling a face that so reminded him of Teddy when she was at her most cheeky that he burst out laughing. That only made her indignant and she shot to her feet to face him. "It is not easy for me to reconcile what you have told me about your past—about your life as a—your life in Italy—with the Squire Bryce of Brycecomb Hall I know. I always suspected your time abroad was what helped to set you apart from other men, and I do not mean just men here in the vale. And now knowing your past, I am even less surprised why you've chosen to keep it secret. You are right to do so. No one would understand, and even those with far broader minds further afield would find your life as a cicisbeo quite shocking—most would condemn it. Tell me: Were you happy with your life in the Italian States?"

"Happy? Not in the beginning, no. I was miserable. But as I said, that was entirely of my own making. I did, however, come to find a certain level of purpose, and in so doing, happiness."

"And these women and their husbands, they were happy with you?"

"Yes, I suppose they must have been. I strove to do my utmost to carry out my contractual obligations to the best of my abilities."

"Of course you did. I have never known you to be anything but diligent and conscientious in everything you do."

For some unfathomable reason, Christopher felt his face grow hot at her emphatic praise. "Am I?"

It was Mary's turn to roll her eyes.

"Need you ask? In the eight years we've known each other you've never deviated from your present life as Squire of Brycecomb Hall. You've always presented as a hard-working gentleman farmer who loves the land and the vale. You care for your tenants' welfare, you've turned around the fortunes of Abbeywood Farm, *and* you've always been there for Teddy and me, even if I've often found your approach at times to be high-handed. No! Do not try to deny it. And I meant every word of what I said at the mill, and still do.

"But there is one aspect of your life that continues to puzzle the women of the vale. It's not something their men folk would usually think about, but from time to time, their wives will put the question to them. Possibly they have appealed to their husbands to discover the truth about you. But as I am not privy to their conversations, I cannot say for certain if this is so. What I do know is your continued bachelorhood and seeming disinterest in the fairer sex, even when they blatantly try to engage you, is a constant source of gossip for the village and the gentry families in the district. And even if the women do not speak to me directly, I am not blind to their admiring glances and their disappointment when you do not engage with them beyond the superficial. They are just as perplexed by you as I once was."

"Perplexed?"

She pouted. "Do you truly have no idea or are you being playful with me?"

He pulled her closer until she stood between his knees, and held both her hands.

"I am not blind, either. I am aware my return to the vale caused consternation amongst our neighbors, but I would have thought that after almost a decade, interest in my marital state would have waned."

"Waned?" Mary huffed. "While a handsome bachelor of means remains without a wife there will always be interest, and absurd rumors will continue to circulate."

"Absurd rumors?"

"Yes. The most absurd is that while you were abroad you became a Papist, entered the priesthood, took a vow of chastity for your faith, and returned here as a spy for the Holy Roman Emperor. And that is why you have no interest in the fairer sex."

Christopher shoulders shook with silent laughter.

"A papist, a priest, a spy, and *no interest* in women? Dear me, what a dour fellow I am, to be sure!"

"Vicar Beasley's wife says you are more monk than man. And even I, who am not quick on the uptake when it comes to veiled meanings in conversations, knew at once she wasn't referring to your ecclesiastical proclivities!"

"Ecclesiastical proclivities?" he repeated. "Oh, my darling, you do have a way with words! And so too does the vicar's dear wife."

Mary peered at him keenly. "You're not about to share more earth-shattering secrets with me, are you?"

Christopher balked, then grinned. "About secretly being a priest?" He pressed her hands. "We've just spent six days together making passionate love at every opportunity—that's not very monk-like, is it? And I don't know if it's earth-shattering or not, but you are the first woman I've bedded in ten years."

Mary gaped at him. "*Ten? Ten* years? *You* have not made love in *ten* years?"

"I see that this disclosure *is* earth shattering," Christopher muttered, then rallied. "My reasoning is simple, and should not surprise you. I indulged in an excess of female flesh from the age of eighteen until my thirtieth year. And while my mind and body were engaged, my heart was not. And so when I retired from my vocation, I made the decision to be chaste. I have not regretted my choice. Chastity would not suit most men, but it suits me. I've since discovered that I have the temperament that requires mind, body, *and* heart be committed to a thing or I am not content. I have put this personal philosophy into practice in running my farm, my mills, and being steward of Abbeywood. And it is the reason that when I did fall in love, and the love of my life was not free to be with me, I was able to reconcile myself to life as a bachelor."

He let the sentence hang, and in the silence wondered if she realized he was talking about her. Mary did, but articulating her feelings did not come easy after such an earnest confession and declaration. And then she said something that made him wish he had never doubted her capacity for insight.

"And while you were reconciled to a life as a bachelor, she—the woman who was not free to be with you—was determined that even though she was wife of a man who was incapable of loving anyone but himself, she would not allow her heart to shrivel and die. She would hold on to hope. And her heart did not wither, because upon meeting her neighbor the bachelor squire, she knew here was a man of principle and benevolence, a man she could admire, and love, if only her life had turned out differently." Her eyes opened wide and she said a little breathlessly, "Are you not, as I am, a little in awe that against all the odds, these two finally became lovers?"

"I am," he replied simply. "Mary. I do not ask you to accept my life as it was, or to even understand it. There are reasons, far deeper than I can explain to you here, why I ran away from the vale as a youth. But I would like to think that my past, particularly my experiences as a cicisbeo, have equipped me with a unique perspective on life and to better understand the wants and needs of females—your wants and needs most importantly—and I do not mean just as a considerate lover."

"Though you are that, very much so," she interrupted with an earnestness that made him blush. "And a wonderful teacher... I was always confounded by those females who actually enjoyed making love. But I could never bring myself to ask about such intimacy. Now I know why Deb is so happy in her marriage to Julian." Leaning into him, as if she feared being overheard, she whispered, "And why she is continually pregnant."

"Is she?"

Mary nodded, saying with a shy smile that made him smile in return, "You have made me very happy."

"And you have made me the happiest of men," he replied, and gently kissed her forehead, saying, all levity aside, "All I ask is that you realize that the life I lead now is the authentic life, the life I intend to have for the rest of my days. It is not my past, but how I choose to live my present and my future that should concern us."

"But that's what I'm trying to tell you," she said with a sigh of exasperation that had him suppressing a grin. "I truly do not mind about your past; it is who I see before me that matters."

"And who do you see before you, Mary?"

"I see Cavendish Christopher Bryce—for that is your name. You told me so yourself. I do not understand why you do not use the name given to you at birth, but I am very sure it is somehow connected with why you ran away. And while that remains a mystery, it does not greatly concern me because that, too, is in the past. To me you will always be Christopher." She touched his cheek, then gently pushed back the curls that fell across his brow with a smile and kissed him. "But above all else," she murmured, "I see a remarkable man. I see the man I love."

ANOTHER DAY AND NIGHT WENT BY BEFORE THE COTTAGE LARDER was so bare Christopher had no choice but to return home for supplies, or he would be boiling nettles for soup. He had been away from home for over a sennight, and while he was comforted by the fact Luke had not arrived with a note from Kate demanding his return, he was oddly disconcerted not to have heard from her. Since returning to Brycecomb Hall ten years ago, he had never been away from home for more than three consecutive nights. So to have been gone more than seven and not had a word from her was surprising indeed.

Mary was all for him checking on his aunt's welfare; she was his only family after all, and relied on him greatly. Besides which, while he was gone, she planned to do some laundering and dry the garments on the warm flagging in the cottage; and she would prefer he was absent while she did so. And while her clothing was drying, she would wear one of his spare shirts she'd found in the clothing chest. He chuckled at her prudery—after all, he had admired her naked in all her curvaceous glory enough times that it was forever etched in his mind's eye.

"But that's different," she argued, blushing and saying quietly, as if one did not raise such topics in mixed company, if at all, "I am laundering my chemise and stockings."

"Ah, yes. Quite right," he replied without a glimmer of a smile at her seriousness. "I could send Luke with a note to the farm to fetch what you need…? Although perhaps that would alert Mrs. Keble, if she isn't already, to ask questions as to your whereabouts. Though the boy would not answer, making it awkward for everyone."

"Mrs. Keble is away from Abbeywood," Mary told him. "While we were visiting your mill, several men arrived with news that her mother—or was it her father?—had taken ill. Though Jane was not entirely certain; all she would say was that the men looked more brutes than escorts. And we were all left wondering why Mrs. Keble needed five such brutes to accompany her to Cirencester. Jane said the woman was in floods of tears one moment and drunk the next, needing assistance to be put up into the wagon. Poor wretch."

Thugs in the employ of the Spymaster General, and who had most likely forced enough spirits down the housekeeper's gullet to render her biddable, was Christopher's guess. A wretched business indeed, and one he was glad Mary had not witnessed.

She followed him to the door, but he paused before opening it and turned to frown down at her.

"Will you be all right here alone? I will be gone several hours. I may not be able to return until nightfall."

She went on tiptoe and kissed his cheek. "Yes. Perfectly. And if you do not go now, I will not have the time I need to have my clothes dry before you come back."

He pulled her to him, hand pressed to the small of her narrow back, and kissed her swiftly.

"Don't go beyond the weir. And stay this side of the stream. I don't want to frighten you, but there are travelers about this time of year and—"

"Silly! Travelers wouldn't dare lay a finger on me for fear of the consequences."

Christopher's gaze swept over her, from free-flowing tangle of long red curls to stained white stockings that had seen better days. She was as far removed from an earl's daughter that few, least of all gypsies, would believe her, no matter how imperious her demeanor and tone. He did not remind her that the highwaymen who had held up her mother's carriage on the way to her brother's wedding had not cared one jot that the consequence of robbing a countess and her daughter was death by hanging. He made no further comment, and after kissing her again, opened the door.

And there under the portico with his knuckles poised to knock was Luke, and behind Luke was a loose-limbed giant of a man with skin the color of burnt caramel. Christopher had no idea who this stranger was. But Mary knew. She was so shocked she blanched and staggered back, a hand to her throat in disbelief. It was her cousin's husband, the Duke of Kinross.

PART II

THE FAMILY

TWENTY-FOUR

The day before, just on dusk, two carriages turned in under the arch of the gatehouse lodge and swept up the gravel drive to the entrance of Brycecomb Hall. The Jacobean manor was at its magnificent best at sundown, when the soft glow of the setting sun turned the buildings' yellow stone a dark golden honey. Visitors always remarked upon it, even those who had been to the house at other times of the day. The occupants of both carriages were no different. They all piled out onto firm ground, and stretched their limbs after a long day of travel, and at speed. They then paused for a few moments to admire the picturesque setting. This said much about the manor's beauty, because these men and women were no ordinary visitors. They were used to residing in homes on such a palatial scale that they were their own kingdoms, and their opulent splendor went beyond the wildest imaginings of everyone except these privileged few.

And then the mistress of this entourage picked up a handful of her delicately-embroidered velvet petticoats from under her fur-lined cape, and swept indoors on the arm of her husband, the family physician a step behind. Following them indoors was the couple's major domo, her lady's maid, two tirewomen, and her husband's valet. A footman directed the two carriages and the eight liveried outriders to the stables at the far side of the main building. Here servants had assembled to offload the mountain of luggage, and stable hands waited to uncouple and clean the carriages of lime dust, and to take care of the more than a dozen horses, while the estate's ostler met the drivers and outriders to oversee that they were provided with enough cider, a hot meal, and had quarters by the stables.

The guests who had entered via the heavy front doors were met in the great hall by a line of silent upper servants and a nervous Carlo, who had been awaiting their arrival since word was sent via a servant of the publican of *The Bear* that two carriages were on their way to Brycecomb. It was the publican's opinion (and everyone deferred to him because he had in his youth been employed in a great household in Bath) that the owner of both and the occupant of one of the carriages was a duke. He knew this by the coronet above the shield and below the helm and crest of the coat of arms emblazoned on the black lacquered doors of each vehicle. Five visible strawberry leaves around the crown were for a duke, the publican would give his good eye tooth, he was that sure of himself.

Watching this arrival from the first landing was Kate's companion Fran, who remained out of sight but within earshot of the conversation. Ordered to report back all she saw and heard to her mistress, Fran was at first surprised to hear the French tongue, not English, and then amazed when Carlo was eventually addressed in his native language. While she had only a rudimentary understanding of Italian, curiosity brought her to the balustrade to peer down at these unexpected but most fascinating of guests, to wonder how far they had travelled and if in fact they might be visitors from abroad known to her mistress.

The little lady, who had swept in on the arm of a tall, lanky gentleman, pushed back the hood of her cape from her upswept blonde hair of many plaits, threaded with ribbons and pearl-headed pins. Her lady's maid stepped forward to remove the cape altogether, and Fran's mouth wasn't the only one to drop open at the lady's gown of rich, dark blue velvet with silver lacings. The servants, too, stared, then quickly looked to the floorboards. Carlo stared longest of all, for this fascinating little lady was possessed of a heart-shaped face, the most unusual green eyes, oblique like a cat's, and a deep bosom. But it was at the roundness of her belly that he stared hardest of all. And then he remembered his manners and brought his gaze back up to her face and saw that she was not in the first or even the second flush of youth, that her blonde hair was lightly streaked with silver threads at the temples. Yet this did not detract from her beauty for Carlo thought her the most captivating elfin creature he had ever seen. And she looked to be in the final trimester of her pregnancy.

"You must please excuse this great intrusion, but we have come to see M'sieur Bryce," Antonia, Duchess of Kinross announced. "And you will please take us to him *immédiatement.*"

Carlo looked to the sun-bronzed giant standing beside her, as if he would provide a translation of her French tongue. But as he was engaged in being divested of greatcoat and gloves by his valet, he had not caught Carlo's unspoken plea. So Carlo bowed again and shrugged, and Antonia repeated her sentence, this time in English. When this received the same non-committal response she turned to her husband and said in Italian,

"I must be mistaken. I presumed a civilized tongue was spoken in this house."

The little man's face lit up, and he so far forgot himself as to speak before being addressed directly, which caused a collective intake of breath from the Duke and Duchess's entourage, but the ducal couple were unmoved. All they cared about was speaking to Christopher Bryce, and as soon as possible.

"*Sì! Sì, Signora!* Carlo speaks the most civilized tongue in the whole world. I am at your service!"

"It seems your presumption was correct, sweetheart," Jonathon, Duke of Kinross quipped. He addressed Carlo. "The Duchessa has come a long way to see *Signore* Bryce, so be a good fellow and don't keep us lingering in the hallway. Just lead the way, and then you can fetch us one of those special coffees your countrymen are so good at making."

"But, *Signore, Signore* Bryce he is not here. I tell you that on my honor."

Antonia and Jonathon exchanged a look and then she said with great patience, "He is not here because he is not here, or because he is away from the house at this time and will return?"

Carlo stuck out his bottom lip and was about to answer when Silvia bustled through from a servant passage. She took one look at Antonia, gaze fixing on her belly for the briefest of moments, then threw up her hands with delight.

"*Signora! Signore!* Welcome! Welcome! All of you are most welcome. Carlo," she reprimanded her husband, "why are these good people waiting to be shown up to their rooms? Their trunks they are being offloaded as I speak, and so you will please take the good lady and her women and his gentleman up to the east wing. This other gentleman who has the look of a *dottore* may have the room down the hall—"

"It is exceedingly important that I have a bedchamber close to Her Grace, so that I may be called upon at a moment's notice," insisted the physician with a sniff. "In her delicate condition and at this late stage, anything could happen! And so it is vital I be on call, and at the ready, at all times."

"I like your diligence, Pratt, but Her Grace could do without your over-effusive attentiveness. Grates on the nerves," Jonathon complained. He looked down at Antonia and said with a wink, "Tell me again, sweetheart, why I allowed Roxton to persuade me to let his personal physician come on this journey with us?"

"You did nothing of the sort," Antonia retorted without heat. "You and my son decided it between you, then presented it *un fait accompli* to me that I could not leave Treat unless he came with us. What choice did I have? But me I think you only agreed with my son so he would not worry excessively while I was away." She dimpled. "Thank-you for that. But I do not thank you for agreeing with him."

"Ah! So you saw through my cunning plan! I should've known you would. But to own to a truth," Jonathon confessed sheepishly, "I'm the one who's feeling delicate."

Antonia looked up at him, and lightly touched his sleeve. "Yes, and I am sorry for it," she said quietly in French, knowing he was fragile with worry for her; his first wife had died in childbed, and so too had their baby boy. "But have I not told you a thousand times I am much stronger than I look? And so too is our little one. I do not need M'sieur Physician here to tell me so, though I know his presence is a comfort to you. But please, his room it must be as far from mine as is possible without putting him in the straw with the horses."

She said this last sentence over her shoulder to the major domo, and when this most trusted of servants nodded his understanding, she turned back to smile kindly at Silvia and Carlo and addressed them both equally.

"I have no wish to cause your household inconvenience but unfortunately it can't be helped and is most necessary. Our *maggiordomo Signore* Gallet, the gentleman in the black coat with the intelligent eyes you see at my back, he will arrange everything to everyone's satisfaction. You are not to worry about any of it. He speaks more foreign tongues than me, which is saying something. But what I most want to do at this moment is to speak with *Signore* Bryce, but you tell me your master he is not here?"

"He is not, *Signora*. But Luke, he knows where he is."

Carlo shot his wife a startled look. This was news to him. "He does? Silvia, why did you not tell me this?"

"It was not your business to know."

"Not my business? Everything here is my business!"

"Not this."

"And yet now it seems that it *is* my business!"

"Please!" Antonia demanded. "You can berate each other later. Now you will attend me." She addressed Silvia exclusively. "This Luke, he can be fetched, yes?"

"*Sì, Signora.* But I do not know if it will do you any good," Silvia apologized. "He knows the whereabouts of the master but he will not say, not to anyone. His mouth it is shut tighter than a sprung rabbit trap!"

Antonia was emphatic. "He will tell me. Now please, I wish to retire to my rooms to bathe and change out of these clothes. And the *bébé* would like a little something for me to nibble on before supper, if that is not too much trouble?"

Silvia beamed and clapped her hands. "Of course! Of course! Silvia will make you a plate of something wonderful and a cup of her special milk coffee. The *bambino* will enjoy it very much, I assure you."

Carlo dismissed the servants to go about their duties—there was much to do. Then he turned to go up the stairs to show the visitors to their rooms, but Antonia had taken Silvia aside, so he stopped and waited; so too did Jonathon, the good doctor, and their clutch of servants. Antonia glanced up the stairs to where Fran was leaning over the balustrade, enthralled, and thus had forgotten she was supposed to be out of sight, and said confidentially,

"There is another who lives in this house. I want you to give her a message from me. And it must be you who tells your mistress. You understand?" When Silvia nodded she continued. "Tell her Antonia she wishes to see her. But only if she wishes to see me."

When Silvia followed her glance up to where Fran leaned over the balustrade then met Antonia's gaze and nodded her understanding, Antonia smiled. "*Bene.* We understand one another. But I will not disturb your mistress this evening. Tomorrow morning will suffice. She needs time to think over my request. And I need time to recover from the journey. The roads in this county they are very bad. But when this Luke he is found, send him up to my rooms. I will not come down again until the morning, unless your master he returns, and then you can get me up whatever the hour. Yes?"

Silvia bobbed a curtsy and beamed. "*Sì, Signora.* It will all be done the way you wish it. You have our complete cooperation."

Antonia returned the woman's smile. "Yes, I know I do. *Grazie.*"

"IT LOOKS AS IF THE LAD CAN'T BE FOUND," JONATHON announced, closing the connecting door to a closet which was crammed with their traveling trunks and belongings, a cleared corner serving as his dressing room. "He may be at Abbeywood Farm," he added, padding across the bedchamber in his silk banyan and Moroccan leather slippers, "which I'm told is in the next vale."

Antonia looked up from the book she was reading, and with a smile rested the pages face down on the rise of her belly. She settled back against the bank of pillows. "Then come to bed, it is late. The boy or his master or both, we will find in the morning."

They had eaten supper in the small sitting room adjoining their bedchamber. And while Antonia enjoyed succulent slices of lamb in a delicious mushroom sauce and a variety of seasonal vegetables, Marc Gallet made certain the kitchen was aware that his master the Duke of Kinross did not eat meat of any kind. Silvia and her two kitchen hands took this surprising news in their stride and Jonathon was treated to one of Silvia's vegetable-stuffed pastas, smothered in a buttery cheese sauce.

And while the ducal couple enjoyed strong coffee and fig biscuits by the fireplace, Antonia's tirewomen, under the direction of her lady's maid, stripped the four-poster bed, remaking it with the Duchess's own down mattress, fresh linens, pillows, and coverlets brought from Crecy Hall. The copper bath by the fireplace and behind a tapestry screen was filled with hot scented water, and a gilt-framed looking glass set on the dressing table along with an assortment of crystal jars, silver-backed brushes, and ribbons. The small pile of books Antonia had brought with her were placed on the bedside table, and her tabouret unfolded and set by the wingchair should she wish to put her feet up and read by the fire before retiring to the bed.

Michelle placed a heavy shawl of India silk and two tapestry cushions on the chair, then stepped back to survey the room that was now filled with those personal possessions the Duchess could not do without. Satisfied the oak paneled room now resembled the bedchamber her mistress shared with her husband at their home in Hampshire, she retreated behind the screen to help the tirewomen ready Antonia for bed.

After coffee, Jonathon slipped outside to smoke a cheroot. He strolled across to the stables in the bracing night air, and there found his major domo in conversation with the ostler. They had then walked back to the house together via an internal courtyard and discussed Jonathon's expectations for the next few days, Marc Gallet adding mildly that in light of the urgency of the situation at hand and the need for Their Graces to return to Treat as swiftly as possible, it was imperative Christopher Bryce's whereabouts be discovered without delay. Would His Grace like him to organize a search party at first light?

"Not at first light, no. I'd be obliged to join you, and I don't want the Duchess woken at the crack of dawn. She needs her sleep. If the elusive Mr. Bryce ain't found by breakfast time, then yes, we'll send out the hounds to sniff him out."

Marc Gallet took this in his stride, and bade His Grace a good night, leaving Jonathon to finish his cheroot.

Seven, almost eight months a duke, and Jonathon was still uneasy when addressed by his title. Except when he was with his wife, because she was every inch a duchess, and so he must be the Duke of Kinross for her—at least in public. When alone together, well, he would be the merchant she had fallen in love with and married, and that pleased them both.

So as he crossed to the enormous four-poster bed to join her, he kicked off his Moroccan slippers, stripped off the silk banyan, letting it fall to the rug, and jumped up onto the bed naked. Antonia did not take her eyes off him for a moment, and giggled when he sprawled out beside her, then propped himself on his side. And as was their practice when they conversed, he spoke in English and she in her native French.

"Did you miss me while I was north of the border?"

"Do you doubt it?"

"No. But I like to hear you say it."

"*Certainement*. I missed you—*very much*. I missed—*all of you*." She dimpled. "Did M'sieur le Duc d'Kinross sleep naked in *Écosse* while he was away from his *duchesse*?"

"I don't own a nightshirt, sweetheart. You know that. Never have. And I wasn't about to start the practice just because I'm a plaguy Scots duke! But I did snuggle up under a bear skin and put myself to sleep by counting the days until I'd be back here with you." He sat up, put out his hand and smiled when she laid her fingers in his. "Being parted from you was unbearable. God what was I thinking to allow myself to be persuaded to leave you behind? Never again."

"Never. I could not bear it either." Antonia's eyes filled with sudden tears. "And look at what greets you upon your return—a-a *grosse femme laide*!" Just as quickly she wiped her lashes and apologized. "Forgive me. As you see I am not myself."

Jonathon's gaze lingered lovingly on her pregnant belly, and then he leaned in and kissed her. He locked his gaze to hers. "I see what others see: A beautiful woman made more beautiful, if that is possible, by the child she is carrying. And I see what others are not privileged to see: My wife. A most desirable, sensual creature whom I love with every drop of blood in my veins." He kissed her again and then asked sheepishly, "May I?"

She knew what he meant without asking and nodded.

He pulled back the coverlet and gently smoothed out the folds of her diaphanous silk night chemise so that her pregnancy was starkly evident. His sheepish grin turned to one of delight as he placed his large hand lightly on her belly and tenderly rubbed his hand over her roundness. The tightness of her skin, as taut as that stretched across a kettle drum, never ceased to surprise him, as did the fact that except for where the baby grew inside her, she had hardly changed at all—this despite her exclamation that she was grossly fat. She was not. He'd forgotten about the changes that occur to a woman's body during pregnancy. In fact he had tried not to think about pregnancy at all for so many years after Emily's death in childbed that he wondered he could be calm thinking about it now.

When he'd first received news from Antonia that she was pregnant he was elated. He had expected it. He had wanted them to have a child. He had walked about for a week as if up on the clouds, smiling at every dour face that greeted him at the ancestral home of the Dukes of Kinross on the shores of Loch Leven. And when he had shared his news with his kinsmen, there had been much rejoicing and toasts made that their new duke was to have an heir. And that's when he was struck by the enormity of what Antonia's pregnancy would mean for her and ultimately for him. He felt as if he had been hit in the chest by a runaway wagon loaded with timber, full force, and it sucked the air right out his lungs.

An heir…

Sixteen years ago, his first wife Emily had done her best to give him a son, and she and the infant had died in labor. It took years for him to come to terms with their deaths, and then, finally numb, he forced himself to forget that traumatic episode. But now, with his fingers splayed across Antonia's belly, the past filled his mind's eye and he could not stop himself from remembering the most harrowing day of his life.

Emily's pregnancy had been uneventful. There was no cause to think anything was wrong or could go wrong. This was her second pregnancy. Three-year-old Sarah-Jane's birth had been long and painful, as all first births are, but Emily had come through that exhausted but happy. And so they approached the birth of their second child with excitement and anticipation. The labor started well, but by the end of the second day, Emily's Indian servants were wailing in despair, and the English physician from the East India Company factory advised him that mother and child were unlikely to survive. He must decide: Mother or child.

How could he make such a choice? He would not. Emily and the baby would both live. He believed that unequivocally. The physician must save them. And if he could not, then the Indian midwife and her helpers would. But the decision was taken out of his control. The baby was a boy, perfect in every way, but he came into the world dead, and then the exhausted mother, upon learning her infant was stillborn, had simply given up, or so it seemed. Later, the physician was of the opinion she had hemorrhaged internally.

They were buried in the English cemetery at Hyderabad, leaving him a widower at twenty-three, with a three-year-old daughter without a mother. And now here he was with a wife several weeks away from giving birth, and she at an age when childbirth came with the greatest risks of all. Emily's death had been traumatic, but should anything happen to Antonia, he would lose the will to live.

He suddenly felt chilled, and pulled the coverlet up over them both. Resettling himself, he snuggled down beside her, resting his ear and his hand lightly against her belly. And there he stayed, content, barely aware that Antonia was lightly stroking his curls while she returned to reading her book.

He dozed. For how long, he had no idea. And then he found himself prodded awake. The prodding continued near his ear, and long enough for him to roll onto his back and look at his wife. She had put aside her book and was lying back against the bank of pillows, grimacing. He sat up and was about to ask if there was anything he could do to help her be more comfortable when she grabbed his hand and shoved it under the covers and onto her belly where his ear had been resting. He wondered why and then of a sudden he felt that same prodding motion but this time it came and went, and then all of a sudden there was a great ripple of movement, and it was all happening under the palm of his hand. It took him several seconds to react and realize what it was he was experiencing, and then he stared at Antonia in wonderment, face splitting into a grin.

"Did you feel that? Did you? She moved! She kicked out at me. I'd lay good odds that was her foot. There she goes again! By Jove, she's quite an acrobat!"

Antonia laughed, any uncomfortableness forgotten in his boyish excitement. "You think this baby it is somehow detached from me? Of course I feel it, all of it, you foolish man. I suspect she has had enough of such confinement. And I do not blame her for wanting to stretch out after so many months curled up, and she is telling me so."

Jonathon fell back on the pillows with a self-satisfied smile, hands behind his head, and stared up at the pleated canopy.

"I predict she'll be a graceful dancer, and an excellent horsewoman who can jump fence for fence with her male admirers. And she'll have many of those, because she'll be the spit of her divine mama. So she needs to be able to defend herself. Lessons in the art of sword play wouldn't go astray. Knowing how to use a rapier, she'll be able to keep at a safe distance all those young dogs who try to make up to her."

"Dancing, riding, *and* fencing? *Parbleu*! While you are making this list why don't you add lessons in how to use a small pistol. There would be no need then for her to dally with these poor puppies in sword play. She can just shoot them dead and be done. Not that I think you, as her doting papa, will allow such men near her in the first place."

Jonathon sat up again and swiftly kissed Antonia's hand.

"Capital notion! Scrap all those years of fencing practice. Target practice is a more practical use of her time. And that will free her up to sit at her books, for I am very sure you have plans for her to be tutored in all manner of learned subjects and languages. Oh dear… Sweetheart, what have I said now to upset you? Or are your eyes watering of their own accord as one of the many wonders of being with child?"

Antonia shook her head and again quickly dabbed her lashes dry. But this time the tears would not stop so readily, and she groped for one of her lace-bordered handkerchiefs from the side table.

"Shall I have Michelle fetch you some hot milk? Tea? Coffee? No…?"

When Antonia had mastery of her voice, she swallowed and said, "You say *she* and *daughter* as if the sex of this baby is a known thing. It is not. Perhaps you do to placate me because you know I want a little daughter very much? But if you want a son you should say so. And you should say so, because a son is what you need. Perhaps you forget you are duke and a duke must have a son to succeed him. Even though I am certain Monseigneur he would have welcomed a daughter because he loved me, he was so very happy I gave him a son and heir to continue the dukedom on after him. He was just as ecstatic when Henri-Antoine he was born. It is the way of all men."

"Is it? Well, it ain't my way!" Jonathon stated categorically. "I want a daughter just as much as you do."

"I love you for saying so. And you say it with such conviction because you know this baby will be my last. It is selfish of me to want a daughter when the needs of the dukedom must come first. You have a daughter and no sons. You are the last of your family. If you do not have a son, the dukedom dies with you. This is what I must focus on—"

"—but in your heart of hearts you want a daughter."

Antonia's green eyes filled with tears again and she nodded.

"I am a disloyal wife to have such thoughts—"

"Rot! Sweetheart, the main thing is that our baby is healthy," he replied buoyantly. "More important for me is that you live through the ordeal. Whatever the sex of the child, I will not be happy or content, and there will be no celebration, until I know you are safe and well. And I will not risk your life to save the child's, so do not ask that of me —ever. And if that's being selfish, so be it. But I can ease your mind on one all-important matter," he added and smiled into her eyes. "The future of the dukedom is secure, whether you give me a son or a daughter."

Antonia struggled to sit up off the pillows. "Oh? Did a long-lost relative come forward to claim kinship with you while you were in Scotland?"

"No. Nothing like that."

"You have that look on your face—smug and secretive—that says you have outfoxed me in some way."

"I can't take credit. My Scottish lawyers told me as a matter of course, almost as an aside. They offered apologies that should the unthinkable happen and you present me not with a longed-for son but with a daughter, all is not lost. And when I rubbed my hands together with glee at what they told me, they wrongly assumed it was because I was thinking of the dukedom, when what I was thinking was that should God grant us our wish, we could both have what we so desperately want: A daughter."

Antonia's eyes went very round.

"You truly want a daughter?"

"Weren't you listening to me just now? Sweetheart, I want a second daughter. I want to have a daughter with you. I love being Sarah-Jane's papa. I raised her without a mother from the age of three. I know how it is with girls. It's all hair, tea parties, and conversation. Can't think of a better way of spending my time."

"But our daughter you say is to learn to fence and discharge a pistol, to have a learned education, and be taught many languages."

"French, English, Gaelic, and Italian should just about suffice for a woman in her position. And she'll need to have much more wit than hair, but that's a burden I'm sure she'll cope with most admirably because girls are smarter than boys. Boys take longer to grow into themselves. We're clumsy clods for the longest time. It's a wonder females can be bothered with us at all until we're at least in our third decade. The Spartans got it right and kept their men away from their women until they turned thirty. But most of all, I want a daughter because it will make you happy. And your happiness is all that matters to me."

Antonia needed no convincing about his love and devotion, and now she believed him about his wish for a girl. But she was still puzzled as to how having a daughter would not be an impediment to the continuation of the Kinross dukedom, and so said, frowning to understand,

"But how is it your lawyers they advise that if we have a daughter and not a son, the Kinross dukedom it will still have a future?"

"Because, love of my life, a Scottish dukedom is not an English dukedom. An English dukedom requires the title to pass down through the male line, so a son is necessary. But a Scottish dukedom stipulates that the title pass to the *heirs of my body*. Male or female is not stipulated, so if a duke—me—has an only child who is a daughter, she will inherit, and be the next Duchess of Kinross, and then it is her son who will inherit after her. Now that's clever! So you, my love, wife to not one but two dukes, and mother of a duke, should you give birth to a female infant, will also be mother of a daughter who will one day be a duchess in her own right."

Antonia gasped and then said, dimpling, "That pleases me *very* much."

"Yes, I thought it would. Now let's get comfortable and sleep. You're forgetting why we're here, and tomorrow is not going to be pleasant, for any of us."

He kissed her, then reached over and snuffed the candle on the bedside table, and in the darkness snuggled in beside her.

But Antonia had not forgotten about tomorrow. She had merely pushed to the back of her mind what had brought them all the way from Hampshire into the Cotswolds, and tried not to dwell on the task that was ahead of her. Tonight she concentrated on being in the arms of the man she loved, and the baby she was carrying; all going well, they would have a healthy baby girl. But as she drifted into sleep, it was not a longed-for daughter that occupied her thoughts but how to tell her cousin Mary the disturbing news about her much-loved daughter, Theodora Charlotte, known simply as Teddy.

TWENTY-FIVE

ANTONIA WAS BEING DRESSED BY HER TIREWOMEN WHEN Michelle returned from downstairs with the news the boy Luke had been true to his word and led M'sieur le Duc straight to the Squire. They had now all returned to the house, and with them was Mme la Duchesse's cousin, the Lady Mary. When Michelle paused on a breath, Antonia looked up from inspecting the sit of the neckline of the pair of jumps secured across her ample bosom. She did not give away her thoughts, but asked blandly,

"Mary she is now here, too?"

"Yes, Mme la Duchesse. She was one of the party that returned with M'sieur le Duc from the cottage in the woods. So it must be assumed she was with M'sieur Bryce because—"

"No, Michelle. One does not assume anything of the sort."

"But her petticoats they are all grubby and her hair it truly is a tangle, so it would appear her ladyship has not had the services of her maid for—"

Michelle stopped mid-sentence and bit down on her tongue, because Antonia's back had stiffened and she had a look in her green eyes Michelle knew very well indeed but rarely saw: A warning—that if she dared to continue her line of reasoning along its present path there would be consequences for her assumptions, regardless if they proved true or not.

So Michelle changed tack and concluded mildly, "—for the many hours she spent on a very long walk."

"Then the Lady Mary will welcome a bath and a change of

clothes while we visit with Lady Paget." She addressed her tire-women. "Finding the Lady Mary clothing will not be a worry, we are very similar, except for this baby, though you will apologize that I cannot offer her a corset. Her maid will bring one in her trunk. Lady Mary's maid she is on her way, yes?" she asked Michelle as she picked up a fan from the dressing table and slipped the silken cord over her wrist.

"A servant was sent at first light with your instructions, Mme la Duchesse. I am told Abbeywood is not far from here, so the Lady Mary's trunks and her maid should arrive by suppertime."

"*Bon*. Tomorrow we must return to Hampshire. But now we go visiting. Oh, and, Michelle," Antonia added quietly as one of her tire-women draped a silk shawl across her shoulders, "as always you are deaf to what you hear."

Michelle curtsied. "As always, Mme la Duchesse."

She followed Antonia out of the bedchamber and across the landing to where a servant waited to escort them to a wing of the house so secluded that it had only ever been visited by one guest in ten years, that guest being the neighbor's daughter, Teddy.

Her ladyship's companion greeted Antonia in the small withdrawing room she kept for her personal use. It was divided from her mistress's large bedchamber, which also served as a sitting room, by a brocade *portière*. This heavy curtain partition used instead of a door enabled Fran to better hear the tinkle of her ladyship's little handbell. When not needed, this small room served as her sanctuary, crammed as it was with all manner of personal objects collected during a lifetime, and mostly from time spent in the Italian States with her mistress. Her two most precious possessions were a singing bird in an ornamental cage, and a ginger cat, curled up in the sun on the daybed, both gifts from the master, Squire Bryce.

Fran bobbed a shaky curtsy and nervously held her hands in front of her. She had never been in the presence of a duchess before, and the imperious little beauty dressed all in velvet and heavy silk was everything she imagined a duchess to be, though the noblewoman's advanced stage of pregnancy was still a shock that was writ large on her long face and had her forgetting her rehearsed speech of welcome.

Antonia instantly put the woman at her ease by leaning in and saying with a smile, and in English, "It was a great surprise to me too."

Fran gave an involuntary nervous titter then became serious and said confidentially, "Your Grace is aware of her ladyship's—*difficulty?*"

"Yes."

"I hope you will not think it an impertinence, Your Grace, for me to ask you to try to understand that there are times when my lady becomes frustrated by her limitations and is not herself. Nothing is meant by these outbursts, but if one is not used to them, they can be confronting. I apologize in advance if Your Grace is in any way offended—"

"I will not be offended in the least."

Fran nodded, curtsied again, and had Antonia, with Michelle close at her back, follow her under the *portière* into a large, long room that had most of its curtains pulled across the windows to keep out the daylight.

"Her ladyship prefers to sit in the dark," Fran apologized. "Her sight—"

"Don't tell fibs, Fran! It has nothing to do with my blindness," Kate retorted. "Women of a certain age look best in shadow. Now run along and fetch the tea—"

"Coffee for me," Antonia interrupted gently.

"Tea for me and coffee for the Duchess," Kate corrected, remaining in deep shadow by a window seat. "Do come closer, Your Grace. I am still able to see parts of you, y'know, just not your face. But I don't need to see that because your delicate features are permanently etched in my mind's eye. But forgive me. I did not curtsy to rank when you entered the room. I am out of the habit, but one should always accord a duchess the respect she deserves."

She made an overt display of dropping into a deep curtsy, in acknowledgment of her visitor's privileged status, but before she was halfway up out of the formal greeting Antonia had the older woman by the elbow and would not let her go.

"No! No! This is most unnecessary between us," Antonia said in a rush of French. "Did not your housekeeper tell you that Antonia wished to speak with you? And so it is as Antonia I am here. We have known each other for far too many years to stand on ceremony. I have never forgotten the great kindness you showed me when I first came to this country, alone and desolate, and to live with a relative who did not want me. If not for you, me I would have been sadder still. Come let us sit and be comfortable," she continued in the same buoyant tone, though she was aware her hostess was shaking and biting her lip as if under considerable duress to keep her emotions tightly bottled. "Michelle! Arrange the cushions, and these curtains open them all. I know you cannot see me as well as you should," she said gently to Kate, "but I wish very much to see you, my lady—"

"It's Kate. It's always been Kate," she burst out, unaware she was clinging to Antonia's arm as if to a life raft in rough seas.

"How long has it been since we were in each other's company?" Antonia asked conversationally, though she knew the answer.

"Twelve years. We last saw each other in Rome."

"Ah yes, Monseigneur and I were on our way home to Paris from Constantinople—"

"—where your eldest son had been living. He was with you, and so too was your youngest boy."

"Henri-Antoine," Antonia told her. "He had his fifth birthday in Rome."

With Kate settled and the curtains pulled back from the window to let in light, Antonia spread out her petticoats and sat in the window seat. Michelle fussed with the placement of a couple of cushions to make her mistress comfortable, then retreated to a chair on the other side of the large Turkey rug and there perched, close enough to be of assistance if required, but far enough to not appear to be eaves-dropping.

Aware that their time alone would be limited now the Squire had returned, and so, too, had Mary, Antonia was even less inclined to waste time in light discourse. But she was sensitive to the fact that the woman sitting beside her was now a recluse and did not receive visitors. So she took a moment to engage her in conversation she hoped would make her feel at ease, particularly when the last time they had seen each other, harsh words had been uttered.

"You look well, Kate," she said truthfully. "The silver in your hair suits. And I see you have lost none of your—how do you say it in English—*sens de l'esthétisme vestimentaire.*"

Kate smiled for the first time since Antonia came into the room. "Dress sense...? Thank-you. Yes, I still strive to look my best, even if I do not receive company."

"You do not think of coming to London occasionally, to see friends, to attend the Opera perhaps? You do not need your sight to listen to beautiful singing..."

"Ha! And this from a woman who locked herself away with her grief for three years. I hardly think you are best qualified to offer me advice, do you, my dear?"

"No? But me I do have a first-hand experience of self-centered misery, and what a burden that is on our loved ones, particularly a concerned son."

Kate's fingers flinched in her lap, tightening about the heavy silk damask of her petticoats.

"Why are you here, Antonia? Why come to me now, after all these years? I kept a respectful distance from your married life with M'sieur le Duc d'Roxton. He and I corresponded, but I am very sure you knew all about it, and accepted it, or he would not have done so. One word from you and he'd never have inked another word to me! He was that devoted, that in love with you. God, to have the singular devotion of such a man is the stuff of dreams for most females. You had that from him and much more, but even you, the great beauty of our age, dared to doubt him the one and only time I ever asked for his help. And how did you respond to my request? You stupidly thought the worst of us both?! *Shame on you*."

"Yes. Me I was very stupid," Antonia admitted in a small voice. "But it is you who are wrong if you think I ever questioned his fidelity or his love. When we married, I knew he had given up his past life, his lovers—you. But his past it was very black. So when you traveled to Rome specifically to see him while we were there, when you sought his help to locate your son, when you were so distressed to think your son he might be lost to you forever and because of your failing sight you might never see him again—*naturellement* I was left to wonder if the two of you were keeping a big secret from me."

"Little fool! You know as well as I Monseigneur never admitted to fathering any bastards, whether it be true or not. So the notion that we shared a secret son and that M'sieur le Duc was keeping this boy's existence from *you* was ludicrous."

"Yes. It was," Antonia replied sadly, letting her shoulders sag. She sighed. "I should never have doubted him, or you."

"Even if you believed it true—and let us for a moment delve into the realms of the fairy folk and say it was—how could you believe I would keep such monumental news from you?" Kate continued, tempering her tone because Antonia's candid admission did much to soothe her animosity. "I know you better than you think. Despite your tender years when you married, you were strong enough to have accepted that truth, had I confided in you that Roxton and I shared a son. I think you would've coped with the news much better than he. Just as you did his nefarious past, as a matter of course and with good grace, confident in the knowledge you were the great love of his life and nothing and no one would ever come between you."

Kate turned her head away and swallowed hard, and Antonia sensed she was not finished scolding her for her poor judgment upon an occasion that had occurred over a decade ago. So she stayed silent and still, the only sign of her unease the way in which her fingers plucked at the closed pleats of her fan. Her intuition served her well. A handful of seconds later Kate turned back to face her, cheeks stained with tears. It took all Antonia's self-control not to offer her lace-bordered handkerchief and to fuss over her.

"I don't care what you think, or if your sensibilities are offended, but I miss him," she stated belligerently. "I miss M'sieur le Duc d'Roxton every day. We were lovers for a short time, but more than that, we were the best of friends for years before you twirled into his life. And we continued as correspondents until his death. He truly understood me, and his letters always had me laughing out loud. I don't know how he did it, but he knew all the best gossip about all the best people! But he was expert at knowing the difference between gossip and keeping a secret. He never betrayed me or my son to anyone—except to you. And he would never have done that had you not demanded it of him. He broke his promise to me because of you, and you humiliated me. I never knew him to have a weakness, but when he had me recount the most painful episode of my life to you— that I'd been forced to give up my only child, a child fathered by a lover—I knew then that you were his greatest weakness of all!"

"What you say—all of it—is true, and I am truly sorry for having caused you distress. It is an episode of which I am not proud. But you must know I would never give you or your son away, to anyone. I have not. And I do not want you to hate me anymore—"

"I don't hate you, you foolish girl! And there is truth in what you say," Kate admitted grudgingly. "I have no right to be miserable. I am alive and in the best of care, and I have the most devoted son."

"I am looking forward to meeting him."

"You will think it a mother's boast, but he is quite out of the ordinary way," Kate said with a warm smile. "You will see what I mean as soon as you see him. He is as far removed from the conventional Cotswold squire that he might as well reside on the moon as be considered one of them! I may not go out into society anymore but I do remember my visits here when I was much younger, vividly. My sister's husband, while a good soul and an excellent man of his type, who was also a good father to Christopher, was a rather dull, plodding fellow who could no more shuffle around a ballroom as fly. Whereas my son has a noble bearing, with a natural grace—"

"He is like you," Antonia stated simply.

"Oh, that is lovely of you to say, my dear. Perhaps he did inherit that from me; his true father had two left feet as I recall..." Kate stopped and sighed, then mentally shook herself free of the past and said flatly, "Christopher, for all his talents, is determined and quite content, it seems, to spend the rest of his days here in this agrarian void, as Squire Bryce. And so I must find it within me to be content here, too."

"*Est-ce une si mauvaise chose*? Kate, this place it is a very pretty part of the kingdom with all the houses made of buttery stone and a landscape that goes up and down like a bed sheet flapping in the wind, so different from what I am used to. Of course, the roads they are atrocious, and here it is remote from life closer to London. And I admit I do not understand a word the rustics say, if they say anything at all because I am told very few of them speak, and when they do it is one or two words only. But if your son he is happy here, and he enjoys being squire of a not inconsiderable estate, what more from life do you want for him?"

"What you mean is: Squire in a picturesque backwater is more than a bastard progeny of an adulterous union between a minor baron and an admiral's wife can expect from life—"

"I meant nothing of the sort! I meant—"

"Antonia, you may be affronted by my bluntness but it does not change the truth in what I say. As a bastard, my son has few if any rights. He is a social pariah. He cannot join our social class, yet he is not of the gentry either. And his neighbors, were they to learn of his true parentage, they would most certainly shun him thereafter. And I am forever relegated to being his Aunt Kate!"

Antonia unfurled her fan with a flick, her agitation showing itself in the way she fluttered it.

"Now it is my turn to be blunt with you, because although I have yet to meet him, what you say about your son's social position and his birth seems to me to trouble you more than it does him. How old is he —thirty-five, forty?"

"He will turn forty in the new year. I remember the day as if it were only yesterday."

"I do not doubt that, Kate. Mothers never forget the birth days of their children. So your son, he is now almost forty, and here he is a prosperous squire. Which would seem to be the life he wants for himself, yes? And from what my son tells me, your son is not only a successful farmer, but he owns cloth mills, too. And Jonathon he tells me your son has an excellent business brain, which is high praise indeed, because he was a merchant before he became a duke—"

"Jonathon—?"

"M'sieur le Duc d'Kinross, my husband. He was an East India merchant before the coronet it unexpectedly fell on his head. He tells me that it is no small feat your son performed to turn around the fortunes of Abbeywood Farm, and in so short a time, too. M'sieur le Duc also says your son he is a financial genius, and he intends to seek him out for advice on his plans for his estates in Scotland. *Voilà!* You have even more reason to be proud. Yes?"

"I am proud of him," Kate replied with emphasis and a trembling smile, gratified to hear such praise. "More than anything I want him to be happy. Isn't that what any mother wants for her child? To be happy? And I do not mean the sort of happiness to be gained from his achievements and his choice to live his life here. I know he is satisfied, even if I am merely reconciled to it. It is his personal happiness that worries me most. I'm afraid his illegitimacy is an impediment that cannot be overcome in this instance, because he can never marry the only woman that matters to him, has ever mattered to him. He has not asked her, and that is probably for the best because she will have no choice but to reject him."

"Why? If he loves her, and she loves him, what is to stop them? Why should she reject him just because of his birth. Has he told her?"

"No."

"If she loves him, his illegitimacy should not matter in the least!"

"Ah. But to her family it will matter a great deal. They set great store on pedigree, particularly her mother."

"So she is much younger than he?"

Kate's lips twitched hearing Antonia's note of concern. "Would it matter if she were? It didn't to you…"

Antonia shut her fan with a snap and leaned in to Kate, intrigued more than ever. "But I did not have parents to stop me."

Kate gave a snort. "As if a parent's objections would have had an ounce of influence in stopping you marrying Monseigneur!"

Antonia's green eyes were alight with mischief. "You are right."

"She is ten years his junior and was married, but is now a widow—"

"A widow?" Antonia grabbed onto the word. "So she is free to marry whom she pleases. Her parents they cannot stop her, whatever their objections."

"If only it were that simple," Kate said on a sigh of regret.

Yet, she was secretly pleased by Antonia's response. Confiding in her about Christopher's love for Mary was a calculated move. She knew Antonia would be affronted to think true love could be hampered by any barrier. The Duchess was an unashamed romantic who had overcome all opposition, even from the nobleman himself, to marry the Duke of Roxton, who had been almost two decades her senior.

Kate had also wanted to discover if Antonia knew that it was her cousin Mary with whom Christopher was in love. And from her responses it would seem not. Which meant either the Lady Mary had no idea Christopher was in love with her, or that she was not in love with him. Or, the third possibility was that the couple, though in love, knew their cause to be a hopeless one. An earl's daughter did not marry down; a squire did not marry up. No one broke that rule. If they did they were socially persecuted and ostracized. That was the last thing Kate wanted for the couple.

She too was a romantic, and she knew the couple needed a champion if they were to have any hope of marrying at all. And she was determined that Antonia would be that champion. After all the Duchess had overcome not one but two scandals in her own marriages. A much-older first husband, and then a much-younger second husband meant she would have an open mind to her closest cousin marrying Christopher. And with the support of the Duchess of Kinross, the match would be sanctioned. Polite Society, and more importantly her family, would have to accept the union then, surely?

She shifted up the window seat and reached out to touch Antonia's silk-clad arm, intent on confiding in her that it was the Lady Mary with whom her son was in love. But she thwarted her own best-laid plans when she made a surprising discovery, one which diverted her thoughts in a different direction altogether.

She finally took a good look at her guest, as best she could, given her disability. And while Antonia's facial features were a dark blur, she was able to make out the upswept abundance of blonde hair framing her face, and take in the richness of her velvet embroidered gown, and the pair of quilted jumps with tight-fitting sleeves and low-cut neckline that came together over her breasts with hook and eye, and cut away either side of the roundness of her belly.

"Good God! You're pregnant!" Kate blurted out, incredulous. Such was her shock that she continued to speak her thoughts. "Serve you to rights for marrying a much younger man, and a virile one at that!"

Far from taking offence, Antonia dimpled.

"Yes, every night I am paying for my sins."

"Ha! I don't doubt your need for repentance is profound, you wicked creature," Kate quipped and patted Antonia's hand affectionately. "News of your marriage was the only topic of conversation in every letter I received from London for months. That you'd married a man ten years your junior, and a duke into the bargain, was enough for some matrons to bemoan the sky had fallen in! But this! You've kept your news very quiet indeed."

"I made no effort to do so. And me I am not ashamed of having a baby at my age because I want this child very much, and so does he— even more so. But I suffered from the morning sickness, and then it was decided it would be best if I remained at Crecy Hall for the duration of the pregnancy."

"When is the baby due?"

"It is five weeks until my lying in, although Michelle she tells me it is closer to three, and she is probably in the right. But I suspect it will be sooner than that. Julian he came three weeks early, and Henri-Antoine, as you know, was early too."

Kate frowned, and as she was still holding Antonia's hand, squeezed her fingers and said with angry concern, "Then what in heaven's name are you doing here disturbing my peace, you silly girl? You should be in Hampshire in your own home, in your own bed, biding your time, not gadding about the countryside!"

"Yes. That is all true. But this cannot wait. I need your help. But I need the help of your son even more."

ANTONIA WAS SAVED GIVING KATE A FURTHER AND FULL explanation and then having to repeat herself to Christopher and Mary because Fran had arrived with the tea things. Not a minute behind her was Christopher, and he was everything Kate had said about him, and more. With introductions made, Christopher took charge of distributing the tea cups for Fran, which gave Antonia time to study him, and it also gave him a moment to hide his surprise because his first thought upon making Antonia's acquaintance was how alike she and Mary were in form, if not in coloring.

With Christopher returned to the tea trolley to make his own cup of tea, Antonia had the opportunity to voice her first thought to Kate. She whispered behind her fan,

"He is very handsome, and has a great look of you."

"When he was born I thought so, too, but later wondered if that were wishful conceit," Kate whispered back and smiled thinly. "But I had my conceit confirmed when I met him again; he was about fifteen. I fell all to pieces."

"I do not doubt that. But it is his eyes, Kate, that intrigue me..."

"Because they are a Cavendish trait."

"*Bon Dieu*! That is so!" Antonia hissed, green eyes wide over the pleated edge of her fan. "My daughter-in-law she has those same eyes."

"Yes. And no doubt she has perfected the Cavendish stare, too,"

Kate drawled, and sat back to take a sip of her tea. "That's the only good thing to have come from my blindness. I may still have to live under the Cavendish stare, but I no longer have to see it. Those gentle but reproachful brown eyes could melt metal—"

"—and hearts."

"Can you doubt that? Too many to count when he lived abroad, and if the females here were given half the chance there'd be melted hearts all over this county! A mucky business."

Both women chuckled at the same time, and that set them off into a fit of the giggles that stopped Christopher in his tracks. It had been a very long time since he had seen Kate be so spontaneous as to laugh out loud. He sipped his tea in the middle of the carpet, enjoying the moment and allowing them theirs before crossing to join them. But the laughter stopped as suddenly as it had begun when Fran interrupted the reverie to announce that the Lady Mary was here to see the Duchess of Kinross. Before Kate could respond, Mary was standing before them. She dropped into a respectful curtsy at her cousin's feet in a billow of silk petticoats.

"Mme la Duchesse, you can only have risked coming all this way in your present condition for one reason," she said breathlessly and in French. Rising up, she lightly kissed Antonia's left cheek and then her right. "Tell me the bad news: Which is it—Dair or my father? But please, I beg of you, don't tell me it's both!"

TWENTY-SIX

"You look very well in my clothes, ma petite," Antonia responded mildly, looking Mary up and down with approval. "You should wear that shade of lavender more often. It complements your eyes and your hair. My lady, does not my cousin have the same glorious shade of red hair as our *grand-mère*?"

She had begun this inane conversation in the hopes of allowing the Squire a few moments to regain his sense of time and place. For no sooner had Mary swept across the room than Christopher's gaze locked on her and remained fixed, as if she were the only person in the room. Antonia knew the look of a man deeply in love, and here it was, writ large for all the world to see. She could have kicked her own shin for not being more attuned to Kate's hints as to the identity of the woman her son was in love with and wished to marry. Well! Here was an interesting turn of events even she would not have predicted. Now it remained to discover her cousin's feelings, and she didn't have long to wait for that to become evident.

"Indeed she has inherited your grandmother's hair, Mme la Duchesse," Kate agreed. "And how Augusta would have hated the competition, to think there was another, much younger beauty with the same fiery red mane." She addressed Mary directly. "I mean no disrespect to your grandmother, my lady, but I was Augusta Fitzstuart's best, and possibly only, friend, so I knew her better than anyone."

"That is very true," agreed Antonia. "And that woman didn't deserve your friendship."

Mary looked from Antonia to the woman seated next to her and made a startling discovery. She was so surprised by it that she turned and looked at Christopher before looking back at Kate and saying, "Oh! How do you do, my lady. I would have known you anywhere. You have a great look of your nephew. Or I should say Chris—Mr. Bryce has a great look of you. I'm so glad to finally make your acquaintance."

"Forgive me, my lady," Christopher said, stepping forward. "I should have made you known to one another at once. This is my—"

"Not yet. This isn't the time," Kate hissed, grabbing for Christopher's wrist.

"This is Kate, Lady Paget. My—aunt," Christopher stated, giving Kate's hand a gentle squeeze. "Let me find you a chair," he continued smoothly, and stepped away to fetch Mary a seat.

Unconsciously, Mary's gaze followed him, and despite her apprehension and preoccupation as to why her cousin had traveled all the way into Gloucestershire to see her, her thoughts were back at the cottage, where she still wished to be, alone with Christopher. Real regret was reflected in her eyes. Their time together had been all too brief, and she had no desire to leave that world behind and reenter this one. Yet, here they both were, freshly scrubbed, hair washed, she dressed in her cousin's exquisite petticoats, while he in his plain buff breeches and dark woolen frock coat with silver buttons was every inch the prosperous squire. Oh, why had they not had a few more weeks together, to enjoy each other's company, and each other's bodies...

"Mary? Mary!? About your brother and your father..." Antonia said quietly, and let the sentence hang, watching her cousin keenly.

And there it was—*that look*; Mary was just as in love with the squire; why had she thought it would be any other way? She waited for Mary's focus to return to her, and was not at all alarmed when the woman blinked at her, as if coming out of a stupor.

"There is no fresh news in that quarter. Julian he received Alisdair's letter officially informing the family of your father's death. And like me, who did so for a beloved uncle, I am sure you have shed all the tears there are to weep for your papa. But after all these months of waiting for this news it cannot come as a shock. And you have read the Duke's letter passing on his condolences, yes?"

"No, Cousin Duchess. I have not had any letters this past week," Mary answered truthfully before she thought much about the implications of her honesty.

"A week?" Antonia glanced slyly at Christopher, who set down a chair for Mary. "You have not had any letters for a week?"

"I—I—That is—I may have received letters, I just have not read any of them." She sank onto the chair without realizing Christopher had placed it there, and put her hands in her lap. "So father is dead, and Dair has proof he is dead?"

"Yes, *ma petite*. It is as we feared. And your brother is now on his way home."

Mary nodded. She was numb. But she had no tears left for a father she had not seen since she was twelve and who had abandoned his family. "I'm pleased. Not that he is dead. But that Dair can now have his inheritance. And that he is on his way home. He needs to be here with his wife. Has Rory been told?"

"M'sieur le Duc wrote to her and enclosed a letter from your brother. So yes, I am sure she knows by now." Antonia re-settled on the window seat, shoulders back, and placed a hand lightly on her round belly. She glanced again at Christopher, who remained standing behind Mary's chair, then said with a frown, "It is unlike you not to have read any letters. Particularly ones from my son, and from your mother... Are you unwell, *ma petite*?"

"No. I am well. It's just—I've been doing a lot of walking recently —and thinking."

"Walking? And *thinking*?" Antonia repeated, incredulous. "And you have been doing this walking and thinking in the woods, yes?"

Again Antonia glanced at Christopher, and this time she caught him staring at her with that Cavendish stare Kate had so derided. But there was nothing bold or smug in his look, and she knew it well. Her daughter-in-law had those same brown eyes, and when she gave someone that look—the Cavendish stare—it was a simple acknowledgment that they were aware the person under their gaze was being less than fair, that they did not approve; and that the person was to modify their behavior or there would be consequences. Deb used it to great effect with her children; once she had even used it on her husband, and to see Julian squirm under his wife's gaze had sent Antonia into a fit of the giggles, which had not pleased her daughter-in-law or her son.

And now here was Christopher Bryce silently chiding her for being less than fair with Mary. He was right, of course. She was teasing her, and this was not the place nor the time for banter. Far from being affronted by his visual reprimand, Antonia liked him all the more for it. The romantic in her saw that he was doing so as a way of protecting Mary, but because he was not in a position to openly do so, he did the only thing he could think of without being impolite. What a shame Kate could not witness this!

"You are quite right, M'sieur Bryce," Antonia said, holding his gaze and inclining her head in acknowledgment of his warning. And when he made her a small bow and respectfully lowered his gaze, a ripeness to his cheeks, Antonia continued, all playfulness gone from her tone. "This walking and thinking is unimportant as to why I am here. If you have not read your most recent correspondence, then you would not have read a letter from your mother, which is what I feared most. And why I had to come, so that either I could tell you the true state of affairs, or if you were still in ignorance of what has happened, that you at least hear the news from a close relative, and not by letter. But promise me one thing, Mary."

"Yes, Cousin Duchess. Of course."

"That you listen carefully to everything I tell you, but know in the back of your mind that she has come to no real harm. That she is safe and being cared for, and she knows I have come to fetch you and—"

Mary rose half out of her chair. "Has something—has something happened to my mother?"

"Your mother?" Antonia shook her head and Mary sat back down again. "No, Mary. Your mother she is in excellent health, despite her constant complaints to the contrary. But she has done a very silly— some would say, *we would say*—wicked—thing, that now requires all of us to do our best to put to rights. And I include M'sieur Bryce and Lady Paget in this, too, because Teddy she has asked for them most particularly. *Naturellement* it is her mama she wants most."

"Teddy? What has happened to Teddy?" It was Lady Paget who blurted this out, and she grabbed Antonia's arm. "I can't see what you are all thinking, so you must tell me, Antonia. Tell me nothing has happened to that sweet child!"

"She is not unwell, Kate," Antonia replied and patted the older woman's hand. She turned back to Mary, who was sitting rigid on the chair, hands clasped tightly in her lap, and she knew her cousin was doing everything in her power to remain in control. "Mary, my dear, that is the truth. Teddy is not unwell, nor is she injured. But your daughter she is a little scared being in a strange place, and she is asking for you, her mother. And you," she added, addressing Christopher. "Teddy wants her Uncle Bryce to come and collect her and bring her home. And I have given her my word that this will happen. And I do not break my word, and never to a child. So, we will all leave tomorrow at first light so this can be done as quickly as possible."

"Where is my daughter, Cousin Duchess?" Mary demanded in a hoarse whisper. "What has my mother done with her?"

"First I will tell you where Teddy is. She is in my treehouse—"

"*Tree house*?" Christopher, Mary, and Kate blurted out in unison.

"That is so. My grandchildren's pirate ship treehouse. Now let me tell you how it is she came to be there, so you will not worry so much."

"How can you tell me not to worry when you say Teddy is scared and in your treehouse, and is asking for me and-and her Uncle Bryce?" Mary demanded, all semblance of control lost. "Oh God, I should've insisted on going to Cheltenham with her. I should not have agreed to her visiting with my mother alone. I should've—"

"Mary, the time for should-haves has passed," Antonia said softly but firmly. "It serves no purpose. You must allow me to—"

"I knew Mother was up to something. I had a feeling, a-a *foreboding* that this visit would not go well. She was so insistent I remain at home, that my presence would only be an unnecessary interference in Teddy's welfare. *Interference?* How can she say a mother—me—is an unnecessary interference in my child's life?"

"I think you can answer that easily enough, *ma petite*, from your own childhood experiences, yes? Your mother she has always acted in the ignorant belief her intentions are for the best, when in fact she has allowed a false sense of pride and self-worth to govern her actions. That has led, as you know, to disastrous consequences for you and your brothers. Your mother *was* an unnecessary interference in your lives that you all could have done without, and that is a great tragedy, for her, and for you. She has tried to do the same with Teddy, and now we must all come together to salvage the consequences of that interference. Do you not agree?"

Mary stared at Antonia, and the sadness in her cousin's gaze brought tears to her eyes, the truth of her words striking her like a blow, so that she was forced to clap a hand to her mouth to stop a sob escaping. She turned on the chair to look up over her shoulder at Christopher, and extended a shaking hand to him, which he readily took in his firm clasp.

"I should have insisted you accompany the carriage to Cheltenham. Perhaps if you had been there you could've put a stop to my mother's foolishness."

"Perhaps. But I doubt it," Christopher told her gently. He wanted to kiss her hand, to press his lips to her forehead in reassurance. But he did not. Reluctantly he let her go, acutely aware of the Duchess's gaze upon them. And yet he could not help offering Mary some comfort by placing his hand on her shoulder, and adding with an encouraging smile, "We don't know the manner of your mother's interference. Nor do we know much about what has been done to counter it. Though I am very sure Mme la Duchesse has done everything in her power to make Teddy as comfortable as possible until we arrive."

"Yes. Yes, of course. I am being foolish—"

"No. Never foolish. A mother's unconditional love is never foolish, Ma—my lady," Christopher assured her. "Kate agrees with me. Don't you, Kate?"

"Are you intent on making us all cry, you wretched man!?" Kate demanded and groped about the layers of her petticoats for her pocket which held her handkerchief. Antonia gave her hers. "Now be useful and have Fran make us all a fresh cup of tea and coffee! And let the Duchess get on with telling us what's happened to Teddy—Oh, and before I forget to tell you, that sweet child so reminds me of you, my dear," she said to Antonia. "Not her red hair and freckles, which I find delightful, but her exuberance for life, and the way she sees the good in everything and everyone! Such a little whirlwind of joy—oh dear," she added when there was a burst of tears she could only assume came from Mary. "Forgive me, my dear. Christopher will tell you I tend to say out loud whatever pops into my head. And that only started with my blindness and not being able to take any visual cues from those around me. I do apologise…"

"The tears this time are from happiness, Kate," Antonia replied. "And your idea of more tea and coffee it is a good one. I fear my little one she is moving about and perhaps that is because me I am in need of refreshment. M'sieur Bryce," she added, staring significantly at his hand on Mary's neck and then up at him, "Please to fetch Mary a cup of tea." She smiled at Mary, who was dabbing her eyes dry, put out her hand to her, and was pleased when Mary took it and held on. "And while you drink your tea, *ma chérie*, I will tell you about Teddy, yes?"

And having their undivided attention, Antonia told them the story of how Teddy came to be living in the pirate ship tree house at the bottom of her garden at Crecy Hall.

"Lady Fitzstuart she gave Teddy into the care of her grandmother at her Cheltenham townhouse, and promised to call on them both in a day or two for afternoon tea," Antonia told them. "But when she returned to the Countess's lodgings two days later, the place it had been shut up, and Rory informed that the Countess and her granddaughter they had quit Cheltenham for Hampshire.

"The Countess she told Teddy she had planned a special surprise for her, one that would see her finally take her place among her noble relatives. They were going to stay in a palace that was far larger than any owned by the King. It was full of wondrous rooms of marble, gilt, and mirrors. There were chandeliers that burned as brightly as the sun, and a theater where the children performed plays for their parents, and there was a ballroom so large that even if you shouted your words they could not be heard at the far end of the room. And surrounding this palace were hundreds of acres of parkland, full of deer and dotted with lakes stocked with fish, fountains that shot water into the air, and peacocks that strutted their plumage on the terraced lawns.

"Charlotte was adamant that Teddy she was just as eager to visit this palace and asked her many questions. Not once did the child fret or ask to be taken home. So Charlotte was confident that what she was doing was in the best interests of her grandchild. She said her only wish was to introduce Teddy to her cousins, and her cousins to Teddy. She could not have foreseen the impending catastrophic consequences of her actions, or she would never, in her words, *in a thousand full moons have taken Teddy to Treat*."

"Against the wishes of her mother and her guardian," Mary retorted. "I am very sure my mother did not add that to the end of her sentence!"

"No. She did not. She knew Teddy's guardian would never give his consent to Teddy visiting Treat," Antonia replied, gaze on Christopher who still stood by Mary's chair. "Which is why she took Teddy without your permission."

"Cousin Duchess, there is good reason why Mr. Bryce thought it best for Teddy to remain at Abbeywood—"

"I do not doubt the reason it is a very good one," Antonia interrupted imperiously, green eyes still on the Squire. "But you will please first allow me to finish telling you how Teddy she ended up in my tree house. M'sieur Bryce may then have all the time in the world to explain to me a few disturbing facts about this episode, not least why a child should be kept from knowing her closest cousins."

"I am at your disposal to answer any and all questions about Teddy's guardianship, Mme la Duchesse," Christopher replied with extreme politeness.

"To continue with the story—and this part, Mary, is most distressing, so please put aside your teacup..."

Mary held out her cup on its saucer expecting a maid to collect it, but it was Christopher who took it from her. As he did so, he came to stand between her chair and the window seat, thus effectively blocking Antonia's view of her. And with his back to the Duchess, he paused in taking the cup from Mary's hand, which made her look up at him. And there, in a single moment, he held her gaze and smiled reassuringly, a finger caressing her wrist. She smiled back, briefly covered his hand with hers to let him know she understood and appreciated the gesture signaling his devotion, then lowered her lashes and sat back, spine straight and hands returned to her lap.

If Antonia was annoyed that the Squire had rudely turned his back on her, she did not show it. And she waited for him to return to stand by Mary's chair before going on with her recounting of events at Treat when Teddy arrived with her grandmother.

"Charlotte she sent on a postilion to forewarn M'sieur le Duc's household of her arrival. And so when the carriage it was met, she and Teddy were taken straight to the Duchess, who was with her children in the ballroom. Rain meant they could not run about the gardens, so, as was their usual practice on rainy days, playtime was spent in the ballroom with their billy carts and toys.

"As you can imagine with four lively children and a baby and their various nurses and tutors, there was a great racket. It all stopped for the new arrivals. And as Charlotte will tell it, everyone was getting on splendidly and Teddy welcomed with open arms by Deborah and her children; and a great fuss was made of her. Charlotte and my daughter-in-law sat down to tea. As Deborah tells it, Charlotte was congratulating herself on the success of her scheme to have her granddaughter known to her Roxton relatives, and that she should have put her plan into action years ago, when M'sieur le Duc arrived. As was his custom at that time of day, my son he spends the hour before dinner with his children. It was with the arrival of my son that this orchestrated meeting of the cousins took a horrible turn."

Antonia paused and stared at Christopher, because at this revelation he took a deep breath and wiped a hand over his mouth as if he were well aware of what was to come.

"M'sieur, let me tell you that while it is Teddy's welfare that most concerns us, she is not the only one affected," Antonia said sternly, addressing Christopher directly. "My grandchildren are distressed and frightened. My daughter-in-law she is perplexed and shaken. And my son, well," she said with a shrug of angry annoyance, "I do not doubt that you of all people can imagine he is greatly troubled; he wonders what he has done to deserve such a damning reception from a child he has never met in his life."

"Cousin Duchess, you cannot blame Chris—Mr. Bryce in the least for Roxton's—"

"Please. Mary. No. You will allow me to finish, and then you may speak."

"Antonia, I hope you know what you're about," Kate warned softly. "For it sounds to me perilously close to an accusation that Christopher is somehow to blame, not only for that sweet child's predicament, but for the wrong done your son. And if that is the case, I object in the strongest terms possible to your tone and to such an allegation!"

"Kate, Mme la Duchesse has every right to her anger," Christopher said mildly. "And while I shall not say more at this point so she may tell us the rest, there is a grain of truth in that of which I stand accused."

"No! I won't believe—"

Kate and Mary blurted this out in unison, and such was their surprise followed by embarrassment on Mary's part, and Kate's secret joy that the Lady Mary was prepared to openly defend her son, that they instantly fell silent and looked down at their hands, allowing Antonia to remain deaf to their exclamation and continue.

"It is from here in the story that Charlotte she was unable to communicate to me in any reasonable manner what occurred. She was too distressed—is still too distressed—to speak about it and has taken to her bed at Treat and has yet to get out of it. If I were to think the worst of her, I could say that her anguish is not entirely on Teddy's behalf—"

"Her distress is self-centered, as always," Mary stated as fact. "Teddy has embarrassed her, and so what most concerns her now is her own position, and what Roxton and others will think of her. She is certainly not thinking about the welfare of her granddaughter."

"Just so, Mary," Antonia replied with a slight raise of her brows, for she was unused to Mary being so forthright or so open in her disloyalty to her mother. As Mary said nothing further, she continued, addressing herself exclusively to her. "Deborah tells me that when my son he was introduced to Teddy, your mother she prodded Teddy in the back and told her to make her curtsy, but the child was unable to move or speak, no matter how many times Charlotte insisted she show M'sieur le Duc the proper respect. Teddy could not move. Teddy was overcome—how did Deborah put it?—and had some sort of fit—

"Oh, my God, no," Mary interrupted with whispered anguish, a fist to her mouth.

"Yes, fit. Her body started to tremble uncontrollably and there was a look in her eyes that Deborah described as *sheer terror*. Yes. They are the words she used," Antonia continued calmly. "Everyone wondered what was the matter, not least of all my son, who, as you know, is a loving papa. He tried to calm her, to ask her what was the matter. But the more he tried to speak with her, to reason with her, and moved toward her, Teddy backed away from him, and the more agitated she became. She avoided looking at him, and kept her eyes to the floor, and the one time my son he put his hand on her arm and asked her to look up, she let out a scream. Deb could not make sense of what she was saying, but she kept saying over and over that she would not be locked up."

"My poor darling dear," Mary muttered, tears streaming down her face.

"Of course, once Teddy started screaming, the grandchildren all began to cry, and so too the baby. There was great pandemonium in the ballroom. So much so that while my son and daughter and the nurses were doing their best to calm the little ones, Teddy ran off, several of the footmen sent after her."

"That would have made her even more afraid, to have liveried servants pursuing her," Mary interrupted. "She was terrified enough as it was. That was unthinking—"

"I am sure you can appreciate my son and his wife they were not thinking clearly with four terrified little children and a baby on their hands. Besides, you, more than anyone else here, can appreciate that once a child—anyone—wishes to be lost in such a place as Treat, it is almost impossible to find them. So Teddy easily avoided capture."

"I remember when they were boys—Julian and Evelyn—they would run off and play hide-and-go-seek and expect me to find them. And I never did. There were too many rooms and so too many hiding places for me to search. I would give up after an hour."

"An hour? I would not have bothered at all and waited for them to find me!" Antonia retorted, recalling a memory from the early days of her first marriage when she had played hide-and-go-seek with Monseigneur. She had simply gone to the library and curled up with a book. He found her there not half an hour later, and for finding her so quickly she had rewarded him there and then, and soon they were making love on the map table…

"One passage is the same as another," Mary continued. "It would be easy to become lost and have no idea as to where you are, or to know which door or window is unlocked that can lead you outside to fresh air and freedom. To a child, to Teddy, being in such a house would feel as if she were trapped in a garden maze. But Teddy found an unlocked door and freedom, didn't she, Cousin Duchess," Mary asked anxiously. "Because she is now safe in the pirate ship tree house?"

Antonia shook her thoughts free of nostalgia and smiled reassuringly.

"Yes, *ma chérie*. She did. Teddy is a resourceful and resilient child. I doubt many children—if any—would have the wherewithal and courage to find their way in a strange place. She went to the lake, and one of the boatmen he obliged her and rowed her across to the pavilion. And once at Crecy she found the tree house. Of course, my son he had all his servants inside and out made aware that Teddy was missing, and M'sieur le Duc d'Kinross did likewise at Crecy. The servants were all ordered not to approach her or frighten her, and if she asked for their help to give it, and then report it. That is how we discovered she had crossed over to Crecy, and how we eventually found her in the tree house. We still do not understand how she even knew about the pavilion, least of all that there is a tree house at the bottom of my garden."

"I told her," Mary admitted. "It was one of our many bedtime stories. She would ask me to tell her stories about my favorite people and places. And one tale she had me repeat often was about my godmother, who I told her was a Fairy Queen who lived in a wondrous old house by a lake, built for her by the Fairy King. This Fairy King also built his queen a pretty pavilion so she would have somewhere to hold tea parties and watch the swans glide by, but most of all so she could read all the books that she loves. I told Teddy the Fairy Queen's house was a very happy place where children were always welcome, so welcome, in fact, that at the bottom of her garden the Fairy Queen had built a pirate ship tree house. And here children would sail the clouds pretending to be pirates on the high seas. It was Teddy's wish to one day visit such a tree house."

"What a wonderful bedtime story, my lady," Kate exclaimed on a sigh and sniffed. When this was met with silence she added, "Not a dry eye in the room...? Is that so, my boy?"

"Just so, Kate," Christopher replied quietly.

Antonia blinked tears off her lashes and smiled at Mary.

"I am glad you told her about Crecy, *ma chérie*, because it seems that she does indeed feel safe there. And she will talk to me, her mother's fairy godmother."

"But how do you converse with the child when she is up a tree, and you are too pregnant to climb a ladder?" Kate asked bluntly

Antonia dimpled. "That was very clever of me. I have allowed Teddy to live in my tree house upon one condition: That she comes down each night to sleep indoors."

"And does she?" Mary was surprised.

"Of course. I gave her my word she may return to the tree house whenever she wishes. I do not break my word. Each night at sundown she comes inside to have her dinner and to sleep in a warm bed. And every morning at sun up she returns to the tree house. I gave her the added incentive of watching over Scipio and Cordelia's babies. So, you see, I am a genius, yes?"

"Scipio? Cordelia?" Christopher asked with a raised eyebrow.

"*Babies?*"

"Oh! Yes! You are a genius, Cousin Duchess! What a splendid ruse," Mary announced, feeling much less apprehensive than she had since learning her mother had absconded with Teddy to Treat. "Teddy loves animals, dogs particularly." She turned on the chair to face Christopher, a hand to the front of his waistcoat and smiled up at him. "Scipio and Cordelia are Mme la Duchesse's whippets. Teddy would not be able to resist keeping an eye on their pups. You know how much she wants a dog of her own."

"Ha! Do I? It is a daily plea," Christopher replied, covering Mary's hand and smiling down into her upturned face. "But she also knows her Mama's aversion for four-legged fiends—"

"I have never called Lorenzo a fiend, and you know it!" Mary retorted lovingly.

"Only because you are so petrified of poor Lorenzo you can't get the words out," Christopher responded with a grin.

"Poor Lorenzo? Oh! That is so unfair. Besides, you can have no idea what I'm thinking!?"

"So you think?"

"What I think is that you both continue this conversation later, and elsewhere," Antonia interrupted tersely, hoping to bring the couple to a sense of their surroundings. And so as to not embarrass them further continued smoothly, "And I am very sorry to tell you this, Mary, but I have promised Teddy she may choose one of the six puppies as her own. And so you will have to overcome your fear of dogs, for she will have the puppy, whatever your objections to the contrary."

"Yes, Mme la Duchesse," Mary replied obediently, much subdued, for she realized she had grossly overstepped the mark with Christopher in her cousin's presence, and now would need to account for her behavior. "And if a puppy will help Teddy overcome her fear, then it is only fair I overcome mine."

"*Bon.* The puppy will help take her mind off her fear, *ma petite*, but she cannot overcome it unless we know what caused her to have this unnecessary and unreasonable dread of M'sieur le Duc my son in the first instance, yes? Which still remains a mystery to me, and to us all. And yet, I feel that perhaps you, Mary, or you, M'sieur Bryce, are the only ones who can provide the answer."

Mary went to respond, but when Christopher gently squeezed her shoulder, she remained silent and let him speak.

"I am best placed to answer that, Mme la Duchesse," he said firmly, gaze steady on Antonia. "While the Lady Mary told her daughter fairy stories that were of happy places and people, Sir Gerald offered his daughter a much darker tale, a fable about an ogre masquerading in the guise of a handsome duke. He told her this tale often and from a young age. And he warned her that her mother was under the spell of this ogre, as were the rest of her family, and so they did not see him as he truly was—a monster—part bear, part wolf, with a hog's tusks and a black heart. Sir Gerald warned Teddy that if she was ever to visit his home—a home that was under his magic spell so it appeared like a shining palace, but which was in fact a dark castle full of unspeakable horrors—she would be locked up in one of the towers, and there she would rot until she was an old maid, and never would she see her mother or her home again."

"Oh, that poor dear child," Kate said on a shattering breath. "No small wonder she is terrified!"

"You knew about this absurd fable, Mary?" asked Antonia.

"Yes, Cousin Duchess," Mary admitted. "But only very recently. I had no notion Sir Gerald was filling Teddy's head with such cruel nonsense."

"And you, M'sieur Bryce, when did you discover Sir Gerald was telling his daughter such damaging drivel?"

"When Teddy was taken ill in Buckinghamshire and her mother went to Treat for Lord Fitzstuart's wedding. She was apprehensive of her mother not returning, and when I asked her why, she confided the tale of the ogre."

"I see. It now becomes obvious to me why a ten-year-old child, who has never met my son in her life before, screams her lungs out and runs away to hide in a tree house and won't come down for anyone or anything! Why did you do nothing to dispel these horrid lies about M'sieur le Duc?"

"Mme la Duchesse, fairy tales, whether tales of good or evil, are not lies to those who believe in them," Christopher said patiently. "They are very real to child and adult alike. There are many who accept as true the existence of fairies, gnomes, goblins, and ghosts. The vale is filled with such spirits and tales. Lady Mary told Teddy happy stories of a Fairy Godmother and her father told her a tale of a handsome duke masquerading as an ogre. You cannot dismiss one tale as utter nonsense without then dismissing the other as nonsense, too. What then do you tell the child? That her parents were lying to her? That there are no such beings as fairy godmothers and ogres—"

"That is exactly what you should have told her!"

"I do not believe the Duke to be an ogre, but how could I tell Teddy otherwise when I have never met your son? Teddy is a smart child. Had I dismissed her father's tale out of hand, she would have instantly asked me how I could do so when I have never seen the Duke for myself. I could have offered her all the reassurance in the world, but I could not offer her the evidence to prove otherwise."

Antonia sat up very straight, uncomfortable as this was, given her pregnancy, green eyes bright with anger.

"*Mon Dieu*! *Je suis incroyablement furieuse*. So, that child continued to believe my son, a man of the highest morals, a loving husband and father, to be an ogre. He is beloved by his family, his tenants, his workers, and his servants, and none have a bad word to say about him. And yet Teddy believes him to be this monster hiding in the skin of a duke, and nothing was done to dissuade her of this belief?! *Incroyable. Et vous l'avez laissée y croire*."

"I did nothing to reinforce the idea," Christopher stated politely but firmly. "But as I said, I could not dismiss the tale as nonsense, for to do so would have called into question the reality behind Lady Mary's fairy story of a good and kind fairy godmother living in a happy place. Which, when you consider it is not so far from the truth, is it? And because Teddy believed her mother's tale, she was able to find sanctuary with you."

"But if you had dismissed both tales as merely tales, then perhaps we would not find ourselves in this predicament in the first place, *hein*? Teddy would have questioned the existence of an ogre and of a fairy godmother. But she would not have needed the latter had she not believed in the former! Which leads me to think that you, M'sieur Bryce, think there is a grain of truth in Sir Gerald's tale about my son —that he is in some way an ogre?"

"Mme la Duchesse—" Christopher began, but was cut off.

"Cousin Duchess, you are justifiably angry because it is your son who was maligned by Sir Gerald," Mary interrupted with uncharacteristic bluntness. "But if you were to ponder the situation with a cool head, surely you cannot be surprised her father would plant such a black seed in Teddy's mind about Roxton? Your son banished Sir Gerald from Polite Society; the only thing of consequence to him was his Cavendish name and his position amongst his peers as the cousin of the Duke of Devonshire, and the brother of the Duchess of Roxton, and thus the brother-in-law of her duke. He only married me because I am your cousin. Social standing and bowing and scraping before his titled relatives is what he lived for, and Roxton stripped that from him. Even in exile here in the remote Cotswolds, he spent his days writing to his titled friends and relatives, his mind faraway in the drawing rooms of London society. He was bitter and angry and he never forgave your son. Refusing to allow his only child to visit her relatives was part of his revenge, as was implanting his black fairy tale so that his daughter would have a lifelong fear of Roxton. That he used Teddy to exact his revenge is appalling, but I am not surprised by it, and neither should you be."

Antonia took a moment to answer Mary, both women regarding each other with a steady gaze, and then she smiled forlornly, no longer angry.

"Mary, I have never told you this before but it has always been a great regret of mine that I gave in to your mother's wishes and left you behind when Monseigneur and I took Henri-Antoine to Constantinople to meet his brother. If you had been with us you would never have married that man. But you did and we had to live with the consequences. But you... you had to live with him, and we did not think enough about that, did we? *S'il vous plaît, pardonnez-moi, ma chérie.*"

She glanced at Christopher, but said to Mary,

"And you are correct. My son he acted impetuously, as young men are often wont to do. At the time, I think he did so as to assert his authority, but he did not think through the consequences of his actions upon you and your baby daughter. I am very sure he would agree with me, and add his apologies to mine. And now, here we are, arrived at a situation that requires the utmost delicacy to resolve. I offer my apologies to you, too, M'sieur Bryce. For although we have only just met, I realize you have Teddy's best interests at heart. That child loves and trusts you as much as she does her mother, and so, too, must I trust you. So I must hope that you can come up with a way to get Teddy and the family out of this sad predicament, yes?"

Christopher bowed his head in acknowledgment of Antonia's apology and smiled.

"I have the germ of an idea, Mme la Duchesse. But I wish to consult with the Lady Mary to ensure she is agreeable. Hopefully it will break the curse that holds the Duke captive as an ogre in Teddy's eyes."

Mary swiveled on her chair and looked up at Christopher. "Oh, yes! If Teddy believes the spell is broken she will no longer fear Roxton. You are clever!"

"I am not surprised you think him so," Antonia quipped, tongue in cheek, adding more audibly, "You have the two-day journey to Treat to come up with a suitable plan. Now, me I must rest. And you, my lady," she said softly to Kate, pressing her hand, "I will scold in the carriage. No doubt this conversation, not its content, has been music to your ears. And you know very well why, and now so do I!"

TWENTY-SEVEN

Just as Antonia was getting used to the idea of Mary being in love with a Cotswold squire, and having confided in Jonathon and asked him to form an opinion of Christopher on the return journey to Treat, her cousin confounded her with a revelation that was so surprising that it left her momentarily speechless.

It was on the second day of travel, and the Duke and Duchess of Kinross, their guests and entourage had been an hour on the road, having set out after breakfast from *The Castle Inn* at Marlborough, where they had spent an uneventful night. The Duchess, the Lady Mary, Lady Paget, Antonia's lady-in-waiting Michelle, and Lady Paget's companion Fran occupied the first carriage, while the Kinross's major domo, Lady Mary's maid, Antonia's two tire women and, much to his consternation, the Duke of Roxton's physician, occupied the second. Jonathon, Christopher, and Jonathon's valet were all on horseback, riding alongside the carriages, with the liveried outriders front and rear.

On a particular stretch of road, Jonathon and Christopher rode side by side and were in conversation, and as they passed Antonia's carriage, Mary's gaze locked on the two men. Antonia, who sat opposite and watched her, knew to which gentleman Mary's attention was fixed. But she said nothing and waited, knowing by the way Mary fidgeted with the fan in her lap that her mind was racing, and that very soon she would end her preoccupation and want to confide her thoughts.

Just as predicted, Mary looked away from the window and about the interior of the silk lined carriage, to where the Lady Paget sat in the far corner, staring out the window. Next to Mary was Antonia's lady-in-waiting, head back against the padded squab with eyes closed, and beside her, the old woman's companion Fran, who had her head in a small volume of poetry which Antonia had loaned her. And there was her cousin, fingers entwined under her belly, as if holding her child against every bump in the road. But her gaze was very much on Mary.

"Evelyn is alive, Mme la Duchesse."

Antonia was more surprised to be addressed formally by her cousin than by the revelation itself. She guessed it was perhaps easier for Mary to confess her disordered emotions in this way.

"Yes, *ma chérie*. Your brother Alisdair he told me."

"Did you also know he is a spy?" When Antonia nodded Mary continued. "He came to Abbeywood. You will be shocked when you see him. He is much altered in body if not in mind, his hair is gray before its time, and he is all but skin and bone. He has the parts of two fingers missing, which makes me wonder if he can still play his viola. But for all that he is still the same Evelyn I remember, with the same eccentric outlook on life."

"I am very happy he is alive, that he is finally home, and that he is still Evelyn. I hope he comes to Treat, to make his peace with my son, and to see me, and to visit his parents."

Mary met Antonia's clear green eyes and leaned in to blurt out in a loud whisper, "He means to ask me to marry him."

Antonia's arched brows lifted slightly. "Is that so? What do you mean by *means to ask*—that he has not done so already?"

"He has given me the month to think over my future, and then he will ask me."

"A wise decision. It seems you have much to think about, *ma petite*."

Mary glanced out the window again, the countryside of hedge rows and autumn trees a blur this time. She took a deep breath and turned to meet Antonia's steady gaze.

"I know what *you* must be thinking—"

"I do not think that is possible because me I am not thinking anything. It is *your* thoughts and actions that will decide what I think."

"But I can imagine what you must think of me after His Grace told you about—" She glanced over at Lady Paget, but as she still had her face turned to the window and seemed to be dozing, she looked back at Antonia and added in loud whisper to be heard over the noise of the carriage wheels, "—about finding us alone at the cottage, and—"

"Mary, M'sieur le Duc has said nothing to me about a cottage. And that is the truth." Antonia dared to smile. "But I do not need to know, do I? Because it is evident to me, and possibly to everyone around us, that you and M'sieur Bryce have more than a—um—*passing interest*—in each other."

Mary blushed. "It was not planned. It just happened. I cannot explain it. I am—he is—Oh! I don't know! I don't know!"

"All I know, Mary, is that it is time for you to consider what *you* want. And that will be difficult indeed. Not because you do not have a mind or opinions or secret desires of your own, but because you must think about what it is you want from the rest of your life."

"It would be an easy thing to marry Evelyn because we care deeply for one another," Mary stated, as if convincing herself. "Such a marriage would be the right and sensible thing for me to do because I will be made a countess, and Teddy will have an earl for a stepfather, and he will take good care of us both. Such a match will be welcomed by everyone of our acquaintance."

"And so it will. You will be Countess of Stretham-Ely, and Society will embrace you with open arms. It will be the match of the season."

Mary frowned. "You want me to marry Evelyn? It would certainly make my mother very happy to see me finally elevated to the social status she deems appropriate for the daughter of an earl—and now sister of the new Earl of Strathsay."

"What I want is unimportant. And you will never make your mother happy, whatever choices you make. Some people are born miserable. They never see the joy that is before their eyes and never will. In truth they like being miserable. That is your mother. My only advice to you is that you realize you have been given a unique opportunity, rare amongst females of our station—one of choice. You can choose the way in which you wish to live your life. But that comes with consequences which you must be prepared to accept. And before you make your choice, be very certain you know everything there is to know about—"

"He has told me everything about his life in Lucca," Mary interrupted matter-of-factly, and when Antonia smiled she realized her cousin had been talking in a general sense and not about Christopher at all. She was so flustered she could not speak.

"Me I am pleased to hear it," Antonia stated. "I am more certain of his feelings for you than I am of yours for him. Naturally he would wish to confide everything in you. But—"

She glanced at Kate, who sat beside her, saw that her eyes were closed and her jaw slack so assumed her to be asleep, and continued, "—it would be wise to ask him if that is all he wishes to confide in you, or if there are other particulars—"

"Other particulars? What other particulars, Cousin Duchess? Do you know of something he should tell—"

"—that is, assuming your choice it lies with him," Antonia finished off smoothly, ignoring Mary's interruption. Her smile widened, and she fluttered her fan prettily and said with a sparkle in her green eyes, "I think, Mary, it is time for you to be less the dutiful daughter and more the Mary who knows what she needs to make her happy. And when you know that, come and tell it to me, and then I will tell you what I think."

THE CARRIAGES DID NOT PROCEED ON TO CRECY HALL, BUT turned in through the elaborate black and gold iron gates proclaiming the entrance to the ducal estate of Treat. As it was almost the dinner hour, Antonia thought it best if they first see the Duke, who would welcome them all to dine, to discuss what was to be done to end Teddy's fear and see her come down from her tree house sanctuary for good.

With everyone indoors and divested of their cloaks, hats, gloves, and muffs, the guests were shown up to the saloon off the dining room where they were given refreshment and waited the arrival of the Duke and Duchess. It was too late in the day to change for dinner. But as there were only family members present, Antonia was certain her son and his wife would not care in the least that they were all slightly travel worn and weary, but just be happy and relieved to see them returned home.

"And you and the babe returned safe and well most of all, sweetheart," Jonathon added, kissing his wife's forehead. He took a glass from a tray held by a hovering liveried footman and handed it to Christopher. "Drink up. You look as if you could do with a bottle, not a glass. It's the scale of the place, ain't it? Had me staggered the first time I came here. This noble hovel has to be the largest privately-owned palace in England, if not the Continent." He leaned in to Christopher and said confidentially, "It's as well the family see their gilt and marble kingdom as a great weight of responsibility, and not as an advertisement for their conceit. Saves me the trouble of popping a few puffed chests and knocking back the odd jutting chin. Same can't be said for the trencherflies who circle 'em. But the main thing is, the Duke, for all his pompous self-righteousness, is a decent fellow. I think you'll like him."

"But will he like me, Your Grace?" Christopher asked seriously, though his lopsided grin belied the seriousness of his question.

"*Naturellement*, M'sieur Bryce," Antonia replied for her husband. "He is his mother's son, and so my son he likes everyone. Kate, shall you walk with me a little?" she asked Lady Paget, who still held on tightly to Christopher's arm since he had helped her alight from the carriage.

Antonia took Kate's arm and wrapped it about her own, and the two women walked a little way from the group.

"This is the first time you have been back here since your stay just before my marriage to Monseigneur, yes?" When the older woman nodded but was too overwhelmed to speak, Antonia understood. "I remember that day as if it were yesterday. You sat with Monseigneur at the head of the table, and across from you was a silly girl doing her best to catch Monseigneur's eye—"

"But he had eyes only for you. It was as if the two of you were the only ones at the table!"

Antonia sighed. "Yes. It was always that way, even with family. We were quite rude at times, I think."

Kate patted Antonia's hand. "But I like this new duke of yours. I suspect he is just as handsome as his voice suggests, and as arrogantly self-assured. Despite his deceptively easy-going manner, he wouldn't suffer fools. And he loves you very much. I can hear that in his voice, my dear. You have been twice blessed."

"Yes. I know it, and never do I take it for granted. The three of us get along very well indeed."

"Three?"

"Monseigneur, Kinross, and me. There will always be the three of us."

Kate smiled and understood. "Of course. I am glad." She squeezed Antonia's hand and added in a breathless whisper, "Do you know, my dear, I was making mental calculations in the carriage, and I am very sure your new duke is younger than my son!"

Antonia giggled behind her fan. "Yes. He is. I am as unbelievably outrageous as ever, am I not?"

Kate gave a snort of laughter and the two women continued up the room, heads close together and deep in conversation.

Christopher continued to watch them, greatly relieved and

delighted to see Kate looking happier than she had been in years, no doubt because the Duchess had put her at her ease and made her welcome. But he also knew it was due in no small part to the fact Kate was back amongst the rarified surroundings and people of the elite, a milieu she had lived in for most of her life. He was so distracted that he was unaware Mary had come to stand by his side. And when he did finally notice her, he smiled and said,

"Do you wish as I do that we had gone straight to the treehouse?"

"I do. I know Teddy is safe, but I am more anxious here, this close to her, than I was before we left Brycecomb."

"Yet, something more immediate is troubling you…"

"How did you guess?"

"I didn't. I can always tell when you are fretful by the way you hold your hands in front of you thus, right hand squeezing the fingers of your left. It is particularly apparent when you wish to say something to me which you think might offend me, and so you have this internal struggle to find the right words. You won't, y'know—offend me."

"Dear me! You've made quite a study of my habits, haven't you?" She glanced down at her hands, even though she knew he was right. When she pulled her fingers apart and whipped them behind her back Christopher chuckled. She pouted and gave his arm an affectionate push with her shoulder. "All right! I'll own to it," she confessed in a low voice, not wishing to be overheard. She continued to lean in against his arm. "I am worried for you—being here amongst my relatives."

"I am touched. But I hope it's not because you think me out of my depth in this exalted atmosphere?"

"No. Not at all. It's because you are here not because you want to be here, but because you've been made to come by circumstance. If not for Teddy up a treehouse, you may never have come at all. And to be utterly truthful, I'm often out of my depth amongst my Roxton relatives, and I am related to them by blood! You have now met my cousin and her husband, and see how they conduct themselves. I do not possess a tenth of their sangfroid."

"I don't begrudge them their place in the world, and I am not awed by it. I like your cousin the Duchess, and I like her husband even more. He may be a duke, but strip him of his ermine and he is straight talking and no nonsense, and knows the value of an acre and the worth of the man who tills the soil for him. I respect him more for that than the fact he's been burdened with an ancient Scottish title. I hope I may have the same respect for your cousin Roxton, regardless of the fact he owns this vainglorious beacon to *noblesse oblige*. But when all is said and done, what I care most about is how they treat you."

"Me?"

Christopher regarded her for a moment, expression giving nothing away of his thoughts, and then startled her by saying with a wry smile, "Surely you must know by now that I would gladly walk into a lion's den—or be here in these lofty surroundings—for you, and for Teddy, if that were required of me."

Mary believed him and was overcome. She did not know what to say. Unconsciously her hands came together again, right squeezing the fingers of the left.

Christopher let her take a moment to digest his heartfelt words, drained his wine glass, and handed it off to a footman. He took a sweeping look about the opulent room with its gilding, crystal chandeliers, and silk-covered chairs up against the painted walls, and found it all a bit overwhelming, even for one who had spent a decade fawning over the wives of Italian aristocrats in their gilded pleasure palaces. Those plastered layer-caked edifices were as hovels when compared to this monstrosity of marble and masonry. He wondered what could be keeping its illustrious owner, and found himself anxious to get on with the pleasantries, and the dinner, so he could implement his plan to free Teddy from her fear.

"I wish we'd had more time together in your cottage," Mary confessed, bringing him out of his introspection. "I wish I could tell you how you make me feel."

"You don't need to tell me, Mary. I know how I make you feel. Just as you know how you make me feel. But I don't want to spend more time with you in my cottage."

"You—you don't?" Mary asked, instantly disconsolate.

"No. Nor do I want to continue as your steward or your squire-neighbor."

Mary's heart sank further into the gloom of rejection. She nodded and sighed and tried to rally herself. After all, if she were honest with herself, she knew from the moment she stepped into his cottage that her time there was finite. But it was so much more difficult to accept that their affair—for want of a better word—was at an end, when he made such a declaration. Still, she tried to rally, as this was not the time nor the place to fall all to pieces.

"I admit it was no easy task having you in the house as steward one moment, and thus my servant, and the next as squire, and therefore my neighbor. Such societal dilemmas always give me the headache!"

He leaned into her and said with a light in his eyes, "I can cure you of that."

Mary stared up at him, eyes wide. "You can?"

He knew she would have no idea to what he was alluding and so was not surprised by her incredulity. But it was her response to what he said next that most interested him, and set his heart racing.

"Yes. Marry me."

His simple declaration was punctuated by laughter coming from somewhere deep in the room. But to the couple, to Christopher and Mary, they could have been atop an isolated mountain peak in the wilds of Snowdonia, for they heard nothing and saw no one but each other. Christopher kept his expression neutral and his gaze fixed on her. Mary stared up at him, face white and lower lip trembling. Finally she swallowed and hissed,

"You cannot ask me that! Not here! Not now! It's not poss—"

"Why isn't it possible? Because I am a lowly squire and you are an earl's daughter, and thus I do not have the right to ask you to be my wife?"

"Yes! No! I don't see you as a-a lowly—anything!"

"What then? Would you have answered differently had I asked you while we were naked in bed together—"

Mary's face glowed pink. "That's unfair!"

"Why? At least in bed we are equals, and I wouldn't have it any other way. Would you?"

Mary shook her head. While they were at the cottage, while they were in bed together, while they made love, there had only ever been mutual respect and enjoyment. Making love with Christopher was a world away from the treatment she had received at the hands of her conceited husband, her social equal. Christopher was light to Sir Gerald's dark. And he was right. She wouldn't have had it any other way.

And here in this gilded saloon she didn't see him any differently. Just because they were clothed and were held by intangible societal dictates that demanded his status in society was less than hers, her rank meant she could not marry beneath her. Beneath her? What did that mean precisely? And why should she be denied personal happiness and the choice of mate when her brother could marry the daughter of a merchant and lift her up to his level, and neither would be ostracized? Why did it fall to the females to be dictated to that they could marry up, not down the social ladder. Where had her mother's social climb gotten her? It certainly had not secured her happiness—a happy marriage, or a happy life. The same could be said of Mary's marriage to Sir Gerald.

And then, just as she was regaining her equilibrium through the strength of her own arguments, and was about to agree with him, he stopped the words in her throat by asking simply,

"Perhaps you do not wish to marry me because you do not love me?"

"Do not love you?" Mary repeated, incredulous, as if there could be any doubt about her feelings for him or that she had never spent a moment's thought on such an idea. She had even told him so in the cottage, so why was he questioning her here and now?

"I love you and have always loved you, since that first day we were introduced in the hall of Abbeywood Farm," he said simply. Then goaded her. "But perhaps loving you must also be restricted to our time at the cottage?"

"You know my feelings, and yet you have the-the—bold-faced cheek to ask me here in public whether I love you?" Mary drew herself up to her full height, indignant. "My heart is not fickle, and you, of all people, know that, Mr. Bryce of Brycecomb Hall!"

Christopher bowed to her with excessive politeness, but when he straightened, he realized a hush had descended upon the room and that their once polite, low-voiced discussion had turned, with every dramatic pronouncement, into a heated argument heard by everyone. And so he did not give her an immediate response but remained tight-lipped. But there was another more pressing reason for his silence. At Mary's shoulder was a stranger who Christopher knew from the familiarity of his green eyes—a trait he shared with his mother—must be His Grace, the most noble sixth Duke of Roxton.

"Dear me, Mary. I can't recall the last time you said anything with such force of conviction," the Duke drawled. "Such a passionate speech deserves a response. But I dare say Mr. Bryce of Brycecomb Hall would prefer to do that in private, not with all your family and relations bearing witness."

Mary spun about in a swish of quilted petticoats and instantly dropped into a curtsy of welcome, eyes to the parquetry, and leaving Christopher face-to-face with Julian, Duke of Roxton, a nobleman much maligned—hated even—by Sir Gerald Cavendish, and with whom, for over two years now, Christopher had exchanged enough correspondence with many a terse sentence that he thought he had a measure of the man.

But Christopher received a severe jolt. He did not know why it was, and later he still could not put into words how he reached such an immediate appraisal, it was just a feeling he had, an intuition, a certain undefinable something he saw in those eyes, that told him here was a good and honest man he could trust with his life.

He made the Duke a respectful bow and said bluntly, the words out of his mouth before he had given them much thought, and thus all the more powerful in their sincerity, "I wish we had met years ago, Your Grace."

Roxton stuck out his hand with a smile. "So do I, Mr. Bryce."

TWENTY-EIGHT

DINNER WAS ALMOST OVER, WITH PUDDING ON THE TABLE, along with platters of seasonal fruits and nuts, when the Duchess finally joined her family.

There was a general hush amongst the diners because Christopher had just outlined his idea for freeing Teddy from her fear of the Duke, and everyone was awaiting Roxton's response. The Duke thought it such an excellent stratagem for helping a child overcome an ingrained fear, that he wondered aloud how it was that the childless squire was attuned to a child's fears, and perhaps he had half a dozen children of his own hidden away somewhere?

Everyone knew this for a quip, but given the earlier heated altercation between Mary and the Squire, no one dared to laugh, and so the joke fell flat, and everyone returned to eating what was left on their plates. Everyone except Mary, who turned to Christopher for the first time since they had sat at the table and teased him with the question she knew the answer to but wished him to tell her otherwise,

"So that's the secret you're keeping from me, Mr. Bryce. You have a brood of brats hidden away in your house—of Italian extraction no doubt?"

"There is no wound to prod, my lady," Christopher stated mildly, though Mary heard the walnut shell crack in his hand and he keep his fist closed. "I wonder why you would pursue it?"

"Because you are keeping something from me, something Cousin Duchess says I should know about if I am to make a decision about my future."

Christopher glanced up the table to where the Duchess of Kinross was deep in conversation with Kate and the Duke of Kinross. He watched as Kate laughed out loud at the Duke's comment and then put her fluttering fan over her mouth as if what he had just told her was equally extremely shocking and humorous. The scene sent him hurtling back to when he was fifteen and had met Kate for the first time, with no idea as to her identity. And how shocked, angry, and disbelieving he had been when told she was his mother. He wondered if Mary would have a similar reaction, and he decided there was no time like the present to find that out.

"Do you want to know here and now, or can it wait until after we free Teddy from the treehouse?"

"Now."

"Why am I not surprised by that?" he muttered, and then he almost breathed an audible sigh of relief when the Duke interrupted their *tête-à-tête*.

"Mary, my dear, I must tell you not to fret about Teddy," Roxton interrupted, unaware the couple were in whispered conversation. "Jack and Harry are with her, which is why they are not here at dinner with us."

"Jack and Harry are in the treehouse with Teddy?"

"It seems Jack and Teddy have struck up a rapport, once she learned who he was, and he asked her about Abbeywood. She has been telling him all about his inheritance, and in return he has been playing his viola for her." Roxton smiled and shook his head. "It was Harry's idea that Jack play at the base of the oak in the hopes that Teddy would find the playing annoying enough to want to leave the treehouse."

"Oh, but Teddy loves music," Mary interrupted. "And Jack is a fine musician."

"Just so. Either Harry has no appreciation for music, or he's tone deaf! No matter. What does matter is that Teddy has some company. Between Jack and Harry's visits during the day and her nightly sleeps with Scipio and Cordelia's pack of pups, she has settled in well. So well in fact, that Frederick and the twins are demanding the girl who lives in their tree be evicted forthwith! Ah! Here you are at last, my darling," he added, pushing back his chair and getting to his feet as his duchess swept through the double doors.

Everyone got to their feet, except for Antonia, who was the first to be acknowledged by her daughter-in-law and receive a kiss to her forehead. The Duchess then asked after her health and the baby, and only when satisfied her mother-in-law was well did she smile upon the assembled company and tell them not to stand on ceremony and to resume their seats. She then went to the head of the table to where the Duke still stood, and said, after kissing his cheek,

"Forgive my tardiness. No sooner had I fed Otto than the boys and Julie needed settling again because they heard one of the nursery maids telling Nanny that Her Grace of Kinross had returned. Of course, they wanted to come downstairs and see Mema for themselves, convinced the baby must have arrived while she was away." The Duchess picked up a slice of apple from her husband's plate and nibbled on it, adding with a smile. "It is as well poor Otto has no idea how neglected he is by his brothers and sister, who think the only baby in existence is Mema's! Oh, and before I forget, Charlotte sends her apologies for not being here at dinner. Apparently she is still nursing a bilious headache. Perhaps she'll be able to find the energy to get out of bed in time for supper," she added, turning to address Mary, "now that she knows you've arrived, Mary dear."

"If she waits until supper she'll find the place deserted," Roxton replied. "We're all needed over at the pavilion at Crecy, where I am to be magically transformed from ogre to handsome—yes, handsome—duke with the help of Mr. Bryce. Let me introduce you to—What is it, Deb?" the Duke demanded, worried when his forthright Duchess swayed and gripped his upper arm. "Darling, you're bleached as white as fresh linen! Here, sit and—"

"Otto?! My God…!"

"I told you with this baby you should've employed a wet nurse sooner—"

Deb shook her head. "Not the baby. My brother Otto—"

"Deb, darling, your brother has been gone for over a decade now," began the Duke patiently, and was cut off.

"Who are *you*, sir?" Deb demanded of Christopher, a glance to the end of the table where Antonia sat, and who by her secret smile let Deb know that she saw what she saw: The startling family resemblance between her daughter-in-law and the Squire.

Christopher made his bow to the Duchess, who now had a shaking hand to her mouth, but it was to Mary he spoke first, and in a clear, strong voice that allowed everyone about the table to hear what he had to say.

"I wanted to tell you at the cottage, and would have done so had we more time. And as I had already confessed to you my life in Lucca, I thought that enough of a revelation for you to manage in those first few days. And then Kate asked that I wait a little longer. I do have a secret to tell you. But this one involves others. It involves Kate, whom

I would not want hurt for all the sugar in the Indies, and there are others—you, Your Grace," he said to Deb, "and you, Your Grace," he said to Roxton, "who may not wish to own to the connection, and I fully appreciate that is your right. But I must and will tell you," he said to Mary, "because you need to know, and I trust that you will understand that it is a circumstance that was wholly out of my control. And while it does not define me, and I have come to accept it, it is still a blemish that can never be removed. The stain of my birth will remain with me for the rest of my life."

"Blemish? Stain of your birth?" Mary responded quietly, up on her feet beside him. She glanced at Deb and saw that she still had a hand to her mouth. She then looked back at Christopher, and into his eyes, and then had to take another look at Deb. It was then that she knew, and felt rather foolish for being blind to it before now. Her own violet eyes went wide with new knowledge, and then she met Christopher's gaze and said, "You once told me your birth name was Cavendish. That you had Cavendish blood and that the connection was *complicated*. But it isn't, is it? It's really rather simple, once you know. Once you *see* the resemblance—" She stopped herself saying it. She wanted to hear him say it.

Christopher looked across the table at Kate, whose hand was being held by Antonia.

"Kate…?"

"I am not ashamed. I never have been," Lady Paget replied. "But I do harbor regrets. I allowed others to persuade me to give you up. I regret I never played any part in your boyhood. That aside, you've grown into a fine, honorable man, worthy of being called a gentleman, and that's all that matters. No mother could be prouder."

The Duchess went to speak but then realized Christopher had more to say, so clung to her husband's arm and kept silent; the Duke holding her closer. Christopher addressed himself to Mary, but again, his voice was steady and loud enough for everyone to hear that he spoke in earnest, and that his words were heartfelt.

"Mary—my lady—I stand before you as Squire Bryce, for that is who I am. But what I did not get to tell you, and which you should know, is that I am the natural son of Sir George Cavendish and Kate, Lady Paget. I was born at Brycecomb Hall and given the name Cavendish Christopher Bryce. I was adopted at three months of age by my mother's sister Sophie and her husband Henry Bryce, and brought up as their son and heir. And those two good and worthy people were my parents in every particular. When as a youth I was told my true parentage—that Sir George was my father, and his son Gerald my brother—it was only natural I would refuse to believe it. For the longest time I lived in a condition of denial, unable to accept that my blood was polluted, that I was not who I thought I was. My life became desolate, and for a time, dissolute. That part I have confessed to you, and I need not repeat it here. And then Kate—my mother— found me, and I—and I—*grew up...*"

He looked at Kate, whose head was turned his way but who he knew could not see his tender smile. "There! I have said it out loud, Kate. My mother. For that is who you are—my mother—and who you have always been. And your son loves you. It's time the world knew, isn't it?"

He then glanced about the table at his silent rapt audience and his wry smile disappeared, realizing there wasn't a dry eye amongst the ladies, and that the Duke of Roxton and the Duke of Kinross both had points of color to their cheeks. He took a deep breath and continued, determined to finish this confessional he had started, if for no other reason than he need not say it again. He returned his gaze to Mary, who was quickly drying her lashes, and when she finally looked up at him, handkerchief scrunched in her hand, he said,

"If I may be exceedingly blunt, I will state the obvious so that there can be no further doubts, and then you may do with this confession what you will. Through my natural parents, I am the bastard brother of the Duchess of Roxton, and through her I am uncle to her children, though I make no such claims on them for that is wholly up to their parents to decide. I am also uncle to Sir John—Jack—Cavendish and to the Honorable Theodora Charlotte Cavendish. And if permitted, I would dearly love to claim kinship to my nephew and most particularly to my niece, whose welfare I have done my utmost to nurture and protect.

"There are other Cavendish relatives too numerous to mention, and I do not care one way or the other if those connections acknowledge me or not. The only relatives—the only persons—I do care about are here within these marbled hallways, or up an oak tree in a pirate ship treehouse. But most of all, I hope that this revelation does not make a cake crumb of difference to how *you* regard *me...*"

There was an awed silence, and whatever their private feelings on the matter of Christopher Bryce's paternity, all eyes turned to the Duke, as head of the family and because they were sitting in his house. But it was Mary who shattered the stillness. She took a series of shallow breaths and collapsed back onto her chair, the handkerchief pressed to her mouth. Christopher immediately poured her out a glass of wine, put it into her hand, and told her to take small sips, which she did. She then pushed the glass back at him and stared up through her lashes with a pout.

"You do realize you've made my headache a hundred times worse!"

He grinned sheepishly. "I don't doubt it."

"And what a complete ninnyhammer I've been for not seeing what was before my eyes—your eyes, in fact! And one of your best features too."

"One of…? Will you tell me the others…?"

"No! Well—not now. *Not here*. Why? Oh why?" she added in an altogether different voice, and loud enough for everyone to hear, though that had not been her intention, "Why would you foolishly believe I would think less of you because of this stain, this blemish of birth which was not of your making, you ridiculous man?! I thought you knew me better—that *we*—knew each other better than to consider such a revelation any more an impediment than the fact you are a Cotswolds squire! And you can believe me when I tell you that to my mother your polluted blood is as nothing when compared to your rustic roots! As for my family—to this family, and to my brothers, and to His Grace and Cousin Duchess—it is your character and your devotion that are most important. Is that not so, Mme la Duchesse?"

"Just so, *ma petite*," Antonia replied gently.

Mary let her shoulders slump, and overcome, put her face in her hands. Yet just as quickly she wiped her face dry, and with a sniff sat up straight. She took a quick glance about the table and saw that her family had eased back onto their chairs and were pretending to do anything but eavesdrop, but were in fact intently listening and watching her and Christopher. She went to get to her feet, and Christopher pulled back her chair before one of the liveried footmen standing to attention up against the wall could get to the chair first.

"Roxton," Mary said, mustering her dignity. "If we are to put Mr. Bryce's plan to rescue Teddy into effect today, we need to do so in the next hour, or there won't be enough light or time to prepare the pavilion—"

"How right you are, Mary," agreed the Duke, coming to life. "I'll tell you all about it on the way to Crecy," he said quietly to the Duchess. He frowned when she was unresponsive. "Are you all right, Deb?"

"I think I am…Yes! I truly am. Though I don't know what surprises me more," she whispered into her husband's ear. "That I have gained a brother, or that Cousin Mary and my new brother are deeply in love."

The rest of the diners had put aside their napkins and were making movements to leave the table when Mary startled them into immobility by making a speech,

"Do you have anything you wish to say to Mr. Bryce, Your Grace? Indeed, do any of you have anything to say? Or I will presume, and so will he and Lady Paget, that by your silence you accept his confessional and that nothing further needs to be said on the matter. We shall go on as before. Though, in my case, while I would dearly love Teddy to know she has an uncle, it would be best left until she is of an age to understand that not all families are created in the same way."

"Hear! Hear!" Jonathon exclaimed, applauding Mary, and with a wink at Christopher. "Well said, my lady. Well said."

Everyone waited to see what Roxton would say and do in response. He looked to his wife, and when the Duchess smiled at him and squeezed his arm and then smiled at Mary and Christopher, his supposition was confirmed. He stepped forward and for the second time that afternoon stuck out his hand to Christopher Bryce.

"Welcome to the family!"

TWENTY-NINE

Mary paced back and forth at the base of the ancient oak, while Christopher climbed the ladder into the treehouse. Everything and everyone was in readiness at the pavilion. It now only remained for Christopher to persuade Teddy to join them there.

Christopher stuck his head up into the treehouse and called out. "Hallo? May I come aboard?"

There was the shuffle of boots on boards above his head and voices, and then Teddy appeared on the ladder that connected the two levels, messy braids framing her face. Her eyes went wide. Her ears had not deceived her! It was her Uncle Bryce's beloved voice. As she scuttled down the ladder, Christopher hauled himself up through the trap door into the treehouse. He had no time to get to his feet. Teddy flung herself at him full force, throwing her arms around him and clinging on for dear life, as if she'd fallen overboard in high seas and found the only raft capable of rescuing her from drowning.

"Now *there's* a greeting!" he said with a laugh, and put out a hand to stop himself falling backwards down the manhole, an arm about Teddy. He managed to keep them both upright and slid across the boards to sit cross-legged against the railing. "How is my ray of sunshine? Your mama and I have missed you."

Teddy muffled something into his waistcoat, where she had buried her face. Christopher tried to detach her, to talk to her. But then he realized she was crying. Great aching sobs of relief wracked her thin little body, and knowing her to be overwrought, Christopher let her sob. He lightly stroked her hair, telling her over and over that she was safe, that he would always protect her, and that her mother was at the base of the oak waiting to give her a hug.

He stayed on the floor with Teddy in his lap, she no longer sobbing but still distressed enough to keep her face hidden, when two youths came down the ladder from the second level. Jack Cavendish and Henri-Antoine were easy to tell apart. Jack had the Cavendish brown eyes and tousle of dark auburn curls, while his best friend Harry was taller, still had to grow into his strong nose, and was fastidiously neat in his appearance for a boy of sixteen.

Both found it awkward to bear witness to this emotional reunion between Teddy and a gentleman they had never met but knew to be her Uncle Bryce, because she had blurted out his name before scurrying down the ladder, and they had heard enough about him from her to feel as if they knew him already. They remained respectfully silent and returned Christopher's nod.

"Would you be so good as to inform the Lady Mary we'll be down in a few minutes. You'll find the family assembled over at the pavilion."

Henri-Antoine needed no further encouragement to quit the treehouse. But Jack hung back. After collecting his viola in its case where he had left it in a corner, he came over to Christopher, a frown between his brows, a glance at Teddy, who still had her face buried in Christopher's waistcoat.

"Will she be all right, sir? I mean truly all right, if you understand my meaning…"

Christopher did understand, and he smiled up at the boy and nodded.

"I do. Thank-you. A little bit of magic, and Teddy and everyone and everything at Treat will return to the way it was."

"Magic, sir?"

Jack was curious. Christopher hoped Teddy would be too. Henri-Antoine was not. From the trap door, where he had started to descend the ladder, but waited for Jack to join him, he rolled his eyes at Christopher's statement and signaled to Jack to hurry up with a jerk of his head. But when Jack ignored him, Henri-Antoine let out a heavy sigh and disappeared down the ladder without another word. Christopher was just grateful the boy's skepticism remained unspoken.

When Christopher did not answer him at once, Jack thought it best to explain himself, so the gentleman knew he was sincere, and more importantly, that Teddy did not think ill of him.

"I've never had the good fortune to come across any magic myself. I know the locals around here say Swan Island is a magical island where the king and queen of the fairies live, protected by the ghost of an old hermit. The island is off-limits, so I've never seen these fairies or the ghost."

"Not seeing them hasn't stopped the locals from believing they exist."

"True, sir. But Harry says there's more truth in the adage, 'Seeing is believing'."

"I presume Harry attends church every Sunday?"

Jack smiled. "He does indeed, sir. I should have said so from the outset—I'm Jack. I know who you are, you're Mr. Bryce and I have a lot to thank you for, for looking after my inheritance."

"I'm glad we've finally met, Jack. And you're welcome to visit any time. I'm sure Teddy would love to show you around Abbeywood, and perhaps take you for a ride into the Puzzlewood. If you're fortunate you may even catch sight of a fairy or two. What do you think, Teddy?"

When Teddy did not respond immediately but snuggled in closer, Jack said to fill the silence,

"I'd like that. And I'd like to visit the Puzzlewood. Teddy told us about the fairy folk who've lived there since before King Arthur's time, and who guard travelers against getting lost. And about the phantom armies of cavaliers and roundheads who come out of the mist each year to fight on the old battlefield near the village green. And then there's the cavalier captain who haunts Tanner's cidermill, cut down by one of Cromwell's soldiers while he was sleeping when he should have been guarding the mill. The whole Tanner family were slaughtered, bar the youngest son who hid himself up a chimney…"

"Teddy *has* kept you entertained with stories of home. Plenty of magical places in our little corner of the country, aren't there, Teddy?" Christopher smiled up at the boy and said with a wink, "And thank-you for keeping Teddy company until my arrival, and for providing her with some musical entertainment. No doubt Teddy told you I'm a woeful musician, so it would've been a pleasant change for her to hear such a talented musician."

"That's a fib, Uncle Bryce! You're not wo-woeful! You play the mandora better than anyone." Teddy sat up, brushing the hair out of her eyes, and quickly wiped her face. She glanced warily over her shoulder, embarrassed Jack would think her babyish and a weeper. "Jack plays a-a viola, which is different altogether, but he does play it very well."

"Then I hope he brings it along when he comes to visit us."

"I will, sir." Jack looked at Teddy. "I will visit Abbeywood one day… That's a promise. But I want you to be there to show me all the places you've told me about. I'll see you both over at the pavilion." He made Christopher a quaint bow and took his leave, viola in its case slung over a shoulder onto his back while he descended the ladder.

In the stillness that followed, voices were heard coming up through the trap door. It was Mary talking to Jack. Both Christopher and Teddy recognized her voice, and it gave them both a sense of comfort, and also one of urgency to want to join her. But first Christopher needed to reassure Teddy all was right with her world, and to secure her confidence and trust regarding the ogre she was convinced was the Duke of Roxton's true form.

He looked down at her and smoothed the mussed hair back off her face to say gently,

"Teddy, you do know that your mama and I love you very much, and that we would never let any harm come to you, don't you?" When she nodded, he smiled and said gravely, "Your granny's only wish in bringing you here was for you to meet your cousins. She had no notion of what your papa had told you about this place, and about the Duke, or she would never have brought you here at all."

"But *you* believe me, don't you, Uncle Bryce?"

"I do. And so does your mama."

"You told Mama? But she is under the Duke's spell so cannot know the truth!"

"That's what your papa thought, too. But would it surprise you to know that your mama has always known the real truth about the Duke?

"The *real truth*?"

"Yes, the real truth… Would it be all right with you if we spoke about the ogre?"

She nodded but added with a frown, "Jack believes me. Harry doesn't."

"That's because Jack wants to believe in magic and Harry does not. If you do not believe in magic, then you cannot believe there are such beings as fairies, gnomes, ogres, and spells, can you?"

"Everyone at Abbeywood knows there's magic, even the vicar. Jack's right. Harry does say that if you can't see it, it can't be real. He's angry because I said the Duke is an ogre. But I didn't make it up. That's what Papa told me."

"He did. But Harry's anger is understandable. He loves his brother. I would be angry if someone said to me that you or your mama were witches, because I know that is not true. Perhaps Harry knows it is not true, too? After all, he has lived with his brother his whole life, so knows him better than anyone—better than we do, and better than your papa did. I just wonder—because I have given it a great deal of thought, too—but I wonder if perhaps your papa may have got it wrong somehow... that the Duke may not be the ogre you think him?"

Teddy frowned, a deep crease between her brows.

"But—but why would Papa lie to me? He said the Duke was an ogre who in his true form has big black eyes and a long tail like the devil. Papa said one look in his eyes and I'd be bewitched and in his power forever and ever, and that he'd lock me up. I'd never see Abbeywood again!"

Christopher squeezed her hand. "I'd never let that happen, Teddy. You'll always be free," adding in a measured tone, "Perhaps your papa didn't lie to you. Perhaps that's what *he* believed. I wonder if you would consider a different possibility. Will you hear me out?" When she nodded, he continued. "I wonder if perhaps your papa believed the Duke was an ogre because it was your papa, and not the Duke, who was under the spell of this ogre. That this ogre cast a spell on your papa to make *him* think your mama's cousin was an ogre in disguise? Do you think that could be what happened?"

Teddy took a deep breath as she thought about what she was told. She shrugged. "Mayhap," she agreed reluctantly.

"It would explain why your papa never came here to visit, and why your papa and only your papa believed the Duke to be an ogre. After all, your mama, your granny, Jack, your Uncle Dair, who was married here to your Aunt Rory—and she is so sweet-natured she is practically a fairy herself—and Mme la Duchesse, who is the Duke's mama— none of these persons believe the Duke to be an ogre, do they?" When Teddy shook her head, he added in the same non-committal tone, "And his wife and children love him very much. I'm told you were there when the children greeted their father in the ballroom. It was raining outside and everyone was playing indoors... Were they happy to see their papa?"

"They were all laughing, and Juliet—she's the only girl—she ran up to him and he picked her up and twirled her round and round, like you used to do with me when I was little. Do you remember?"

"I do."

They sat still and quiet for a moment, and then Teddy said, "Mme la Duchesse has promised me a puppy of my own. Will Mama let me take the puppy home with me do you think?"

"Your mother has already agreed to it."

Teddy shifted to sit opposite Christopher, eyes wide and smiling for the first time since he had climbed up into the treehouse.

"Has she? Oh! I can't wait to show you! Will you come and see the puppies with me? There are six and they are all the dearest little dogs, and Mme la Duchesse said I could choose whichever one I wanted."

"That must have been a very difficult choice to make."

"It was! I don't think I've had to decide anything so hard, *ever*. But I finally chose a black bitch because she is the runt of the litter, and being small, I thought Mama would not mind her so much, and would be less frightened of her."

"That was thoughtful of you. Have you decided on a name?"

"Mme la Duchesse says all her dogs are given Latin names and she drew up a list for me. I chose Nera, which means black. Jack has a dog called Nero. Nero's a whippet too, and seven years old. Mme la Duchesse said Nera was a very good name for my puppy. What do you think, Uncle Bryce?"

"I agree. It is a lovely name, and Silvia and Carlo will think so too. Oh! And I nearly forgot to tell you: Kate is here—

"Here at Treat?" Teddy could not keep the breathless excitement from her voice. "Truly?"

"Truly. She has come to see you, and been invited to stay for Christmas. We—your mother, you, Kate, and I—have all been invited to stay as the guests of Mme la Duchesse and the Duke of Kinross here at Crecy Hall. But there will be occasions when we will travel across to the big house, to attend church, and whatever Christmas celebrations there are for the children and the rest of the family. But only if you are comfortable with these arrangements. Of course, the Duke would very much like all of us to be part of the family gatherings, but if you wish to stay behind here, then that will be up to you."

"Do you like him, Uncle Bryce? Do you like the Duke?"

"Do you really want to know what I think?" When Teddy nodded, he smiled. "I do like the Duke, Teddy. I believe he is a good man with a good heart."

"Then why would an ogre put a spell on Papa to think the Duke an evil man who would want to lock me up?"

"I wish I had an answer for you, but I cannot with any certainty tell you why. Perhaps your papa upset the ogre in some way? What I do know is that ogres are mean for the sake of being mean. They exhibit all the worst traits of human kind: Jealousy, pride, vanity, greed, slothfulness, and they are miserable for its own sake. They certainly don't want people to be happy. In fact, they are quite the opposite in nature to good fairies, who are kind, loving, giving, and want everyone to be happy—"

"Just like Aunt Rory, and Mme la Duchesse, and Mama!"

"And you."

"*Me?*" Teddy stuck out her bottom lip and made a noise signaling her incredulity, a noise her mother would not have approved, but which made Christopher grin. "Uncle Bryce, I can't be a good fairy, I'm not pretty enough. Everyone knows good fairies have hair the color of spun gold and big blue eyes and skin as smooth and as white as whipped cream."

"Not the fairies I've seen," Christopher stated emphatically, which made Teddy sit up and take notice. "The fairies I know have ruby kisses to their cheeks, and sometimes across their nose, too. And their hair is the color of spun copper or sometimes the same dark rich red as ripe cherries. And their eyes are big, but not blue. They are the color of the harebell, which is more purple than blue. Those fairies are uncommon and the most beautiful of all."

"They must look just like Mama."

Christopher touched his nose in a knowing way. "Just like your Mama."

Teddy hunched her shoulders and smiled. Christopher smiled back. And then both of them were startled when a beloved voice from the trapdoor said conversationally,

"You forgot to mention fairies have wings. Though I do not possess any, and wish that I did because this is the highest I have ever climbed in my life and I am very sure I shall fall if you don't help me up or take me down at once!"

WHEN MARY WAS BACK ON FIRM GROUND AT THE BASE OF THE oak, she pulled the woolen shawl closer about her shoulders to ward off the chill night air, now that the sun was low on the horizon, and looked up into the tree, anxiously waiting for Teddy to join her and Christopher. Teddy scrambled down the ladder as one who was used to going up and down it all day long, and eagerly fell into her mother's open arms.

Mary's reunion with her daughter had not been as emotionally fraught for Teddy as it had been with Christopher, and her daughter seemed in much better spirits than she had expected from a child scared out of her wits by her father's vile lies about her cousin Roxton.

She knew this was all due to Christopher's careful handling of the situation. She could have hugged and kissed him in thanks just for putting a smile on Teddy's face, never mind he seemed to have persuaded her that Roxton was not a monster who wanted to lock her up after all. Teddy skipped alongside her mother, who had shyly taken the crooked arm Christopher offered her, and proceeded to tell her all about Cordelia and Scipio's litter, and how Uncle Bryce liked the name Nera for her puppy just as much as Mme la Duchesse, and would Mama come with her to visit the puppies to see Nera for herself tonight...?

They arrived at the pavilion in time to witness several gardeners scrambling about, putting the finishing touches to a bonfire positioned in the middle of the lawn between the pavilion and the lake. Under supervision of their nurses and tutors, the Roxton children were restlessly waiting for the bonfire to be lit, along with half a dozen children belonging to the household servants invited to join in the celebration of the winter solstice. All the adults were gathered on the pavilion steps, in capes, hoods, fur muffs, and gloves. Betsy broke from the cluster of upper servants with Mary's fur-lined cape. Christopher put it about her shoulders and affixed the clasp, and then they went forward to join the rest of the family.

Christopher noticed Teddy hanging back. So he put out his gloved hand to her with a smile, and she eagerly took it, but he did not go up the steps with her to join her mother.

"Do you want to come up into the pavilion, or would you rather be with the children by the bonfire? I see Jack and Harry are with them."

"Where's Kate?"

"Sitting over there with Mme la Duchesse. Do you want to sit with them?"

Teddy shook her head. Christopher saw that she was scanning the faces of the adults, and he guessed whom she was looking for because she was suddenly still and quiet, and Teddy was never still unless she was ill or upset or nervous.

"There's the Duke. He's talking with the other duke. I'd never met a duke before coming here, and now I know two. Are there any more dukes in the family to meet?"

"I don't think so. Do you want me to come with you to see him? The other is the Duke of Kinross—"

"He's married to Mme la Duchesse. I like him. Did you know, Uncle Bryce, that he lived in India, and that's why his skin is brown? He rode elephants, and kept monkeys, and he has a daughter who has hair the same color as mine! And when Mme la Duchesse is not about he smokes a cher—che-*root*. He showed me his tinderbox and how he lights his cheroot so he can smoke it. But he said I was to keep it between us because Mme la Duchesse would be displeased with him." Teddy cocked her head in thought. "But I think Mme la Duchesse knows about the cheroots, Uncle Bryce, don't you? And I don't think she is displeased with him at all. I think he was funning with me."

"You may be right."

Teddy took a breath and nodded and said resolutely,

"I want to see the Duke of Roxton, and I do want you to come with me."

"Of course."

They went hand in hand across the front of the pavilion steps to where the Dukes of Roxton and Kinross were deep in conversation, and stepped into the pool of warm light from the burning tapers and waited to be noticed. It was Deb Roxton who saw them first, and had a quick word in her husband's ear. Conversations amongst the adults hushed, the only noise coming from the children who were getting restless down by the bonfire. Kinross stepped back, and Roxton, seeing Teddy and Christopher, went slowly down the steps to meet them. He flicked out the skirts of his velvet frock coat and sat on a low step, so that his face was level with Teddy's, who had come up one step and now stood before him.

She let go of Christopher's hand and after looking up at him and receiving a smile of reassurance she went forward and dropped a curtsy before bravely raising her eyes to meet the Duke's gaze. And it was then that she noticed what she had failed to see in the ballroom, all because she had been too scared and upset to notice anything other than that the Duke was tall and wide and loomed large over her. But now, looking into his face, she saw that he had a friendly smile and kind eyes, eyes that were the color of emeralds. He had the same kind green eyes as his mother, Mme la Duchesse, who, to Teddy's mind, if anyone was queen of the fairies it was she.

So when the Duke smiled and put out his hand to her, she smiled back and tentatively took hold of his fingers. He did nothing more than that, and remained very still. But it was all that was required for Teddy to let out a little sigh of relief. Because although she trusted Uncle Bryce's word that the Duke was not the ogre her father had told her he was, there was something about the power of touch, that if something were to happen to turn the Duke into an ogre, it was this, and she would see him alter before her eyes.

But when he remained as he was, her heart quietened. And when the Duke bowed over her hand, Teddy's shoulders relaxed. She took another glance over her shoulder, to reassure herself Christopher was still there, and then she bravely leaned into the Duke and put her cheek on his shoulder. He lightly held her, not wanting to frighten her, or make her uncomfortable, and they stayed that way for a few moments, before Teddy straightened and glanced about at the silent adults at the Duke's back. She saw her mother wipe a tear from her eye, then smile brightly, and she smiled back.

There wasn't a dry eye in the pavilion.

"I'm so glad you and your mother and your uncle could be here with all the family tonight, Teddy," the Duke said quietly, a glance up at Christopher who was again at Teddy's side. "Because do you know what special day it is today?" When Teddy shook her head, he said, "It's the winter solstice. A very special night Mme la Duchesse my mother began when I was a small boy, much younger than you—and *that* was a very long time ago now."

"Winter solstice? Is that the longest night of the year?"

"It is."

"Then I do know something about it because Cook says that if you light a fire on winter solstice, it helps rid the house of the evil spirits that have been lurking in dark places. And she said that from now until spring the days become longer until it is spring and there is sunshine and then the evil spirits have nowhere to hide; that's when the good spirits come to stay." She glanced over her shoulder at the unlit bonfire. "Is that why you have a bonfire, too?"

"Something like that, yes. Mme la Duchesse had the ancient Roman festival of Saturnalia in mind, but I like Cook's explanation," Roxton replied. "You're very clever, Teddy. At your age I don't think Jack or Harry had any idea why we lit a fire on this of all nights, nor did they enquire. They just liked running about and watching a giant fireball."

"That's because they're boys. Uncle Bryce will tell you girls are smarter than boys. Isn't that true, Uncle Bryce?"

The Duke chuckled and so did the rest of the assembled adults, Roxton adding, "I agree with you and your uncle. And so does everyone here. The females in our family have always been far smarter than us fellows." He nodded to a liveried servant who stood as a sentinel at the base of the steps holding a lighted taper, and then said to Teddy, including Christopher in his conversation, "I wonder, Teddy, if you and your Uncle Bryce would do the honors and light the bonfire?"

"Can Mama come with us, too?"

"Of course. That's a splendid idea."

Rejoining the adults on the top step of the pavilion, Roxton stood with his wife behind the chaise where his mother and Lady Paget sat, and watched Teddy walk towards the bonfire, holding aloft the lighted taper, her mother and Christopher a step behind. And while everyone from the adults in the pavilion to the children running about on the lawn in the fading light watched mesmerized as Teddy dipped the flame to the bonfire, Antonia's gaze was on the couple flanking Teddy, and most particularly on Squire Bryce who had his hands clasped behind his back. For all his outward appearance of elegant calm, his thumbs would not still, and that telling sign made Antonia smile.

She looked over her shoulder at her son, and put up a hand, which he took in his, and she gave him a little tug so that he leaned in to hear what she had to say.

"Julian, it is time to write to Cornwallis."

He knew to what she was alluding, but he said it aloud anyway, and with surprise, though he wasn't at all surprised by her demand or the reason for it. "You do realize this will be the third Special License I've requested in eight months."

Antonia shrugged. "That is not important. What *is* important is that your family is happy. Yes?"

"I agree."

"And Mary deserves to be happy."

"I agree with that too." He hesitated, a glance over his mother's coiffure at Lady Paget. But as that lady and Deb were deep in conversation, he felt able to proceed. So he went on his haunches beside the chaise and said with a frown, "If she marries him, there will be consequences that will be beyond my—our—power to control. There will be people who will turn their backs on her regardless of our public support for the match—"

"Julian—"

"Maman, there is only so much I—we—can do. There will be houses, gatherings, social occasions to which she won't be invited, least of all welcome as the wife of a squire, never mind as a couple. And who knows if she'll ever be received at Court again."

"Julian, I know all this, but—"

"And they'll be talked about, and not in a nice way. I wouldn't be surprised if news of their marriage ends up in the newssheets to become gossip fodder for the masses. Ghastly petty scribblers! And God help them if it ever gets out about his base birth—"

"*Assez*! Julian! All this I know only too well, *mon chou*. You worry too much as always. Do you think she cares? That he does? Perhaps you forget that your own grandparents, your father's parents, were disowned by their families. Your papa's maman—your French *grand-mère*—was forbidden the French court by Louis himself. She never went to Versailles again. Monseigneur was a boy before his maman's parents acknowledged the marriage had even taken place, and that your papa was not the product of a liaison, and that he was not in fact a bastard. *Mon Dieu.* Can you believe such a thing? It was horrible for them, and truly horrible for your papa, who was deeply affected by it all. He saw daily the anguish his mother suffered at being denied the comfort and company of her mother and her sisters. But we, Julian, are not like that. We support our family and their choices. And as long as Mary has her family, and we welcome him, and they love each other and are happy, then that is all that should matter, *hein*?"

"I don't disagree with you, *ma mère*. And I will give my blessing to the match if Mary does indeed want to marry her squire. But why can't their union wait for the reading of the banns? It would put a more respectable distance between the death of her father and her marriage. There does need to be some period of mourning for his lordship, regardless of what we all thought of Strathsay as a man. In fact, I would prefer they wait until after your happy event, and the christening. Dair will have returned, and can attend his sister's wedding ceremony. So why do they require a Special License?"

When his mother giggled behind her fan, eyes bright, his cheeks warmed and he knew to what she was alluding but he could not quite believe it. He looked out across the lawn to the blazing bonfire and the silhouettes of adults and children gathered about the fiery orange flames, but could not discern which of the couples was his cousin Mary and her squire. He looked back at his mother, who was still regarding him with amusement.

"Good—God! How—I don't know how you know these things… Are you certain?" When Antonia put up her brows in response but said nothing, he wiped a hand over his mouth. "It is Mary we're talking about. And he strikes me as much a stickler for the proprieties as I am. From reading his letters these past two years, I think he has all the hallmarks of a hair-splitting pedant!"

"I do not doubt you will become firm friends," Antonia quipped dryly, her dimple showing itself. She shut her fan with a snap and squeezed her son's wrist. "I am not talking about him as a squire, or you as a duke, *mon chou*, or that the two of you have a great drive to do your duty. I am talking about you as *men*. I am very sure that he is just like you in that regard, too. Just as Monseigneur he had a strong physical appetite, so too do you, and so does M'sieur Bryce. Such men when they fall deeply in love do not think of consequences when the need to satisfy—"

"All right, Maman. I'm convinced," Roxton interrupted curtly, and shot to his feet. "A Special License it is. I'll write to Cornwallis tomorrow."

"*Mon Dieu*! Not yet… *Julian*!"

"But you just said they needed a Special—*Mon Dieu*!" It was only then that he realized she was clutching her round belly and her eyes were squeezed tight. "Maman!? *Maman*, are you all—"

"Jonathon! *Jonathon*. Where is Jonathon?"

Those nearby heard the anguish in Antonia's tone, saw the Duke look wildly about as if he'd lost something, and the bonfire was forgotten by all in an instant. Everyone crowded in around her.

"Stand back! Stand back! Give her air!"

It was Kinross, and he shouldered his way to his wife's side and dropped to his bended knee. He could see she was in great pain. One hand gripped the side of the chaise hard, knuckles white, the other she had flung out to grip Lady Paget's hand, needing human contact and reassurance.

Antonia took a few deep breaths and opened her eyes.

"Jonathon, I need—I need—Gabrielle. Please to have her fetched. *Immédiatement!*"

"She's here, sweetheart," Jonathon said with a reassuring tremulous smile, snatching up her hand and kissing her fingers. "Gabrielle's here. She knew. Said you were early with your sons, so you'd be early this time, too. She arrived an hour ago and is settling in." He searched Antonia's face, eyes troubled and brow furrowed. "But—*it is* too early, isn't it?"

Antonia breathed a sigh of relief knowing her previous lady's maid, who had attended on her at the births of both her sons, had arrived in time for this birth. Seeing the apprehension in Jonathon's eyes, she managed a smile, but then she again caught her breath as another contraction robbed her of speech. When she could talk, she said breathlessly, "We do not decide these things, *mon chéri*. The little one she has made up her own mind—It is time."

THIRTY

Kinross, Roxton, Lord Henri-Antoine, and Christopher Bryce sat in a row, perched on the edge of a settee on one side of the drawing room, backs straight, fists on their knees, and staring ahead, silent. Across the room Lady Paget sat by the fireplace, taking tea and talking in hushed tones with Deb Roxton, who was breastfeeding her seven-week-old son, his little lordship's nurse and a nursery assistant by the draped window with Lord Otto's traveling crib.

Lady Mary had come and gone several times from the drawing room, but with nothing new to report, other than the Duchess's labor was progressing as well as to be expected. This information the two women took in their stride, but it left the men feeling even more anxious, as everything was out of their control. When Mary disappeared back down the corridor towards Antonia's bedchamber for what seemed the umpteenth time, Jonathon could no longer contain his thoughts and burst out in annoyance,

"Why are we waiting here, and not there—at least we should be in her sitting room next to the bedchamber, damn it! I can't hear a thing from here!"

"I gather that's the point," Roxton replied. "So we can't hear what's going on."

"Why not? Why can't I be in there—now? I should be in there with her, not sitting here like a prize stuffed pheasant!"

"You'll be in there soon enough—"

"Will I? Will they let me in there, d'y'think, eh? You were in there from the off, weren't you? A plaguey physician and a pack of women wouldn't have stopped you from being with your wife at such a time."

"I realise this is none of my business, Your Grace—" Christopher began and was cut off.

"It seems it's everyone's bloody business but mine, so speak up!"

"From the short time I have known her, I would suppose it is Mme la Duchesse who is making the decisions, and so it is she and not her attendants who will determine when you are to join her—or not."

"Ha! Y'know, you're damn-well right, Bryce. I'd not thought of that. Thank-you."

Jonathon was suddenly less troubled than he had been in the previous hour. But then Roxton negated Christopher's verbal calmative with an unguarded observation.

"I know I should be telling you not to worry—that all will go well. And I'm sure it will. But I can tell you from experience that even after five children, being in the stalls and not on the stage doesn't get any easier. Every birth is different, every infant, too. So even though I was there with Deb, I was never any less apprehensive with birth number five than I was with my firstborn's welcome into the world. Bloody harrowing business—and this birth has to be the worst time of all!"

"Why? Why is this worse?" Jonathon demanded, turning to stare at Roxton. "Why do you say so? Has the physician said something to you that he hasn't said to me? Has *she*?"

"No. It's because it's my mother in there, that's why! That changes everything. Deb has given birth to five healthy children, with as little drama as possible. Whereas my mother has had two births, and neither one was particularly uneventful. And here she is at age fifty about to give birth again. To say the prospect scares me witless is putting it mildly."

Jonathon shot to his feet. "Jesu—I feel bloody useless!"

"She's my mother, too," Henri-Antoine said through his teeth, fingers curled about the edge of the settee cushion.

All three men stared at the youth, who had not spoken since Antonia's labor pains had begun in the pavilion a couple of hours ago. He was paler than usual, and biting his lower lip as if to keep himself in control. Roxton was instantly contrite, and affectionately pulled his brother to him and kissed his temple.

"I'm sorry, Harry. Of course she is," Roxton murmured near his ear. "We're not going to lose her, too. You know that, don't you?"

Henri-Antoine nodded quickly, then pulled out of his brother's embrace and got to his feet.

"I'll see what's keeping Jack and Teddy."

"Excellent notion. Tell them to join us here for supper, and if Teddy wants to bring her puppy to show her Uncle Bryce, she's most welcome."

Henri-Antoine nodded, and in a rare show of sentiment he gripped Jonathon's shoulder.

"She'll be fine, sir. She has to be. I think Mr. Bryce is in the right. Maman will send for you when she's ready."

Jonathon acknowledged the boy's affectionate gesture, patting his hand and smiling.

"Thank-you, Harry. Your mother always knows what's for the best —and what's for my own good."

In the silence that followed Henri-Antoine's departure, Roxton said, to fill the void and divert their thoughts,

"I've had a letter dispatched to Martin. He'll be here by tomorrow night. I had it written and ready to send at a moment's notice before Audley went away. Bryce! A note from Shrewsbury said my secretary is helping him with his enquiries, and that he'd tell me all about it when he came visiting just after Christmastime. You wouldn't know anything about that, would you?"

"Your Grace…? About Philip Audley or Lord Shrewsbury's visit?"

"Either or both. I'm mystified."

Christopher smiled in spite of himself.

"What I do know, Your Grace, is that you're a far more congenial fellow than your secretary."

"Am I? I'll take that as a compliment."

"You should. Bryce was being diplomatic about your secretary. I won't be. Audley's a muckworm," Jonathon stated bluntly, pacing before them. When Christopher gave a crack of laughter, he added, "There. He agrees with me." He patted his frock coat pocket and breathed a sigh of relief to feel the outline of his silver cheroot case. "I need to smoke… Think the ladies will mind?"

"Under present circumstances? Not a whit," replied Roxton.

Jonathon moving to the fireplace to light his cheroot gave Roxton and Christopher the excuse to follow him and join the ladies. The Duchess had finished feeding, and the Duke welcomed the opportunity to take his infant son and to pace the room with him at his shoulder, rubbing his little back to settle his stomach. This gave Deb the chance to speak with Christopher, who returned from the tea trolley with a cup of tea for her, one for Kate, and one for himself.

As ever with Deb, she came straight to the point.

"Would you have come to Treat if not for Teddy's predicament?"

"Perhaps…" Christopher smiled over his cup. "If I'd been summoned to give an account of myself."

Deb chuckled. "No you wouldn't! You'd have found an excuse not to. Of course you'd have written Julian a long and detailed letter with a polite refusal as a postscript."

"Ha! Ha! So you read your husband's correspondence, Your Grace?" Kate asked with a grin.

Deb smiled cheekily. "Only when it is thrust under my nose and I am asked to agree that the correspondent is the most frustratingly annoying obscurantist His Grace has not had the pleasure yet to meet. Naturally I agree with him, but had I known the correspondent was my brother, I may not have been so quick to do so. Is it true you play the lute?" she added quickly, because she could see Christopher was uncomfortable with her familial appellation.

"A mandora, Your Grace."

"Musicality must run in the family. And it's Deborah. Deb. I would like you to call me by my Christian name. We are brother and sister after all."

Christopher glanced at Kate. "Half-brother and sister. But thank-you."

"Otto and Gerald were brothers, but they were my half-brothers. We all share the same father but different mothers. So other than the fact Sir George was married to their mother, you and I are as related by blood as I was to Otto and Gerald, and as you are to them." Deb looked to Kate. "Did that make sense?"

"Perfect sense, my dear."

"It is very generous of you to say so, Your Grace—"

"Christopher! The Duchess is not being generous, she is stating fact," Kate countered with annoyance, then turned to Deb and said with a smile, her hand out across the sofa, "Thank-you. I hear the sincerity in your voice. But you must understand it will take my obstinate son far more time to adjust to your welcome than it will for you to accept him into the family fold."

"Obstinate? Kate! I would never be presumptuous—"

"Wouldn't you? It simply won't wash, my boy," Kate interrupted dismissively. "How can you not be presumptuous when your greatest wish is to marry into the family?" She turned to Deb and asked lightly, "Is he blushing with embarrassment or fury?"

Deb chuckled. "I fear it may be a bit of both, my lady." When Christopher turned his head, jaw tight, she asked him gently, "You have asked her?"

He met her open look.

"I have."

"And she has yet to give you a response?"

"She is presently occupied with something of far more immediate importance, Your Grace. If you will excuse me. I had best see how Kinross is holding up."

He bowed and walked off, depositing his teacup and saucer before crossing to Jonathon's side just as the door at the far end of the room opened, and in stepped the physician; behind him was the Lady Mary. Both looked worn thin, and both were worried, though Mary did her best to hide her apprehension for fear of upsetting everyone concerned. The physician had no such qualms.

Jonathon flicked his cheroot into the fire and strode over to meet the physician, Roxton giving his infant son into the care of his nurse, and joining Jonathon on the other side of the room.

"Well? Can I see her now?" When the physician took a moment longer than Jonathon presumed he needed to say yes, his breathing quickened and he rasped out, "What? What?! Tell me! Out with it!"

"Everything is progressing as it should, Your Grace."

Jonathon wiped a hand over his mouth and let out a deep breath that saw his shoulders drop.

"Thank God."

"So while Her Grace is having a moment of respite I thought it prudent to enquire again that if the circumstance arose where there was cause for alarm—"

"Alarm? What alarm?"

"—what would be your wishes if it came to the unspeakable—"

Jonathon looked about, but saw nothing. "Unspeakable? What are you blathering about, Pratt?"

"You'll save my mother, that's what you'll do, Pratt!" the Duke of Roxton growled.

The physician cowered but managed to say with a sniff, "Your Grace, my question is directed at His Grace of Kinross. He is the Duchess's husband and thus legal guardian, and thus it is to him—"

"Don't be ridiculous! You'll save my mother's life, and that's an end to it!"

Jonathon turned on Roxton.

"I don't interfere in your marriage, so stay out of mine!" He took a step closer to the physician, towering over the short man in his brown bob wig who leaned back to look up into the sun bronzed face. "Are you a blockhead, Pratt? We've had this discussion. You know my wishes. You save the life of the Duchess. If there is any risk—*any*—you save her. She is all that matters."

"Just to be clear—"

"Oh, for God's sake!"

"—after all, I must point out that she is carrying your heir, and giving birth to an heir is what is of paramount importance to most men."

"Well I ain't most men, *wiseacre*. The Duchess's life is what's important—*to all of us*. Got it?"

"Understand, Pratt?" the Duke of Roxton added menacingly, standing at Jonathon's shoulder.

The physician looked from one furious ducal face to the next and nodded.

"Perfectly."

"So can I see her now?"

"Soon, Your Grace. Allow me to return to the bedchamber and speak with Her Grace. I'll send out one of her women…"

Jonathon threw up a hand in frustration and turned away, pulling at his head of auburn curls as if he meant to yank them out.

The physician left, but Mary remained, and she came up to Jonathon and put a hand on his sleeve, which made him turn and look down at her. She smiled up at him reassuringly, a look over at Roxton to include him in their conversation.

"She is as comfortable as to be expected for a woman in labor. Gabrielle and her ladies are providing her with the confidence she needs to get through this. And she did call out for you—"

"She did?" Jonathon interrupted, hopeful.

"—to be consigned to the gates of hell for putting her through this," Mary quipped, smile widening when Jonathon's face fell. "At least that is what I think she said… Her French tongue becomes ever more rapid when she is agitated. I believe there were a few other *more colorful* words thrown in there for good measure, because her ladies clapped their hands over their ears. Gabrielle's response was to laugh and encourage Cousin Duchess to shout those words as loud as she pleased, and while she was at it to add a few of the more *interesting phrases* picked up from Parisian gutters which Monseigneur had taught her, and which she had hurled back at him while in labor with her firstborn."

"Did she, by Jove?" Jonathon said with a chuckle and a shake of his head. "I wish I'd been there to hear that string of abuse."

Roxton was surprised. "I can't imagine *mon père* teaching her such language—"

"Of course you can't! She's your mother." Jonathon grabbed Mary's arm. "Walk with me, Mary." He led her away, down the room, to have a private word and stopped out of earshot of everyone else and came straight to the point. "You're in a better position than anyone else to know—What is that blockhead physician not telling me, eh? And what do you think I should do about it?"

Mary took a moment to formulate a considered response and it was almost a moment too long for Jonathon, who was so tense he wanted to cross to the fireplace and light another cheroot just to have something to do. But then Mary spoke, and her soothing delivery coupled with her sensible counsel was enough to ease the tension in his limbs, and he relaxed his grip on the silver cheroot case.

"Cousin Duchess knows what you went through with your first wife," she said calmly. "And while she has not said so openly, I sense that the traumatic experience of losing your wife and child weighs heavily with her. I believe that is the reason she has stopped herself from asking for you to be at her side until the last possible stages of the birth. To be perfectly candid, and this should not surprise you," she added, looking up into his troubled gaze, "Cousin Duchess is afraid. She is afraid for her life, for the life of her baby, and afraid for you. And who can blame her? Childbirth is a terrifying experience for most females. It is sixteen years since she gave birth to Harry. And he was born under—under *trying* circumstances—"

"I know all about that episode," he interrupted brusquely.

Mary nodded, relieved not to have to elaborate.

"Then you are aware that she had a very short labor with Harry. It was almost over before it began, and she was so ill afterwards she hardly remembers any of it. And then there is the fact she was only eighteen when she had Julian—a lifetime ago now… So that this labor is for her as if she is experiencing childbirth for the first time. Is it any wonder she is frightened?" Mary squeezed his arm. "What she needs at this time is *you*. Now more than ever you need to be brave, for her, and for your baby."

Jonathon's dark eyes sparked. "So I should storm m'lady's bedchamber, to hell with the physician and everyone else?"

Mary smiled and nodded. "To hell with everyone, Your Grace. But do take your armor. You'll need it against the verbal abuse which will inevitably be flung at you."

Jonathon grinned, slapped his hands together and rubbed his palms with glee. "Good. Looking forward to it! Thank-you, m'dear."

He gave Mary an impetuous kiss to the top of her head, turned on a heel and strode away. Without a word to anyone, but with a wave of acknowledgement above his head, he followed the physician down the hallway that led to the bedchamber he shared with his wife. Arriving at that apartment, he flung wide the door without warning or ceremony and went into battle.

Mary did not immediately return to the bedchamber, though she wished to be a moth on the wall, to see the faces of the physician, her cousin's attendants, and Gabrielle de Crespigny, to have her intuition confirmed when Antonia berated her husband, only to then throw her arms about his neck and hold on for dear life, relieved he was finally there by her side and to make him promise not leave her until their baby was born.

Mary hoped that if she were ever blessed with more children, her husband would want to be with her, holding her hand during child-birth. Giving birth to Teddy had been a lonely and terrifying experience that did not bear repeating, and would not be with Christopher by her side. He would most certainly want to be with her when she gave birth to their child... *Their child*... She was already thinking of children, and yet she still had to accept his proposal. But she owed it to Evelyn to speak with him first, to tell him her true feelings and where her heart lay. She loved Christopher—no, she was *in love* with him. She loved Evelyn, too, but she was now very sure her love for her cousin was not the same as the love she had for her neighbor.

She dared to let her gaze wander across the room to where Christopher had rejoined the Duke on the settee. She smiled to herself to see them in amenable conversation. She would never have predicted they would like each other on sight. But it should not have come as a surprise, because both were sticklers for exactness and truthfulness, both were honorable and honest, and both could be frustratingly pedantic at times, and she admired and esteemed them equally.

Why, when Christopher had asked her to marry him, had she not thrown her arms about his neck and kissed him and said yes, and told him he had made her the happiest woman alive? That's what any free-thinking, free-spirited female would have done. That's what she should have done if not for her ingrained self-restraint. This constant need to think through the consequences of her actions had surely drained her of spontaneity? If only she would allow herself to be who she wished to be rather than who she had been taught she ought to be...

"Mary! Who is that individual talking with the Duke?" asked a strident female voice at her shoulder.

Mary let out a tiny sigh of contentment, gaze still very much on Christopher. "The man I wish to marry."

THIRTY-ONE

"Don't mumble, Mary! Did you say *Wishart*? Did you say his name is Wishart Manly?"

Mary went white. She had voiced her thoughts aloud, and to none other than her mother—the last person to whom she would ever confide. Flustered, she blushed at her ineptitude. Yet, force of habit kept her agitation in check. Her back stiffened, she put up her chin and lowered her lashes. Taking hold of her petticoats, which she lifted slightly, she bobbed a respectful curtsy to the Countess of Strathsay, and then enquired after her health, which she hoped would deflect her mother's need to have her question answered.

"How are you, Mama? Has your bilious headache subsided?"

"No, it has not! But what is a headache—my health—of consequence when history is to be made this night? One must rise above one's own wants and needs upon such an occasion as this, to know that one has been part of something greater."

"I don't understand. If you are still unwell, you should have stayed in bed."

Charlotte Strathsay rolled her eyes and made a familiar clicking sound with her tongue that instantly further stiffened Mary's back and gave her a presentiment of what was to come.

"The Duchess of Kinross is about to give birth to the heir to a Scottish dukedom, Mary," her mother enunciated as one does to a small child when cross. "Her Grace has already provided an English duke with an heir. Surely even you have managed to figure out that with this birth your cousin will be the ancestress of not one but *two* different dukedoms from two different kingdoms. Now *that* is something to crow about!"

"I doubt Cousin Duchess cares for any of that at this moment, Mama. All she wants is a healthy baby and to come through the birth alive, and that is what His Grace wants too."

"And how would you know what their wants and needs are when—"

"Because that is what any new mother would—"

"Do stop talking drivel. You never fail to surprise or disappoint me with your commonplace observations. Sometimes I wonder if you are my daughter at all. You always manage to take something of great significance and reduce it to the mundane. Your cousin is not just *any woman* about to give birth, she is a duchess."

"I know that, Mama."

"Then you also know that in her exalted position she is required to think of the greater good of the dukedom. Though dearest Antonia does occasionally forget who she is and fails to take her position seriously enough. After all, trundling off across the country to fetch *you,* just because *your child* has had some sort of infantile fit, was an unnecessary risk to her and the baby, and why, no doubt, she has gone into an early labor. Be it on your head, Mary, should any harm come to the Duke of Kinross's heir."

"My-my—*head?*" Mary stuttered and was momentarily lost for words.

"You don't look well, my lady," Deb Roxton stated mildly, sweeping up to join mother and daughter. She smiled kindly on Mary, then said to Lady Strathsay, "Perhaps a cup of tea would help?"

"Yes, I do believe you are quite right, my dear. An excellent notion," the Countess agreed with a smile and a sigh, and in an altogether different voice she used with her daughter; this voice dripped with obsequiousness. "If you would be so kind, I am sure a cup of tea will help keep the thud in my temple within the limits of tolerance."

Mary looked from her mother to Deborah, then glanced across at Roxton and Christopher and saw that both men had broken off their conversation and were also an audience to this exchange.

Always having been one to concede, to back down, to take on the chin her mother's petty public criticisms and be put in her place because she never won with her mother, and it was far easier to say nothing than offer an alternate point of view, tonight Mary was having none of it. She was unsure as to what prompted her defiance—her heightened anxiety for her cousin about to give birth, or because Christopher was witness to her mother's appalling behavior, or because she had finally reached the limits of her tolerance that her family members took in their stride the manner in which her mother spoke to her, and then would intervene on her behalf, as if she were incapable of defending herself. Whatever it was, and she suspected it was a combination of all three—although having Christopher bear witness to her mother's humiliating behavior did spur her on to take umbrage—upon this occasion she was not going to be belittled.

Still, such determination did not stop her feeling sick to her stomach and weak at the knees. In truth, her mother terrified her just as much now she was an adult as she had done when she was still in the schoolroom. Anticipating her reaction to any challenge to her parental authority was almost as crippling as the challenge itself. But for once Mary was not going to buckle, and with her hand holding tightly to her wrist she said quietly but firmly,

"Mama, if you wish a cup of tea, I will fetch it. Deb should not wait on you. It is a conceit and feeds your vanity to have her at your beck and call. Deb has just suckled her infant, so could do with a cup of tea herself; which I shall also fetch."

"Mary, I was only trying to—" the Duchess began, then stopped and changed tack under Mary's determined gaze. "That would be lovely. Thank-you, Mary. Your mother and I will sit by the fire to take our tea."

The Countess stood her ground.

"You are clearly not yourself, Mary, to dare to speak to me in such a disgraceful tone, and to the Duchess, too. You owe us an apology."

"No, Mama, I do not. I have nothing to apologize for. Sit by the fireplace as Deb suggests and I will bring your tea. Then I must return to Cousin Duchess."

The Countess of Strathsay stared at her daughter as if she were mad to have interrupted her twice in as many minutes, face flooding with embarrassment. And then she caught the smile exchanged between the Duchess of Roxton and her duke, and was convinced they were having a laugh at her expense, that Mary, whom she had never considered very bright and thought socially inept, had, in one unwitting sentence, unmasked her, and in public.

Charlotte did indeed enjoy having the Duchess of Roxton wait on her. It reinforced her self-worth and bolstered the delusion that she was an important member of the Roxton inner circle. But to have her daughter draw attention to this vanity was more than she could tolerate. Momentarily stunned, she was lost for a suitable rejoinder, but she knew she had to do something to realign the planets to her worldview.

"I will sit when I want to sit and not when *you* tell me to do so," she retorted, gloved hands clasped tightly about the closed sticks of her fan. She looked down her long nose. "This is as good a time as any to tell you that because you have done nothing to curb your child's flights of fantasy—which caused a most embarrassing episode I cannot bring myself to repeat—I was compelled to interfere on her behalf. If her mother cannot see what is best for her, then I must step in as that child's grandmother and do what I see fit."

"Are you talking about Teddy?"

Charlotte made a face at her daughter as if she lacked basic levels of comprehension.

"Do you have any other children? No! More's the pity. Of course I am talking about your daughter—"

"Then please use her name. And I do know what is best for her, so your concern is unnecessary."

"Unnecessary? Dear me, perhaps it is you who are living in a fantasy world. That child is not normal by any stretch of the imagination. Naturally I do not blame her, I blame her parents—her father for not allowing her to socialize with her Roxton cousins, and you for not caring in the least that she spends her time cavorting with the unwashed and unkempt brats of pig farmers and woodland dwellers and the like."

"I do care. I care very much. And you have never been to Abbeywood so you would not know—"

"I know *her*. I don't want or need to know *them*. It is as well I had the foresight to correspond with a reputable school for young ladies in Cheltenham. The headmistress has been persuaded to take the child, particularly given my rank and that she has ducal relatives. And you can thank me the woman did not request to inspect Theodora before she accepted her, because one look and she'd have thought she was admitting the sister of Peter the Wild Boy!"

Mary was aghast, but kept her temper in check.

"You should not have gone to so much trouble on Teddy's behalf without first consulting with me, because if and when she goes to a seminary for young ladies, it will be because she wants to, and because she has the approval of her guardian Mr. Bryce."

"Oh, for pity's sake, Mary! How can you be such a sapskull as to think an intermeddler from the depths of the Cotswolds holds any sway with civilized people? Roxton merely amuses himself with that supercilious rustic and could, with the snap of his fingers, dissolve that ridiculous guardianship. And after your daughter's barbaric display upon first meeting the Duke, where she acted like an untamed animal escaped from its cage, I would think now is the time to put an end to that man's intolerable influence. If you allow this situation to continue upon its present course she will be unfit for good society—Good grief!" she continued with a scoff and a look about the room to make certain she had an audience and they were being attentive to her, and thus would be just as scandalized, "I was never more shocked than when the child told me she wears breeches under her petticoats so she can climb trees. How perverse!"

"I made them for her—"

"More fool you! That tells me you are even more shatterbrained than I thought possible. Why you would indulge her with—"

"—for the precise purpose she told you. So she can climb trees."

The Countess shuddered her disgust. "Barbaric!"

"I beg to differ. It is not barbaric. What *is* barbaric is forcing a child to sit straight for hours with a heavy book balanced upon her head to give her correct posture—"

"It was not in vain. You do carry yourself very well indeed."

"—and if the book should slip, to receive correction with a caning across the shoulders for the infraction. That, Mama, is barbarism."

"There is nothing wrong with disciplining a child; anyone will tell you so. And if you continue to indulge *your child's* ridiculous whims, not only will there be talk of her having a lame brain, but you'll never be able to marry her off. I am telling you this for your own good, Mary, and for the good of that child. Something must be done about her unconventional behavior before it is too late and you will be forced to hide her away in that Cotswold backwater for the rest of her days."

Mary took a deep breath and set her spine straight. It was one thing for her mother to malign her—she had become immune to her constant hurtful insinuations about her intelligence, her looks, and her behaviour—but to turn her talons on Teddy was thoroughly unacceptable and beyond her tolerance.

"Teddy is just a child, a child who enjoys being outdoors. Dair won't be confined within four walls, neither will Teddy."

"Do be sensible! Your brother has just inherited an earldom. He can say and do and stay outdoors all he likes. Teddy is a mere female and thus must know her place is in the drawing room."

"No, Mama. Her place is wherever she is comfortable. And I am appalled you would suggest your only grandchild is mentally deficient. Nor have you any right to speak so disparagingly about her guardian."

"I would not need to speak about such an individual at all had you done your duty and remarried by now, or at the very least have had an offer of marriage from a suitable suitor!"

"You'd be surprised at just whom one meets in the country," Mary quipped and smiled, and pleased with her jibe, she went so far as to glance at Christopher.

The Countess saw that glance and the handsome stranger return her daughter's smile with a smile of his own and a slight bow. This interchange intrigued her and deepened her curiosity to know just who he was. He was not young and while his sober attire suggested a serious disposition, the quality of the fabric and its well-fitted construction, the polish to his shoes and the whiteness of his stock and shirt proclaimed a man of independent means. That he and the Duke were in easy conversation led her to presume they were social equals. It was evident he was interested in her daughter, he had not taken his gaze from her since she had entered the room. So perhaps here was a potential suitor. She decided to test her hypothesis.

"No doubt by remaining in the wilds of Gloucestershire since Sir Gerald's death you've attracted the sort of riffraff who wouldn't know a baronet from a barrow boy. But now you're amongst your own kind," she said, tapping Mary on the arm with her fan, "you may yet find a gentleman of title and fortune worthy of your pedigree. Though I will not hold my breath; your indifferent looks and age are against you, so that you'll have to settle for a suitor who is the other side of fifty and gouty."

She ended what she thought was a witty remark with a smug smile directed at Deb Roxton, as if the Duchess would be in accord with her depressing summation of her daughter's chances of finding a new husband. Not only did her remark fall flat, there was a lingering embarrassed silence because all the Countess had done was humiliate herself.

It caused Mary to blurt out an unguarded remark which had the unwelcome consequence of making her appear fickle and capricious, and before the only man who mattered. And when sometime later she realized this she was mortified. But in the moment, she was too angry to care whose feelings she hurt as long as her mother was put in her place.

"As it so happens, I am in expectation of receiving an offer of marriage by the end of the month from just such a nobleman. But he is not old nor have I seen any evidence of gout. And if I accept his proposal I will be his countess in the new year. So you see, Mama, I am not as unattractive or unworthy as you suppose."

"A countess? Wonders never cease! As the daughter of the Earl of Strathsay I would hope you would not accept anything less," proclaimed the Countess, contradicting her earlier statement. "Marrying a nobleman in possession of an earldom will go a long way in rehabilitating you and Theodora in society. Naturally you told him you will accept the offer when it is made. But it won't happen if he discovers you are deferring to a rustic about your daughter's welfare, so I hope he is ignorant of present arrangements—"

"Mr. Bryce is a gentleman of infinite good sense, who cares deeply about Teddy. And you will stop referring to him as a-a *rustic*. He was educated at Harrow, and spent many years on the Continent, so is a man of considerable address and—"

"Oh! I am very sure he has considerable address and cares *deeply*. That he has spent years abroad amongst foreign types only increases my suspicions. I am the child's grandmother and thus I have every right to voice my fears."

"Suspicions? Fears? Whatever do you mean?"

"The child tells me her guardian is teaching her the minuet and that you allow her to make unchaperoned visits to his house."

Mary frowned. "What is there to be suspicious and fearful of in dancing and visiting? Teddy derives great pleasure from both."

The Countess let out a trill of forced laughter.

"La! You simpleton! How naïve you are. Don't you see he has designs on her—"

"*Designs?*" Mary blinked her incomprehension.

Her mother moved closer and hissed in her face.

"She is a child *now*, but in two years' time she'll be of legal age. Have you thought of *that*? Of course you haven't! This nobody bumpkin could very well marry her out from under your nose, and take her sizeable dowry—well, it would be quite a sum for a yokel farmer's needs. And as he has already begun to school her with dancing lessons and unsupervised visits, her head would easily be turned and she would give in to his demands. But if you marry this unnamed earl and Theodora is sent off to a seminary, then his plans will be thwarted and the child safe from his deviousness."

Mary staggered back apace, as if struck. Dawning realization as to the meaning behind her mother's lurid insinuations sent her into shock. But she forced herself to find her voice, a hand to the base of her throat which was hot and tight.

"Oh! You—you—wicked, wicked—*wicked*—woman," she uttered. "How—How could you have such—Why would you have such—*evil* —thoughts? What an *appalling* accusation to make against a-a gentleman—yes, a *gentleman*—whom you do not know in the least! If you were not my mother I would think you the very devil—"

"Oh, do stop these dramatics, Mary! You are being ludicrously naïve," the Countess stated coldly, unmoved by her daughter's distress, though when the others in the room crowded in about them, her arrogant self-assurance wavered, but not enough to dissuade her from continuing, adding with a sniff, "You know as well as everyone here that arranged marriages between children are commonplace."

"Between children, yes! But what you insinuate is—"

"—and it is not uncommon for men to be much older than their brides. No one lifts an eyebrow. I need not remind you of your own marriage at eighteen—"

"No, you need not remind me!"

"—or the marriage of your cousin to a much older husband."

"Cousin Duchess and I were young women, not children of ten or twelve! But whereas I was absurdly naïve, Mme la Duchesse knew her own mind and was educated beyond her years for what was usual for our sex. She was also deeply in love; I was not and never was with Sir Gerald," Mary enunciated, and such was her angry disgust with her mother that she dared to put up a hand to the Duke to not make comment when he opened his mouth to do so, because she was not finished. "I put it to you that what bothers you most is not the age difference between Cousin Duchess and M'sieur le Duc, but the fact that they had a loving, happy marriage, something you were denied, or denied yourself, the truth be told. And if you want the brutal truth, M'sieur le Duc d'Roxton was more of a parent to me in the short time I lived here than all the years under your roof, Madam!

"Nor will I allow you to make scurrilous and malignant suggestions about the innocent love between my daughter and Mr. Bryce, a gentleman who has loved Teddy as a daughter all her life, and who has been a far better father to her than her own ever was! And if you wish to continue to have contact with her and with me, you had best find it within yourself to seek out the good in people rather than always insulting them, as if by such hateful assessments it somehow makes you appear better and more decent than you are. Now I will leave you with those thoughts, as I must return to Cousin Duchess and—oh dear! How silly of me..." she muttered when she turned away too swiftly and felt suddenly light-headed.

Unaware until that moment that her heightened emotional state had left her giddy, she pitched sideways, knees buckling. But Christopher had seen her sway and kept her from falling by taking her arm and holding her close. He whispered for her to lean into him, and hearing his calm deep voice, Mary looked up and around, and when he winked at her, all the emotional fight drained away and she was no longer angry but relieved.

"Thank-you... I'm—I'm sorry you had to hear such-such *vile* and-

and *preposterous* suppositions, and from no less a person than Teddy's grandmother," she said, then looked about and saw as if for the first time that not only had Roxton moved to stand by the Duchess and both were regarding her with concern, but that Lady Paget was up off the settee and leaning lightly on her walking stick beside the ducal couple. "I would dearly love to make excuses for my mother and blame a megrim, or brain fever, anything but state the sad truth that she is a self-absorbed *cold-hearted* wretch—"

"You ungrateful child! Stand up straight and stop your theatrics. And who is this gentleman that he dares hold your arm as if he has ownership?"

"*Enough*," Roxton hissed with menace, which had Lady Strathsay staring up at him in surprised fright and closing her mouth in an instant. "You have badgered and berated your daughter for the very last time, Charlotte. She is no longer a child, though I suspect you would continue with your ridiculous parental pestering were she sixty! But if you wish to continue as part of this family you will find some humility and circumspection, and you will leave your daughter alone. It falls upon me to remind you that you are part of this family through marriage only, not blood. Unlike Mary, whose blood connection gives her claim on my protection and munificence without question, you are here under sufferance and barely tolerated. Dear God, even her husband had a greater claim to his seat at my table as the Duchess's half-brother, and I wouldn't have Sir Gerald within twenty miles of here! One word from your daughter and I would be happy to never again admit your carriage through my gates. Do you understand *me*, Madam?"

The Countess glanced swiftly about at the mute faces and saw that they were all in agreement with the Duke. She understood that he was furious with her but not why, because she blamed Mary for his anger. Just as her parental conceit meant she was unable to comprehend why Roxton would favor her daughter over her, when she believed herself to be in the right. Yet she knew when to respectfully cower to ducal authority. So she bobbed a curtsy and said meekly, mouth set in prim line, "I do, Your Grace."

"Good. Then I will no longer hear you voice such ridiculous and thoroughly reprehensible assertions about the gentleman you maligned. And now I will let him speak for himself, for I am certain he has been itching to tell you precisely what he thinks, and you deserve everything he cares to throw at you, Madam."

When the Duke nodded to Christopher, Christopher let go of Mary's arm with a smile, waited to see that she was steady on her feet and no longer fighting dizziness, then turned to greet the Countess. He executed a bow of extreme politeness, the effortless grace in which he conducted himself softening the prim line about the Countess's mouth. But not a minute later the pucker returned, and more severely because when he straightened and met her gaze with an unblinking stare, she saw the contempt in his handsome face. But that was as nothing compared to the embarrassment she experienced when he addressed her.

"Your spiteful and defamatory remarks have forfeited you the right to a civil introduction, my lady. But for the sake of your daughter and your granddaughter, Their Graces, and my mother, who have listened with forbearance to the muck issuing forth from between your teeth, I will tell you precisely who and what I am. As Squire Bryce of Brycecomb Hall in Gloucestershire, with an income of ten thousand a year, I am anything but a simple rustic. And I mean to marry your daughter, if she'll have me."

"Rustic? Gloucestershire? *Squire?*" The Countess blinked. "Ten *thousand* a year? But-but you're not an earl."

"I am not. Nor shall I ever be." Christopher grinned. "But I must be the one with brain fever for I still want to wed your daughter, very much, even though it means gaining you for a mother-in-law."

This quip was met by a collective chortle, and then punctuated by the loud clap of a door hitting hard up against the gilded molding of the wallpapered wall. A liveried footman yelped and jumped in fright as the door narrowly missed hitting him. Everyone else in the room was also shaken and they turned as one to face the doorway to see who or what had caused the commotion.

And there was Jonathon, Duke of Kinross, swaying in the doorway, face white and staring without blinking. His eyes were brimful of tears, and his cheeks were wet. He took a step into the room, staggered, then crumpled and dropped to his knees. And when he covered his face with his large hands no one dared to breathe.

THIRTY-TWO

Mary was the first to rush forward, and she, too, dropped to her knees in a billow of quilted silk petticoats, to press her handkerchief on Jonathon and to put a soothing hand to his back. Everyone else crowded around and stared down at them, except for the Duke who hung back, gazing through the open doorway. If not for Deb holding him fast, he would have taken off down that darkened corridor to his mother's rooms to find out for himself why it was her husband was in a crumpled heap on the carpet.

"Breathe, Julian," Deb whispered.

It was what Mary was telling Jonathon. Christopher strode to the tea trolley, found a decanter of lemon water, and poured out into a tumbler. This he gave to Mary, who gave it to Jonathon to take a sip so that he would have occupation to calm his nerves, and so that he might then be able to speak to them. He drank up, and Christopher took the tumbler from him, and then Jonathon swiftly wiped his face dry. And when he made motions to stand, it was Roxton who gave him his hand, while Christopher helped Mary to her feet.

And still no one spoke, and all eyes remained on Jonathon, waiting for him to tell them the news of the Duchess, and not wanting to ask or speak for fear that to do so would elicit a response they did not in the least want to hear. And when Jonathon again covered his face with a hand before wiping his eyes dry, it was too much for the Duke, who grabbed him by the sleeve and gave him a shake.

"For God's sake! End this excruciating wait one way or the other!"

Jonathon nodded and took a deep breath, but then his mouth

began to tremble and again he was too overcome to speak; he put up his hand and then buried his face in his sleeve. The Duke could take no more. He broke from his wife and had taken a step toward the door when Mary spoke. Her words and her calm assurance stopped him, and he returned to stand by the Duchess.

"Wait, Roxton! Please. It is the Duke's right to give us news of his wife and child. Please. Give Kinross a few moments to collect his thoughts. It has been an emotional day for everyone, but most of all for him and for Cousin Duchess." She touched Jonathon's hand and smiled up at him and said confidently, though inside she was a quaking mess of anticipation. "Take your time, Your Grace… It is not every day a man becomes a father, and this for the second time. Every birth is a wondrous thing, as Roxton will attest, but we all know just how special this birth is for you, is that not so?"

At that Jonathon again wiped his face, and this time when he took a deep breath he gazed about at the expectant expressions gathered around him, and his face split into a grin. And with his smile everyone in the room relaxed and smiled back, even Lady Paget, to whom Christopher whispered the happy news that His Grace of Kinross was grinning from ear to ear.

Jonathon next fixed on Roxton and grabbed his shoulder and pressed it then shook his hand. He repeated this with Christopher, and then kissed Deb's cheek, and then Mary's. And with the kiss to Mary's cheek he picked her up, and twirled her about on the spot before setting her down again, she taking a step back with a breathless laugh and falling into Christopher's arms.

"I must return to her… She'll be wondering what's taken me so long… But I had to come and tell you," Jonathon finally blurted out, finding his voice in a series of breaths. He then laughed and shook his head and rattled on, as if he had already told them what they were all waiting to hear and was following up with the details. "I almost didn't make it! Gabrielle scolded me; so did Michelle. And Antonia—ah! What a divine creature my wife is! Mary? Mary! It's as well you weren't there—how your poor little ears would've burned. Those final few pushes saw her curse like a French sailor! Tremendous! Now excuse me —Mary, you are wanted. She's asked for you. And, Roxton—she asks that her sons wait just a little longer." He grinned sheepishly. "Females. Got to have their faces scrubbed and their hair threaded with ribbons. Her women are attending to her now. She don't want you seeing her until she's your mother again, if that makes sense—"

"Perfect sense," Deb agreed with a smile. "Isn't that so, Julian?"

"Sense? Bloody hell! None of it makes sense to me!" blurted out the Duke, wiping a hand over his face. "For God's sake, Kinross! You've not told us how she is. What's most vital. Tell me she's all right. Tell us all that Maman and her babe came through it and are all right!"

"Ah! Oh? Didn't I? Apologies. Yes! Must do that of course… Harry! Jack! Come in! Come in and hear the news!" Jonathon called out and beckoned as the two youths, with Teddy skipping before them, entered the room. He waited until they joined the group and then looked down into Henri-Antoine's grave face with a reassuring smile. "Everything is fine, my boy," he said gently. "Your mother did splendidly. She and the babe came through it all just splendidly—"

"Oh, thank God!" Roxton announced with a heavy sigh of relief and promptly collapsed onto the nearest chair.

"—and she wants to see you. I'll send someone out to fetch you and your brother when she's ready."

"Thank-you, sir," Henri-Antoine replied and let out a soft breath. He flashed a rare smile. "And did Mama's dearest wish come true? Do I have a sister?"

Jonathon looked about at the eager faces and was again overcome. He patted Henri-Antoine's shoulder gently before clearing his throat and mentally pulling himself together. He stared over the youth's head at Roxton, who still remained seated and was holding his wife's hand, then addressed the room.

"Mme la Duchesse has given me a daughter. The dukedom of Kinross has an heir, and she's the most beautiful creation on God's earth."

Everyone erupted into applause.

THE FOLLOWING HANDFUL OF DAYS WAS A BLUR OF ACTIVITY AND tiredness for Mary, who supervised the coming and going of visitors to the Duchess's bedchamber, ensuring family and guests alike were able to coo over the ducal infant but that the new mother was not left exhausted, and there was still time for Antonia and Jonathon to be alone to enjoy and become acquainted with their newborn. Gabrielle de Crespigny took charge of the infant's needs and the nursery and its nurserymaids, Michelle supervised the maids, and the major domo Marc Gallet soon had the household returned to its daily routine, given there was a newborn in the house.

Come Christmas Day, two of the Duke of Roxton's carriages arrived from the big house to collect Mary, Christopher, Lady Paget,

Teddy, Mme de Crespigny, Marc Gallet, and the upper servants for the family service in the Treat chapel, to be followed by a lavish Christmas banquet and games and gifts for the children. It was the first time Antonia was left alone with her infant with only Michelle for company —she refused to leave her side—and without Jonathon, whom she sent off to spend the day with the family as he had not been outside their apartment since the birth, and who, in her opinion, needed a dose of winter air to unfuddle his brain so that they could come to a firm decision as to their daughter's names for the christening ceremony. Besides which her grandchildren, particularly Frederick, was missing his company and would want news of his Mema and the baby from him and no other.

And so the corridors and rooms of Crecy Hall were quiet for the first time in a very long while, allowing Antonia to enjoy the quiet and do nothing more than gaze wonderingly at her baby daughter. It was while she was dozing with her infant nestled in the crook of her arm that she dreamed her nephew was seated on the edge of the mattress facing her. He was cross-legged and smiling in that way peculiar to him, head cocked to one side, like an enquiring parrot, bright blue eyes so like his father's, full of undisguised mischief. Only this time his eyes were glassy, and he was much older and more gaunt than her remembrance of him. He had also acquired a scar to his eyebrow and left cheek. She did not remember his hair being streaked with gray, but then he had always worn a wig or powdered his own locks.

With a sleepy smile she put out her hand to him across the coverlet. He smiled back and took hold of her fingers, and after kissing the back of her hand, kept it in a firm clasp. As always, aunt and nephew spoke in French, their first language.

"Boy or girl?"

"A daughter."

"I know nothing of infants. But she looks beautiful and serene, just like you."

"I am glad you are here, *mon chou*. It has been far too long."

"And I'm glad you are happy, and have a new family. You deserve nothing less. Mary tells me your new duke is a good man, and in his own indomitable and unique way, not unlike M'sieur le Duc Roxton."

"He is and I love him; all the more because he accepts I will always love Monseigneur, too. And when my time it comes, I will return to him. Until then, I am Jonathon's, and he has given me this most precious gift and we are very happy."

"I went to the mausoleum to pay my respects. It is a fitting place for my parents. It is good to see them keeping company with

Monseigneur. I asked their forgiveness… I wish my life had been different—that *I* had been different—for them. But there is no point in wishing the impossible, is there? That way madness lies…"

"Do you wish you had told them you were alive?"

"My father knew. He always knew. After my—um—*death* we continued to correspond. I made him swear not to tell Mama."

"That was wise. Your mother she would have pestered Vallentine unto death to tell her your whereabouts. Better that she mourn and leave him in peace, than worry about you."

"Aha! So *mon père* he did confide in Monseigneur, and in turn he told you! Of course he would. And yet you never said a word to anyone, not even to your son?"

"It was not my place to say anything to anyone. You wished to be dead. *Il n'y avait aucune discussion possible.* Just as it is not my place to tell Mary that your offer of marriage, while sincere, was made in a bid to have Christopher Bryce act upon his feelings, yes?"

"And we all thought Monseigneur he was the omniscient one!"

Antonia dimpled.

"I do not know everything. But I know my son, and M'sieur Bryce his disposition it is very similar to Julian's. Honor and duty and doing what is right, even if it is to their detriment, that is what is important to them."

Evelyn smiled crookedly.

"I don't doubt they are getting along splendidly. A mutual admiration society of sorts."

"*Absolument.* But you knew that too, did you not, *mon chou*?"

"It was just a matter of herding them into the same room… And has Squire Worthy found his ballocks to finally declare himself to Mary?"

"*Pouvez-vous en douter*? They are in love and so they are lovers. And he has asked her to marry him. But they are not betrothed—yet."

"Whyever not!?"

"It was you, was it not, who told Mary you would return within the month to ask her to marry you? And so like a good girl she waits to speak with you, to tell you herself about her squire's marriage proposal. She will only accept him after she has refused you. She too can be just as obdurate. *Mon chou*, she loves you but—"

"—it is in a different way to her squire. I know and I'm glad. Truly. I would've married her, made her my countess, and looked after her, had matters with him turned out differently. You have always known about Mary and me. We grew up under your very nose. Our first and only kiss was here at Treat. But I make a poor husband. And this you also know. Oh, she'd have put up with me, and loved me, and tolerated my selfish eccentricities. That is because she is a sweet creature—a good girl, as you say. But after her deplorable first marriage, she is deserving of a man who not only loves her deeply but worships her, who will be a devoted husband and father to their children, and to her daughter. I would be a poor substitute for the Squire. Christopher Bryce is a worthy man, and he is worthy of Mary."

"All that is very true, *mon cher neveu*. You speak from the heart, because despite how you present to the world, I know you, too, are a good man with a good heart."

"Only to those I love. To others I am the very devil." He kissed her hand again and smiled into her eyes, a glance at her sleeping infant. "I hope one day to have the privilege of seeing her grown."

Antonia's fingers convulsed in his and her green eyes misted with tears.

"You are leaving us again." When he nodded but did not speak she added, "I would ask you to write but I fear that may not be possible, yes?"

"I cannot promise, but I will do my best in my self-absorbed way to send you word that I live, if nothing else. Should you have news for me, send it via Shrewsbury. He'll know where I am."

Antonia was surprised, and yet also strangely not, that he was in the service of the Spymaster General. She made no comment, and said only,

"And Mary? Will you take your leave of her?"

"That would be unwise. But I am not a complete coward. I have written her a letter." He took a folded parchment from a pocket of his frock coat and placed it on the sidetable. "I could've had it delivered but I had to see you for myself, *ma chère tante bien aimée*; to be satisfied you are well and happy, and content."

Antonia smiled down at her infant, who was starting to fuss. "As you see, I have not been this happy or this content in a very long time."

Michelle appeared in the doorway then, and behind her was one of the nurserymaids. Seeing a stranger sitting on the edge of the Duchess's bed, both women bustled forward in alarm. But when Evelyn hopped off the bed and made them a sweeping bow before putting a finger to his lips for them to remain mute, they brought themselves up short and waited. And as the baby continued to fuss, and the Duchess gently rocked and cooed over her daughter, they stood in frozen dread of the stranger's motives.

And then the stranger, still with his finger to his lips, and his blue eyes wide and unblinking, tiptoed up to them, then passed them, the two women turning to watch him go, mesmerized. And as they followed him with their eyes, he twirled about, grabbed an edge of the tapestry *portière*, and with a wink and smile, jerked the curtain across the doorway in their faces.

The stranger disappeared as he had arrived, with not a word spoken or a sound made, much in the manner of an apparition.

Both women let out a sigh of relief when he was gone, the nursery-maid daring to take a peek behind the curtain to make sure the stranger had indeed left. She then whispered loudly to Michelle that Mme la Duchesse had been visited by a ghost. To which Michelle, who was trembling inside and had had the same thought, told the girl in an audible hiss that she was being ridiculous and to get on with her tasks.

At that, Antonia looked up and found only Michelle and the nurs-erymaid were with her, leaving her to wonder if indeed she had dreamed the entire conversation with her nephew. The letter on the bedside table addressed to the Lady Mary Cavendish was forgotten in the fuss that comes with attending to the demands of a newborn, until many hours later.

THIRTY-THREE

Two days after Christmas Day, on a cold and silent winter's morning, the servants, masters, children, favored guests, and honored tenants of both households, Treat and Crecy Hall, were up and making ready for the christening and celebrations to mark the birth of an heir to a Scottish dukedom—Elspeth Henrietta Jane Strang Leven: Elspeth, the Scottish form of Elizabeth, after the fourth Duchess of Roxton; Henrietta for Henry, the fourth Duke, both Jonathon and Antonia's ancestors in common; and Jane for Antonia's mother, to be formally known by the courtesy title of the Marchioness of Leven, and by her doting parents, half-brothers, and close family simply as Elsie.

The christening was taking place in the Roxton family chapel, followed by a celebratory dinner hosted by the Duke and Duchess of Kinross at Crecy Hall. And after dinner there would be dancing. Teddy had asked that she be permitted to perform the minuet in honor of her baby cousin. How could Antonia and Jonathon refuse her, particularly when this minuet would be danced with her Uncle Bryce, who she assured them was the best dancer in the whole of England, if not the world.

Teddy was even prepared to dress for the occasion and suffered to be put into stays and her best winter gown of green velvet, with white clocked stockings and velvet embroidered shoes that had heels and paste diamond buckles. Her waist-length red hair was brushed until it shone and was then braided and tied up with matching green silk ribbons. She then promised her mother she would remain uncrumpled so that when the time came for Christopher to lead her out to the dance floor, he would be dancing with her as a young lady.

It was as a young lady she descended the stairs with her mother to enter the waiting carriage to take them across the bridge to Treat. Christopher and Kate were already awaiting them in the hall. Seeing Mary and Teddy on the first landing, Christopher led his mother over to greet them, he noticing that Mary wore a velvet gown of the same lavender hue as she had worn at Brycecomb Hall the day of the Duchess of Kinross's visit. The color complemented Mary's eyes and the fiery red of her hair. He wanted to tell her how beautiful she looked, but it was to Teddy he directed his admiration and delight, for he could see the girl had gone to a great deal of trouble to look her best. He bowed to her and she grinned and bobbed a curtsy in reply, which had her mother smiling. Kate, too, offered Teddy her compliments and in a deft move that did not go unnoticed by the couple, she took Teddy's hand and walked away with her to the fireplace, all the while asking questions about her new puppy Nera, and when would she be permitted to take her home; was she weaned yet?

And so Christopher and Mary were able to have a few minutes together before the Duke and Duchess with their infant daughter, Gabrielle de Crespigny, Michelle, and Nurse finally came downstairs and joined them to set off for the chapel.

It was the first chance the couple had to be alone in a sennight, if by *alone* they ignored Kate and Teddy by the fireplace and the clutch of servants lined up by the entrance doors, ready and waiting to help shrug them into fur-lined cloaks, gloves, muffs, and hats. They had seen little of each other since Elsie's birth, not even at meal times, because Mary spent her time in the Duchess's apartment. The few hours she had to herself she shared with Teddy, or with family from the big house come across to visit.

Christopher, too, was rarely alone. His time was taken up at the big house with Kate, who was invited by the Duchess to reacquaint herself with the house. He would leave her chatting with the old Duke of Roxton's former valet and the present Duke's godfather, Martin Ellicott. The old man was only too happy to sit with Kate over tea and cake and talk over the glory days of Monseigneur, the lives of mutual acquaintances, and most importantly to trade anecdotes about M'sieur le Duc d'Roxton and his many scathing aphorisms, which had them both chuckling and shaking their heads.

And while Kate was kept entertained by the spritely old gentleman, who had the cadence and mannerisms of an ancient aristocrat, Christopher joined the Duke for a ride about the parklands, played at billiards with him and spent several hours shut up in his library. Here, surrounded by thousands of leather-bound volumes, seated in comfortable chairs by one of two fireplaces, they discussed the surprising unmasking of Philip Audley as a traitor, both in accord that if the secretary was indeed guilty of treason, it was for purely pecuniary gain; the man did not have an idealistic bone in his body. An inner voice warned Christopher that it would be imprudent to mention Evelyn Ffolkes's involvement in Shrewsbury's spy network, or that the man had returned from the dead; that revelation he would leave to others. But he was keen to press upon the Duke the sincerity of his wish to marry the Lady Mary. Her future and that of her daughter, marriage settlements, Christopher's financial situation, and the future of Abbeywood Farm were all discussed, and such was the accord between them that they were left with the feeling they had known each other for years, not days.

Christopher had the Duke's blessing to the match, though Roxton felt duty-bound to warn him that such an unequal marriage would not suit the sticklers of Polite Society, who would forever shun one of their own marrying beneath her. But, and this was more important to him than anything else, he wanted Mary to be happy, and if her happiness was dependent on marrying Christopher, then so be it. The couple would always be welcome at Treat. And then the Duke gave him the startling news that the Archbishop had been applied to for a Special Marriage License.

Roxton suggested the marriage take place as soon after the christening as could be arranged. All the family were gathered, so why delay? Not even confirmation of the death of Mary's father, the Earl of Strathsay, was reason enough for a postponement until a suitable period of mourning had elapsed. As far as the Duke was concerned, and he admitted to be a stickler for protocol, the Earl had forfeited an appropriate period of mourning, given he had abandoned his wife and children, and there was the fact that he had died almost six months ago now. Dair, Mary's brother and earl presumptive, would agree. And with good fortune and good winds, Major Lord Fitzstuart would be back in England in time to give his blessing and to attend the ceremony.

Thus Christopher came away from the library in a buoyant mood, knowing he had the Duke's blessing to his marriage with Mary, and the ceremony was practically arranged. All that was required was for the prospective bride to agree to sharing her future with him. It was this future that was uppermost in his mind as he and Mary stood by the base of the hall stairs and faced one another. And while his head reminded him that she had told him on numerous occasions in that week spent in the cottage that she loved him, and not only while they were a tangle of naked limbs amongst the bedcovers, and that he was confident she would say yes, his heart, which was beating inordinately fast and hard at that very moment, still wanted to hear her say it, here, now, out loud, that *yes*, she would be his wife.

Yet such was their nervous expectation that neither spoke, waiting for the other to do so first. Finally, Mary turned her back on the room and moved closer. She tilted her chin up and said with a tremulous smile, a gloved hand lightly to the front of his embroidered wool waistcoat,

"I hardly know where to begin... I have so much I want and need to tell you... And I will tell you *now* because I've kept you waiting my response to your proposal for far too long already, though events—the early arrival of baby Elsie—did conspire against me. You have been so patient and—"

"Mary, I have waited eight years to finally arrive here—at this moment—with you, that a few more days, or even weeks, are of little importance. What is important and of the greatest interest is your response. And I will admit there is little else I think about—"

"But surely you know what it is!?"

"I can surmise and I can wish, but you must tell me for me to know." He smiled when she looked confused, and leaned in to say gently, "Yes, I am being pedantic, but for good reason. You did tell your mother you were in expectation of an offer of marriage from an earl—"

"Oh *that*! I shouldn't have allowed foolish misplaced pride to get the better of me and made such an announcement," she interrupted with a pout and a guilty blush. "But my mother has a way of getting under my skin, like a pebble in my shoe. One walks on, trying to ignore the irritation, but then it becomes too annoying to bear and I just have to rip off my shoe and shake it to get rid of it. Or in the case of my mother, to blurt out a response I hope will at least give her pause." She sighed. "It rarely works..."

"Do not be so hard on yourself. I suspect she has that effect on most people. I'm ashamed to admit that I used the same tactic on her myself and made public a topic that is not discussed openly in polite circles, and should only ever be mentioned upon two occasions: When discussing marriage settlements, and at the reading of a will. I had the ill manners to announce my annual income. That was a vulgar display, and my only excuse is that it was also an attempt to give your mother pause as to her prejudices about the gentry. We do not mix in the first circles, but there are many of us with incomes that match and often exceed those of noblemen."

"Would it surprise you to know that I had no idea as to your wealth, nor have I ever wondered?"

Christopher grinned. "No. How could you? Your first visit over the ridge into my little corner of the world was the picnic at my cloth mill. Though Brycecomb Hall must've given you an indication that I was a man of some means."

"It did," she replied truthfully. "But my first thought upon seeing your lovely house was not a vulgar one. I was puzzled as to why a man with your wealth, who has manufacturing concerns as well as an estate —with all the necessary time and energy that is required for such enterprises—would agree to take on the stewardship of Abbeywood Farm. Why do you spend two days out of every fortnight away from your own interests, your own home—and your mother?"

"Surely you know why? I agreed to be steward, not because Sir Gerald asked it of me—though that put me under an obligation and I was sincere in wanting Jack to have an estate worth inheriting—but so I could be near you."

"Oh, you darling man!"

"It gave me a legitimate excuse to be at Abbeywood. It mattered not to me if I spent them locked away with Mr. Deed, tearing at my curls over the deplorable state of the account books, or dealing with a household overrun with unnecessary ill-tempered and resentful servants. What did was that you were there somewhere in the house, and just knowing that was enough. I was there, and so were you, and I dared to dream that one day we would live under the same roof, but in a different way, in the only way that mattered to me, as husband and wife."

Mary was so overcome she looked away, a shaking gloved hand to her mouth, and swallowed down a sob. She did not know whether she wanted to cry or laugh or do both, she was filled with such joy. It was the same sort of extraordinary happiness she had felt at the cottage. But joy such as this did not stem from an occasion or a place, or even the wondrous experience of making love with this man, but came from deep within her because she loved him to her core, and most impor-tantly for her, she knew his love for her was just as deep and abiding. She had never experienced anything like it, and she wanted to hold onto it for dear life; it was the most precious thing in the world to her. She had to tell him, to let him know, but she was so overcome by such profound emotion that she did not know how to begin or where to start.

Christopher saw her distress in her inability to articulate herself and purposely grounded her with the statement,

"I know about your cousin's impending offer of marriage."

This brought Mary out of her breathless awe to look up at him wonderingly. "You do?"

"Apart from the fact I would have to possess less intelligence than a chicken not to realize the earl you spoke of to your mother was your cousin, there is the small detail that he told me."

"Evelyn told you? Why did he do that?"

"Only he can answer with any certainty, but if I were to hazard a guess I would offer a two-fold reason. He has a competitive streak, and he can be mischievous for its own sake. Yet I suspect him of the best of intentions. But I don't care that he means to make you an offer. I only care about your answer—to him, and to me."

"He sent me a letter, and I have written him a reply. I think he always knew what my answer would be. Despite his self-absorbed distracted temperament, he is a keen observer of human nature." She smiled up at him. "He would have married me, too. Had his intuition failed him upon this occasion. But it didn't, did it? I love you with all my heart and—"

"—I love you with all my heart." He caught up her gloved hand and after pressing it to his chest, kissed it, saying in a rush, "God knows I want you to say yes, you will marry me, but I would be failing in my duty if I did not remind you that you will be marrying a man with a tainted pedigree, who is so far removed from the *beau monde* that there will be places you will no longer be welcome, events you can no longer attend, and people who will no longer speak to you. I gave my word to the Duke that I would remind you what he told me—that in marrying me, a farmer of bastard birth, you retain your title but you forfeit your social status amongst your peers. And that in marrying you, the daughter of an earl, I will forevermore be branded as a toady who has dared to reach too high up into their world for a wife. In so doing, I've pulled you down with me into mine—not unlike Persephone's abduction by Hades. But even she was permitted to return from the underworld for part of the year; you will not be given such latitude. There is no climbing back up to join them, Mary."

"And my family? What did Roxton say about them? Will he turn his back on us? Will they?"

Christopher shook his head. "Not at all. He and they will support you—us." He smiled shyly and blushed. "It seems the Duchess has taken a liking to having a brother, regardless our connection is through base means. But despite the support of Their Graces and the Duke's power and influence over his peers, we cannot expect him to do anything that would compromise his position and authority."

"I do not expect it. I welcome his support because my family do mean the world to me, and I would be very sad to give them up. But I would—I would give them up, to spend my life with you."

Christopher pressed her hand. "My darling, I would never ask or expect you to make such a sacrifice—ever."

"I know you would not. But you forget I have already done so before, and not because I wanted to. Living in exile with Sir Gerald was tedious, but not because of where I was living but because of whom I was living it with. Dare I say, since being widowed, I came to the realization that social events of the season, cards of invitation, and the latest gossip and London hairstyle are rather trivial ways to fill my days. You know how much I enjoy the day-to-day running of a household and its myriad of tasks, and how much I love living in our corner of England. I could think of no better way to live a fulfilled life than to be of help to you in realizing your dreams for your cloth mills and your estate. You are creating something worthwhile and wonderful for the people of the vale, and I am so very proud of you. Life in the Cotswolds suits me— suits us—very well indeed, and I cannot wait to return."

"As my wife?"

Mary leaned into him, went on tiptoe and kissed him. "As your wife."

"Then your answer is *yes*," he asked rhetorically, hands going about her waist and drawing her against him, "you will marry me."

"We must not forget those whose blessings are important to our future happiness."

"If you're referring to Kate—my mother—the truth is she had almost despaired of me ever asking you. She'll be over the moon with happiness. As for Teddy..." Christopher frowned. "I've wondered how she would feel about having me for a stepfather. It is one thing to be her Uncle Bryce, but in marrying her mother I become something else entirely."

"Well, I am glad about Lady Paget because I like her very much. And you need not frown over Teddy. I thought it best to discover her opinion before giving you my reply because had she objected, it would have delayed matters, though the outcome would eventually have been the same. But I am happy to report she only had good things to say about you as a possible father, and was unsurprisingly excited at the prospect, and almost as happy as I am that we will all be living under the one roof as a family."

Christopher glanced over Mary's head across the hall to where Kate and Teddy were by the fireplace. Predictably, Teddy was not still, but showing Kate the steps of the minuet. Christopher looked back down at Mary, his frown returning.

"She does not object to living at Brycecomb Hall?"

Mary shook her head, mirth lighting up her eyes. "It would seem not. She tells me that it would only be for a short while, because she means to return to live at Abbeywood when she marries Jack. She says it is the best outcome for everyone."

"Good—God! What a little schemer! Does *he* know this?"

Mary shook her head. "Not yet. And best he doesn't know until Teddy is *at least* eighteen."

Christopher began to chuckle, then the frown returned when Mary added,

"There is one other matter Teddy says I must take into account before I agree to marry you and we move to be with you at Brycecomb. I see her point. It may take me some getting used to, particularly when the attachment to you is very great indeed. In fact, it may necessitate a delay to our marriage because—"

"No it won't! Tell me what it is and it will be dealt with immediately."

It was Mary's turn to giggle, such was his despondency, and she briefly rested her forehead against his chest to control her laughter, before raising her chin and feigning surprise.

"But how can you be so cavalier as to sweep aside such devotion? I won't allow you to do so. It would be inhuman!"

Christopher's frown deepened as he racked his brains for who or what she was talking about. He did not have long to wait to find out because Mary's teasing was cut short by her daughter, who had skipped up to them, and wishing to be noticed, loudly cleared her throat, then ruined the effect by giggling behind her gloved hand. The couple instantly sprang apart, coming to a sense of their surroundings, both blushing and feeling awkward. Teddy saw none of this, such was her excitement and need to know.

"Did you say yes to Uncle Bryce, Mama? Kate and I are anxious. And you have promised Uncle Bryce you will do your best not to be frightened of Lorenzo, haven't you?" Before her mother could respond she turned to Christopher adding earnestly, "Mama is getting better and better with dogs. She held Nera yesterday and allowed her on her lap for the *longest* time. So I'm very sure that if you introduce her to Lorenzo *in the right way*, she will see that he is a most obliging animal and get used to having him around, too. Look! Here's Cousin Duchess and the baby!"

Everyone in the hall turned to the staircase. There on the landing was Antonia, Duchess of Kinross, in a froth of white silk-embroidered quilted petticoats, and behind her the Duke, grinning from ear to ear and holding in his arms his baby daughter, wrapped up in soft layers, her thatch of soft dark hair covered by a beautifully embroidered pink silk christening cap.

Teddy gave her mother's arm a tug, and when she looked about, whispered loudly,

"Did you say yes, Mama? Did you say yes, you'll marry Uncle Bryce?"

Christopher looked down at her, and then looked to Mary with a raise of one eyebrow, but said nothing.

Mary smiled and put her hand on his sleeve, "Mr. Bryce, there is nothing on this earth I want more than to be your wife, and so my answer is—yes!"

She smiled at Teddy who was clapping and jumping on the spot, and in the next moment found herself swept off her feet, Christopher so overjoyed and relieved he lost all sense of decorum. He twirled Mary round and round before setting her down again. But he did not let her go. She did not want him to. Her arms went up about his neck and held fast. They enjoyed the moment, so long in coming, and the world around them melted away as they abandoned themselves to a long, lingering kiss.

"*Bon*. You see now, Jonathon, why I told you this christening it would not be the only event this week," Antonia said mildly as she joined the kissing couple at the base of the staircase. "Elsie's godmother she is to be married, and to a gentleman I approve, and that pleases me very much."

THE CHRISTENING AT THE ROXTON FAMILY CHAPEL WAS AN intimate affair, attended by family and upper servants. Elspeth, Marchioness of Leven, was on her best behavior and slept in her father's arms throughout the service. When she protested, she had every right to do so when her forehead was sprinkled with holy water. Her godparents solemnly swore to watch over her and to bring her up in the ways of the Church of England, Lord Henri-Antoine swallowing hard and looking more stern, if that were possible. But his mother saw how proud he was to have this honor bestowed upon him and to share it with his cousin Lady Mary, and her eyes filled with tears thinking how equally proud her beloved Monseigneur would be of their son, and more than a little conceited that he had such a great look of him.

At the conclusion of the service, everyone bundled into their coats and into carriages that had hot bricks wrapped and placed on the floors to ward off the winter cold. The short journey back across the bridge to Crecy Hall was uneventful, and the guests were treated to hot punch and a warm fire in the Great Hall, to the accompaniment of the Duke of Roxton's string quartet, while they waited for the banquet to begin.

It was delayed by half an hour because two carriages, one containing the Duke and Duchess of Kinross and their precious bundle, and the other their closest servants, took a diversion to the family mausoleum. Only Antonia and Jonathon with Elsie entered the tomb. They were there for several minutes before Jonathon and his baby daughter emerged first, Antonia joining them in the carriage a few minutes later. Nothing was said. Nothing needed to be said. And the party continued on their way to Crecy Hall.

After dinner, Teddy danced the minuet with Christopher and everyone applauded, not least because the girl danced well, but also because Christopher Bryce was an elegant and masterful practitioner of the art. Kate smiled knowingly, Martin Ellicott providing her with a running commentary of the reactions of various family members— ranging from awe to dumbstruck surprise—to her son's skill on a dance floor.

It then came time for the newly-engaged couple to perform the minuet, Mary too happy to be apprehensive about dancing in front of her family. Her one regret was that her brother and his wife were not there to share in her happiness. This she voiced to Christopher as he led her out into the middle of the room, only for a commotion at the double doors at the far end of the hall to halt the music and the dance before it began.

Everyone turned as one and were stunned into silence when a large man with a full dark beard, who had in his arms a white blonde nymph, came through the open doors and strode towards them. Mary picked up a handful of her petticoats and rushed to meet them.

"Apologies for our tardiness. Fallen tree right in front of the gates. Rory said I should ride on ahead but I wasn't going to leave her behind, now was I?"

"Dair! Dair, oh thank God you're finally home!"

Alisdair, Major Lord Fitzstuart, heir presumptive to the earldom of Strathsay, showed a white smile in his black beard. "I am, Mary. And for good." He put his wife gently to her feet, but kept an arm about her waist while his gaze scanned the happy smiling faces of his family. He leaned in to his sister's ear, "Rory tells me you know our wonderful news—"

"I am so happy for you both," Mary replied breathlessly and impulsively kissed his cheek. She unintentionally grimaced. "Oh dear, but I do think you'll have to shave that off before the baby arrives."

Rory laughed behind her hand at Mary's reaction to her beloved's beard. "Don't fret, Mary. The new Earl of Strathsay will be clean shaven before the ink dries on his letters patent." She looked up at her husband. "Though I do love you as a pirate…"

Dair winked at his wife, then said to Mary in all seriousness, "I'd like to tell everyone our news, and then meet the newest member of the family, but first Rory says there's a fellow I need to meet, and that he'll be here. Says he's in love with you. And you feel the same way about him."

Mary regarded Rory with no small surprise that she had been able to make this assessment from her short stay in the Cotswolds. She smiled and blushed. "It would seem I am the last to know my own feelings!" And before her sister-in-law could respond, glanced over her shoulder, sensing a presence, and there were Christopher and Teddy.

Teddy broke from Christopher and ran up to her uncle and threw her arms around him. Dair picked her up and kissed her, then set her down and kept hold of her hand. He laughed when she pulled a face.

"Don't tell me you don't like my pirate beard!"

"I do, Uncle Dair! But I don't want to kiss it! But you're just the captain our pirate ship treehouse has been looking for. Isn't he, Uncle Bryce?"

"Dair, may I introduce Mr. Christopher Bryce of Brycecomb Hall in Gloucestershire, and the man I am to marry in two days' time. Mr. Bryce, this is my eldest brother, Major Lord Fitzstuart."

Dair stuck out his hand. "Congratulations! Glad to make your acquaintance, and to have you as a member of the family."

"That is very generous of you, my lord. And may I add, surprisingly unquestioning."

"Generous? Mayhap. But unquestioning? Ha! Mary is my older sister. I've never questioned her judgment or offered her advice in my life. Not about to start now. That she wants to marry you, Mr. Christopher Bryce of Brycecomb Hall in Gloucestershire, is enough of a recommendation for me. Besides," he added, smiling down at Rory. "My wife likes you. So I will too." He looked back at Christopher and suddenly balked, losing his train of thought; so much so that he glanced about the room, as the rest of the family came up to welcome him home, to search out the Duchess of Roxton. Finding her he blinked, then regarded Christopher anew. "Good—Lord! Good. Lord. It's—it's *uncanny*! Has anyone—has anyone ever told you how much— how very much you resem—"

"Yes, my lord, they have," Christopher interrupted, with a smile and a wink at Mary. He took hold of her hand. "And that is a story for another day…"

EPILOGUE

"I still maintain the odds are in my favor!" the Duke of Kinross announced.

Antonia looked up from the book she was reading and smiled.

"So you have said more than twice in as many minutes, *mon chéri*," she stated mildly and set aside *Cassius Dio's History*. "But I told you how it is. And me I am rarely wrong in these matters, am I, Martin?"

Martin Ellicott placed his chess piece on the board and nodded solemnly, though there was a twinkle in his eye. "I do believe you have been correct upon every occasion there is a birth in the family, Mme la Duchesse."

Antonia smiled and nestled against the cushion at her back. She reclined on the chaise longue in the pretty pavilion by the lake, mules kicked off to the marble floor, and her stockinged feet upon the silk cushions. With her book closed on a silk ribbon to hold a place, she took a moment to gaze out at the view of sweeping lawn and tranquil lake, where ducks with their ducklings were winding their way through the waters of the reedy bank. The sun was high in a cloudless sky and a cool breeze stirred the green fingers of the willow branches. It was an altogether blissful summer's day, made all the more happy by the distant sounds of her grandchildren scampering about the pirate ship treehouse, and the more immediate noises of her baby daughter gurgling with delight as her papa carried her about in the crook of his arm while he paced the steps before her maman's chaise.

"What do you think, Deborah?" Jonathon asked the Duchess of Roxton.

Deb Roxton was seated on a wingchair, her youngest child sprawled out asleep across her light silk petticoats, his chubby cheeks glowing red with the contentment that comes from a deep sleep. She sat opposite her husband's godfather, a chess board on the table between them. She was sure Martin was about to put her in check, so when she looked up, it was with a frown of concentration between her brows.

"I truly cannot say. But Julian thinks it will be a boy."

The Duke, who was seated near them on the cool marble slab between two fat columns, hair falling into his eyes, was tackling a knot in the strings of a kite belonging to his twin son Gus, and did not look up. "I have ten pounds riding on the outcome."

"Ten pounds you are going to lose!" Jonathon stated with glee. "Your brother," he said in a different voice as he opened wide his eyes and smiled, addressing his baby daughter and tickling the underside of her chubby chin, "is about to make your papa ten pounds richer."

"No, he is not," Roxton stated and sat up. He pulled back his hair and let out a satisfied sigh. "There! Knot undone and kite back in full working order." He handed it off to one of the footmen who was waiting to return it to Lord Augustus at the treehouse. "Tell my third son that if he wishes his papa to fix anything else, he is to bring it to me himself and not have you waiting on him, Peter."

"Why are you so confident, Julian?" Martin asked, intrigued. "I grant you have yet to be wrong in your predictions with your own children, but this is Lady Mary and Mr. Bryce's progeny were are talking about."

"He may have foretold the sex of our children, *mon parrain*, but his prediction fell miserably short with Rory and Dair's babies."

"You disloyal wretch, Deb!" Roxton threw at her lovingly. He stood and stretched his long legs, hands on his slim hips. "Twins! Who could've predicted *twins*? She's such a waif. And one of each, too."

"And you lost twenty pounds..." Antonia said airily.

"It's all the fault of Uncle Lucian!" Roxton stated without heat. "He started this wager business with Julie's birth and as far as I recall he never managed to win once."

Antonia giggled. "Not once. He would be a great deal poorer today, too."

"If I may correct a presumption, Julian," Martin offered, sitting back after placing Deb's king in check. "It was not with Julie's birth but with your own that the tradition of the ten-pound wager began. Lord Vallentine dared to wager Monseigneur a pound that you, Mme la Duchesse, would be delivered of a son. M'sieur le Duc was most offended at the amount, and suggested ten. To which his lordship readily agreed. But in so doing, he found himself out–maneuvered, because your father wagered him ten pounds that your mother would deliver him a son and heir, and his lordship agreed. It was only on the handshake that Lord Vallentine realized what had occurred. With your birth, Julian, and the subsequent loss of his ten pounds, Lord Vallentine was determined to win it back from your father; he never did."

"*Naturellement.* Monseigneur he has never lost a wager in his life."

Martin inclined his head. "That is very true, Mme la Duchesse."

Jonathon came up the stairs and placed Elsie into her mother's arms then sprawled out beside her. "Well, I'll be having words with Vallentine the next time I see him!"

No one made comment but no one thought it odd, either. It was well-known Kinross often accompanied his wife on her visits to the family mausoleum.

He leaned in and asked her quietly, "And where have you placed your ten pounds, sweetheart?"

Antonia smiled into Elsie's beautiful face with her large blue eyes and mop of dark hair and kissed her chubby cheeks before settling her on her lap, little head supported against her drawn-up knees. She held her daughter's hands and addressed her husband. "But you know where I have put my pounds, Jonathon. Mary and Christopher they will have a son. And I know his names, too. David Henry Renard Bryce. Mary, she told me."

"What?! She wrote and told you her son's name?" Jonathon was aghast. "Then why are we having this wager if you know it's a boy and you know his name?"

"Because we do not know. We await Jack and Henri-Antoine to arrive from the big house with the news."

"At least they are not so far away, and nowhere near the birth!" Roxton stated. "But they again find themselves in the right place at the right time to deliver the news."

"That is true, *mon fils.* They were with you when Julie she was born. And then they came here with the news." Antonia smiled wistfully and leaned in to kiss her daughter's fingers. "I remember that day as if it were yesterday, *mon petit chou.*" She glanced mischievously at Deborah and Martin and raised her brows before saying on a sigh that was at odds with the light in her green eyes, "Vallentine he lost ten pounds that day, too, and today, Elsie, your poor papa he will lose ten pounds also."

Jonathon frowned. "How? How do you know that?"

"Because, my love, I do. And here comes my son and Jack across the lawn from the jetty. Which means they have rowed over to get here the quicker."

Jack and Henri-Antoine were indeed striding across the lawn, Henri-Antoine with a sliver of paper between his fingers, which he held up and waved at the occupants of the pavilion. This seemed to bear out Antonia's prediction that they had news to share of the impending birth of Lady Mary and Mr. Christopher Bryce's first child.

Roxton came to stand behind his wife's chair, and stared down at their sleeping fourth son, a hand lightly on Deb's shoulder. "All I care about is that Mary came through it, and so did the baby."

"She had no trouble with Teddy… I am confident all will be well. And by the boys' smiles everything is. So," Deb asked them, "you have news from Brycecomb Hall?"

Lord Henri-Antoine gave the letter to his mother. "We do. But we do not know what it is—yet."

Antonia broke the seal and read the short note, which was written in Christopher's strong hand. She then folded the paper and kept it in her fingers, but said nothing.

Jonathon sat forward. "Sweetheart? Well?"

Antonia teased him. "How much will you pay me for the news contained in this note?"

Jonathon sat back against the chaise longue with a huff. "Oh, no you don't! If you're going to play at that game, all bets are off!"

Antonia giggled. "In that case, you will save your ten pounds." She handed the note to her son and announced to all present, "Mary was delivered of a son. A healthy baby boy, and mother and baby they are very well indeed."

"Aha! I knew it would be a boy!" Roxton couldn't keep the glee from his voice. "Your Grace owes His Grace ten pounds!"

He handed the short missive to his wife, who read it and then handed it to Martin, who dug in a frock coat pocket for his spectacles and propped them on the end of his nose. He looked up over his rims, the note still in his hand, in time to see the Duke of Kinross wipe a hand over his face in defeat and then stick out his palm to his duchess with a sheepish grin.

"Antonia—sweetheart—I need ten pounds."

*Behind the Scenes—explore the places, objects,
and history in* Proud Mary *on Pinterest.*
www.pinterest.com/lucindabrant

*Concept to Cover—costumes, jewelry, models, & photoshoot.
Discover how the* Proud Mary *cover art was made.*
www.youtube.com/lucindabrantauthor
www.lucindabrant.com/blog/proud-mary-cover-reveal

The Roxton Family Saga continues…

www.ingramcontent.com/pod-product-compliance
Lightning Source LLC
Chambersburg PA
CBHW060734190726

48285CB00001B/207

9 781925 614824